I0654131

Her Convenient Forever

Her Convenient Forever

A Touches of Austen Novel

LEENIE BROWN

LEENIE B BOOKS
HALIFAX

Cover design by Leenie B Books. Images sourced from Deposit Photos and Period Images.

ISBN (print) 978-1-989410-65-3; (ebook) 978-1-989410-66-0

Contents

Dear Reader,

This novel is part of my *Touches of Austen* Collection of Austenesque stories. These stories feature original characters and plots that have been touched in some way by the influence of Jane Austen and her novels.

Several of the characters in *Her Convenient Forever* pay homage to Jane Austen's *Sense and Sensibility*. We have a hero who has loved and lost and who has lived abroad. Our heroine, much like Maryann or Eliza, has been foolish and fallen prey to a Willoughby-like rogue. And then, there is the villainess of this story. She might make Lucy Steele look slightly less evil.

Along with the intentional nods to Miss Austen's work in this story, there may also be some which are purely serendipitous, and, then, there is one special nod to a character from *Emma* for the true lover of Jane Austen to discover.

If you would like to share your observations about which elements you thought were Austen-inspired, you can do that in my *Touches of Austen Readers Group* on Facebook.

Happy Reading!

Chapter 1

The sea lapped at the sand below her. A group of gulls dipped and soared before landing just out of reach of the rolling waves. A breeze steady, but gentle, pulled at her skirts, and tugged at her bonnet. The sun peeked out from behind a light grey cloud. If only her heart felt as perfectly lovely as the weather.

Felicity Love opened the small box she held but quickly closed it again. This must be done, but...

She turned away from the edge of where the land dropped from where she stood to the beach far below. Perhaps tomorrow she would feel more prepared.

Turning yet further away from the cliff, she walked in the direction of the road which would take her to the small cottage her father had rented.

This place and this time away from home was

her reprieve – her place to grieve and her place of solace, where her heart was supposed to mend enough to face the future. But how could a heart, which had been shattered as hers was, repair itself in just two months?

She stopped, blew out a breath, closed her eyes, and drew in another breath only to once again blow that one out slowly before repeating the process with a new draught of salty sea air. She listened to the cry of the gulls, the soft whisper of the wind, and the rolling of the ocean. If she focused on those things, it might be possible to outlast this wave of nausea without retching.

For two minutes she stood there, thinking of nothing but the bits of nature she could observe without the use of her eyes. A small longing for her bed crept into the back of her mind. To sleep away all that she had experienced in Bath and at home, as well as the future she faced, would be a blessing of immeasurable size.

A tear escaped her closed eyelids. She let it slide down her cheek and did not bother to even attempt to keep more tears from joining it. She had had her fill of pretending – pretending to be well, pretending not to care, pretending that the future would not be as horrid as she knew it would be. Pretending was tiring and not as a long walk might be. No, pretending to be well when one was not was the sort of exertion that caused one's bones to ache and muscles to collapse from their strength being completely exhausted.

The box in her hand grew heavy as she allowed her sorrow its freedom.

She turned back toward the sea. It had to be done. She could not continue as she had been.

Slowly, with steps that seemed to be weighed down by bricks in her boots, she made her way to the cliff's edge once more. Upon reaching her destination, she opened the box and cast the lid out into the void of space before her so that she could not replace it on the box.

Next, she removed the lock of hair – *his* hair – from the box. Holding it securely in her closed hand, she lifted her fist to her lips and whispered goodbye to what was supposed to have been, before opening her hand and allowing the breeze to lift each piece of hair from her outstretched palm until not a strand remained.

The box was next. She hesitated, remembering the day he had given this to her. Then, she held it out as far as she could over the edge of the cliff and allowed it to drop. It took several minutes before she heard it splinter on the ground below her.

Everything was gone. Every sentimental reminder of the man, who had claimed to love her but had abandoned her, had been destroyed.

Nausea gripped her again, and just as she had last time, she closed her eyes and drew a breath. She placed a hand on her abdomen. Not every reminder of Simon Ramsey was gone. There was one that would remain with her for the rest of her life. Oh, to be able to wake from this dreadful reality and find it was not reality at all but rather an appallingly horrid dream!

How stupid she had been! How utterly stupid! But Simon had sounded so sincere when he had pledged his undying love to her. He had not wavered in passion when declaring that he would marry her. There had been no sign at all of his deception – not a single hint had betrayed his duplicity.

And now, because of her willingness to believe his pretty words, she would bear his child and all the shame that went with such a thing.

She peeked over the edge of the cliff to the shore

below. Would it hurt much to cast herself off the cliff? Would she suffer for a long time, laying bloody and broken on the beach, or would death come quickly?

She clutched her queasy stomach. She might deserve, and even welcome, such an end, but this child – the one that was growing within her through no fault of its own – did not deserve such a fate. He or she would be loved. Her father had promised that neither Felicity nor her child would ever want for anything – ever. He would see to it, for he loved her no matter what wrongs she had committed.

She stumbled backward and sank to her knees as nausea began to make her head spin. She leaned forward onto her hands, breathing deeply.

Could she ever love as deeply as her father did? She shook her head and allowed the wave of anguish, which accompanied such a thought, to crash over her while pushing down the thought of throwing herself off the cliff and ending her pain even if it took more pain to find that end.

She buried her face in her hands as sobs shook her body. She was a selfish creature. She always had been. There was not a time in her life when she could remember doing anything to please someone other than herself. However, she would not continue to be so. She would endure this present torment, not for herself or even for her father or mother, but for her child.

"Miss, miss, are you well?"

The sound of someone calling and boots crashing through the long grass filtered into Felicity's awareness.

"Miss, are you well?" A gentleman knelt beside her and placed his hand on her shoulder.

"I barely know," she answered. She was breathing and not dead, but she did not know whether that was a good thing or not.

"What can I do to help you?" He asked as he removed his hand from her shoulder.

"There is nothing which can be done," she answered honestly, more to herself than to him. "I must just bear this." There really was no other choice, was there? How she longed for there to be another choice.

The warmth of his person, which lingered inside his jacket, wrapped around her.

"Do you live far from here?"

"Quite far," she replied. "My home is half a day's

drive from here, but my parents and I are staying in a cottage just down that road." She pointed behind her and to the left. "It is the first house you come to." She attempted to smile at him. He was not so handsome as some, but he had kind brown eyes and longish, windblown brown hair with tinges of golden sunlight, that gave him a sort of dashing appearance.

"Then, allow me to assist you in finding your way home. Can you walk?" His hand was on her elbow.

"I am sure I can so long as the dizziness does not return, and my stomach does not churn too much." With his help, she rose to her feet.

"We can stop so often as you need," he assured her.

"Thank you." She began to remove his jacket, but his hand on hers stopped her.

"No, put it on. You are unwell, and, therefore, you must stay warm."

"I am quite recovered," she lied.

Her protest was met with a raised eyebrow and a stern expression.

"Very well," she acquiesced, putting her arms into the sleeves of his jacket with his assistance.

"And now, you must take my arm. A lady who falls to her knees on such a fine day as today requires assistance." He held his arm out to her and smiled.

"I appreciate it." And she did. Having an arm on which to lean was a very helpful thing when one was feeling wobbly.

"You were standing very close to the edge," he said after they had walked halfway to the road. "When I was coming up from down there," he used his walking stick to indicate the direction to the left of them, "I was fearful you might slip and plunge over the edge."

"There was no need for your concern, sir. I was not going to fall." At least she was not going to fall by accident.

They walked on in silence until they reached the road.

"Forgive me," he said, "I have just realized that I have not yet given you my name. It was a terrible oversight on my part; however, now that my heart has returned to beating as it should rather than as if it wished to outrun a prize stallion, my mind is free to remember what I should be doing."

She had frightened him – a stranger who did not know the first thing about her?

He stopped, removed her hand from his arm, and, said with a bow, "Mr. Boyd Hedrington at your service, ma'am."

Felicity curtseyed. "Miss Felicity Love."

He presented her with his arm once again. "It is a pleasure to make your acquaintance, Miss Love."

"I find I concur, Mr. Hedrington."

He glanced at her skeptically. "Are you certain?"

She blinked. "Why would I not be certain that I am happy to meet you?"

"You looked over the edge of the cliff as if contemplating something of a grave nature." He paused, before adding softly. "I thought perhaps I had prevented you from holding to your purpose."

"You have a very unusual accent," Felicity replied, turning the subject. "I am sure I have not heard it before."

"Ah, yes, it is difficult to hide that one is not originally from England if one does not sound English."

"You are not from England?" She had never met anyone who was not from England before. She knew several people who had travelled to various destinations and returned, but they were from England no matter where their journeys had taken them for a time.

"No, indeed, I am not."

"Then, where are you from?"

"Nova Scotia by way of the American Colonies." He gave her a lopsided grin. "Which I do know are not colonies any longer. However, they were colonies when I was born and were only recently not colonies any longer when my family fled to Nova Scotia."

"You were there during the war?" She had met soldiers who had been in a war, but this was the first person she had met who had lived where there was a war.

"I was, though, I really had very little idea what war was or was not at the time. I was only four when we moved." He straightened his shoulders. "And now, my son is four, and we are here."

"You have a son?"

He nodded. "He is a quiet little scamp."

"Do you have any daughters?"

"No. It is just me and Matthias."

Her brow furrowed. Did he mean to say he had

no wife? Felicity wished to ask but knew it would be far too forward.

"My wife died shortly before we were set to sail for England."

Felicity gasped. "How sad!"

"Indeed. The loss of a life always is, is it not?"

"I suppose it is."

Their conversation lapsed into silence as Felicity considered a young child losing his mother and a husband being left suddenly without his wife. Had he loved his wife? She glanced up at him.

He caught her glance and held her gaze. His expression was as serious as any she had ever seen. "Did you think about death when you were looking so intently over the edge of the cliff?"

Her eyes widened, but she did not look away. She could not. Her lips trembled as tears welled in her eyes.

"What prevented you from falling?"

Should she tell him?

"I shall not judge you."

"I fear that is an impossible promise to keep," she replied.

"I will do my best to keep it," he assured her.

She looked ahead of them. They were nearly to

the cottage. She drew a breath and released it as she considered if she should reply or not. It was not as if she would see this stranger again, and it might be best to discover what censure she would face once her condition became obvious to all.

"What prevented you?" His voice was soft and gentle.

She placed a hand on her abdomen, and without lifting her eyes from the study of the path before her, she admitted her folly to him with two simple words. "My child."

Chapter 2

Her child.

The weight of such an admission settled on Boyd like a blanket of iron. Silence encircled the two of them as he struggled with exactly how to respond to such a confession. She had introduced herself as Miss Love, and she had also said it would be impossible for him not to condemn her. While he was not the sort to immediately cast judgment, he had to admit the thought that she must either possess loose morals or lack intelligence did enter his mind. However, he pushed those thoughts aside quickly as a third more likely option came to him.

"What did the child's father promise you?" He suspected he knew the answer. It would not be the first time he had seen a young woman desperate to be done with life because of some rogue's pretty promises.

Her brow furrowed. "What did he promise me?" She repeated the question as if it had taken her by surprise.

"A lady does not contemplate throwing herself off a cliff because she planned on being pregnant and unwed," he responded in as gentle a tone as he could while, inwardly, he wished to run through whoever had done this, just as he did whenever he met or heard of a lady in such a state. It had been so since Viola had died after passion, which had been aroused purposefully by a scoundrel who was seeking only to pleasure himself, had led to a similar consequence.

"What did the scoundrel promise?" he repeated.

Her lips quivered. "You do not condemn me?"

Fear of condemnation was what had prompted Viola to do as she did. He would never immediately condemn a lady for an error such as Miss Love had made.

"No, not out of hand," he answered. "You are responsible for your actions, of course. We all are. However, sometimes those actions follow the leading of another and, therefore, I find myself condemning the one who leads another into folly far more than the person who has been led."

She blinked at him and then, a small smile tipped her lips for a moment before she became serious and sad once again. "Marriage."

It was only one word, but it was a powerful one, especially when used as a promise to a young lady whose heart had been touched by some rogue.

"Had he offered for you?" Likely not. Usually, it was merely a promise of an offer that was used.

"Not officially, but he did speak to my father after and had set a time to speak with me privately."

Whoever this blackguard was, it seemed he had done more to appear honorable than most. Unless...

"Did your father say he had spoken to him?"

She nodded. "We all expected Simon to offer for me, but he disappeared the night before our interview was to take place."

And that had been, judging by her still slim figure and the nausea she claimed to have, about two months ago.

"He has not contacted you since then, has he?"

She shook her head and tears slid down her

cheeks. Her heart must have been greatly touched by this man.

"I am sorry he has not," Boyd said softly.

They walked on a few steps.

"Thank you," she finally whispered through soft sobs.

"Is that why you are here? Has your father taken the cottage so that you might bear your child in obscurity?"

Again, she shook her head. "I was secretive about..." Another shake of her head. "My father has decided it is not something from which I am allowed to hide."

"I see." They stood now at the door to the cottage. "Is he a hard man?"

"My father?" Her eyes were wide with surprise. "No! Not at all. He has promised to love and care for me and my child, but it will not be done in secret." She looked down at the ground. "I hope to one day be so good a parent as he is."

That was a relief. There were parents who would not be so reasonable. "I am glad to hear it. May I meet him?" There was something he wished to tell the gentleman.

"Oh, yes," she said eagerly, "I am sure that both

he and my mother would enjoy a visit. We have not had any visitors since we arrived two weeks ago."

She seemed to brighten somewhat, and a pleased smile tipped her lips, giving Boyd the faintest glimpse of the lively young lady she must have been before she had fallen into her current circumstances. She was pretty even in her sorrow, but that smile hinted at the possibility of an enchanting sort of beauty.

He followed her through the cottage door, down a short hall, and into a small and welcoming sitting room at the back of the house.

The gentleman in the corner – he assumed it was Mr. Love – placed his book on the table and stood. His eyes were wary, but he smiled – it was similar to the small smile his daughter had given Boyd at the entrance to the cottage.

"Welcome," Mr. Love said.

"Mr. Boyd Hedrington," Boyd said with a bow. "I came upon your daughter while I was out walking. She was not feeling well, so I offered to escort her home."

"Are you ill?" Mrs. Love asked her daughter.

"No more than normal," Miss Love replied.

"If I may be so forward as to suggest it, a spot of

tea and a bit of something to eat might do her some good," Boyd offered. "It worked for my wife when she was in a similar condition."

"You know about that?" Mr. Love did not even try to hide his surprise.

"I do." He paused and looked at Miss Love. She would likely hate him for what he was about to say, but that could not be helped. She had considered taking her life, and that was not something which he would hide from any parent, let alone a parent who had been proclaimed as loving by his daughter. "Miss Love told me of her condition when I asked what kept her from ending her life."

Mrs. Love dropped into her chair. "What?" she squeaked.

Miss Love turned furious eyes on him.

"She was at the cliff, looking over the edge rather intently when I first saw her. I hurried as quickly as I could in her direction, but thankfully, before I could reach her, she had stepped back and sunk to the ground." He expelled a great breath. "It is not the first time I have witnessed someone intently gazing into the arms of death."

He closed his eyes for a moment as he recalled the pain Viola's family had suffered at her passing.

How many weeks had his dreams been disturbed with the scene – Viola standing on the precipice and then falling while he ran towards her – playing itself out over and over in his mind? "I was thankful that this time, rational thought prevailed, and two lives were spared."

Miss Love's angry glare faltered and fell away, turning into sorrow while her eyes shone with unshed tears.

"A friend's sister listened to her despair," he explained. "The death was not instantaneous. She lay in pain for nearly a week until a fever, induced by her injuries, claimed her life." He took Miss Love's arm and guided her to a seat for she was looking rather faint.

"Forgive me," he said softly, "but you needed to hear that story, and your father needs to know how much care you require." He turned to Mr. Love. "I apologize for the less than pleasant impression I know I am making, but a life –" He shook his head. "It is far too precious to take lightly. I did not wish to live with the guilt of hiding your daughter's anguish from you in the event that rational thought does not win the next time she wrestles with her heartache."

The tears in Mr. Love's eyes spoke to the truth of his daughter's assessment of him.

"I have spoken frankly and indelicately about what transpired with Miss Love today. However, I want you to know that I do not gossip. Not a word of this will be shared with anyone other than you." He placed his hat back on his head. "I should go. My son will be waiting for me."

"Will you have some tea before you do?" Mr. Love asked.

"I think it is better if I do not." They needed time to speak with their daughter and digest the information he had told them.

"If that is what you think is best. However, I should like to thank you for the service you have rendered my family. You will call on us again, will you not?" Mr. Love's smile was kind. "You may bring your son." It was said as one might when adding an inducement to get a child to agree to a plan.

A chuckle bubbled up from Boyd's chest. "I would be happy to call on you. Matthias might not be so willing a guest, but it would be good for him."

"He is a shy fellow, is he?"

Boyd nodded. "Since his mother died, he is. Of

course, the crossing from Canada did not help with it any."

"Ah, that is the accent," Mr. Love said with a smile. "Have you been in England long?"

Boyd shook his head. "Less than a year. Just long enough to know that my experience growing crops in Nova Scotia on a small parcel of land is not quite enough education to feel capable of running the estate my uncle left to me."

"Oh, my!" Mrs. Love cried. "A wife and an uncle gone in close succession?"

"I am afraid so. Although, to be honest, I only knew my uncle from my mother's accounts and his letters, so his passing was not felt so deeply as Anna's was. I think the hardest part of my uncle's passing was leaving my wife behind, though she was no longer living, and coming here – not that I do not like it here. I find the winter to be quite agreeable actually."

"You simply must call on us at your earliest convenience," Mrs. Love declared. She seemed the sort of lady who did not like anyone to feel alone.

Miss Love had loving parents, though he suspected they might be a touch indulgent.

"Yes, please," Miss Love agreed.

"Are you certain? I have told your secret to your parents."

She nodded. "You were so helpful today."

"Very well, then. It is settled. I will return... tomorrow?"

"Oh, yes!" Mrs. Love cried. "That would be perfect, would it not be, Mr. Love?"

"It must be if you say it is," Mr. Love teased with a laugh. "So long as there are tea and sweets, I will be content."

Boyd bowed his leave and exited the room, but not alone.

"Thank you," Mr. Love said to him in the hall. "I knew Felicity was unhappy, but I had not realized she was so desperately unhappy."

"Viola – my friend's sister – seemed well until it became painfully, and fatally, obvious that she was not." He turned to leave but then turned back. "I am glad I could be of service." And with that, he finally made his way back to the road that led to his home.

He had walked further than was his normal wont this morning and had been gone for hours, therefore, he hastened his steps. In half an hour, he had reached Grenwood Hall.

"Papa!" Matthias, who was in the garden with his nursemaid, ran towards him.

Papa was one of the few words that Matthias ever uttered. Boyd smiled at him and, squatting down, held out his arms so that his son could run into them. However, the smile Boyd wore was only an expression to let his son know how happy he was to see him. Inside, the weight on Boyd's heart grew heavier as he remembered the sweet babbling boy Matthias used to be when he was three – before Anna had died.

He squeezed Matthias tight. "Did you have a good morning?"

Matthias nodded.

"And did you have any biscuits yet?"

Matthias shook his head.

"Then, I think we should find some because my stomach is beginning to rumble. I walked a great distance."

Matthias wiggled out of his father's embrace. Gone were the days of him wishing to be carried everywhere. Boyd knew it happened eventually with all children, but he had hoped that it might last a bit longer. He supposed he would just have to content himself with the fact that Matthias still greeted him with a hug and allowed him to hold his hand.

"I saw the sea," he said as they walked. "And I met some friends."

Matthias looked up at him.

"I am going to take you to meet them tomorrow."

Matthias stopped walking and swung his head back and forth.

"You are going," Boyd said firmly. "They are very nice, and I know they will have tea and sweets. You like sweets."

Matthias scowled.

"I will not leave your side while you are there unless you wish it."

Matthias's shoulder sagged. Boyd knew that meant his son would go without protest, but he would not go happily. It would have to do for now. Together, they proceeded down the path to the house in silence.

They did not need words to enjoy one another's company, but a few words would have been nice for they would assure Boyd that his son would eventually be able to face the world as everyone else did. How did he help his child heal a heart that was so broken – especially when his own was still grieving more than a year and a half after having lost Anna?

"Sir," Mrs. Feasby, the housekeeper stepped into the study where Boyd and Matthias had gone upon entering the house, "I have the menus when you have a moment."

"I will see them now." He sighed.

Menus. Food orders. Issues in the dairy and laundry. The décor of the master's chamber. He scrubbed his face. There was so much that would be less arduous if his wife were with him. Anna had always excelled at managing a household, and he knew that even faced with a larger home such as Grenwood was, she would have had it running smoothly. He poured himself a cup of tea and half a cup for Matthias but put it aside so that it could cool.

"You need a wife," Mrs. Feasby echoed his thoughts.

He shook his head. "I cannot."

"You must consider it. If not for yourself, for your son."

He knew she was right. He was not the sort of man who just went on his merry way by himself. He liked having a companion to help him through life. He longed for someone with whom he could share his struggles. He had friends, but that was not the same.

"There is no one..."

"There will be more families coming to take cottages as the weather grows warmer. Many will have daughters," Mrs. Feasby interrupted his protest. It was not the first time he had attempted to protest that there were no females who suited him in the area.

"But they will only be here for a few months. That is not enough time to get to know any of them." He sighed. The thought of meeting young ladies to determine if he could love again or, at least, find a companion for himself and a mother for his son made him feel quite ill. To love again meant the possibility of suffering yet another devastating loss, and he truly did not know if his heart could love again or if it had been lost forever when Anna died.

"A few months will have to do. You must marry," his housekeeper said softly. "You know you must. Unless you are planning to return to Canada."

"I am not sailing anywhere ever again!"

The experience had been torturous. He had

never been so ill in all his life. Had he known it would be so bad as it was, he would have sent a letter telling the solicitor to dispose of his uncle's estate. However, he had not. He had, instead, sent word that he and his wife would be arriving in August to claim his inheritance.

Anna had been excited about the adventure and the beautiful house which awaited her. And then, she had become ill and died before their passage could be purchased.

Again, he would have written to his uncle's solicitor and told him to dispose of the estate, but Anna had begged him in her final hours to take Matthias to the land of his ancestors. He had promised without hesitation. How could he not?

Of course, now, along with living in the home for a year before any of it or the proceedings from the sale of it would become his, he also needed to acquire a wife to meet his uncle's demands. Apparently, having been married and widowed was not enough to satisfy his stipulations. Boyd must have a wife at the time of possession. There was no way around the demand. He had read the will himself a dozen times while trying to find a way out of that requirement.

"Maybe you will meet someone who will suit," Mrs. Feasby said hopefully. "Or, I know how much you like to help others, perhaps there is a lady who you could help by marrying her." She laughed. "Not that I think that is truly an appropriate reason to marry, and not that I do not approve of charity. I just think marriage should be founded on more."

Boyd took a sip of his tea, added his initials to the menu before him, and said, "No, no, I think you might be onto something there, Mrs. Feasby." He nearly laughed at how quickly she snapped her mouth shut when he looked up at her. "I shall have to consider it." And he knew just where to begin his consideration.

Chapter 3

The breeze made the shadows cast by the tree overhead dance in the sunlight. A bird trilled from somewhere close by, and the fragrance of lavender which grew in the bed to the right of the bench, on which Felicity sat, wafted through the air. She inhaled the soothing scent. If she could stay right here like this for the rest of her days, she would. Here, in the garden, everything seemed at peace and welcoming.

"Miss Love."

Felicity turned toward the gentleman who called to her. She had done a lot of thinking about him last night when the day had drawn to a close and the sun had slipped below the horizon. One could not see much when the moon was merely a sliver of light in the sky, but one could ponder things that seemed as vast and unfathomable as the blanket of stars overhead. Her thoughts had been as dark as the night sky for many days, but yesterday, Mr. Hedrington had been her sliver of moonlight.

His words about life being precious, coupled with his story of his friend's sister would not leave her. She could not push them away or bury them underneath her sorrow. She had seen the pain in his expression when he had spoken of Viola and again when he had mentioned his wife. She had no desire to be the source of such an expression for anyone simply because she had decided that the trials of life which lay ahead of her were too much to bear. Had not Father reassured her again last night that she would not walk her difficult path alone?

She rose to greet Mr. Hedrington and his son.

"I wanted Matthias to meet you before he met your parents. He finds it easier to greet strangers when there are not too many of them all in one place. Do you not, Son?" The little boy, who clung to Mr. Hedrington's hand, looked up at his father and nodded.

However, the nod did not seem very confident to Felicity. She could relate to that feeling for it was how she had felt yesterday when her father was promising his love and support. She trusted him, but she still did not want to be in the situation in which she found herself.

"Miss Love, this is my son, Matthias. Matthias, this is Miss Love, the lady I met on my walk yesterday."

"I am pleased to meet you, Master Hedrington," she said with a curtsey and a smile.

"Matthias. Please, call him Matthias."

She arched a brow in surprise and question that was met with a look of concern and a nod. Mr. Hedrington had said his son would not be happy to be calling on them today.

She crouched down so that she was Matthias's height. She had seen her father do this very thing with children – especially the quieter, more reserved ones – though until now, she had thought it silly. But then, there were so many things she had not understood until recently. "Would you like that? Shall I call you Matthias?"

The question earned her a smile and a nod.

"It is a pleasure to meet you, Matthias." She held out her hand to him, and after a moment of consideration, he took it. She gave his hand a squeeze, smiled reassuringly at Matthias one more time, and then, rose to greet his father.

"You are looking well," Mr. Hedrington said.

"I am much improved over yesterday. I have confined my activity to watching a maid in the kitchen garden, the sheep on the hill, and a butterfly flit from flower to flower today."

"That seems a wise decision. Too much exertion can cause one to feel unwell."

Wide eyes filled with worry peeked up at Felicity.

"My mother said the same thing, and since I did not wish to feel so dizzy as I did yesterday, I listened, and I am as well as well can be."

Matthias looked somewhat mollified by her comment but not completely reassured of her well-being.

"I promise," she said to him. "I am well, though I am hungry, and, therefore, I am happy you are here so I can have tea."

There, he was smiling, which was a better expression than worry for a youngster to wear.

"Shall we make a circuit of the garden before we go in?" Mr. Hedrington asked. "Would that be too much for you? I am certain it would be beneficial for Matthias."

"It would be perfect," she said as she placed her hand on his proffered arm.

It seemed that despite what he knew of her, Mr. Hedrington had proclaimed himself to be her friend. Still, she held herself at a bit of a distance, not knowing exactly how to act or what to say. And that was an extremely uncomfortable feeling. Until recently, Felicity had known exactly what to say, who to accept, and what to do. However, now, it was not just her stomach which often felt topsy-turvy. Every piece of her did not know which way to stand.

"You may run ahead of us if you stay on the path," Mr. Hedrington said to Matthias.

The boy's only response was a wag of his head.

"You will not mind walking slowly, then?" his father asked.

Again, the boy shook his head.

"He does not speak at all?" Felicity whispered.

"Rarely, and only a few words."

Matthias peeked around his father to look at Felicity. His eyes seemed to dare her to say something, though she was not precisely certain what he wanted to hear. Was he unhappy that she had been talking about him? That was the only reason she could think of for him to be looking at her as he was. She supposed she would not like to be whispered about – no, that was not true. She knew beyond a shadow of a doubt that she did not like to be whispered about. It was one of the things that she was dreading. Once she was no longer able to conceal her growing child, there would be whispers – horrible, horrible whispers. The thought nearly brought tears to her eyes.

"I am not certain I could ever be so silent," she said to Matthias. "Is it very hard?"

Matthias hesitated but then shook his head.

"Truly? Do you not wish to tell your father about the games you played or the things you saw?"

The child's brow furrowed.

"It just seems too difficult for me," she said with a shrug and then turned the subject so that Matthias would smile again. He had a beautiful smile that showed his dimples. "Do you like cake?"

Matthias's eyes lit with delight, and she knew he liked cake even before he had nodded his head.

"Cook has made some delicious oatcakes," she added. "I hope you like oatcakes."

Again, Matthias's head bobbed up and down.

Felicity released a breath that allowed her shoulders to relax, and her worry about not knowing what to say to a child dissolved. She had just survived a challenging conversation with a child who did not speak. If she could do that, she might just be able to speak to her own child once he or she was born. Maybe, Mr. Hedrington would allow her to visit Matthias so that she could practice holding a conversation with a child. It really did not seem so difficult as she thought it might. She really should have paid more attention to the children in the houses her mother had taken her to when doing calls. She sighed. It was just another way in which she had failed herself.

"Perhaps we should go in the front door," Mr. Hedrington said when she dropped his arm and stepped toward the side door.

"Oh, of course." Her cheeks warmed. She should have thought of that. How stupid of her! "Forgive me. I was not thinking."

He held his arm out to her again. "If I had done the proper thing and called at the front door to begin with, it would not be an issue. However, I skipped propriety for the sake of my son, and were it not for him..." His tone was apologetic.

Her eyes grew wide as understanding dawned on her. It was not her actions that he was correcting. It was his own because of Matthias. Together, in what felt to Felicity like awkward silence, they exited the garden and made their way around the shrubbery that flanked the front step to the door of the cottage.

"Should we knock?" Felicity asked.

"I think it is acceptable if we just enter since you do reside here." His smile was kind, and his tone was gentle.

Felicity opened the door and once again, after removing her bonnet, led Mr. Hedrington down the short hall to the small sitting room at the back of the cottage.

"Mother, Father," Felicity said as she entered the room. "Mr. Hedrington and his son, Matthias, have arrived."

"Oh, how delightful!" her mother cried.

There was likely only one person in all the world who enjoyed entertaining callers more than Felicity did and that was her mother. Hopefully, Felicity's disgrace would not take that pleasure away from both her and her mother. Oh, what a mess she had made of things! Again, tears threatened, but she refused to give in to their demands.

"I shall have our tea and sweets brought in straight away," Mrs. Love added after she had been properly introduced to Matthias. "Please, do be seated."

"Where shall we sit?" Mr. Hedrington asked Matthias, who looked at Felicity.

"I am going to sit on the sofa near the hearth," she said.

Matthias smiled and nodded his head.

"Will three fit?" Mr. Hedrington said with a laugh.

"I should hope so," Mr. Love said with a chuckle of his own. "My Felicity has always charmed the young gentlemen, but I was not aware that her abilities extended to such young gentlemen."

He was teasing, and three months ago, Felicity would have rolled her eyes and giggled. However, at present, her cheeks flamed as she forced a small laugh.

"I am pleased to see Matthias wishing to sit with you," Mr. Hedrington said softly as they sat down. "He has not found it easy to accept new acquaintances. I have had several neighbours call on us since our arrival, and aside from Mrs. Jones, he has not warmed to any of them."

"Felicity is hard not to like," Mr. Love said with a smile.

Again, while Felicity knew her father was praising her, she blushed and could not accept it. She had not been easy to like. In fact, she had been dreadfully difficult and even impossible to like for some people. One only needed to ask her sister, Grace, to discover the truth of it. There were many sins she had contemplated while looking at the stars when sleep would not come.

"Miss Love said you live a distance from here," Mr. Hedrington said.

"Ah, yes, a little further than a day's drive to the northeast into Kent," Mr. Love said. "But we come here nearly every summer. There have been a few summers where we have not been able to make the journey due to other obligations, and we have missed our time here."

"Is it always this cottage at which you stay?"

Mr. Love nodded. "We enjoyed it so much on our first trip that we have never considered any other place. Of course, our first time to the ocean was after our marriage. Mrs. Love had never seen the sea, and I could not resist being the first to show it to her."

Felicity loved the way her father's eyes grew soft when he looked at her mother and spoke of their wedding and first trip to this cottage. How many times had she asked him to tell her that story when she was young? It was likely why she had fallen so deeply in love with the idea of marriage. What girl would not wish to be so treasured as her father's look said her mother was? Of course, as it turned out, Felicity had not gone about trying to find such a situation for herself in the right way, and now, she would never have someone to look at her in such a fashion.

"If you will excuse me," she said before rising quickly and leaving the room, for she knew that those tears which had threatened before would not be refused this time.

Chapter 4

"Oh, um," Mrs. Love looked from the door, through which her daughter had fled the room, to her husband and then Boyd. The lady was clearly startled and uncertain about what to do.

For his part, Boyd was glad he had had his hand on Matthias's leg when Miss Love had made her hasty exit, or his son would have also run from the room. It was how he was. If there was a reason for him to worry about someone being well, he would follow that person to the ends of the earth to make certain they did not disappear. Crossing the Atlantic had been trying for Boyd because of his seasickness, but it had been a torment to his son because he feared his father would leave him as his mother had.

"I am certain she will be well," he said both to

Mrs. Love and his son, whom he scooped up and placed on his lap.

It did not matter if his son usually did not like to be held in such a way when they were not alone in the library or nursery at Grenwood. Boyd knew that Matthias would be anxious, and this was the best way for him to judge the extent of Matthias's worry without asking him any questions. As he made Matthias comfortable, he pressed his hand against his son's chest. Matthias's heart was racing, just as Boyd suspected it would be.

"Do you think I should go to her?" Mrs. Love's question for her husband was asked softly.

He shook his head. "She likely just needs some fresh air. She will return when she is ready."

Boyd could feel every muscle in Matthias's body tense and knew his son was listening as carefully as Boyd was to what was being said.

"Miss Love is sad, not sick," he whispered in Matthias's ear. He had seen Miss Love's face just before she had risen. She had not looked nauseated. Her expression had been one of grief.

Wide eyes that shone with their own sadness turned toward Boyd.

"She will return," he assured him. And if she

did not return, then Boyd would find her so that Matthias could see that all was as well as could be under the circumstances in which Miss Love found herself. To be honest, he would not seek her out just for Matthias's benefit. He also wished to see that she was well.

"The sweets will be here soon," Mr. Love said to Matthias. "I love sweets. Do you?"

The man seemed to have a very natural talent for conversing with anyone of any age and making them feel at ease. It was a skill for which Boyd was excessively grateful at present, for Mr. Love's question and mention of treats had distracted Matthias for at least a few moments, and often, it only took a small distraction to help him relax. Even as he thought it, Boyd could feel a portion of the tension drain from his son.

"I am glad to hear it," Mr. Love said in response to Matthias's nodded answer.

He rose and crossed to the window where he stood at one edge of the window frame and leaned forward to peer out. He looked back at Matthias.

"Did you know that if you look out this window just like this," he once again leaned forward and peered out, "you can see the corner of the garden where my daughter likes to sit? It is the very place she was when you found her earlier."

"Did you see us?" Boyd asked in surprise.

Mr. Love nodded his head. "I did, but you must not tell my daughter." He chuckled. "I like being able to check on her without her knowing." He motioned to Matthias to join him. "She is there now."

To Boyd's surprise, Matthias pushed off his father's lap and went to join Mr. Love at the window.

"You may climb up on the ledge here. I will make sure you do not fall," he offered Matthias.

Boyd had not seen his son respond so easily to anyone in over a year. However, both Mr. Love and his daughter seemed to have some sort of magic about them that drew Matthias out of himself. That was a promising thing.

"Do you see her?" Mr. Love asked.

Matthias nodded his head. His brow furrowed with concern as he stood on the deep windowsill looking out at the garden. "Sad."

The air in Boyd's lungs rushed out in a surprised but soft "oh." A smile tipped his lips. His son had spoken – and to someone other than Boyd.

"Yes, my boy," Mr. Love said, "Felicity is sad." He drew a breath and released it. "You see. She made a poor decision that caused some trouble."

Boyd could not help but be impressed with the way the gentleman was presenting the situation in terms that a child would understand.

"And that trouble has made her feel very sad." Silently, he and Matthias continued to look out the window. "But I still love her."

Mr. Love's final words, which were spoken softly as if just for the boy standing there with him to hear, tugged at Boyd's heart. That was how a father was supposed to respond to his children. He would not mind being tied to a lady who had a father like Mr. Love – even if that lady had been allowed too much freedom and had behaved badly – for he knew that such a parent would have instilled some good principals within his child.

Again, the room fell into silence until the tea service was brought in and Matthias's attention was drawn away from the window.

"Sweets!" Mr. Love cried in delight as if he were the expectant child. Then, he helped Matthias down from the windowsill.

Such a man who could insert himself into a

child's world with such ease would make an excellent grandparent for Matthias. That was also a good thing, for if Boyd decided on Miss Love as his wife, he would not only be gaining a mother for Matthias but grandparents as well.

"Shall we sit at the table?" Mrs. Love asked.

"That would be best, I should think," Boyd answered. "Matthias is careful, but managing sweets and a cup might be a little much even for the most careful lad."

"You have such a smart father," Mrs. Love said to Matthias before she went to the table to begin pouring. "Do you allow him tea? We have milk for it."

"More milk than tea if you would."

The tea was poured, and Matthias was given a cup filled halfway with milk that was tinged with the colour of tea. Then, the oatcakes were offered. The sweets and tea kept Matthias occupied and happy for some time while the adults talked.

"Did you leave many relations behind when you came to England," Mrs. Love asked.

"A few."

"I imagine that was not easy." Her eyes darted to Matthias, who was taking a sip of his milk.

"No, it was not. For either of us. However, it was the right decision." Or so he continued to hope. "We have made a few friends here already."

"Oh, that is good." Mrs. Love's relief was evident in both her tone and expression. "We have just recently parted with our youngest daughter, Grace."

"Did you?" He had wondered if Miss Love was an only child.

Mrs. Love nodded. "She recently married and lives in Bath with her husband, Mr. Blakesley. He has a lovely estate, as well as several other properties that he rents to those who do not regularly live in Bath. He is a perfect gentleman and so good to our Grace." She was quite obviously pleased with the arrangement.

"Do you have other children?" Boyd asked.

"No, it is just Felicity and Grace," Mr. Love replied in his wife's stead.

"I had no brothers or sisters," Boyd offered. "It was just my father and me for much of my life." Much like it was just he and Matthias. "Although, for a time, we had my grandmother."

He watched his son put the last bit of oatcake into his mouth and remembered how he had always wished for a mother like the other children. However, his father had never remarried. Boyd had asked his father about it once – after his grandmother had died when Boyd was fourteen.

His father had simply said he had never met anyone who could fill Boyd's mother's place, and while Boyd now intimately understood the void that could be left by the death of a spouse, he had not when he was fourteen. That being said, he had understood the emptiness that he had felt when his mother had died. It really was not so different from the emptiness he had felt since Anna had died. The two griefs were different in many ways and yet alike in others.

"He never remarried?" Mrs. Love asked.

Boyd shook his head.

"Will you?"

Boyd blew out a breath and turned his eyes toward Mrs. Love. "I must."

"You are a good father," she said with a smile.

"Matthias is part of it," Boyd admitted. "I knew a life without a mother, and I would prefer that he not know that same life. However, it is also part of the stipulations in my uncle's will that I have a wife before I can become the official owner of Grenwood Hall."

This was the first time he had shared that detail of his uncle's will with someone other than Mrs. Freasby and the solicitor. It was not exactly a secret. Many in the area, as well as all of Grenwood's staff, seemed to know about that detail, and several neighbors had hinted that their daughters were available to him. However, the Loves were not from the area, and the only way for them to know about his need of a wife was for him to tell them or wait until the gossip mill had done the job for him. Seeing as he was hoping to approach Mr. Love with an offer for his daughter, it was probably best if Boyd presented the fact himself.

Mrs. Love leaned forward. "But you had a wife when your uncle died, did you not?"

Boyd nodded. "But the estate is not to be mine until one year after the quarter day nearest to, but not preceding, the day of my arrival in England. My uncle wished to give me time to determine if running an estate the size of Grenwood was to my liking before I claimed my inheritance."

"I suppose that was considerate of him," Mrs. Love said.

"I suppose it was," Boyd agreed. "And I have been thankful for the opportunity to make the decision even if the voyage from Nova Scotia made the decision for me before I ever set foot on English soil."

Mr. Love chuckled. "A rough journey was it?"

"I have never been so ill in my life," Boyd admitted with a laugh. "Matthias was ill for a day and a half. I, on the other hand, was unable to stand on my feet for a week after we left Halifax, and then, I never did completely lose that unsettled feeling until sometime after we had arrived in England. I vowed that I would never leave England until they have devised some means to travel that is not sailing."

He and his hosts all laughed at that.

"It seems you will always be with us, then," Mr. Love said. "For there is no other way to cross an ocean. I am sure a hot air balloon could not make such a distance without the need to set down."

"No, I suppose it would not, and I cannot imagine that it would be a more comfortable way to travel."

"Oh, I should think it far more uncomfortable and dangerous!" Mrs. Love cried.

Matthias who had finished both his oatcake and milk was watching and, therefore, listening carefully to the conversation around him.

"Far too risky for me," Boyd assured Mrs. Love. "Which is why I must marry." He paused. "Before Michaelmas."

"Oh! That is not so very long from now, but it is not as if you are without ample time," Mrs. Love said. "Why my Grace was only in Bath for a few weeks before she was promised to Mr. Blakesley." Her brow furrowed. "Have you anyone in mind?"

"My dear," Mr. Love said, "that is really not our concern."

"But I might meet someone and be able to make recommendations to Mr. Hedrington," his wife protested. "I am not prying for my own sake I assure you," she said to Boyd.

"I thank you for your generous offer, but there is someone who I am considering." And contrary to what her husband said, whom Boyd was considering was very much her concern. Of course, he was not fully decided and would not say anything until he was.

"Oh, I am happy for you, but should you find yourself in need, I would be delighted to be of assistance. I take great pleasure in helping others be as happily settled as Mr. Love and I are."

"I will keep that in mind." He looked at Matthias, who was looking a trifle bewildered by the conversation the adults were having. "Do you think it would be allowable for Matthias and me to take a walk in the garden? He has been an excellent young man, and I think a reward of running and playing might be just the thing after sitting for so long."

"That is a capital idea," Mr. Love agreed. "And then, we can see if Felicity is still in her favourite spot." He winked at Matthias. "Do you think we should take her an oatcake?"

Matthias's eyes lit with delight and his head bobbed up and down.

"And maybe we can take an extra for ourselves for later," Mr. Love whispered as he stacked three oatcakes in the middle of a napkin he had spread out on the table and then tied the corners to make a neat little package before handing it to Matthias. "I can trust you to carry these carefully, can I not?"

Again, Matthias nodded.

"I thought I could." Mr. Love stood and extended his hand to Matthias. "Shall we, sir?"

Matthias placed his hand in Mr. Loves, and, before his father had done more than rise from his chair, left the room with Mr. Love.

Boyd shook his head in wonder as a smile spread across his face. "He has never taken so easily to anyone," he said to Mrs. Love.

"Ah, but he has never met anyone so charming as Mr. Love," she assured him. "My husband has a way with children. It is quite endearing if you ask me."

"I cannot disagree."

"With such a grandfather," Mrs. Love said as she put her hand on Boyd's proffered arm, "Felicity's child will not want for affection despite not having a father." She sighed. There was a note of sorrow in the sound. "I am confident Felicity will make a good mother, for she is a great deal like her father. But oh," she said wistfully, "if things were different, she would have made someone an excellent wife."

And the truth behind those two things was what Boyd hoped to discover, for he had to agree with Mrs. Love. Any child who claimed Mr. Love as a grandfather would be a very fortunate child indeed, and he had to admit that he also found himself somewhat charmed. It had been a long time since he had felt so at home as he had for the past three-quarters of an hour. And that was promising. Very, very promising.

Chapter 5

"Mrs. Adams has sent an invitation," Mrs. Love called from where she sat on Felicity's bed. "It is for the day after next."

"What kind of gathering is it?" Felicity tied her bonnet's yellow ribbon under her chin. She had no great desire to attend any gathering, but to not attend a function with her mother would be reason enough for people to question what was wrong with her. Right up until the end of her time in Bath, Felicity had enjoyed fetes and soirees. The more lively the company she kept, the better life was. That was how she had always lived her life – in constant pursuit of pleasure.

"A garden party." Her mother entered Felicity's dressing room and handed her daughter the invitation. "Your father has already agreed that we should go, but if you are not feeling well enough, we can decline this one in favour of a later date."

"Nothing is going to change between now and tomorrow or even two weeks from now," Felicity retorted.

"No, most likely not, but you might feel better than you do now. Your heart might have healed a piece more."

"Please, do not look at me like that."

"Like what?" Mrs. Love asked.

"Mr. Ramsey is not worth pining after." Although she was. Daily. Or more specifically, nightly. "He treated me very shabbily and without any regard for my heart."

"Oh, I most heartily agree! He is the most despicable person I have ever met," her mother agreed. "But you have not answered my question. How was I looking at you?"

Felicity sighed. "As if you feel sorry for me."

Her mother's mouth dropped open, and she gasped. "I do not see why I should not feel sorry for you. I am your mother, and I am feeling nearly as disappointed as you." She pressed her lips together. "And there is the baby." That was all she said, but Felicity felt all that was left unsaid.

"I would rather not think about that at present." Not that it was actually possible to not think about the fact that she was with child.

If she was not attempting to keep food inside her stomach, she was wishing to eat. Her stomach was never satisfied. Her mind swung like the erratic arm of a grandfather clock from thinking the world was sunny to wishing the world and everything in it would go away and leave her alone. And most days it was difficult to tell which caused her more discomfort – her head or her breasts.

"I will say no more," her mother assured her. "But about the invitation. Will you go?"

Felicity studied her reflection in the mirror for a moment. To look at her right now, one would not know that she was not the same girl she had always been. Soon enough that would not be the case. Then, invitations would be infrequent if any came at all.

"Yes, I will go. A garden party might be just the thing to lift my spirits, and if we are fortunate, maybe Mrs. Adams will have those lovely berry tarts that she had last year." She closed her eyes and drew a breath. She was certain she could still smell the tempting sweetness of those berry tarts.

How she would love to eat a full tray of them right now.

"Do you think there is time for a piece of bread and jam before we leave?" Jam and bread was often what her mind settled on as an agreeable option for eating, and Felicity knew if she did not appease that craving, it would not go away. Instead, it would become more intense and cause her to be cranky or worse – ill. She certainly hoped there was time for a piece – or two – of bread with jam on it.

"I should say there will have to be time," her mother replied with a knowing smile. "We cannot have you feeling unwell while at Grenwood Hall." She held the door open for Felicity. "I must say I am excited to take a tour of the estate. I have heard Mrs. Adams mention it with such admiration that I cannot wait to see the place for myself."

She followed Felicity out of the room and down the hall to the stairs. "According to Mrs. Adams, while Grenwood Hall is by no means insignificant in size, it is not overly large, and the grounds and house are well-proportioned and delightful."

Ever since yesterday, when Mr. Hedrington had issued his invitation for the Loves to visit him, the delight of seeing Grenwood Hall had not been far from Mrs. Love's mind if one could judge such a thing correctly by the number of times she had cried her anticipation about the visit. Felicity's mother was not one to keep her delight to herself. In fact, her mother was not one to keep silent on most things, and she was easily distractible – most pronouncedly so when the distraction was of an entertaining nature such as a tour of a house was. That last fact was one that Felicity had often used to divert her mother's attention. One only had to find a fascinating topic or activity to suggest to Mrs. Love, and whatever thing for which she was scolding her daughter would vanish into thin air as quickly as the steam rising from the laundry cauldron on wash day.

Felicity placed a hand on her stomach. What sorts of tricks might her child attempt to play on her? Oh, that was not a pleasant thought! She did not like to be tricked. And yet, that was exactly how she found herself with child, was it not?

"We must have some bread and jam," Mrs. Love said to her husband, who was waiting for them at the bottom of the stairs.

"We must?" His eyes moved from his wife to his daughter who nodded.

"We most certainly must," his wife replied.

"Can it be eaten in the carriage?"

Mrs. Love looked at Felicity for an answer.

"Yes, Father, I can eat it in the carriage."

"Then, hurry on. I am not fond of being late." He pulled his watch from his pocket and opened its face while Mrs. Love scurried to the kitchen. He held out his arm to Felicity. "Come. We will get you settled into the carriage while we wait for your mother."

Felicity placed her hand on her father's arm.

"Other than being hungry, are you well?"

"I am."

"And are we accepting the invitation to Mrs. Adams's garden party?"

"We are." She put a foot on the step to the carriage.

"You are not fearful of being in public, then? It will not find it to be overly taxing, will you?" he asked as he made certain she was safely inside the vehicle.

She blew out a breath and shook her head. "Not yet."

"I am happy to hear it." His words were gentle even if his smile was sad. The mixture was nearly enough to make her want to run back inside and not face the world. However, she was visiting someone who would not make her feel fearful even if she were obviously with child, which she was not.

She closed her eyes and, as she waited for her mother, willed herself to think of something, anything else, rather than how much her life was and would be changing.

~*~*~

Half an hour later, and after having consumed two large slices of bread with jam sandwiched between them, Felicity was feeling somewhat refreshed and ready to step out of her father's carriage to greet Mr. Hedrington and Matthias.

Father's and son's looks of pleasure at the Loves' arrival were equally as bright. To Felicity, it was a joy to see, not only a handsome gentleman, but also his retiring child, smiling with delight to welcome her to their home. She paused as she exited the carriage, trying to store such a sunny scene in her memory for later when the grey clouds of gloom would once again gather.

"Matthias had no desire to stay in the nursery when he knew that he had friends arriving." Mr.

Hedrington beamed at his son. "And how could I refuse him, when he asked very politely to meet his friends."

"He asked?" Felicity felt a small jolt of excitement at the news. Mr. Hedrington had mentioned to her yesterday in the garden, when Matthias had brought her an oatcake, just how delighted he was that Matthias had taken to her father and had actually said a word that was not *Papa*. It was a small revelation to her about how much parents must care for their children, and she had once again hoped she would be equal to the task of being a mother.

"Yes," Mr. Hedrington said. "He asked in as few words as were necessary, but he asked."

"That is very good, Matthias." She crouched down to his level. Doing so yesterday had been welcomed by the child, so she hoped it would also be welcomed today.

"How many words did it take?" She held up a finger. "One?" Then, she added a second finger when Matthias shook his head. "Two?"

This time, her question was met with a nod and a smile.

"Hmmm..." Mr. Love said when Felicity, who

was feeling quite proud of herself for once again being able to successfully interact with a child, had risen. “Which words would those be?”

Oh, that would have been a good question to ask!

“Do not tell me,” he added quickly. “I think one word might be…” His face scrunched, and he tapped his lip. “*Meet*. Was one of them *meet*?”

Matthias’s head bobbed up and down.

Her father’s brow furrowed. “If only I could think of the other word.” He sighed. “But I cannot.”

The little boy giggled. “Friends,” he said.

“Oh yes! That would be the best word.”

For so far back as Felicity could remember, her father had always sought out the children in a room and made certain to spend a few minutes greeting them. She had often watched him and wished he would behave more like the other adults in the room who ignored the children, but now, as she saw him interacting with Matthias, she wished she had paid better attention to how he had spoken to those children. There was much she was certain she could have learned from him which would be helpful to her as a mother. Thankfully, she would have him to help her learn what she needed to know.

"You are a miracle worker, Mr. Love," Mr. Hedrington said and then waved toward the front door. "Shall we? I see Susan is waiting to take Matthias back to the nursery." He looked down at his son. "We will come to visit you on our tour." Then, he nodded to the nursemaid named Susan who took Matthias by the hand and led him into the house.

Mr. Hedrington extended his arm to Felicity. "Miss Love," he said.

Felicity accepted his proffered arm.

"I thought that we could start our tour in the drawing room with a glass of lemonade and a biscuit if you wish."

"I just ate something on the way here," Felicity admitted softly. It was not something she would have admitted to just anyone, but Mr. Hedrington had not judged her harshly for being with child. Therefore, she suspected he would not care one bit if she had consumed a full meal while travelling the few miles from their cottage to his home. "However, I would not refuse a glass of lemonade."

"Then, we shall have lemonade and save the biscuits for later." He paused before he reached the door. "Did you get a good look at the façade? It is quite grand, is it not?"

"It is lovely, simply lovely," Felicity's mother cried. "Mrs. Adams – do you know her?"

"I do," Mr. Hedrington said.

"Mrs. Adams told me that the house and grounds were well proportioned, and she was right. Oh!" One of her hands rested just above her heart. "It is so delightfully proportioned. Even spacing on the windows and each matching the other. The symmetry is exactly as it should be."

"You do not mind a flat front?" Mr. Hedrington asked. "Some have said it would look better if there was perhaps a portion protruding or a rounded room on both corners."

Her mother looked aghast. "You should not listen to those people, for their taste in architecture is wanting. No, no, no. Leave it just as it is, and if you should ever decide to add on, I would suggest an extension that is set back a bit from the front, lower than the house itself – two floors, not three – and longer than it is tall." She tipped her head. "One on both sides would be lovely." She nodded. "Yes, that is just what I would do."

"I will keep your recommendations in mind should I ever find such a large house in need of more rooms," Mr. Hedrington said with a laugh.

"One would be surprised how many rooms one needs once his family grows," she added as she followed him and Felicity into the house. "And you did say you intend to marry."

"For Matthias's sake and to satisfy the will," Mr. Hedrington said. "My son needs a mother, and my uncle requires me to have a wife."

"Oh, yes, that is right." She did not protest what he said with words, but the smile and sparkle in her eye spoke loudly of her not believing him at all that a new wife would only be so that Matthias had a mother or that some requirement might be met to keep his inheritance. Last evening, as they ate dinner and when she was exclaiming her delight over being invited to tour Grenwood, she had told Felicity about the requirement that Mr. Hedrington had to marry.

"The drawing room is just here."

They turned left out of the grand entrance hall, which was in want of a few decorations, as it was rather plain, and into a very prettily decorated yellow drawing room.

He drew Felicity across the cream rug to a sofa next to which there was a small round table with a pitcher of lemonade and glasses on it. He was prepared. The thought of a gentleman preparing to entertain guests made Felicity smile. Her father was excellent at socializing, but she had yet to see him know exactly what needed to be done to prepare to entertain guests.

Mr. Hedrington waited as she took a seat before pouring the lemonade into glasses and handing them out. He served himself last and took a sip, but then placed his glass back on the table and wiped his hands on his breeches. His cheeks puffed out, and he expelled a breath. Perhaps he was as nervous as his son was to have company, though she had not thought him the anxious type.

"I have come to a decision," he began, looking nearly calm but more flustered than he had at any point since she has met him, except perhaps when he had first come upon Felicity near the cliff. "When I married Anna, I married for love." His lips tipped upward. "Now, I find myself in a position where I do not have the luxury of finding love and then marrying. I must think of my duty to my son and Grenwood Hall." He stopped and took a visible breath.

He was most certainly nervous.

"I am a gentleman of newly found fortune who, in order to keep that fortune, is in want of a wife and a mother for his son." He smiled at Felicity before turning his attention to her father. "Your daughter would do well to have a husband and her child, a father."

Felicity's eyes grew wide as her heart stumbled in its rhythm and climbed into her throat while the glass she held came very close to being dropped. Was he proposing that they marry? Her head spun.

"Therefore," Mr. Hedrington continued, "I would like to marry your daughter."

Cool glass slid through her fingers, and the faint realization that her slipper was wet flitted through Felicity's mind before everything went black.

Chapter 6

Out of the corner of his eye, Boyd first saw Miss Love's glass hit the rug. Then, he saw her slump in her seat. This was not how his presentation was to go! He expected both Miss Love and her parents to be surprised by his offer. It would only be natural. However, he had not thought it would be so shocking as to cause Miss Love to swoon.

"Oh, my!" Mrs. Love was the first to move, but her husband was the first to reach his daughter's side.

With some effort, Boyd willed himself to not remain rooted to his spot. Bending, he retrieved Felicity's glass and, with hands that he could not completely still, placed it on the table. He was unsure what else to do. Miss Love's parents were attending to her. He was certain there were other things which needed doing, though what they were escaped him at present.

"I will get Mrs. Feasby," he muttered before crossing the room and poking his head into the hall. His housekeeper would know what to do.

"Are you ready for me, sir?"

He shook his head. "We need..." He glanced over his shoulder. What was it that he needed? Surely, he could think of one thing that was needed. His eyes fell on the wet patch of carpet. The spill. Ah, yes. "Towels. There was a bit of a spill."

He glanced back at the Loves once again. Miss Love was stirring. Salts would not be needed.

"Do you need anything else, sir?" Mrs. Feasby had not yet moved from where she had been waiting to be summoned to assist in the tour of the house.

"I am not certain." Anna had never fainted. His grandmother had never fainted. None of his friends' mothers or sisters had ever fainted. He knew that salts could help revive a person who had swooned, but he had no idea what was needed beyond that.

"Perhaps if you told me what the trouble was," Mrs. Feasby suggested.

Boyd blew out a breath and ran a hand through his hair. "My proposal did not go as planned."

"Did it not?" The question was asked flatly without a hint of surprise.

A furrow formed between Boyd's eyes as a scowl settled on his face. Mrs. Feasby had warned him that springing the idea of marriage on any lady was not a good idea.

"Miss Love fainted," he admitted. "What do I do?"

"Offer her mother a glass of something that can be given to her daughter. I will bring towels and a blanket in case Miss Love needs to lie down for a bit. Offer one of the pillows if she does need to lie down."

Boyd nodded and turned to return to his guests.

"We can conduct our tour when she is well," Mrs. Feasby added before her master could move away from her.

He nodded without turning around. Then, he drew a fortifying breath and crossed the room.

"Would you like some lemonade for Miss Love?" he asked Mrs. Love.

"Please," Mrs. Love said as she held her daughter's hand and spoke softly to her.

The pitcher clinked rather loudly against the glass into which he was pouring, causing him to grimace. Why would his hands not stop shaking? He paused a moment before turning and handing the beverage to Mrs. Love.

The sight of a groggy Miss Love once again shouted at him to be of assistance.

There was something else he was supposed to do. His eyes shifted from the scene before him and searched the room for the answer. Ah! There on the chair where Mr. Love had been seated. "Does she need to lie down? There are pillows if you need, and Mrs. Feasby, my housekeeper, is bringing a blanket."

"That might be best," Mr. Love replied.

Quickly, Boyd snatched the pillow he had seen and thrust it at Mr. Love.

There, he had done what he was supposed to do, and now, he once again felt helpless. He hated feeling helpless. "What can I do? Tell me what to do."

"I suggest you sit down, young man," Mr. Love said. "We shall see that Felicity is comfortable, and then, you can explain yourself to me further."

"Of course." Boyd wiped his hands, which were once again sweaty, on his breeches and perched himself on the edge of a chair. He took up his glass of lemonade which he had neglected earlier and took a large swallow of the sharp, yet sweet liquid, while wishing that the glass contained something much stronger.

"Are you certain there is nothing else I can do?" he asked.

"Not a thing, son," Mr. Love said as he removed his daughter's slippers and handed them to Mrs. Feasby who had arrived with a blanket and towels.

"I did not mean to harm her." Boyd's heart raced and something very like panic settled upon him.

"She will be well, sir," Mrs. Feasby assured him. "Place this on the rug, if you will." She held out a towel to him.

With a nod, he did as instructed just as a maid entered the room.

"Would you and Mr. Love prefer to speak in the library?" Mrs. Feasby asked.

"There is no need," Mr. Love answered. "I think Felicity should hear whatever is said."

Mr. Love moved to return to his chair, but when Boyd did not immediately follow, he said, very softly, "She will be well. You may relax on that account."

"Is she given to swooning?" he asked in a whisper.

"No. Felicity has never swooned until recently. I suspect it is the emotional burden she currently bares which is the cause."

That made sense.

"I knew my suggestion would be a shock, but you must believe me that I did not think for one moment that it would cause your daughter so much discomfort." He motioned for Mr. Love to be seated.

"I have seen you with your son, Mr. Hedrington. I know that you are not the sort to purposefully harm another." Mr. Love said as he settled into his chair.

It was amazing to Boyd just how at ease the man always seemed to be. Other than the speed with which he had reached his daughter's side, there was nothing about his demeanor that spoke to anything being wrong.

"Now, about your offer," Mr. Love began. "It will come down to Felicity's decision, of course."

"Of course," Boyd agreed.

"However, I doubt she will get any other offers."

He shook his head. "I love her, but I must admit that I am not certain why you wish to take her on."

Boyd opened his mouth to reply, but Mr. Love waved his words away before they were even spoken.

"I know there is the stipulation of the will, but a fine-looking young fellow who has a fortune, such as you do, could have his pick of the local beauties."

That was true. He had been presented with several of those beauties since his arrival.

"Why my daughter?"

"Matthias does not hide from her." That was the thing which had promoted Miss Love to him above anything else.

Mr. Love's head tipped while he silently studied Boyd. "You are only looking for a mother for your child, then?"

Boyd felt warmth creeping up his neck. "I also wished to help Miss Love."

"So, this is a charity project."

Boyd shook his head. "No, no. It is not that exactly. Though I suppose there is an element to it that is, for doing good for others is part of my nature. It always has been."

"Then, am I to assume that there is something in this match for you? Other than securing your inheritance that is."

"I have enjoyed the few times I have spoken with your daughter, and I truly believe we would get on well. I find the thought of having a companion to help me through life to be a satisfying and comforting thought."

"Friendship?" Mr. Love arched a brow. "You are proposing friendship."

"What else can I promise at present? Miss Love and I have not known each other long enough to love one another." He paused and lowered his voice. "I do not know if I can ever promise anything more. Anna has not even been gone two years yet." Not until next week.

Mr. Love held Boyd's gaze. "It is hard enough to take the place of a ghost, but my Felicity will have more to deal with than just replacing a well-loved wife and mother. What about her child and all that entails?"

"I will care for her child as if it were my own. He or she would be subject to the same care I have given Matthias."

"But the whispers will not go away just because

Felicity has married. The child will be born before the expected time, and that will bring its share of trouble. You have not known Felicity long enough for the child to be yours. Anyone who knows anything about children being born will know that the child is not yours."

"I have considered that, and I believe I can withstand the wagging tongues."

"Can your son?"

That was a far more difficult question to answer. "I do not know for certain."

"Are you willing to risk it for him? An untainted mother might be better, and as I said, there are plenty of ladies who would be willing to marry a handsome man with a fortune."

Boyd shook his head. "I do not want any of the others. Surely you must know what a father would do for his child. I would endure far greater than the discomfort of a few whispers for the sake of my child. Matthias has barely spoken since his mother died, and a smile has been a rare expression. However, since meeting your daughter and you, he has smiled more than he has in over a year. There is something about you and your daughter which draws him out of himself and poses the greatest hope for his recovery. Your daughter could help my son's heart heal. That is the risk I am taking – the risk that my son will once again smile and bubble over with words."

"And what of your heart?"

"My heart will be satisfied to see my son well, and it will be pleased if my son and I can play any part in bringing a happier future to Miss Love and her child than the one which might lie before her."

Again, Mr. Love tipped his head and studied Boyd. Silence, which was only interrupted by a whispered request to be allowed to rise, followed by a refusal of that request, enveloped the room for a full two minutes.

"I like you," Mr. Love finally said. "You are honest, and you seem to have some idea of what you might face if this marriage happens. I can see your care for your son, and I do not doubt that you will care for my daughter just as well as you do for Matthias." He sighed. "I had always hoped for a love match for my daughter, but, as things stand, I do not see that as a possibility. I will not live forever, though I do expect to have another forty years at least." The man chuckled. "And it would be a comfort to know Felicity will be cared for even when I am gone." He shook his head. "You would think it would be easy to accept the offer you present, considering the state in which my Felicity finds herself, but it is not. I will be adamant about seeing her well-settled upon in the marriage papers."

A small bit of relief washed over Boyd. He just might meet his uncle's requirement, and in a fashion that was more than tolerable for himself. "As you should be."

"It will be Felicity's choice," Mr. Love cautioned. "I will see to her care if she chooses to carry on as she is."

"I would not wish for Miss Love to feel trapped, nor do I wish to mislead her into thinking that this marriage would be more than a companionable arrangement. She has been duped enough for one lifetime."

"Yes."

Boyd turned his eyes toward the lady lying on his sofa.

"Yes," she repeated. "I will marry you."

"Are you certain?" her father asked.

"What other option for my own home will I ever have?"

"One never knows," Mr. Love hedged.

Miss Love laughed a small bitter laugh. "I think one does know." She turned her eyes back to Boyd. "Do you really think I can be a good mother to Matthias?"

In her eyes, he could see the fear that lay behind the question. "I would not ask you to be his mother if I did not. I think you shall be an excellent mother both for Matthias and your own child." A small smile played at her lips. How lovely it was to be the cause of such an expression, but then, she was lying on his couch because he had also been the cause of her swooning. "You have just suffered a shock. It is perhaps best if you take some time to consider your reply."

She shook her head. "I do not have the luxury of time."

"I believe a few hours or even a few days would not be postponing your response too long."

Her eyes narrowed. "When do you wish to wed?"

She seemed determined to accept his offer. This was good, was it not?

"I should think the sooner the better," Mrs. Love

answered. "We can see about extending our stay, of course, to help you get settled if necessary."

"Most certainly," her father agreed.

Boyd looked from one parent to the other and then to their daughter. This would be his family now. "Since you are open to entertaining my offer, I would suggest that we get to know one another better for say... a week? And then we can set a date."

"Are you attempting to withdraw your offer, Mr. Hedrington?" Miss Love pushed herself up into a seated position.

"No, not at all. I am confident in my decision to take you as my wife. I only wish for you to know that you may refuse me if you discover that I am too much of a bore or that my son and I are too great a responsibility to take on."

"And what if you find I am too difficult?"

"I have no doubt that you are, but I am not afraid of a challenge. Anna was no wilting wallflower." Indeed, she had been deemed too opinionated by most of the elderly matrons in their village. And, at times, she was. However, they had weathered the storms between them well in their short marriage.

"Then, we will set the date next week," Mrs.

Love agreed on behalf of her daughter before clapping her hands. "Oh! Two daughters married. The Lord has been good to us, has he not, Mr. Love?"

"I should say He has, but I will reserve my exuberance until Felicity is actually married."

"Of course, of course," his wife murmured while smiling as if there was not a concern in the world. "Now, if Felicity is feeling up to it, shall we see this house which she will call home?"

Mr. Hedrington chuckled.

"My mother loves architecture and design," Miss Love said. She was looking perfectly recovered from her swoon.

"Everyone should have something they find fascinating, I always say," Mrs. Love said before launching into a discourse on the various items, which she found most appealing, in Grenwood's drawing room.

Chapter 7

"You must not be shy about asking to see things again," Mrs. Feasby said to Felicity when they had finished the tour of Grenwood Hall. "There has been a significant amount of information presented to you today."

Indeed, there had been. Felicity had arrived at Grenwood Hall as a neighbour and new friend of the owner. She was leaving all but formally betrothed to the man, and, well before the summer was over, Grenwood Hall would be her home.

"Thank you, Mrs. Feasby. I am certain I will find something which I cannot quite remember and must look at again. It is a lovely house."

"I am happy you like it, miss." The housekeeper who appeared to be only a few years older than Felicity's mother looked at the others in the group who seemed to be occupied with the scope of the garden. “There are furnishings appropriate for an infant in storage. They are far from new, but I can have them brought out and cleaned so that you can view them when you call next. If they are not to your liking, something will need to be ordered quickly I assume.”

Felicity bit her lip and nodded. Heat crept up her cheeks.

“You have nothing to fear from me, miss,” Mrs. Feasby said with a small smile. “I was made aware of your circumstances, but nothing has been said to anyone else just yet. There was no need to have too many made aware of the arrival of a new resident of the nursery since I was not certain if you would accept Mr. Hedrington’s offer – what with not knowing him for very long and all.”

“That is kind of you. It is rather a sudden thing.” Shockingly sudden but not unwelcome. She had given up any hope of ever having her own home.

“But it is a good thing, I think,” Mrs. Feasby said.

It was good to hear someone other than herself thought so. “Do you truly think so?”

“Mr. Hedrington needs a wife, and Matthias needs a mother.” She peeked around her again before lowering her voice further. “I should not say it, but both of them seem happier for knowing you."

Felicity's eyes shifted from Mrs. Feasby to Mr. Hedrington. "Have you worked at Grenwood Hall long?" she asked while she watched Mr. Hedrington's lips curl into a smile at something her mother had said.

"I started in the kitchen when I was just a girl."

"You have been here nearly your whole life, then?"

"The previous Mr. Hedrington was as good as the present one. I did not stay because I had to. Grenwood Hall has been a wonderful place to work. However, I will admit to never having served a mistress."

That was surprising! "I did not realize that Mr. Hedrington's uncle did not have a wife."

But then again, there was much she did not know about the man who would be her husband.

"That is why he insisted that his nephew be married to claim the estate. He always felt the vast emptiness of the house and regretted how lonely it could be. Not that he was unhappy," she added.

That seemed a very personal thing for a housekeeper to know about her master, but then, he was not married and had no one else with whom to share his thoughts.

"Miss Love," Mr. Hedrington interrupted before Felicity could think to ask anything else of Mrs. Feasby, "if you are not too fatigued from your tour of the house, I would like to show you at least part of the garden and hear your thoughts about Grenwood."

"I think I can tolerate a walk."

"We will have some refreshments on the terrace when we are through," he said to Mrs. Feasby, who assured him that it would be taken care of and then, with a bow of her head, returned to the house.

"She seems very nice." Felicity placed her hand on Mr. Hedrington's proffered arm.

She felt somewhat out of sorts. Strolling through a garden on a gentleman's arm was not an unusual activity for Felicity. She had done it many times with many gentlemen over the years. However, she had always done so with the ability to share as little or as much of herself as she chose. That was not a possibility at present for the gentleman, who walked with her, knew one of her darkest secrets already.

"Mrs. Feasby has been a treasure," Mr. Hedrington replied. "I knew very little of what I was doing when I arrived at Grenwood Hall. She made certain I knew who was who and what was what. She still does, for that matter. I fear you are not considering marriage to a man who knows all there is to know about estate management, Miss Love."

"Are you attempting to withdraw your offer, Mr. Hedrington?" Flirting was allowable when speaking with a gentleman who had offered for her even if she was pregnant with another gentleman's child, was it not? It felt as if it should be both proper and improper.

"I would have you know who you are considering. I am not a man without limitations and faults."

"None can be so great as mine," she said softly. Flirting felt wrong. She would try something new. She would converse with him as a friend and not as she would a gentleman who needed to be drawn along. Theirs was not to be a marriage of attachment. It was to be one of convenience and companionship.

"Perhaps not," he replied. "But I assure you I have many. I had a farm in Nova Scotia. A farm. Not an estate. The two, as I am sure you know, are quite different. It would be the same as if your father gave his estate to one of his tenants. There are skills which transfer, but the scope..." His words trailed off as he shook his head. "I thought I understood it, but I did not."

They paused under some trees where there was a bench.

"You should rest," he said.

"I am well. We can continue walking."

He shook his head. "I am afraid I am the sort to cosset others when they are not completely well, and since you did swoon earlier, I feel it necessary to insist that you rest for a few moments while we talk."

She gave him an appraising look. While his features and form were not soft, there was a gentleness that shone in his inquisitive brown eyes. But then, she had noticed the kindness of his eyes at their very first meeting. Perhaps that was why she felt no trepidation about accepting his offer when she knew so little about him.

"Please, Miss Love." He motioned to the bench.

"I apologize," she muttered as she took a seat.

"For what?" He settled next to her.

"I was remembering the day we met and forgot

what you had asked me to do. I was not trying to be obstinate." Her lips tipped up on one side. "Not this time."

He chuckled. "You will find we have that trait in common then. I am not easily swayed from my position."

"Do you suppose we will have many arguments?"

"Most likely. Once we are more familiar with each other."

He was honest to a fault. "You truly are trying to persuade me to refuse you, are you not?"

"I promise I am not. I need you to marry me as much as you need me to marry you. On that ground, we are equal."

He was also direct. He did not avoid the topic of her indiscretion. He had not since their first meeting. Oh, how she had wanted to scream at him when he first told her parents about her contemplation about hurling herself off the cliff, but then, he had softened the blow by sharing the story of Viola.

"I can be quite unreasonable," she cautioned him.

"Do you pout?"

She grimaced. "I do – or, I did. I am not certain what I would do now. I have not had an argument with anyone since before..." She placed a hand on her stomach. "Since before we left Bath, and I see things so differently now than I did before."

"Some things alter us forever." He glanced back at the house. "Take my son as an example. He used to babble constantly before Anna died." He shrugged as if he understood it and yet not quite. "And now, he is silent."

"And what about you? What things have altered you the most?"

He blew out a breath. "Death. My mother's death, Anna's death, Viola's death. Each has left an indelible mark on me."

How much grief this man had suffered! She placed a hand on top of his.

He smiled and covered it with his other hand.

"How have they marked you?" she asked softly, hoping to catch a glimpse inside him.

"Well," he said, "my mother's death taught me that I would never allow my child to grow up without a mother."

"Your father did not remarry?"

He shook his head. "He said he could never love

again." He closed his eyes. "Anna's death has taught me why my father said that." He looked down at their joined hands. "I may never be able to love you as you have been loved or deserve to be loved as a wife."

Her brow furrowed. Did he mean…? She opened her mouth to ask but then closed it again. How did one ask a gentleman if he was talking about what happened in a marriage bed or if he was just speaking of affection?

"And Viola's death taught me to never judge harshly," he continued.

"I am grateful for that."

He squeezed her hand.

She turned her head and studied the profile of his face – the way his nose jutted out sharply, the deep set of his eyes, and the firmness of his jaw. She had deemed him not so handsome as some when she had first met him, but he was not deficient at all. There were small lines by his eyes that spoke of his age, but he was an excessively attractive fellow. Or maybe that was his kindness which was colouring her opinion. He would not think less of her if she asked an improper question. She was certain of it.

Her eyes lowered to look at their still joined hands. "Do you wish to have children in the future?" There that should clear up her confusion about what he had said about being unable to love her as a wife. She peeked up to see him looking at her.

He smiled and shrugged. "I do not know and not because I have not considered it. I have thought about it, but I am unsure."

"Oh." Her gaze dropped to their hands again.

"We have only just met," he said softly. "My wife has not been gone a full two years yet. I thought I would have more time to discover how a heart heals before I would take a wife so that Matthias would have a mother." He blew out a breath. "It sounds ridiculous does it not? Vows are until death, but it still feels..." He shrugged. "The deficiency is not in you."

Felicity blinked against the tears that gathered in her eyes. How she longed to be loved so greatly that even death would not break that bond. However, she had given up that hope when she allowed Mr. Ramsey to take her to bed. That she was even being given the opportunity to be a wife to a gentleman of upright character and a mother to his son was blessing enough.

"It is not ridiculous." She wiped a wayward tear from her cheek. She had never been such a watering pot until recently. "I think it is beautiful." Another tear coursed down her cheek. "I had thought I had found such a love with Simon."

"I am sorry you did not." He released her hand and fished out his handkerchief. "I have done a horrible job of being a good host. First, I cause you to swoon, and now I have overset you again."

"No, no. It is not you. My mind has been so muddled since… since Simon left me, and I never imagined I would ever find someone, anyone, who would not judge and condemn me, let alone offer to marry me and allow me to be his child's mother." The tears were falling in earnest now.

Mr. Hedrington stood and drew her up and into his embrace. "It is not proper, I know, but you require comfort. I am still capable of such things."

He smelled lovely, and his grip was as firm as the chest against which she rested her head.

"I do not need a week to decide. We can marry whenever you would like." Here, in his arms, she felt protected. Protected and cared for. For what more could she ask? It was truly all she needed to be content.

He rubbed her back. “You may not need a week, but you will have it anyway.”

She felt his lips against her hair as he kissed the top of her head.

“I am an obstinate man, and I require you to give my offer its due consideration.”

“My answer will not change,” she protested.

A chuckle rumbled softly in his chest. “Then, you may tell it to me again in a week.”

Chapter 8

The day had begun with a gloomy greyness that wrapped snuggly around everything it touched. However, when the sun burned its way through the fog, a pleasant aspect was revealed. Gone were the rain clouds from yesterday, and a clear blue sky spanned the horizon. If it were not for the mud that clung to Boyd's boots and the water that still filled ruts and depressions in the ground, one would never know that, yesterday, Boyd had been required to dash between raindrops when entering and exiting his carriage which had carried him between home and the parish church.

Before next Sunday, he would need to call on the parson and arrange for a license and an appointment to be married. Barring any unwillingness of the parson to perform the ceremony, within two week's time, he would once again be married.

It would be a quick affair. There would be no banns called. All would be over and done with before anyone knew of Miss Love's condition. There would be questions eventually, but there was no need to reveal Miss Love's secret until it must come to light. She seemed far too fragile on that front at present, and he would be the last person to cause her harm. It just was not his nature to do so.

"Mr. Hedrington, I do hope you are enjoying this gathering." Mrs. Adams stood at his side.

"How could I not? You are a consummate hostess." He turned toward her with a smile. Behind Mrs. Adams, stood the lady he had seen with Mrs. Adams at church yesterday.

"I was hoping I could introduce you to my cousin's daughter. She very unexpectedly and delightfully, I might add, arrived for a visit on Saturday." She pulled the lady forward. "It has been years since she has visited, which means she is unfamiliar with many of my friends and neighbours. Therefore, this party could not have come at a better time, do you not think?" She looked to her cousin's daughter, who assured her it was as if it was designed just to welcome her.

There was something in the way the young lady

said it and how she looked up through her lashes at Boyd which put him off. She was practiced, and he had no desire to be any lady's plaything, which is what a gentleman often became when he attached himself to a lady who was proficient in flirting and flattery. Unless, of course, the young lady had given up those ways. His eyes shifted to follow Miss Love as she strolled with her father. He was certain she was very good at flirting and flattering. Her father had said she was known for charming gentlemen. However, she had yet to attempt to charm him. She had teased a bit, but all in all, she had been very unaffected in her interactions with him.

"May I introduce her to you?" Mrs. Adams asked.

Boyd's thoughts snapped back to the ladies before him. "Yes, of course."

"Mr. Hedrington, this is Miss Flint. Mallory, this is the new owner of Grenwood Hall, Mr. Hedrington."

"Was not the old owner of Grenwood Hall also Mr. Hedrington?" Miss Flint's lips pursed in an amused fashion while she peeked out the corner of her eye at Boyd.

Practiced. Very, very practiced.

"That does seem to happen in families where estates are passed from one gentleman of the family to another until it becomes necessary to pass the inheritance on to a cousin or the like," Boyd replied.

"Yes, yes, of course." Miss Flint seemed somewhat flustered that her prey had not responded with a laugh and some simpering reply. "Was the former Mr. Hedrington your father?"

"No, he was my uncle, who I only knew through my mother's accounts and his letters."

"Your mother's accounts? Was he her brother?"

Boyd shook his head. "As my name suggests, he was my father's brother, and my father did speak of him on occasion. However, my mother was best at telling stories, and she was the better correspondent."

He had taken over the task of replying to all his uncle's letters after his mother had died. His father wrote as well, but not as either Boyd or his mother had. Boyd had worked diligently to do as his mother had done, sharing small mundane details about life – things which Boyd's father would not have thought to include. The exercise had taught him to pay attention to details and remember them. For that, he was thankful.

"Then, I assume if you corresponded with your uncle through the post, you are not from this area. Where do your mother and father call home?" She had stepped closer to him. He did not like it.

"Nova Scotia."

Her eyebrows jumped up. "Indeed?"

He nodded.

"Do you find England to be strange?"

"Not overly so. In fact, I quite like it."

"Have you taken a turn of the garden yet?" Mrs. Adams asked.

He wanted to lie and say he had for he knew what the woman was doing. However, lying was not something of which he approved, even when it would keep him from having to spend more time with Miss Flint.

"I have not."

"Excellent. Mallory was just telling me how she was desirous of a walk, were you not, dear?"

"Indeed, I was," Miss Flint answered brightly.

"Perhaps you might walk together?" Mrs. Adams prompted.

"I promised Miss Love I would walk with her."

"Surely, you may do that later," Mrs. Adams said. "She is occupied with her father for now."

"Miss Love?" Miss Flint batted her eyes and looked around as if searching for something.

"Yes, my dear, do you not remember meeting her? She is the lady just there in the blue dress."

"Oh, yes! I remember her now. She seems lovely. A little quiet and reserved, but lovely."

"She is quite lovely," Boyd said as he extended his arm to Miss Flint.

Displeasure flitted across Miss Flint's face but was quickly hidden.

"Tell me, Miss Flint, how did you come to arrive unexpectedly at Mrs. Adams' home?"

"It is quite the story I can assure you. Not more than a month ago, I was thinking I would be doomed to spend the whole summer with my grandmother in Bath. Not that Bath is a horrible place or anything, nor is my grandmother an unwelcome companion, but Bath is not here. The seaside in summer is so much nicer than any town, even one as lovely as Bath."

"I have never been to Bath; you will not offend me if you do not like the place."

Miss Flint tittered. "I have already forgotten that

you are not from here. How foolish of me! You really must visit Bath if you get the chance. It is a fine place. There is nowhere quite like it."

"Perhaps one day." That was where Miss Love's sister lived, so the possibility of visiting was not inconceivable. In fact, it would most likely happen at some point.

"As I was saying, I thought I was going to spend the summer with my grandmother, but then, my mother had a letter from her cousin, Mrs. Adams, who mentioned how nice it would be to see each other again. Unfortunately, my grandmother is not well, so my mother did not think it was wise for her to travel so far. Therefore, she sent a letter to Mrs. Adams saying I would be coming alone. However, the letter did not arrive until after I did!"

"Mrs. Adams seems pleased to have you visiting her."

"She does, does she not? Mother has always spoken so highly of her, and I can see why."

"I find Mrs. Adams to be a very fine sort of lady." A little bit of a busybody but not more than any other lady who liked to know everything about everyone.

They were nearly to where Miss Love was sitting

on a blanket with her mother and father. She looked a trifle fatigued. He tipped his hat and smiled at her when he and Miss Flint walked past. He would rather just leave Miss Flint standing on the path and go sit with Miss Love, but that was not the best idea. Be that as it may, the desire to do so was excessively encouraging to him as it confirmed yet again that he had not chosen incorrectly for Miss Love to be his lifelong companion. He truly did enjoy her company.

"Is there something I should know?' Miss Flint asked with a cunning grin. "Mrs. Adams said you were unattached, but..." She let the idea waft on the breeze rather than completing it.

Mr. Hedrington pulled his eyes away from Miss Love. "Not yet."

"My, that sounds promising." There was an edge to her tone which detracted from the lightness that he expected it was intended to carry.

"One can hope," he replied simply. He really did not care for Miss Flint, and perhaps if she knew that he was not completely unattached, she would go away. It was, more likely than not, a wish that would be left ungranted, but he thought it worth the effort to attempt.

"Does anyone else know you are hoping?" Miss Flint whispered conspiratorially.

"Yes." He smiled, knowing that such a short answer was not what she sought.

"Will you tell me who?"

"No."

"Is it Miss Love?"

She was persistent. Annoyingly so.

"I will not say."

She gasped. "But you did not say no, so I will assume it is."

"You will not trick me into revealing more than I have."

"You were sitting with them at church yesterday."

"I was, and my son and I dined with them last evening."

It had been a very comfortable dinner at the Loves' cottage, one where Matthias had played with toys all by himself on the carpet while the adults talked. Not once had he clung to his father, and more than once, he had taken his place at either Mr. Love's or Miss Love's side. Since Anna had died, Boyd had not enjoyed a soiree so much as he had last night's.

"I fear you have revealed all, Mr. Hedrington. It is Miss Love who is hoping as you are."

Boyd shrugged. "I will not say, for it is not for me to say."

A scowl touched Miss Flint's features before being quickly tucked away. "You mentioned you have a son."

"I do. Did not Mrs. Adams tell you?" He doubted that very much. All good matchmakers shared all they knew about the gentleman they were promoting to their hopeful charges. He was certain that was just as true on English soil as it was in Nova Scotia.

"She may have said something about you being a widower."

"I am. My Anna died before Matthias and I left Nova Scotia."

"My deepest sympathies."

"Thank you." It seemed as if she were genuinely offering her condolences.

"How old is your son?"

"Four, and he has not been unaffected by his mother's passing. I am afraid it weighs on his young mind quite heavily."

Her brow furrowed as she nodded, seemingly

very concerned. "And how will he feel when his mother is replaced by Miss Love?"

"I have told you; I am not speaking any more on my hopes in that regard." He suspected that his son was going to happily welcome Miss Love as a new member of their family, but he was not about to tell the conniving Miss Flint that.

"Oh, I did not mean to bring that up again."

Boyd did not believe her, but he held his tongue.

"I was just thinking about how challenging it might be for a child to accept a new mother, no matter who she is."

"You are correct, of course. I know I likely would have found it strange, at first, had my father remarried. However, if the lady had been a kind woman who treated me as her own, I would have been very happy to have welcomed her as a second mother. She would never replace my mother, but she would have filled a void." A void that he had always felt greatly.

"And is that how it is when one looks for a second wife, Mr. Hedrington? Are you seeking to fill a void?"

He did not answer immediately, for until just now, he had not truly considered his marrying

Miss Love in such terms. He knew he needed a wife to fulfill his uncle's demands, he knew he needed a mother for Matthias, and he knew that he wanted whomever that lady happened to be to be his companion. However, now that he thought about it, that desire for a companion was likely his own way of seeking to fill the hole that had been ripped in the fabric of his life when Anna died.

"I suppose I am, Miss Flint. I suppose, in a way, I am."

Miss Love would bring him the friendship and assistance he had lost when he lost Anna. The only questions which remained were whether or not she could ever fill the emptiness in his heart and whether or not he could allow her to even try without feeling as if he was betraying his Anna.

Chapter 9

"Mr. Hedrington most certainly dotes on you, Miss Love," Mrs. Adams said upon joining Mrs. Love and Felicity where they stood waiting for their carriage to be brought up. Mr. Love and Mr. Hedrington were occupied a short distance away speaking to some gentlemen.

"We have become fast friends," Mrs. Love answered. "He is an excellent addition to the neighbourhood."

"He is," Mrs. Adams agreed. "Grenwood Hall will be in good hands if he claims it." She allowed her eyes to rest on Felicity. "And it seems he might just be planning to do so. We ladies had nearly given up hope that he would remain in the area. Of course, there are several young ladies who had hoped to claim Grenwood Hall as their home, but none seemed able to make any sort of impression with Mr. Hedrington. I dare say they are destined to be disappointed." She sighed. "I had even hoped when Mallory arrived that she might catch the gentleman's eye. Such an arrangement would have brought my cousin to visit. I have not seen her in years. We correspond, of course, but it is not the same. We were inseparable as children whenever we were together, which was quite often."

"Close relationships are delightful, are they not?" Mrs. Love replied. "I was not fortunate enough to live close to any of my cousins, but my sister and I were close and then we each had our particular friends."

To Felicity, Mrs. Adams and her mother had always seemed very alike. Both loved nothing better than to socialize and talk.

"Perhaps if your daughter succeeds where no one else has, you might be a frequent visitor here," Mrs. Adams said.

"I should like that very much." Mrs. Love's face bore the evidence of her delight at the prospect in a bright smile.

"Is it true, then?" Miss Flint asked, directing her question at Felicity. "Has Mr. Hedrington asked you to marry him?"

Felicity felt her cheeks grow warm. "There is nothing to announce at present." In a week, there would be an announcement but not today.

"But do you wish it to be true?" Miss Flint pressed eagerly.

"I would not be disappointed if it were."

"You and Mr. Hedrington seem to be of a like mind on that account."

There was a particular set to the lady's mouth and a glint in her eyes that warned Felicity away from confiding too much in Miss Flint. She had seen that look before, and it had usually meant that the lady was a schemer who thought herself better than most everyone else. Felicity had even affected that look herself on occasion when she thought it was needed.

"Are we indeed?" Felicity allowed her eyes to open wide in surprise. Pretending was not something that was new to her.

"I think you know you are," Miss Flint said with a practised laugh.

Felicity allowed a brief pause before giving a small shrug and saying, "Perhaps."

One of Miss Flint's brows quirked upward in interest. "I had heard that you were quite the temptress when you were in Bath. I had not thought it an accurate description when I first met you, but you have caught Mr. Hedrington's eye rather quickly."

"Mallory!" Mrs. Adams chided. "This is not the halls of the Assembly rooms."

Felicity's heart was galloping at a rapid pace. What did Miss Flint know of her stay in Bath and how?

"Have you been to Bath?" Mrs. Love asked.

Bless her mother for being inquisitive!

"My grandmother lives there. She is not well, and it seemed like it was the best place for her."

"Do you live with her?" Mrs. Love continued.

"No, but my mother is there now. Our estate is not far from Bath, so it is no inconvenience for my father to travel there and back to visit her."

"That is fortunate," Mrs. Love said. "Of late, my youngest daughter is of Bath. She married Mr. Blakesley. Do you know him?"

"No, I am afraid I do not, but I have heard the name."

"And Mr. Norman," Mrs. Love said with some excitement, "do you know him? He is reportedly the best physician in Bath."

Miss Flint shook her head. "I have not acquainted myself with the physicians. I only know that my grandmother has one."

"Mr. Norman is a dear friend of Mr. Blakesley, so if you do know Mr. Norman, it would be no trouble at all to gain an introduction to Mr. Blakesley. My Grace is blessed to be the wife of the one and friend of the other."

"I will have to remember that," Miss Flint said in a tone that was nearly convincing, though Felicity was certain that Miss Flint did not care one jot if she were to meet either Mr. Blakesley or Mr. Norman.

"Oh! How wonderful for Miss Grace," Mrs. Adams cried. "It is important to marry well and have good connections. Does Mr. Blakesley have an estate or does he also hold some sort of profession like his friend Mr. Norman does?"

"I know Mr. Ramsey," Miss Flint whispered to Felicity while Mrs. Adams was busy discussing Mr. Norman and Mr. Blakesley with Felicity's mother.

Was that how she knew of Felicity's stay in Bath? Felicity blew out a breath slowly and quietly before drawing another. Mr. Ramsey's was not a name she had expected to hear.

"Almost as well as you do," she added with a smile. "But that will be our little secret, will it not?"

"I am sure I do not know of what you speak," Felicity lied.

Miss Flint merely chuckled.

The world was tipping a mite as Felicity drew another breath and willed herself to stay upright and not swoon. She thought she would have more time before she would have to face whispers and viciousness. Had Simon told Miss Flint about his secret rendezvouses with her? Oh, she had been stupid to trust him!

"How do you know him?" she asked when she thought herself able to both speak and stay upright with the same breath.

"I will tell you but not here." She cast a significant look at Mrs. Adams. "You do wish your relationship with him to remain a secret, do you not?"

"Another time then?" Felicity replied.

Miss Flint gave a small nod of her head.

"Are you well?" Mr. Hedrington was at her elbow.

Miss Flint smirked and dropped her eyes to Felicity's abdomen. She arched an eyebrow as if asking a question.

How could she know about the baby? It was not as if Simon had known that he left Felicity with child. It had only been a possibility when he had left her. There was no way he knew, and no one else in Bath knew except for Grace and Walter. Her mind whirled, trying to figure it out.

"Are you well?" Mr. Hedrington asked again.

"Yes, I am well," Felicity assured him, though she was not. She very much was not.

"I came to take my leave," he said. "Mrs. Adams, I would like to thank you for the delightful party."

"You are leaving us already?" Mrs. Adams said. "There is no rush."

There were few who remained. It was not as if Mr. Hedrington was departing early. However, Mrs. Adams' comment sounded exactly like something Felicity's mother would say. Her mother was never eager to have all her guests leave. She liked to have parties continue for just as long as they possibly could.

"My son is waiting. I have already stayed longer than I had intended." He smiled at Felicity.

"Yes, it did seem as if you found *something* to be of particular interest to you today," Mrs. Adams said.

“Not just today.” His gaze left Felicity for a moment but returned as he was replying. “I will call tomorrow if that is acceptable to you.”

“It is. Will you bring Matthias?”

“Not tomorrow, but perhaps the day after that.”

“Tell him I look forward to his visit.”

“He will be delighted to hear it.” His brow furrowed as he studied her. “The top is down on my carriage. May I ask your father to escort you home?”

“That would be a lovely thing,” Mrs. Love replied. “A ride in the fresh air – there is nothing quite like it on a day so fine as this.”

“Miss Love?”

Felicity nodded. “I would like that.”

“I will only be a moment.”

“Have you met his son?” Mrs. Adams asked.

“We have,” Felicity answered.

“That is promising. Not everyone gets to meet his son. I understand he is a bit of a strange child who does not talk and often hides behind his father. I thought he was just shy when he first arrived – that is when I met him – but I hear he is still that way and it is nigh unto a year since he arrived.”

Irritation pricked Felicity's mind at the woman's comments. "Matthias is anything but strange," she said, doing her best to keep her annoyance out of her tone. "He is a lovely boy with a beautiful smile and a tender heart that has been touched by grief." She took her mother's hand. "Far greater grief than any of us ever knew at such a young age. I know I could not imagine suffering the loss he has, and I am much older than he."

"I suppose you are right," Mrs. Adams said. "However, it is odd that he does not speak."

"He will speak when he is ready," Mrs. Love assured her friend. "He has had several conversations of a half dozen words with my husband, but then Mr. Love is very good at drawing people out – even children."

"That is the truth! Your husband is a master at starting and holding a conversation. I know when I invite him to any of my parties that my guests will not lack for a welcoming smile and a friendly word or two."

Felicity had to agree with Mrs. Adams. Her father was a good guest to invite to any soiree.

"Your father has agreed," Mr. Hedrington said as he offered his arm to Felicity. "And, Mrs. Love, he assures me that he will be with you in five minutes. There is just the conclusion of a story to hear about smugglers who once frequented a cove near here."

Mrs. Love laughed. "Is he telling the story or listening?"

"Listening."

"Good, then five minutes it will be. However, if he were telling the tale, it could be much longer."

Mrs. Adams and Mrs. Love had a good laugh over that while Mr. Hedrington chuckled and Felicity smiled at the image of her father entertaining someone with a story. He was good at storytelling. She wondered if she would be so good as he should she ever try to tell a story which was not gossip.

"Are you well?" Mr. Hedrington whispered as they strolled away from the ladies and toward his waiting carriage.

"Can it wait until we are well away from here?" she whispered in reply.

"Has something happened?"

"Yes, but can it wait?"

"Of course, it can."

Miss Flint likely did not know that Mr. Hedrington knew about Mr. Ramsey or Mr. Ramsey's child. It seemed best in Felicity's mind to keep it that way.

"Did Miss Flint question you about me?" he asked as he helped Felicity into the carriage.

"Yes."

"And does she seem to think we are getting married?" There was a playful smile on his lips.

"She does."

"Good. I had hoped to leave her with that impression." He settled into the carriage next to Felicity. "I do not like her."

"It seems we agree about that, Mr. Hedrington," Felicity said with a light laugh.

"But that is not what has you looking ill, is it?" The carriage was making its slow way down the second half of the circular drive.

She shook her head. "You cannot let her know I have told you this."

His brow furrowed. "Why?"

Again, she shook her head. "I do not know, but I feel as if she must not know more than she does. I have seen her sort before." She looked heavenward as tears filled her eyes. "I have been her sort of lady before."

He took her hands in his. "What sort of lady is that?"

"A lady who uses anything she can to scheme her way into getting what she wants." It was such an ugly truth. "How can you wish to marry me? I am not good enough."

"Would you still use whatever you could to get what you want?"

Felicity shrugged and shook her head. "I hope not, but I do not know."

"But you see such behaviour as improper?"

She nodded. "I do, but I think I always knew it was. However, that knowledge did not keep me from acting shamefully."

She knew what she needed to do. He deserved to know all her darkest secrets before he tied himself and his son to someone like her. "I was nearly engaged before Mr. Ramsey."

"Were you?"

"Yes." She dared to peek at him and see the condemnation on his face, but it was not there. Not yet. "I teased and flirted with Mr. Clayton until he liked me."

"That does not seem so bad."

"I did it knowing full-well that my cousin was in

love with him, but I wanted him. So..." She could not bring herself to finish her thought.

However, Mr. Hedrington did not hesitate to finish it for her. "So you used what you could to get what you wanted."

"No matter the cost to my cousin." Oh, the weight of guilt was heavy, and she was not yet wearing all of it.

"Why are you not engaged to Mr. Clayton if you were successful in drawing him along?"

"I never loved him, for if I had, then when I met Mr. Ramsey, my heart would not have been able to be touched. I was smitten with Simon nearly from our first meeting, and I treated Mr. Clayton very poorly while being drawn along by Mr. Ramsey so that finally, Mr. Clayton gave up on me and walked away." Literally. She could still remember him, walking away and looking excessively dejected. At the time, the sorry sight had only brought her a fleeting moment of remorse.

The carriage fell silent with Felicity's completion of her confession. Mr. Hedrington was likely trying to decide how he would withdraw his offer, and the thought made her want to weep. He was such a good man, and if he did not marry her, she would likely never marry, never have a house of her own, never have a father for her child.

"You do not have to marry me," she offered when he remained silent for some time. "I will not hold you to your offer."

"I am not withdrawing my offer."

How could he not?

"I was merely considering what you have told me."

She looked at him expectantly.

"When we marry, I expect you to remain faithful to me – if not for my sake, then for the sake of my son."

"Of course."

"Even if I find I cannot take you to bed?" His jaw clenched, and he grimaced.

"Even then," she agreed.

"Even if Mr. Ramsey were to reappear?"

That was a hard question, but she nodded. "A vow is a vow, Mr. Hedrington. I will keep my vows to you."

His shoulders relaxed as he exhaled. "And I will keep mine to you."

"Must we truly wait a week?"

"Would you honestly promise yourself to me

now – not as one might give a small assurance to a friend but as someone who swears her troth?"

"Yes."

"It is tempting," he said with a smile. "However, I think a week is still a good period of contemplation." He squeezed her hand. "I will not withdraw my offer."

"And I shall not change my answer."

He lifted her fingers to his lips. "Now that we have that settled, tell me why you were looking faint earlier. I feared you would swoon on the spot where you stood next to your mother."

"I thought I was going to," she admitted, "when Miss Flint said she knew Mr. Ramsey and had heard about my stay in Bath."

Mr. Hedrington's eyes grew wide. "She knows about Mr. Ramsey?"

Felicity dropped her eyes to look at the strong hand which held hers. "She intimated that she knew I might be with child."

Mr. Hedrington blew out a breath. "No wonder you looked ill and wish to marry sooner rather than later."

Felicity nodded. "I know it will not erase the stain that I bear, but to have something settled."

She shrugged. "It is foolish. Marriage will change very little in that regard."

The carriage turned into the drive at the cottage.

"I fear you are right about that." He waited until the vehicle drew to a stop, and then hopped down and offered his assistance to her. "Do you think it would be too much for you to take a turn of the garden with me while we wait for your parents. Or if you prefer, we can sit in your favourite spot while you tell me which treats and conversations you enjoyed the most while at Mrs. Adams."

"I am a little fatigued." Whether that was a result of her condition or purely due to emotions, she was not sure.

He wrapped an arm around her shoulder and pulled her closer to his side. "Then, lean on me, and we will make it to your favourite spot where you may rest."

She nestled close to him as they walked slowly toward the bench on the edge of the garden. His warmth enveloped her, and his care touched her heart as no other gentleman had ever done. *This – this giving of one's self for the benefit of another,* she told herself, *must be something like what it felt like to be truly loved.*

She yawned, and he rubbed her shoulder. He was such a good man. She did not deserve him, and yet deep inside, she hoped one day to be so good as he and prove herself worthy of his offer.

Chapter 10

A tug on his coat returned Boyd's attention to the room in which he sat.

"Do you need something, Matthias?"

His son held up a pencil with a dull lead. They were both *working* in the study. Matthias had paper and pencil to write with on a table near the window, while Boyd had his ledgers spread across his desk. From what he could see of Matthias's paper, his son had been far more successful at accomplishing his *work* than Boyd had been.

"Paper?" Matthias asked while his father was trimming the tip of his pencil.

"Not that one." The folded piece of paper on which Matthias's hand rested was of great importance. Miss Love had not changed her mind regarding accepting his offer, and the parson had been willing to grant to Boyd both a license and an appointment to perform the ceremony.

"Special?"

"Yes, that paper is very special."

Special was what Boyd called all the important things he had to do. Matthias was allowed to write on ordinary paper, but the child knew not to mark on anything Boyd had declared special. "In fact, that is likely the most special paper on this desk. Would you like to see it?"

Matthias nodded.

"Take your pencil to your table while I clean up the mess I have made trimming it, and then I will show you."

Eager curiosity was faster than meticulous cleanup, and Matthias was back at this father's side in an instant. Boyd wiped his hands on his handkerchief to remove anything which might smudge the precious document. Then, he carefully unfolded it and smoothed it flat.

"Do you know what it says?"

Matthias giggled and shook his head.

"We shall have to work on that. A master of an estate must know how to read." He tapped Matthias's nose. "And one day, you will be the master of this estate – once I am done with it, that is." He pointed to the line that held his name. "This is my name, here." His finger shifted. "And this is Miss Love's name, here."

Matthias's brow furrowed.

"The rest of it says that she and I are to be married, and once I have a wife, then I can claim our home outright. All the stipulations will be met."

The crease in his son's brow had not faded.

"Do you remember what I told you about the special papers my uncle had written that said we could live here at Grenwood Hall?"

Slowly, Matthias's head bobbed up and down.

"One of the rules on that paper said I needed a wife and you needed a mother."

"Mama?"

"Yes, a new mother. Do you understand?" This was the one moment in all of this arranging for his inheritance that had worried him the most. As much as he had wished for his father to remarry, he also knew that accepting a mother in place of his own would not be easy.

Matthias's face scrunched up as he attempted to put it all together.

"Miss Love has agreed to be my wife and your new mother."

This news was met with a shaking head.

"I thought you liked Miss Love?"

Matthias nodded.

"Then can you tell me what you find so disagreeable about her being your new mother?"

Tears clung to the rims of Matthias's eyes. "Not Mama," he said, through trembling lips.

Boyd gathered him into his lap. "No," he said softly, "she is not and cannot be the mama you had. She must be who she is – a lady who cares very much for you and wishes to be part of your life." He rubbed Matthias's back while he held him close. "Your Mama is in heaven, but we have been granted someone to help make us a whole family again."

"Not Mama."

"I know." He missed Anna, too. Taking a wife was something he had to do and which he knew was best for Matthias. However, doing what was best was not always easy.

"Mr. Hedrington? Mrs. Feasby said I could find you here. Mother is in the garden. I am not unchaperoned."

Miss Love's eyes were filled with questions when Boyd met them with his own.

"I can come back," she offered softly. "I was just anxious about the license."

"I have it. Come in."

"Are you certain?"

Boyd nodded. She needed to be part of all the challenges that becoming a family would entail. The license was purchased, but that did not mean the wedding had to take place.

"I was just telling Matthias that we were getting married."

Her hand flew to her heart. "And it made him cry?"

"Not Mama," Matthias said for a third time.

Much to Boyd's surprise, Miss Love came around the desk and dropped to her knees.

"No, Sweetling, no, I do not want to be your Mama. I want to be your mother but not your Mama, though you may call me that if you wish. Indeed, you can call me whatever you want."

"Not Mama?"

Miss Love brushed at a tear. "No, not Mama. Felicity. Can you say that?"

Matthias shook his head, but it was a slow and not-altogether-certain refusal.

"Maybe someday," Miss Love assured him with a smile as she dashed another tear from her cheek.

Matthias held out Boyd's handkerchief to her, the same one he had just used to dry his eyes and nose. Miss Love paused for a moment but then took it and thanked him before drying her eyes.

"Are we still friends?" Miss Love asked Matthias. "Even if I am to come live at your house?"

Matthias's eyes grew wide, and he looked between her and his father.

"When we marry, Miss Love will come to live with us." He had thought that part of the explanation about a new mother would have been understood. "Would you like that?"

Matthias nodded.

"We are friends then?" Miss Love repeated.

Again, Matthias nodded. Apparently, so long as Miss Love was not attempting to take his mother's place but was promising to be a friend, Matthias was happy to have her come to live with them.

"Now," Boyd said, giving Matthias one more hug and then placing him on the floor next to the kneeling Miss Love, "we are going to the garden. You may go ahead of us."

Matthias stood for a moment looking at Miss Love. Then, he wrapped his arms around her neck in a quick hug. It was so quick that Miss Love barely had time to place one arm around the child before he had released her and moved toward the door.

"He hugged me," she said as she once again dried her tears with the soiled handkerchief.

"He did, indeed, and that is no small thing. Even I rarely get one of those. Anna, however, was showered with them." Boyd held out his hand to her to help her rise. "You are going to be a wonderful mother to him. How did you know to tell him he could call you something other than mama?"

"My father."

"Your father? I am not certain I understand."

She straightened her skirts after rising. "Mrs. Adams and her guest came to call yesterday." She placed her hand on his proffered arm.

"And this has to do with your father?"

Her answering smile was filled with humor. "Yes, it does. If you will allow me to continue, I will explain it fully."

He chuckled. “Please continue, Miss Love.”

“Thank you, sir. As you know, Miss Flint is such a charming young woman.” Contempt dripped from every word.

“Charming is perhaps too kind a word,” he offered in agreement, earning him another amused smile. This being together and talking about whatever needed to be discussed was beginning to feel very welcome to him.

“She mentioned something about my taking the place of Matthias’s mother and how I must be very brave to be taking on such a challenge. I did not let it show that such a thought bothered me, or, at least, I thought I had not. However, my father brought it up after Miss Flint had left. He guessed that I was uneasy with it, and he mentioned that Matthias would probably be feeling similarly.”

“That is wise.”

“He is.” She sighed. “If only I had paid better attention to him while I was growing up, perhaps I would not find myself where I am.”

“You are likely correct, but then, who would I marry?”

She shook her head. “It is not as if I am the only lady willing to fill the position.”

"There may be those who were hopeful, but they were not for me." Despite their short acquaintance and her delicate condition and the issues that could pose, marrying Miss Love was beginning to feel right. The thought was both comforting and disturbing. He, like his son, did not wish to replace Anna.

"I think Miss Flint would not say no to an offer," Miss Love teased.

"Miss Flint would be the last to receive an offer," he assured her with a laugh. "I would take my chances with seasickness and return to Nova Scotia before offering for her."

"I am flattered that I am a better option than seasickness."

"That is not what I meant!"

Her laugh was as becoming as her smile. It was no wonder that she had had her pick of gentlemen.

"I am happy to have you as my wife."

"Truly?"

He nodded. He was happy to have her as his companion for life. They already seemed to fit together quite well as friends. Perhaps that was why marrying her felt right. That was a much more calming feeling than thinking of her as a replacement for Anna.

"Now, tell me," he said, "has Miss Flint revealed to you how she knows Mr. Ramsey." He hated to bring up the name, but it had been several days since Mrs. Adams' garden party and still, Miss Flint had not related that information to Miss Love.

She drew and released a deep breath. "No, and while I am curious to know, I also am afraid to ask. Truthfully, I hope that she will forget about him, though I do know that is unlikely. If it were me trying to do harm to another lady, I would hold the information until it could do the most good for me."

That was precisely what he expected Miss Flint was doing.

"Mr. Hedrington, you have guests, and I do not mean the Loves," Mrs. Feasby was looking rather put out as she joined them on the garden path where they were strolling. "I attempted to hint that you were not available, but it seems some ladies will not be put off."

"Who is it?'

"Mrs. Adams and Miss Flint, sir. I believe Mrs.

Adams would have taken her leave if it had not been for Miss Flint."

It seemed that Mrs. Feasby did not like Miss Flint either. It made Boyd wonder if the lady had any friends at all, for she did not seem to be making a favourable impression on any of the people he held as close confidants.

"They would like to wish you happy."

He grimaced. Small towns and gossip were a familiar pair. "I see. I suppose we must allow them."

"I suppose we must," Mrs. Feasby agreed. "They are with Mrs. Love, sir."

He looked at Felicity. "Shall we?" With a nod from her, he led her the short distance across the lawn to where Mrs. Love sat, conversing with her friend Mrs. Adams.

"We must apologize for the intrusion, but Mallory wanted to be among the first to congratulate you on your betrothal." Mrs. Adams smiled broadly. "I knew how it would be when I saw you together, and I was right. Oh, what a happy thing it is! First, Mallory receives news that her sister is finally married – it has taken years to get that young man to the point – and then we hear that you, Mr. Hedrington, had been to see the parson about a license." She glanced at Felicity. "When will the happy day be?"

"Seven days hence," Boyd answered.

"So soon!"

"I am impatient to see my estate settled." He squeezed Miss Love's hand, hoping she would understand why he was being so blunt with the lady. It was best that no one tried to concoct any other reason for the quick nuptials. There would be plenty of speculation later, but Miss Love did not need that now.

"Oh, yes. Oh, yes. I can understand that, but is there not also a hint of attraction?" Mrs. Adams asked. "I thought I had noticed some at my party."

"I think that goes without saying," Boyd answered.

"So long as it was not too much attraction which spurs you to settle your estate so quickly." Mrs. Adams winked at him. "I fear that might be the thing which finally brought Helen's young man to the point," she added in a whisper.

"Mrs. Adams," Miss Flint chided.

"I am only repeating what your mother said in her letter when she sent the marriage announcement to me, and Mrs. Love and I have been friends for years! From her first arrival with her new husband on their wedding trip."

"Your sister is married, and you were not there to witness the ceremony?" Mrs. Love asked in surprise.

"No, I was not." There was a sharpness to the reply. "Father thought it best if I was not."

"That is odd," Mrs. Love said. "Was your mother able to attend despite your grandmother's failing health? It would be a very sad thing indeed if your mother was not in attendance."

"She was there. Grandmother even joined her for it. Our estate is not far from Bath, you know."

"Yes, yes, you told me. Is your sister's husband handsome?"

Miss Flint's eyes rested on Miss Love. "Quite."

"And does he have an estate?"

"He does."

"Is it close to your family's estate?"

"No more than twenty miles away. His father and mine have been good friends for their entire lives, and my sister was promised to Simon before either was out of leading strings. My father has always wished for a familial connection with his friend. However, Simon was less than willing to just fall into step with the plan, you see." She was still looking at Miss Love. "Therefore, his father allowed him some time to participate in the season and dance with other ladies before demanding he did his duty. It seems that with the right inducement, he finally saw reason and now my sister is happily Mrs. Ramsey at long last."

Mrs. Love gasped and looked faint, and next to him, Miss Love swayed and required his assistance to steady herself.

Simon Ramsey.

Good heavens! *That* was how Miss Flint knew Mr. Ramsey.

Chapter 11

Pull air in. Push it out. Felicity concentrated on breathing and staying upright. Miss Flint had delivered a powerfully hurtful blow, and she likely knew she had. However, Felicity was not of a mind to allow her to know how deeply Simon's marrying another cut.

"Have we said something amiss?" Mrs. Adams asked.

Felicity looked at her mother and gave a small shake of her head.

"No, no, it is..." Her mother looked at a loss for how to continue.

"We are surprised is all," Felicity forced herself to say. She could do this. She had concocted fabulous stories before. "We knew Mr. Ramsey when he was in Bath. In fact, we had met him earlier in the summer at a house party."

"Did you?" Mrs. Adams's expression was all startled curiosity while her guest looked only mildly surprised and even that was likely feigned.

"Oh, yes," Mrs. Love agreed.

"And he seemed quite smitten with a young lady in Bath the last time we saw him." Felicity gave her mother a pointed look, willing her to add to the story. Unfortunately, her mother did not appear to be able to figure out where the story was leading.

"Was Helen in Bath?" Mrs. Adams asked Miss Flint.

"No, it has always been just Mother and me."

Though her legs were feeling a bit less wobbly, Felicity dared not remain standing for too long. She glanced at Mr. Hedrington. "Do you wish to sit down?"

"If you do," he said. His eyes held a great deal of concern.

"I do," she said with a smile, hoping to ease his mind a trifle.

Mrs. Love scooted as far to the end of the bench on which she sat as she could to allow room for both Felicity and Mr. Hedrington to be seated, albeit not comfortably. However, it was better than standing when a lady was still not certain she could keep her senses and not dissolve into tears or fade away in a swoon.

"How long were you in Bath?" Felicity asked Miss Flint while running a hand along her skirt to smooth it. Grace's description of a blonde beauty standing altogether too close to Simon in the carriage corridor at the Upper Rooms flitted through her mind

"Oh, four months I suppose," she replied.

"Did you visit the theatre?"

"A couple of times." Miss Flint eyed her warily.

"Is not the theatre entertaining?" Mrs. Love cried. "I would be content to see a play once a week if it were possible."

"I think you said the same about the concerts, Mother."

"I did," Mrs. Love agreed with a nod. "Did you get to take in a concert? I know it is not always possible to participate in all the pleasures an area might hold when one is tending to an infirm relation."

"My grandmother enjoys music, so we took her to two concerts while I was there."

"How lovely. There is nothing like music to lift the spirits. That is, of course, if one cannot go to the theatre." Mrs. Love laughed lightly, and Mrs. Adams joined her.

"Did you ever attend a ball at the Upper Rooms?" Felicity asked. Again, she ran a hand along her skirt. It was simply impossible not to do so, for her agitation must find some release.

Miss Flint's lips curled into a sly smile. "Not recently."

"But you have seen the rooms?"

Miss Flint nodded.

Felicity tipped her head and furrowed her brow. "Are you certain you did not attend a ball there recently?"

"She has already said she did not," Mrs. Love inserted. "Why do you ask such a thing?"

"I was just thinking of a lady Grace described to us as being stunningly beautiful."

"Which lady was that?" Mrs. Love asked with interest.

"Do you not remember the one she saw at the last ball we attended?"

Her mother's lips parted, and her eyes grew the tiniest bit wide as she looked at Felicity. Then her gaze shifted to Miss Flint before returning to Felicity. "I believe you are correct."

"But you were never at a ball," Felicity said with a small laugh, "so it could not have been you. However, I must say you do look like the lady my sister described. She and I were walking in the hallway..." Felicity shook her head and smiled.

Oh! She must not do that again. Her head was still far too light feeling to be shaken.

"It matters not. It was not you as you did not attend a ball at the Upper Rooms, and that may be why you did not see Mr. Ramsey with his lady," Felicity added.

Miss Flint's lips parted as if she was going to retort, but then they closed again.

"Did Mr. Ramsey know you were in Bath?" Mrs. Love asked. "He must have known your grandmother was there if your families are so close."

Miss Flint turned a smile on Mrs. Love. "He did know we were in Bath. He even visited us, but he made no mention of a lady. It was likely just a flirtation."

Mrs. Love leaned forward. "Oh, no," she said most intently, "I had heard that he had spoken to the lady's father about marrying her." She glanced at Mrs. Adams and nodded her head. "I fear, Miss Flint, that your sister has not married so well as she could have if Mr. Ramsey is the sort to play with one lady's heart while he is betrothed to another."

Mrs. Adams gasped. "How dreadful! I hope for Helen's sake he is not such a fellow!"

"It would be no more than she deserves," Miss Flint muttered.

Curiosity about Miss Helen Flint – she would not call her Mrs. Ramsey, not even in her mind – rose within Felicity.

"What was that my dear?" Mrs. Adams asked.

"I just said it is not something anyone deserves," Miss Flint lied.

"What is your sister like?" Felicity asked as she once again smoothed her skirt. "I find I miss Grace greatly some days. We have never been apart for very long until now."

Miss Flint pressed her lips together and was silent for a moment before replying. "Helen is Father's favourite. She is very much like our mother," she directed that part of her reply to Mrs. Adams. "She has darker hair than mine, but we are enough alike in stature to share gowns without any alterations."

Was it Felicity's imagination, or had the lady actually drawn her shoulders back as she smiled at Mr. Hedrington? There was only one reason for doing such a thing. Felicity was well-versed in flaunting her figure in such a fashion. She slipped her hand into Mr. Hedrington's, drawing both his attention and a smile. He was hers. Miss Flint and her sister may have stolen Mr. Ramsey from her, but there was no way Miss Flint was going to take Mr. Hedrington. She smiled and fluttered her lashes when Miss Flint's eyes narrowed.

"Does your sister have any particular accomplishments?" Mrs. Love asked. "Felicity is very good at drawing and painting, while Grace is better at stitching and singing. Both are quite good at playing the piano."

"Helen plays the piano and the violin. The violin is my mother's favourite instrument." She again looked at Mrs. Adams. "And, of course, she draws and sings and the like. However, playing the piano is her favourite thing."

"A house that has music is blessed," Mrs. Adams said. "Our house, I must admit to my shame, is not such a house unless my daughters are home. I never could get my mind to coordinate the notes I saw with the action my fingers should take to produce the correct sound."

"You sing," Mrs. Love said. "I have heard you. Music is music no matter the instrument used to make it. Do you like music, Mr. Hedrington?"

"I do. In fact, I play piano myself. I do not play it well, but I can pick out a tune." He squeezed Felicity's hand. "You will have to play for Matthias and me. We have not had someone to play for us in a long time."

Two years, Felicity thought. He meant two years – since his Anna had died.

"Did your wife play well?" Mrs. Love asked.

"She did, but she did not sing. She refused to do so, though I heard her when she did not know anyone, save for Matthias, was listening." His lips curled into a soft, reverential smile.

Tears pricked Felicity's eyes. How was she ever supposed to compete with his sweet memories of his wife? Would she ever be able to make him smile like that when he was not thinking of Anna?

"It must be challenging to think of replacing her," Miss Flint said softly as if she genuinely cared for Mr. Hedrington's heart.

Mr. Hedrington's brow furrowed, and his smile faded. "I am not replacing her."

Miss Flint blinked. "Are you not getting married?"

His hand squeezed Felicity's tightly. "I am. However, I am not replacing Anna." He released Felicity's hand. "I should check on tea. I cannot remember if I told Mrs. Feasby when to have it ready."

Felicity looked at him in question. She knew he had told Mrs. Feasby that they would have tea as usual. Her heart sank. He must be just as reluctant to have her become his wife as Matthias was to have her as his mother. She swallowed, willing the tears to say where they should.

"It must be very difficult," Miss Flint said with a small triumphant smile for Felicity.

She was wrong. She could not do this. She could not continue this battle of wits with Miss Flint when Mr. Hedrington was not at her side. Without him, what was she? An unwanted, former lover, who had not been anything more than a lady to seduce.

She rose on legs that still did not feel as if they could support her. However, she would have to trust them to do their duty for she could not stay here any longer. "If you will excuse me," she said before hurrying off after Mr. Hedrington.

Though it likely appeared to the others that she was chasing after him, she was not. She needed to find a place where it would be safe to feel all that she was currently pushing down. She wound her way down the paths in the garden toward the kitchen garden. She had seen a bench near some trees over there, and in all the times she had been at Grenwood, she had yet to see anyone sitting there. Therefore, it seemed a safe place to collapse, and collapse is what she did when she reached it. Her legs crumpled under her, and she sat down heavily on the bench. With tears already flowing, she buried her face in her hands and allowed herself to feel everything.

Her heart cracked and crumbled as she replayed the news that Simon was married. She had known he was not coming back for her because he had not sought her out since she had last seen him in Bath, but hearing that he was not returning because he was married to someone else somehow felt darker and heavier than just being abandoned had.

Her child fluttered in her abdomen. It had started doing that yesterday. She pulled one hand from her face and caressed her child. "I will love you," she whispered. "I will love you," she repeated. Even if no one else ever did, she added silently.

And that was likely the thought that hurt the most. Her heart longed for someone to love her. No, she thought, not just someone. She longed for her husband to love her. A sob made her shudder and, then, much to her chagrin, her stomach retched. It had been a few hours since she had eaten. There was not much in her stomach to expel, but the silly thing insisted on attempting to rid itself of nothing.

When her body had finally relaxed, she slid from the bench and sat on the ground resting her back against the wooden seat. She drew in a breath slowly and expelled it just as slowly while she wondered if she could slip into Grenwood Hall through the kitchen and find a place to wash her face and maybe lie down before she had to see anyone. She turned so that she could rest her head on her arms on the bench.

She would sit here for a few more minutes to make certain her stomach was done roiling and to give her face time to dry in the breeze and begin to cool. She closed her eyes, concentrating on the steady inhale and exhale of air. Weariness washed over her. She would just rest here for a moment. Just a moment. But as her breathing slowed while she relaxed, slumber overcame her.

Chapter 12

Of all the vile and obnoxious creatures one might find in England, Miss Flint had to be the most loathsome! How could Miss Love sit there and be so pleasant? Oh, Boyd knew Miss Love was not really delighted to hear about Miss Flint's sister. How could she be? He had felt her tremble and sway. Yet, she sat there, keeping her composure and carrying on a discussion with *that* woman.

He slowed his pace as he neared the house. He did not need to check on when or where the refreshments were going to be laid out. He knew Mrs. Feasby had her instructions and would see that they were completed in fine fashion. He just could not sit on that bench and keep his tongue from telling Mrs. Adams precisely what he thought of her guest and her guest's sister! He still wanted to, but that would not do anyone any favours. And so, he had removed himself from the temptation.

"Mr. Hedrington?" Mrs. Feasby was near the garden door speaking to Matthias's nursemaid. "Is something wrong?"

"*That* woman." He pointed back toward where Miss Flint, Mrs. Adams, Mrs. Love, and Miss Love were seated. "*That* woman," he repeated, "needs to be gone, and I am not certain I can remove her from my garden without insulting Mrs. Adams."

He liked Mrs. Adams. He did not wish to ruin a friendship with a resident of the community over the actions of a visitor, especially when he was nearly certain Mrs. Adams had no idea what her guest was doing. Miss Flint was sly and hateful, while Mrs. Adams, though somewhat of a matchmaking busybody, was pleasant and kind.

"I will see to it, sir," Mrs. Feasby said. "I will have Miss Love and Mrs. Love in the drawing room..." She looked at the watch which hung on her chatelaine. "... in ten minutes as expected, and with any luck, Mrs. Adams and Miss Flint will be on their way home. I may, however, have to tell a half-truth or discover some unnecessary task that must be done."

"I frankly do not care how you accomplish the removal of that woman." Boyd only wished Miss Flint gone and quickly before she could do or say anything further to harm Miss Love.

Mrs. Feasby gave him a questioning look before turning back to Susan to finish her instructions about bringing Matthias to the drawing room in ten minutes. Then, when Susan had left them, she turned back to Boyd.

"Has Miss Flint done something dreadful?"

Boyd scrubbed his face. "She brought news which she joyfully delivered, knowing full-well that the news would be painful for Miss Love."

"What news might that be?"

"You know about Miss Love's need to marry."

"I do."

He shook his head and blew out a breath. The anger he felt at Miss Flint's delight in Miss Love's suffering would not leave him. "Mr. Ramsey has married."

"Mr. Ramsey is...?" The look Mrs. Feasby gave Boyd told him that she knew who Mr. Ramsey was, but she would not proceed without clarification.

"The baby's father."

Sadness mixed with displeasure settled on Mrs.

Feasby's face, furrowing her brow and causing her to frown as she shook her head. "And how did Miss Flint know that Mr. Ramsey is married?"

Boyd closed his eyes, allowing himself to feel the sorrow he imagined had gripped Miss Love's heart at the news. "He married Miss Flint's sister."

Mrs. Feasby's eyebrows lifted high. "Oh, well, that is unfortunate, is it not?" She tsked softly and muttered, "The poor dear."

Boyd paced back and forth in front of the garden door. Mr. Ramsey's being married was far more than unfortunate. It was utterly earth-shattering for Miss Love. He knew it had to be.

He rubbed the back of his neck. It was not as if he wished Mr. Ramsey to be free to return and claim Miss Love. Indeed, the thought of such a thing made Boyd wish to revisit the parson and move up their appointment to be married to tomorrow morning, and it was not because he needed to marry her for the sake of his inheritance that he wanted to hasten their wedding. Miss Love deserved better than Mr. Ramsey. She deserved to be loved.

He stopped mid-pace.

She deserved to be loved.

"Was there anything else, Mr. Hedrington?"

Boyd blinked. Was Mrs. Feasby still standing there waiting to be dismissed? He shook his head, and she began to walk away.

"Wait," he called to her.

"Yes, sir?"

"I am certain you are not the person of whom I should ask this, but I have no one else at present to question." He swallowed. "Can a person love twice in one lifetime?" If not, perhaps he was doing Miss Love a disservice by marrying her. That thought made him wish to weep. He did not want to be another source of sorrow for Miss Love.

Mrs. Feasby's replying smile was understanding. "It has always been my belief that the capacity of the heart to love is only restricted by the mind's willingness to allow it. I am not saying that each time one loves it will be the same. We change as life changes and so changes the way we love." She stepped closer to him. "I have never been married, sir, but that does not mean that I have never loved someone as deeply as a wife loves a husband."

He looked at her curiously, wanting to ask her more on the subject, but not daring to.

"Open your mind to what your heart is saying,"

she added. "Do not let love slip past you if you are free to grasp it."

He nodded and thanked her.

As she walked away, Boyd considered allowing himself to love another as he had loved Anna. The thought was both comforting while at the same time being terrifying. He longed to love and be loved as he had been. However, to love again brought with it the possibility of grief and loss. Could he withstand such pain again? He was not certain he could, but...

He blew out a breath. Miss Love deserved to be loved. If he was not brave enough to face a shattered heart once again, then he was most certainly doing her a disservice in marrying her. It was not a thought he wished to contemplate, but it was one which he had to consider.

He entered the house and made his way to his study. The license was still lying on his desk. The arrangement had been agreed to by all parties, and nobody had entered it blindly. He had even told Miss Love that he was uncertain if he could love her as a wife.

He sat down in his chair and read the license to himself, remembering his relief and delight at having received it. He had been relieved to know that his inheritance and, by extension, that of Matthias, had been secured, but his delight had come from knowing that the lady with whom he would share his life was a lady who loved his son and whom he looked forward to seeing each day.

Rising from his chair, he replaced the license on his desk. Even if the wedding could be easily called off, he did not wish it to be. He *wanted* to see Miss Love every day for however long the Lord granted them time together. Was that because he loved her, or was it merely because they were good friends? He was not certain, but, whatever it was, it felt hopeful, and as if it could be the beginning of love.

He thought of Miss Love kneeling on the floor, right where he was now standing, and telling his son that she did not want to take his mother's place, and Boyd knew it was true. Miss Love would make her own place both in Matthias's life and his. As he had told Miss Flint, he was not replacing Anna. No one could ever be to him what Anna was. She had been and always would be his first love and the mother of his firstborn. However, that did not mean that Miss Love could not be just as dear to him as Anna had been. If he could allow these hopeful feelings to take root, she could very likely be his second love. He blew out a breath. And hopefully, she would be his last.

A smile curled his lips. He should thank Miss Flint, he thought as he exited the study. For without her questions about replacing his wife the thoughts that had just sorted themselves out, but had troubled him for days, might still be plaguing him with questions and doubts.

"Miss Flint and Mrs. Adams are departing. You, along with Mrs. Love and Miss Love, will have to look over some receipt books with me to find just the perfect meal to serve in celebration of your marriage," Mrs. Feasby said when she met him on the path.

"I will?" He looked from his housekeeper to Mrs. Love.

"Oh, most certainly," Mrs. Love assured him. "I doubt our cottage is large enough for a wedding feast, so having it here would be much better. That being said, I still wish to plan the breakfast. There are a few items that Felicity adores, and I will provide, but this is a joining of two families. Therefore, it is absolutely necessary that we discover what both you and Matthias would like to have on that day."

"That seems logical."

"And it was an excellent excuse to get rid of that horrid Miss Flint," Mrs. Love added. "Mrs. Feasby was brilliant to think of it. You know I adore Mrs. Adams, and we are as close as two distant friends can be. However, that does not mean I have to like her relations. In fact, I think I am allowed to despise the one staying with her at present. Did you know that my Grace saw that woman being very cozy with Mr. Ramsey at the Upper Rooms? I am shocked and appalled on Felicity's behalf, but my sentiments are greatly deepened knowing that Miss Flint was doing such a thing when she knew her sister was to marry him. It is no wonder her father did not want her at the wedding. Can you just imagine the scene that would have been? One daughter pledging her troth to Mr. Ramsey while the other was winking at him?" She shuddered at the horror of it all.

Boyd could not blame her for shuddering. When the details of the situation were laid before him in full, he also found himself wishing to shudder. The sooner Miss Flint returned to Bath, the better. He would have to make a point of not calling on Mrs. Adams until her guest was gone.

"Where is your daughter?" he asked Mrs. Love.

"Why with you, is she not?"

His eyes shifted to Mrs. Feasby, who only shook her head. Boyd turned his attention back to Mrs. Love.

"She is not with me. Why did you think she was?"

"Not with you?" Mrs. Love cried. "How can she not be with you? She followed behind you when you left us. She might not have shown it, but she was quite distraught. I always could tell when she was truly unwell by the way she would smooth her skirt over and over for no reason."

He had seen Felicity do that while they were sitting on the bench and she was presenting herself as if she had very few cares in the world. The rhythm of his heart picked up a pace. He had known she was upset, yet, he had thought her well enough to be left in the care of her mother. The agony of having left her when she needed him gripped him, causing his breathing to be laboured while panic raced through him.

"I did not see her," he admitted. "But then, I was

rather angry with Miss Flint and not paying attention as I should have been." His eyes searched the garden.

"Maybe she went to check on Matthias," Mrs. Love suggested.

"She was not with Matthias when I saw him," Boyd said. Where could she be?

"Mrs. Love and I will search the house. Miss Love could have wished for a morsel of food or a drink of water," Mrs. Feasby said.

That was a possibility.

"You can canvas the garden," Mrs. Feasby continued.

He would begin with the parts of the garden which would be hidden from Miss Flint's view, for he was certain Felicity was looking for someplace to hide from that woman.

Up one path, down another, around a bend, into the wildwood, and back. He had begun his search walking quickly, but by the time he was certain she was nowhere in the garden and beginning to wonder if she had walked toward the cliffs, he was running. His heart pounded, and his mind cried out prayers that he would find her and that she would be safe.

"You, there!" he cried as he saw a footman carrying a bucket through the kitchen garden.

"Yes, sir."

"Have you seen Miss Love?"

"No, sir, but Molly has."

Boyd bent over and rested his hands on his thighs as he breathed heavily both from the exertion of running and the relief of knowing Felicity had been seen.

"Where is she?" he called to the footman.

"Molly said she was on the bench yonder but needed help to come to the house. I am taking a pail of water to clean up a bit of a mess, and then, I was to help Miss Love to the kitchen."

"Is she ill?" his heart climbed into his throat. She had not seemed ill when he had left her, but the strain of what Miss Flint had revealed might have precipitated an illness. He scolded himself again for leaving her when she needed him. How reckless he had been.

The footman nodded. "Molly said she was."

Boyd did not wait for any further information. He ran ahead of the footman and found Felicity sitting on the ground with her head resting on the bench. Her bonnet was in her lap, and next to her, was what he assumed had at one time been the contents of her stomach.

"Oh, my darling Felicity," he said as he knelt beside her.

"I was tired," she said softly.

"Allow me to help you to the house." He offered her his hand to help her rise.

She seemed steady enough when she rose, but he wrapped an arm around her shoulder and drew her to him. "Put your arm around my waist and lean on me, or shall I carry you?" Perhaps that would be better.

"I can walk. I was just tired and fell asleep. I assure you that am well. I am hungry, but I am well."

"Are you positive you are well?"

She nodded.

He was not sure he believed her. There was so much sadness in her eyes when he looked at her.

"I have had Mrs. Feasby rid us of that heinous Miss Flint."

"She is gone?"

"Yes, and hopefully, she will never be back."

They walked in silence for half the length of the kitchen garden.

"You do not have to marry me if you do not wish it." Felicity's words were barely above a whisper.

"Why would you think I did not wish to marry you?" Boyd asked in surprise.

"You were smiling about Anna, and then, Miss Flint asked you about replacing her, and then..." He felt her shoulders lift and lower in a shrug as if she could not say the rest.

"And then, I left you?"

She nodded and brushed at her cheek. She was crying, and it was he who had made her cry. He was the source of her pain.

He stopped walking and scooped her into his arms so that he could hold her close.

"I can walk," she protested.

He did not care. He was not letting her go when she so obviously needed comfort.

"Forgive me. Please, forgive me," he said. "I only meant to find a way to get rid of Miss Flint. I was not walking away from you nor will I ever walk away from you. You will be my wife."

A maid stepped out of the kitchen door.

"Hold the door," he called.

The startled maid did as she was told.

Before entering the house, Boyd pressed a kiss

against Felicity's hair and whispered, "You will be my wife, for I want no other."

Chapter 13

Felicity blinked to adjust her eyes from the brightness of the out of doors to the dimmer light inside the house.

"I see you have found her." Mrs. Feasby stood inside the passageway into which Mr. Hedrington had carried Felicity. "Is she well?"

"I am perfectly well," Felicity said. "I told him I could walk." Not that she minded overly much being held by Mr. Hedrington. She just did not like looking foolish if it could at all be helped.

"I preferred that she did not," Mr. Hedrington said. "She needs some food and drink, as well as a place to wash her face."

"Would my room work?" Mrs. Feasby asked. "I know it is not grand, but there are a chair and a washbasin."

Felicity opened her mouth to protest once again

that she could walk, but Mr. Hedrington spoke first.

"That seems a wise choice."

"I can walk," Felicity said, but her words fell on deaf ears.

"Bring her in here. Molly, fill the water pitcher and bring a glass of something sweet." Mrs. Feasby opened the door to their right. "Use whatever you need," she said to Felicity as Mr. Hedrington finally allowed her to stand.

"You should sit," he suggested.

"I am well."

"Please."

Concern etched such a deep furrow between his eyebrows that Felicity could not bear to refuse him, and so she sat down on a rocking chair in the corner of the room.

"Will you forgive me?" Though they were alone, Mr. Hedrington spoke softly since the door was still open. "I thought it would not be a problem for me to leave you with your mother while I saw to the disposal of our unwanted guest." He shook his head. "I was not thinking clearly, but you seemed so composed. Surprisingly so, truth be told."

Felicity smiled at him and held out her hand,

which he took with alacrity. He bore such a marked resemblance to Matthias when he was anxious about something. "I have had many years of practice at pretending."

"You are very good at it." He stepped close to her, released her hand, and knelt on the floor next to her before once again claiming her hand in his.

"I am not proud of the skill," Felicity said, "and I would not have used it except that I could not allow Miss Flint to know how deeply her news affected me."

Mr. Hedrington's free hand joined the hand which was already holding hers. "It grieves me to know that you were treated so ill, both by Mr. Ramsey and by Miss Flint." He paused. "Will you forgive me for leaving you with Miss Flint?"

She nodded. "Of course." How could she not forgive him? He had only been attempting to spare her from having to put up with Miss Flint.

Molly entered and placed a pitcher of water near the basin and then gave Mrs. Feasby's prescribed sweet beverage to Felicity. While Felicity was happy to have something to drink, she was sorry that holding the glass required Mr. Hedrington to release her hand.

"I thought I had lost you," Mr. Hedrington whispered as she sipped the sweet and fruity vinegar from her glass. "I am so glad I did not." He cupped her cheek and caressed it with his thumb. "I want to marry you, Felicity, and not just so I can claim this estate, but because I love you."

"You love me?" Her hand trembled as it lowered the glass from which she had been sipping. Had she truly heard him say that he loved her?

He took her glass from her. "I believe I do. I was considering the possibility of loving you while Mrs. Feasby was getting rid of Miss Flint, and as I considered it, it seemed, in all likelihood, that I was already falling in love with you."

"But..." She did not want to ask it, but she felt she must. "What about Anna?"

Again, he cupped her cheek. "I will always love Anna, but that does not mean I cannot also love you. When I saw you sitting next to that bench with your head resting on it, the dread I had felt upon hearing you were missing fled from me, and I knew to the very core of my being that all would be well so long as you were by my side."

"It was just relief." Again, she did not want to say such a thing, but she had to be certain that he was not misconstruing his feelings. She did not want to allow her heart to hope only to have it crushed once again when the love that it expected in return for the love it wanted to offer turned out to be nothing more than a passing fancy.

"No." He shook his head adamantly. "It was not just relief at having found you. I do not want to live without you, Felicity. I need you."

Hope welled up within her. Could he truly love her?

"Why?" She pressed. "Why do you need me?"

"Do not ask me to explain it at present, for I cannot. I only know that to be completely happy as I move toward my future at Grenwood, you must be part of it."

Happy tears filled her eyes. "How can you love me? You know that I have been a selfish creature who carries the result of my foolishness in the form of another man's child."

He laughed as he held her face between his hands. "I do not know how I love you. I cannot explain that any more than I can tell you why I need you. I only know that I do, and that I do not care what errors you made in the past if you will promise yourself to me from now until the Good Lord parts us."

"I have already agreed to marry you."

He shook his head. "I am not asking you to marry me. I have already done that. I am asking you to love me and allow me to love you. Be mine. Forever."

She could not have held back her tears is she had wanted to. The fulfillment of her longings to be loved and adored so greatly as her mother was by her father knelt before her.

"Do not cry," he said as he wiped at her tears with his hands.

"It cannot be helped for my happiness cannot be contained and must be allowed some release."

He became perfectly still as he looked at her expectantly.

"I would be honoured to be yours, but only if you will be mine. My heart for yours."

He closed his eyes. "I no longer believe I love you." He drew a deep breath as a smile overtook his features. He opened his eyes, and for so long as she lived, Felicity was certain she would never forget the love she saw there. "I know I love you, for the joy and peace your words have brought me could have no other source."

He drew her face forward and kissed her forehead and then her left cheek, after which he whispered, "I will kiss you properly on our wedding day." Then, he placed a final kiss near the ear into which he had whispered.

Of all the kisses Felicity had ever received – and she had received many – she could not remember a single one which rivaled Boyd's for speaking to her heart and binding her to him. The others had stirred her emotions and flamed her desires, but none had touched her heart as the three gentle kisses he had given her did.

"Are you ready to join your mother and Matthias?" Boyd asked.

"After I wash my face." Felicity rose and went to the washbasin. She poured water into it and dipped a cloth in the water.

"What is wrong?" Boyd asked when Felicity paused before applying the cloth to her face.

She peeked over her shoulder at him. He was still kneeling next to the chair, looking quite content to watch her. "You will think me foolish."

"I may, or I may not," he replied.

Felicity could feel the heat of embarrassment rising in her cheeks. "I do not want to wash away your kisses."

As expected, he laughed. "Wash your face. I will replace them."

And before they went to spend an hour discussing recipes over cups of tea and a plate of treats, each kiss was replaced – one for her forehead, one for her left cheek, and one near her ear after he whispered an "I love you."

~*~*~

"You are both looking satisfied with your outing," Mr. Love said when, later that day, his wife and Felicity joined him in the sitting room at the cottage.

"It was a great success," Mrs. Love said, "though it began in quite a different fashion. I thought for sure it was going to be a disaster."

Mr. Love laid aside the book he had been reading. "How did it begin?"

"With a call from Mrs. Adams and Miss Flint," Felicity's mother replied. "I do not mind a call from Mrs. Adams. She and I are quite good friends after all these years." She shook her head as she settled into a chair near her husband. "However, I do not like her cousin's daughter. She is a malicious schemer."

Mr. Love's eyebrows flew high. "Is she indeed?"

"She most certainly is."

"Would you agree?" he asked Felicity.

"I would."

"At the risk of promoting gossip, may I ask why you have come to this opinion?"

"Do you remember the lady Grace said she saw in the hall with Mr. Ramsey at the Upper Rooms?" Felicity asked her father.

His brow furrowed. "I do."

"That was Miss Flint. She has not confirmed it, but I know it was her."

He looked to his wife, who nodded her agreement.

"Mr. Ramsey is married." Felicity blew out a breath. It still stung somewhat to admit that he had cared so little for her, but not as it had when she first heard it. "He married Miss Flint's sister."

"Oh, my." Mr. Love fell back in his chair as if overcome by the news. "I had not taken Ramsey for a fellow who would play with your heart. He seemed quite sincere when he asked permission to propose to you."

"We were all duped," Felicity said.

"You do not look so despondent as I would think this news would make you," her father said.

"Oh, I was. I cried quite a lot after I got away from Miss Flint." However, her tears had not all been for the way Simon had used her. Her true heartache had been from thinking that Boyd did not truly want to marry her. "In fact," she added, "I was so distraught that I retched."

"You did?" her mother cried. "Why did you not tell me this before?"

"We were having tea with Matthias."

"Oh. Well, yes, I suppose it would not have been good to speak of such things when he was present."

Mr. Love chuckled. "I believe you have the right of that, my dear."

"You will be such a good mother," Mrs. Love said to Felicity.

"I hope you are correct."

"Your mother is right. You possess a quick wit. Being a good mother is not a skill that is beyond you."

"But I have made so many foolish choices."

Her father shrugged. "Do not make them again."

"But how will I know to make the proper choice?"

"Why did you not tell your mother earlier that you retched?"

Felicity's brow furrowed. Had she not already answered that? "It was because Matthias was present, and for him to hear that I was ill, and not merely tired, might have caused him to fear."

"That, my dear daughter, is how you make the proper choice. You think of how what you do or say will affect others." He smiled. "It is both that simple and that hard. Now, tell me why you are not still in tears and pleading a headache or some such thing over that cad Ramsey."

"I dare say it has something to do with Mr. Hedrington," her mother said with a waggle of her eyebrows. "He was very attentive to you this afternoon, and you did a great deal of blushing."

"This sounds promising," her father said, pulling himself forward and looking excessively interested in what Felicity had to say.

A smile spread across her face. "It is completely because of Mr. Hedrington. He loves me."

Her father's eyes grew wide. "He loves you? Well, I knew he would eventually – who cannot love you." He gave her a wink. "However, I must say, he has come to that conclusion much faster than I thought he would." He leaned back in his chair once again and folded his hands comfortably in front of his stomach. "I must agree with your mother. It seems you had a most successful visit. Most successful, indeed."

Chapter 14

Four days later, despite the activity going on around him at home as Grenwood was prepared to receive its new mistress Boyd still found himself feeling at peace.

Today, a cart laden with crates and trunks, as well as a few pieces of furniture had arrived from Kent. Mr. Love had sent instructions to have Felicity's belongings delivered so that his daughter would have everything she needed to feel at home in her new home. Boyd still maintained that Mr. Love was indulgent as a father at times, but he also would never deny that the man loved his family ardently.

"Mr. Hedrington." A silver-haired man dressed in a drab brown set of clothes extended his hand in greeting when Boyd approached the table in The Broken Lantern.

"Mr. Dootson, thank you for agreeing to meet me here."

"I am always happy to let someone else pay for a pint," the man said with a grin.

"I will buy you two pints if our meeting goes well."

Mr. Dootson laughed. "Who told you that ale was an effective bribe?"

"Mr. Love mentioned you were fond of the beverage." Boyd seated himself across from Mr. Dootson. "He also assured me that you are not the sort to overindulge. In fact, according to Mr. Love and everything I have seen and heard myself since arriving here, you are an upstanding individual, which is why I hope we can come to some sort of agreement on this item."

Two pints of ale were placed before them by a man wearing an apron.

"I hear we must wish you joy, Mr. Hedrington," the man said.

"And from whom do you hear such things, Mr. Jeffries?" Boyd inquired of the tavern owner.

"My wife had it from Mrs. Hunt who had it from Miss Shaw who had it from Mrs. Adams. The news of a wedding does not travel slowly, especially when there will be so many disappointed mothers." He pulled out a chair and joined them, though he had not been invited to do so.

The Broken Lantern was not completely empty, but, since there were still a few hours until dinner, the number of patrons were few. Mr. Beck, Mr. Jeffries' right-hand man, was sweeping the floor near another group of men three tables away from Boyd, who were enjoying an afternoon drink. Mr. Beck stopped his sweeping and leaned on his broom when laughter erupted from the group of men.

"Cooper must be telling tales again," Mr. Jeffries commented.

Mr. Dootson took a drink of his ale and wiped his mouth on the back of his hand. "Cooper always has a yarn to spin. Some of them are even true." He chuckled along with Boyd and Mr. Jeffries.

It had not taken Boyd long to learn that Mr. Cooper was an excellent entertainer, who would keep you from doing what you wished to do by telling story after story and rarely allowing time for his audience to escape between tales.

"But Mr. Hedrington is not here for stories." Mr.

Dootson pulled a pile of paper from his bag. "They are just as you wished."

Boyd's eyebrows rose. "Indeed? No negotiating."

"We can argue a point or two if you want," Mr. Dootson offered, "but as I was telling Mr. Love when he arrived this summer, the place is getting to be too much of a burden in upkeep for one of my age."

"Your age?" Mr. Jeffries inserted with a snort. "You are not so very old."

Mr. Dootson smiled broadly. "I am a babe compared to Methuselah, but I assure you that I am quite decidedly ancient compared to what I used to be. Just because I am spry does not mean I have not aged. Martha and I would like to do less fussing, and none of my daughters and their husbands live near enough to see to the cottage. They will be happy to have the money." He paused and looked sheepishly at Boyd. "That number is slightly higher than we had discussed. Martha thought it would be better to have a price that was easily divided by three."

"Three daughters?" Boyd asked, peeking up from the papers he was reading.

Mr. Dootson nodded.

"Why are you buying Dootson Cottage?" Mr. Jeffries asked Boyd. "Is Grenwood too large for you?" he teased.

"The cottage is a gift," Boyd answered.

"That is a mighty expensive gift," Mr. Jeffries said.

"It is for his new wife," Mr. Dootson whispered.

Mr. Jeffries whistled. "I thought you were only marrying to claim your inheritance."

"That is how it began," Boyd assured him before taking a swig of his ale and continuing to scan the documents he held. "However, even if that were still the only reason I was marrying Miss Love, having a place near Grenwood for her parents to stay as they have always done would be a good idea. I know there are rooms enough at Grenwood Hall, but the cottage is where they came on their wedding trip."

"I didn't have you down as a romantic," Mr. Jeffries said.

"I would say we all are to some extent romantics when it comes to the ladies we love," Boyd replied.

"Then, what my wife said about you being smitten with Miss Love is true?"

Boyd only nodded. He had papers to read, and

the inquisitive Mr. Jeffries was hampering that task.

"It seems you are marrying in haste."

There was no mistaking the implication in Mr. Jeffries's words.

"I have a deadline to fulfill for my inheritance, and the Loves will not be here much longer. Summer does not last forever."

"Dreadful thing that," Mr. Dootson said. "My spry old joints prefer the summer to the dampness of winter." He shook his head. "Growing old and enjoying life at the same time is not for the faint of heart."

Mr. Jeffries rubbed the back of his neck. "There is a lot of truth in that."

The table fell silent for a few minutes after that.

"You know," Mr. Dootson said, "if Mr. Hedrington were marrying in haste for the reason I suspect your wife has supposed to you, Mr. Jeffries, it would not be the first time the masters of Grenwood have withstood a scandal involving a child."

Boyd looked up at the tavern owner. "Is that what the ladies are saying?"

"It was just a theory my wife had." The man

shifted uneasily in his chair. "So far as I know, she did not hear it from anyone."

"But she has likely shared this theory with others," Boyd grumbled. He had hoped Felicity would not have to face those sorts of whispers until it became impossible for everyone not to notice that she was with child.

"I would like to say you are wrong," Mr. Jeffries said, "but I know my wife, so I cannot."

Boyd turned back to Mr. Dootson. There was no point in pursuing the gossip about him and Felicity as it would only lead to one of two impossible outcomes. Either he would end up having to deny that Felicity was with child, or he would have to admit to the pregnancy. Neither was a thing he wished to do.

"What other scandals have my relations been a part of?" he asked.

"Your uncle nearly lost Grenwood over a girl," Mr. Dootson replied.

"Did he?" Boyd placed the documents he held on the table. "These look acceptable. Will you see they are delivered to my solicitor?"

"Of course."

"And the money will be given to you when

everything to make the transaction legal has been completed."

"I would not expect it any sooner."

Boyd picked up his pint. "How did my uncle nearly lose Grenwood over a lady?"

"Technically, she was not a lady. She was a maid," Mr. Dootson said. "He was young and willing to defy convention. However, his father – The Old Curmudgeon – that is what your uncle always called him – was not. From what I understand, the maid was sent away – some say she was with child when she left – and your uncle was told that if he had anything to do with the girl, he would be written out of his father's will. Your uncle loved Grenwood, and he decided not to chase after the maid. However, there are rumors that he kept up a correspondence with her for some time after she left." Mr. Dootson smiled softly. "He loved that maid all his life, and always said he could never find another to compare to her."

"He seemed happy enough," Mr. Jeffries said.

"He was to a point," Mr. Dootson agreed. "He made his peace with his lot in life and began preparing to see his brother's son as his heir." He looked at Boyd. "You are a lot like him. I have never known a more kind-hearted man. Laurence would go out of his way to see that those within his care were well. Grenwood Hall's staff is loyal for a reason."

Boyd had noticed that about Grenwood's servants. They had welcomed him with caution, but once they knew he was to be trusted, he could have asked them to do anything for him and they would have. It felt more like he had gained a great family rather than a staff. "Could my uncle not have married the maid after his father died?"

Mr. Dootson shrugged. "Laurence said it was impossible when I asked him that once. I do not know why, and he would not say. I assume The Old Curmudgeon had written things so well that it was not possible." He rose, drained the last of what was in his pint, and replaced the mug on the table with a thump. "I will take my second pint when I come to visit you at your home after you have married," he said to Boyd. Then, he gave a tip of his head toward the door.

It seemed the man had more to say to Boyd but was not willing to say it here.

"Can I walk with you?" Boyd asked. "I have to

stop at Poole's to purchase a gift for Miss Love from Matthias."

Mr. Dootson smiled. It was a look of relief. "I would welcome the company. I will be outside." He put his documents in his bag and then, with a nod and a good day to Mr. Jeffries, he left the tavern.

Boyd finished his ale and followed.

"I was not completely truthful in there. Jeffries can be as loose-tongued as his wife." Mr. Dootson started walking in the direction of Poole's. "There was a child. It was not a misplaced rumour. Shortly before his death, your uncle charged me with telling you about the child if you proved to be so good a man as he suspected you were." He tipped his hat at some ladies as he passed them. "Your purchase of the cottage was the final piece that made me know that you care for more than gaining an estate."

"Why must I know about this child?" It seemed a strange thing for his uncle to wish to tell him about an illegitimate child.

"There is a school for girls a good distance from here. The maid and her child were taken in there, and the child was educated in the school. The reason your uncle did not pursue the maid was so that his father would provide for both the maid and her daughter. Miss Smith, that is how your uncle referred to the child, has since married and left the school, but until his father's death, your uncle continued to provide a yearly allowance for her and a yearly donation to the school where she lived for her whole life until her marriage. He hoped you would be amenable to carrying on the tradition."

That was most certainly a good reason for his uncle to want him to know about the child.

"What happened to the maid? Did my uncle ever say?"

Mr. Dootson chuckled. "I think you may wish to ask Mrs. Feasby about that. She has probably told you that she spent her whole life at Grenwood."

Boyd nodded. Suspicion tickled his mind.

"She did not."

Was he correct in interpreting what Mr. Dootson had shared to mean..."Mrs. Feasby is the maid?"

Her comments about having known what it was like to have loved so deeply as one who had been married made sense if it were true that she was the maid. He also understood now why she had been so adamant that he fulfill his uncle's requirements and become the master of Grenwood Hall. She knew that his uncle was counting on him to help provide for her daughter.

He shook his head as all the pieces fell into place. Mrs. Feasby being the maid would also explain why she had not batted an eyelash upon learning that Felicity was with child.

"I am never to say who the maid was or is," Mr. Dootson replied, "It is a promise I take very seriously. Therefore, I cannot answer your question."

It was a refusal to answer that was as good as a confirmation.

They stood together just outside of Poole's where Boyd was going to purchase something pretty for Miss Love's hair as per Matthias's drawing which was tucked into Boyd's breast pocket.

"If there is a child," Mr. Dootson said softly, "it will not be the first time Grenwood has withstood the whispers."

Though it was not a question, Boyd knew that the gentleman was asking if the rumors about Felicity were true.

"How long have you held my uncle's secrets?"

Mr. Dootson smiled. "I knew the maid was with

child before she left Grenwood, and I mailed the letters to her."

He was trustworthy. Boyd looked at the store and then back at Mr. Dootson. He nodded.

"Yours?"

Boyd shook his head. "But it will be."

"The work of a scoundrel?"

Again, Boyd nodded.

"Your uncle would be proud to hear it. There is usually at least one young lady of unspecified parentage at that school your uncle supported. His donation helps see to their care." He lifted his satchel. "I shall see that your solicitor gets these while you make sure your future wife has a gift from your son."

Chapter 15

"You should bring down your bonnet and dress." Mrs. Love placed the brown paper wrapped parcel she carried on top of her workbasket. "The light is good in here in the afternoon, and we only have today and tomorrow to get your wedding ensemble finished."

"Could I have a few minutes to rest before we begin?"

"Of course, you may," her mother agreed with alacrity. "It was an eventful trip."

"Yes, it was," Felicity muttered as she removed her gloves and bonnet.

Their outing to the village to purchase a few more embellishments for Felicity's wedding dress and bonnet had been far more trying than Felicity had imagined it would be. The lifted eyebrows and questioning looks that accompanied several words of congratulations on having been the one to finally capture Mr. Hedrington should not have been unexpected, and she knew she must harden herself to the whispers and glances. However, the fact that she had encountered such open looks of disdain so soon had taken her by surprise.

"It seems Mr. Hedrington was correct about the gossip," Mr. Love said before Felicity could make her escape from the sitting room. "I am sorry you have to endure it."

Felicity nodded as she wrestled with keeping her emotions regulated.

"I think both your mother and I are equal to the challenge of hearing your thoughts and bearing your tears," he added softly.

She shook her head. "I do not think *I* am equal to it."

He caught her hand as she turned toward the door. "You are loved. Remember that."

"I will." She looked toward the ceiling to keep from crying. "I just need some time to rest." And think. She had a decision to make. A very difficult decision. One which she knew would likely break her heart.

Her father gave her hand a squeeze and then

released it. "We will be here when you are ready, and perhaps, when you return, you can bring your bonnet, your dress, and whatever it is that Miss Flint said to you."

Felicity froze at the doorway and turned slowly back toward her father. How did he know about that?

"I saw her whisper something to you," he said as if her thoughts were written for one and all to see on her face, "and from how you responded, I would say it made you fearful. I will not have some bitter harpy causing you undue anxiety."

Felicity moved three steps to the side and sank down onto the chair that stood near the door. Her heart cried out to tell someone what Miss Flint had said and for someone to take her decision from her.

"When did Miss Flint whisper to you?" Mrs. Love asked as she unwrapped her parcel.

"It was while you and Mrs. Adams were admiring that piece of lace on the bottom of your pile," her husband replied. "Miss Flint is calculating."

That was the truth put gently if you were to ask Felicity. To think that, at one time, she had been just such a lady. How often had she whispered just the right thing at the right time to cause another lady some unease so that a particular gentleman could be secured for a dance or a drive?

Her shoulders sagged under the heavy weight of such a realization. "I was just like her," she admitted aloud.

Her father shook his head. "You could never be like her."

"But I was. I was."

He gave her a disbelieving look.

"Perhaps I was not so cruel as she, but I was just as calculating. Do you not remember what I did to Beatrice and even my own sister!" She laughed bitterly. "And I was no better to Miss Abernathy, a lady who was supposed to be my dearest friend. I whispered about her shortcomings to more than one gentleman so he would see me as the better choice since I could not compete with her dowry."

"I will not deny you have, in the past, done some shameful things." From the look on her father's face, Felicity knew that admitting such a thing was painful for him. "But that is neither here nor there at the moment, for presently, I do not want to know what you have done in the past. What I want to know is just how cruel Miss Flint is.

Miss Flint's insinuations were not mere barbs

about the lack of some lady's accomplishments. She was, for some reason, far more desperate than that.

"She will deny ever having said anything," Felicity cautioned. That was the only response someone could give to being accused of threatening the wellbeing of another.

"I suspected as much," her father assured her.

Felicity dried her eyes and pulled in a deep breath, which she released slowly. Fear, mingled with anger, rose within her as she remembered what Miss Flint had said and how she had said it.

It is very courageous of you to try to fill the void in a gentleman's heart left by the dear mother of his child.

Felicity swallowed. She was not replacing Anna. Boyd had said as much. However, the anxiety from that moment in the garden five days ago was too freshly put aside and, therefore, easily aroused.

Her father, with his eyebrows drawn close together in concern, watched her expectantly.

"She said I must be a very brave person to be willing to take the place of a dearly loved mother and wife."

Her father's head tipped as he continued his observation of her. "That can be a challenging thing to do unless, of course, you know that you are equally as loved – at least by the gentleman you are marrying, though I suspect his son also loves you."

That was how the best schemes to defeat a rival for the attention of another began. With a bit of truth.

Miss Flint's next words sprang to mind. *I would be so afraid to do something which could injure the child and thereby, end up being hated by my husband. Not that I would purposefully hurt a child, of course, but accidents do happen, and if it looked as if it were my fault... Well, I am sure you understand.*

Felicity ran a hand over her skirt, smoothing it unnecessarily. "But what if something I do causes that son to be harmed?"

"Mr. Hedrington knows you would never harm his son purposefully."

"What if it appears that I have?" Her heart felt as if it had climbed into her throat just as it had when Miss Flint had hinted at something like that happening.

"Did Miss Flint threaten to harm Matthias?" Her father's features were suffused with horror.

"Not in so many words, but I am certain it was her meaning."

"We must tell Mr. Hedrington." Mrs. Love was on her feet and putting on her hat. "Shall we go all together? I think that would be best, do you not agree, Mr. Love?"

"I do think it would be best if we went together," her husband said. "However, it can wait a few minutes."

"Wait a few minutes!" Mrs. Love cried. "I would box the ears of anyone who said that telling me that my child might be in danger could wait a few minutes!" She huffed. "And when we are through telling Mr. Hedrington, we must stop to see Mrs. Adams. She must be told how dreadful her cousin's daughter is."

"I understand your impatience, my dear, but please, sit. Just for a few minutes." He turned back to Felicity. "What else did Miss Flint say?"

It is enough to make one not wish to marry a widower with a child, even if he does have a large estate and one was desperate for a father for one's own child. That is what she had said, and she had said it with an amused smirk as if she knew that she had struck a mortal wound.

"She suggested that I not marry Mr. Hedrington."

"Not marry Mr. Hedrington, indeed!" Mrs. Love cried. "We will stop at Mrs. Adams's before we go to Grenwood."

"And you considered her suggestion?" Mr. Love asked his daughter, ignoring his wife's state of agitation.

Felicity nodded.

"Do you not wish to marry him?"

"I do. With all my heart I do want to marry him, but is it right for me to take what I want if it could put Matthias in danger?" She had been a selfish creature all her life but had been determined not to continue as such.

Her father smiled. "I could answer that for you, but I think you will come to the correct conclusion."

Of all the frustrating, bothersome responses! Why could he not tell her what to do?

"Of course, Felicity will marry him!" Mrs. Love was once again on her feet. "If she does not, they will lose their home."

That was no help either. Did she choose to save Boyd's home or his child?

"Mr. Hedrington could marry someone else," Mr. Love poked his head out the door to speak to the footman in the hall. "We will need the carriage again." He turned back to his wife. "From the sour faces I saw today on several young ladies, he would not be hard-pressed to find someone willing to help him keep his home."

That was true, but Boyd had said he would not marry anyone else. Maybe when he knew that it was the only way to protect Matthias, he would consider another. Felicity's heart physically ached at the thought of giving him up.

"Oh, Mr. Love, you are being impossible." Mrs. Love crossed to the door. "Felicity go up and wash your face. I will be in front of the house in the carriage." She paused. "Do you need some bread and jam?"

"I do not think I could eat it." She was uncertain at this point if she ever wished to eat or breathe ever again. To give up Boyd was to give up her heart, but she also could not bear the thought of something happening to Matthias nor could she withstand losing Boyd's love in the process. And then... She placed a hand on her stomach which over the past few weeks had begun to swell quite a bit. If she gave Boyd up, she would also be giving up a father for her child.

"We will bring some just in case. Mr. Love, could you send for some, please?"

"Mrs. Love," her father's tone was slightly stern.

"I am not being unreasonable," she retorted. "That woman is trying to harm my child and my future grandson."

Felicity slipped out of the room while her father wrapped her mother in his arms and assured her that he would not let any harm come to either her child or her grandchildren. A year ago, Felicity would have rolled her eyes at such a display, but not now. Now, it made her smile for she knew how wonderful it felt to be wrapped in the arms of a gentleman who loved her, and then, it made her cry as she considered the fact that she might not ever be held so again.

She raced up the stairs to her room and tossed herself on the bed so that she was staring up at the ceiling through her tears. She could not give him up. She simply could not give Boyd up. She would be selfish just this one more time and hope when they told Mrs. Adams about Miss Flint, her tormenter would be sent back to Bath posthaste.

She rubbed at her tears with her hands. She was being foolish. Of course, Miss Flint would be sent back to Bath once it was known how horrible she was, and if not, Mr. Hedrington would certainly take precautions to ensure his son's safety.

She sat up. There was no choice in the matter. Her child needed a father, Mr. Hedrington needed a wife, and Matthias needed a mother. Marrying Mr. Hedrington was the only way to see all of those things happen.

"It is the right thing to do," she said to her empty room and allowed the audible confirmation to bounce off the walls and furnishing and settle into her mind. "I know it is." She expelled a great sigh. "But it if is the right thing to do, then, why do I feel as if I am only trying, once again, to please myself?"

Chapter 16

"Is everything how you wished for it to be?" Boyd stood at the door to the mistress's chamber at Grenwood Hall, watching Felicity inspect the room and the dressing room beyond.

Tomorrow, this would become her home, and he was anxious that she would feel at ease here. The last time his heart had beat so forcefully about a change of residence had been when he and Matthias had boarded that ship in Halifax. He supposed that his marrying Felicity had a great many things in common with that departure from Nova Scotia. He was, after all, leaving part of his past behind while seeking a happy future for those he loved, and he knew that the journey ahead would not be without its trials.

"Mrs. Feasby has done an excellent job arranging everything," Felicity replied with a smile.

He had seen several of those truly happy expressions today, and it did his heart good to see it. It made him worry less about her happiness. What she and her father had told him just yesterday about Miss Flint's veiled threats, along with Felicity's revelation after that she had considered not marrying him to protect his son, had given him a restless evening and a less than sleep-filled night.

"I find that she is exceptional at her job," Boyd said. "I do not know what we would do without her."

Mrs. Feasby smiled and blushed at the compliment.

"I quite agree," Felicity said. "You have made my welcome here very warm, Mrs. Feasby." She pulled a corner of her bottom lip between her teeth, picked up a figurine of a woman holding a basket, and studied it carefully.

If Boyd had to guess what was going through his future wife's mind, he would say she had something more she wished to say but was hesitant to say it. He had been attempting to notice the things she did when nervous ever since that day in the garden when he had not realized that the smoothing of her skirts indicated she was uneasy.

"It is especially kind of you to welcome me, knowing what you do about my condition." Her eyes were shimmering when she finally lifted them from her inspection of the figurine. "And it is not just you. The whole staff has been so kind. I feel as if I do not deserve it." She pulled in a breath and released it. "I have not always been so kind as I should have been."

"You have been nothing but kind to me," Mrs. Feasby replied. "It is not as if we do not all make some errors in our youth."

"But mine is so great!"

Mrs. Feasby shook her head. "It is no greater than..."

She glanced at Boyd. He had asked her about the donation to the school after talking to Mr. Dootson, and she had shared the full story with him about falling in love with his uncle, being sent away, and returning to Grenwood with a new name but without her baby.

"It is no greater than mine," Mrs. Feasby finished her thought.

Felicity's brow furrowed.

"I am just happy to know that you will get to marry Mr. Hedrington," their housekeeper continued, "and that you will always be known to your child as its mother."

"I apologize, but I do not follow your meaning."

"Mrs. Feasby has never married but that does not mean she has never been a mother," Boyd stated simply.

Felicity's lashes fluttered over wide eyes. "You had a child?"

Mrs. Feasby nodded. "A daughter. It is a secret that stays within Grenwood's walls."

"Oh, of course, I would not dream of telling anyone." Felicity had crossed the room and taken Mrs. Feasby's hands.

"It was years ago. It is best if we do not dredge up the past."

Felicity lifted Mrs. Feasby's hands, and Boyd was certain he saw her squeeze them tight.

"If you ever wish to share your burden," she said softly, "I will listen."

"I will keep that in mind, miss." She turned away from Felicity once Felicity had released her hands but then turned back. "I am so pleased that you will be Mrs. Hedrington."

There was another one of those happy expressions curling Felicity's lips. Boyd wondered how long it would be before he would take those pretty smiles for granted instead of marking them as precious. He hoped it would never happen, but he knew better. He knew life would fall into a routine eventually. It always did.

"I am quite pleased about that myself," Felicity admitted with a blush. "No matter how selfish it makes me feel to be so delighted at the prospect of marrying Mr. Hedrington."

"Why does it feel selfish?" Mrs. Feasby asked in surprise.

"Because it is what I want," Felicity said with a shrug.

Mrs. Feasby smiled and shook her head. "My dear, sometimes what we want and what is right are the same things, and marrying a man who loves you and you love in return is the proper thing to do. I only wish I had been given the opportunity to do so. Oh, but do not fear," she added when concern overshadowed Felicity's features. "I spent as many days as I was allotted with the man I loved. I just did not get to wear his name. It just was not possible."

Boyd had learned from Mrs. Feasby that his uncle would have lost his claim to Grenwood Hall had he ever married her. There was an alternate heir named by the Old Curmudgeon, and it was not Boyd's father, the second-born Hedrington son, as one would expect. Boyd's grandfather had been too shrewd to allow that to be how things would fall if his eldest insisted on sullying the Hedrington name by marrying a servant.

Again, Felicity's lashes were fluttering over wide eyes. "Do you mean Mr. Hed –" She pressed her lips together on the name when Mrs. Feasby put a finger to her lips, indicating that it was a secret.

"That also remains within Grenwood."

"Of course," Felicity agreed with alacrity.

Mrs. Feasby smiled. "Honestly, it feels good to share that with you both. The former Mr. Hedrington would be so pleased to have you for a niece. I know he would be. He was not one to judge harshly."

"Neither is his nephew."

"They are a lot alike," Mrs. Feasby agreed, "but now, we must not spend the day in idle chatter. I have to see that all is ready for tomorrow's wedding breakfast, and I believe, your mother and father are expecting you and Mr. Hedrington for dinner."

And with that, Grenwood's housekeeper left

Boyd and Felicity standing alone in the mistress's chamber.

"Do you wish to go with me to see if Matthias and Susan are ready to leave?" Boyd held out his hand to Felicity.

"I would love to," she said as she placed her hand in his.

He lifted her fingers to his lips before he wrapped her arm around his and drew her close to his side. It felt as if she were perfectly designed by the Almighty to be there next to him, but did Providence work though deaths, wills, and secret liaisons between lovers?

Matthias, who was ready and waiting in the hall outside the nursery, raced toward them. "Papa!" he called excitedly before adding an equally as eager, "Felicity!"

If the smile on his son's face and the small expansion of his vocabulary to include Felicity's name were the answer to Boyd's question, then he would have to say that God could indeed use even dark circumstances to bring about what was good.

"Shall we go to the cottage?" he asked Matthias.

"Yes, please."

Those words had recently replaced Matthias's

normally mute nod of affirmation. Matthias was not bubbling over with words, but Boyd had hope that one day soon, he would long for silence instead of wishing for it to be gone.

"Are you ready, Susan?" he looked past his son to Matthias's nursemaid.

"Yes, sir. We have been ready this past half hour."

Boyd chuckled. "Come along then, son."

Matthias slipped his hand into Felicity's, and, with a heart that was overflowing with gratitude for the mysterious workings of Providence, Boyd led his little family, with Susan trailing behind, toward the staircase and then, to the carriage that waited for them in front of Grenwood Hall.

~*~*~

"Were your parents expecting more than us to dine with them this evening?" Boyd asked as they came to a stop in front of the Loves' cottage but behind another carriage.

"They did not tell me if they were," Felicity replied. "I wonder who it could be?"

Boyd was wondering the same thing. "Would you like Susan to take you to the garden before you come in?" Matthias did not always do well with surprises, especially if that surprise came in the form of a stranger. The Loves knew this, which was why Boyd was feeling uneasy himself about that carriage.

"Yes, please." He held his arms out to his father to lift him from the carriage.

"Shall we stay in the garden long?" Susan asked Matthias, who shook his head.

To Boyd, that was an encouraging sign since it meant Matthias did not intend to hide himself away.

"He is doing well." Boyd turned his eyes away from his son and toward Felicity. "I have you and your family to thank for that."

"My father is very good with children."

Boyd shook his head. "It is not just your father's doing. It is yours, too. The biggest change I have seen in him was after you asked him if you could be friends even if you came to live with us, and do not tell me that your father prompted you to say what you said that day," he added with a lifted eyebrow and a challenging look that made Felicity smile and laugh softly. "You spoke from your heart. You were not just repeating some lines in a play."

"Are you certain?" she teased. "I am very good at play-acting – or I was."

"I am absolutely certain."

She stopped walking just as they were about to reach the door. "You trust me completely?"

"Yes."

A smile lit her face. "That is a novel and wonderful feeling."

"And one you need to harden yourself to feeling," he teased before adding, "The Felicity you were is not the Felicity you are."

"You are right," she agreed just as the door to the cottage opened and a handsome looking fellow stepped out.

Felicity clutched Boyd's arm tightly.

"Simon," she whispered.

The name hit Boyd full in the chest, forcing out a breath. This was him? This was Ramsey, the cad who had run away?

"Felicity!" Mr. Ramsey cried.

"Miss Love," Felicity corrected.

"I am so glad to have found you at last!"

"Found me? I do not believe I was lost."

"You were to me." Mr. Ramsey cast a curious look at Boyd.

"Boyd Hedrington," Boyd offered by way of introduction. "Felicity's betrothed," he added by way of warning Ramsey off.

Mr. Ramsey gave him an assessing look. "Simon Ramsey."

"I figured as much," Boyd replied.

"Since you seem to know who I am," Mr. Ramsey said, "you will understand if I ask to speak to Felicity privately."

"I might understand why you would wish to, but that does not equate to being allowed to do as you wish."

"She is not your wife yet."

That was an unfortunate thing.

"No, she is not. However, I suspect, from the fact that you were departing when we arrived, Mr. Love was not eager to allow you to speak to his daughter."

The comment was met by an uneasy shifting that Boyd found somewhat satisfying. This Ramsey fellow had a disagreeable air of self-importance about him that would not have recommended him to Boyd had they met under any circumstances, let alone now.

"Felicity, it is your choice. You can speak to Mr.

Ramsey, or you can send him away, knowing that your father likely did just that."

"Please, just for five minutes," Mr. Ramsey inserted.

Boyd watched Felicity's eyes flick from his to Ramsey and back. The sadness he saw in them tugged at his heart.

"Whatever you choose," he assured her while his mind cried out against allowing her to choose. What would he do without her?

"Just five minutes," she said. "But not alone." She slipped her hand into Boyd's.

Willingly, he squeezed her hand. He would give her whatever support she needed to do whatever had to be done, even if her choice utterly shattered his heart and life.

"You may begin, Mr. Ramsey, by telling me why you abandoned me."

"As I told your father and mother, I did not abandon you. I wrote you a letter explaining everything, but it arrived after you had left Bath."

Boyd would like to see that letter as proof – if it did, indeed, exist.

"Why did you leave Bath?" Felicity pressed.

Boyd could feel her trembling slightly.

"I had to go home to attend to some business."

"Such as getting married?"

Boyd squeezed Felicity's hand, hoping she could feel his pride in her for confronting Mr. Ramsey with what she knew rather than playing ignorant.

Mr. Ramsey smiled softly. "I did not get married."

"Yes, you did. You married Miss Flint's sister."

Ramsey shook his head. "It was a show. Helen was married secretly to my cousin and needed my help to get her portion."

Boyd clenched his teeth to keep his mouth from gaping at the nonchalant way Mr. Ramsey spoke of what seemed to Boyd to be a rather large and well-planned deception.

"You are not married?"

Boyd could hear the utter disbelief in Felicity's voice.

"No. How could I marry another when I had promised myself to you?"

"But you left."

To Boyd, Felicity sounded both confused and unsure of herself.

Ramsey dared to take a step closer to Felicity. "I

left Bath, but I did not leave you. I love you. Marry me. It is not too late. I thought it was, but it is not."

Felicity turned her eyes to Boyd. What he saw in those beautiful eyes could only be described as grief tinged with uncertainty.

He closed his eyes and swallowed. "Whatever you choose." The words scratched and clawed their way out of his mouth. "So long as you are happy," he added softly as he opened his eyes to meet hers. He blinked against the tears that wanted to be shed.

"I am so relieved I have found you," Mr. Ramsey said.

Obviously, he was not interested in sharing Felicity's attention with Boyd.

Felicity's brow furrowed. "How did you find me?" she asked as she turned her eyes away from Boyd's with what seemed to Boyd to be some reluctance.

"Mrs. Adams mentioned her friends the Loves."

"You have been to Mrs. Adams's house?"

"Yes."

"Why?"

Once again, Mr. Ramsey was satisfyingly uneasy looking.

"To visit a friend."

"Miss Flint?"

"Yes."

"She was in Bath."

Mr. Ramsey blinked as if he was uncertain where this line of questioning was going. "I know."

"My sister saw you with her at the Upper Rooms the night before you left me."

"I did not leave you," Mr. Ramsey said with some frustration. "I left Bath because Miss Flint mentioned her sister had married."

"Did Miss Flint also tell you that her sister needed you to pretend to marry her?"

Ramsey shook his head. "No, my cousin told me that in a letter. I was just waiting until I heard that Helen was married, and I knew I had to help her as soon as possible since I was planning on marrying you."

"Though he was planning to marry Miss Flint before he planned to marry you."

Boyd turned his eyes to the cottage doorway. How long had Mrs. Love been standing there?

"I believe my husband said you are not welcome to offer for my daughter."

"My wife is correct." Mr. Love stood behind his wife.

"Were you betrothed to Miss Flint?" Felicity asked.

Ramsey looked a bit like a fox that had been cornered by the hounds. "No. We spoke of marrying, but we were never betrothed. We were young. It was a mere infatuation. I swear I have never wished to marry anyone but you, Felicity. Please. Please give me a second chance before it is too late."

Felicity pulled her hand away from Boyd and moved toward Mr. Ramsey. Both Boyd's hand and heart felt empty at her actions.

"You broke my heart," she said softly.

"I never will again. Please," Mr. Ramsey begged.

"I had hoped you would chase after me, and we would go happily into our future together."

"I did come after you."

Felicity shook her head. "No, you came to visit a friend. I just happened to be here."

"Come away with me, Felicity. Marry me."

"No!" Matthias pulled away from his nurse and ran to Felicity. "Do not leave me," he cried as he wrapped his arms around Felicity.

"I apologize," Susan said. "We were going to join you in the cottage."

Boyd moved to pry his son away from Felicity.

"Leave him," Felicity said as she placed a hand on Matthias' head. "As you can see, Mr. Ramsey, while I am not yet married, you are too late." She looked down at Matthias. "I have no intention of ever leaving you."

Boyd sucked in a quick gasp of air. She was choosing him and Matthias?

"Never?" Matthias asked.

"Never." She looked up from his son to Boyd's face.

"I will not force you to hold to our agreement." He had to be certain she was choosing him because she wanted to choose him and not because she felt obliged to do so.

"It is what I want," she replied. "If you will still have me?"

"Gladly." He took the hand she held out to him.

"Mr. Ramsey, I think it is time for you to leave," Mr. Love said from the doorway.

"My father is right."

"But what about our child," Mr. Ramsey protested. "Mallory said you were with child."

Felicity squared her shoulders and lifted her chin. "Give my regards to Miss Flint when you see her. I wish you both happy."

"That is it? You will dismiss me so casually after all we have been to each other?"

"Casually? Casually?" Felicity laughed bitterly. "I have spent a great deal of time getting over you. I wished to die because of you, and then, you appear because you fortuitously happened to hear I was in the area when you were calling on a friend – a friend, whom, by the way, you at one time spoke to about marrying and were seen being cozy with while at a ball with me. And this is after leaving me without a word of explanation to perpetrate some elaborate deceptive scheme!"

"You know you love a good scheme, Felicity."

Felicity shook her head. "No. No, I do not. At least, I do not any longer. I have had my fill of schemes and deceptions." She exhaled. "Please, Simon, please, just go. I find we no longer suit."

"She is no longer a maiden," Mr. Ramsey said to Boyd.

"I know," Boyd replied. "And not for the reason you suppose," he added when Mr. Ramsey's eyebrows shot to his hairline. "She told me."

"Is that so?" Mr. Ramsey said with a sneer. "I wonder how many will believe that?"

"Mr. Ramsey, allow me to see you to your carriage." Mr. Love had taken Mr. Ramsey by the elbow. "I think Mrs. Love will allow you one biscuit before dinner," he added to Matthias.

"Papa?"

Boyd nodded.

"Abandoned for a biscuit," Felicity said with a laugh as Matthias raced to the house.

Boyd wrapped her in his arms. "Thank you," he whispered. "Thank you, for choosing me."

"I will always choose you," she replied, "for I love you. Most dearly."

He kissed her forehead and held her against his chest until his heart had recovered from the events which had just taken place. Then, he pressed one more kiss against her forehead and, with his arm around her shoulders, led her into the cottage.

Chapter 17

Clouds hung low when Felicity woke on her wedding day, rain plinked against the cottage windows while her mother helped her into her dress and cooed about how beautiful she was, and a gust of wind made the shutters covering the sitting room windows rattle. And yet, it was the most wonderful day Felicity had ever hoped to see, for today, she would marry a gentleman who loved her and whom she loved in return with every ounce of her being.

She sat in front of her mirror after both her maid and her mother had left her room, thinking about her future husband. She had known Boyd loved her. He had told her that he did, and she had felt it in his actions and heard it in his words. However, until yesterday, when she had watched the pain of losing her wash over his features as he gave her permission to choose what would make her happy, she had not known the depth of his love for her. Her happiness had been his first concern – far above his own desires. She patted at her eyes.

"You are not crying on your wedding day, are you?" Her father stood at the door to her room which her mother had left open.

"They are happy tears," she assured him as she rose to join him. "Is the carriage waiting?"

He nodded and held his arm out to her. "Along with two pieces of bread with jam on them. It would not do for the bride to become faint during the ceremony." He covered the hand which lay on his arm with his. "I am very happy for you, my dear. You have chosen well."

"Are you certain?"

"Do you not think that Mr. Hedrington is a good choice?"

"No, I know he is. That is not what I meant."

"We have discussed this. Mr. Ramsey is a charlatan. He does not know what love is. He plays a game which no one, but most especially he, will win." He stopped with her at the bottom of the stairs. "I visited Mrs. Adams this morning."

"You did?"

He nodded.

"Why?"

"I wished to hear what she had been told by Mr. Ramsey when he returned to her house."

"What did she say?"

Felicity knew the sort of rumours that might have been started by Mr. Ramsey. She had travelled in the circles where many damaging stories had begun. She was certain that by this morning, the whispers about her being with child would have been confirmed. She also figured such confirmation would come with an elaborate tale of how she had been a willing fortune hunter, moving from gentleman to gentleman before choosing the one with the best situation and bank account. She smiled to herself as she realized that she had no idea what sort of fortune Boyd had beyond inheriting Grenwood Hall, and the most astounding part was that she did not care. She had no fear of want. Boyd was not the sort to promise where he could not fulfill.

"Mr. Ramsey said he had a pleasant visit, and that we had been delighted to hear he was getting married."

Felicity ducked under the umbrella her father had opened. "He is getting married?"

"That is precisely what I said to Mrs. Adams."

"How did she answer?"

He waited until Felicity was seated inside the carriage next to her mother before he climbed in behind her.

"Apparently, Miss Flint and Mr. Ramsey have been secretly engaged for years."

Mrs. Love sucked in a quick breath of air.

"But he said –" Felicity began to protest before her father cut off her words.

"I know what he said, my dear. It was either a lie, or the story about being engaged for years is a lie. Either way, he is a gentleman who should not be trusted." Her father looked out the window. "And he is gone. You have nothing to fear from either him or Miss Flint. They had left Mrs. Adams's home not an hour before I arrived."

"In this weather?" Mrs. Love cried.

"He was in a hurry to get back to Bath and marry Miss Flint. Her mother and grandmother were expecting them."

It seemed to Felicity that there were a great number of tangled webs decorating the corners of Mr. Ramsey's life.

"Did Mrs. Adams tell you how he explained the fact that he was not married to Miss Flint's sister?" Felicity asked.

"She did. It seems his cousin could not perpetrate the charade so easily as the other Miss Flint and Mr. Ramsey could and stopped the wedding with a confession that he and the lady standing before the parson were married and an announcement that he was to be a father."

"Oh!" Felicity and her mother said in unison.

"To appease his father and Mr. Flint, Ramsey assured them that he would do the right thing and marry the Miss Flint who was at Mrs. Adam's to join the two families as required to inherit all that was being offered for such an arrangement. Mr. Flint has no sons and there is no entail, so he is free to dispose of his holdings as he wishes."

"But he offered for Felicity when he arrived here," Mrs. Love said. "How is that in keeping with his father's wishes?"

"It is not, but our daughter has a sizable fortune, which he knew about, and I truly believe he fancied himself in love with Felicity."

"But he could not be," Felicity inserted. "If he had truly loved me, he would not be going to Bath to marry another so soon after being rejected, would he?"

Her father shook his head. "I very much doubt that Mr. Ramsey understands what love is. We, including your child, are well rid of him."

Felicity placed a hand on her abdomen. "Then, I have made the right choice." She had worried about that. For her choice to marry Mr. Hedrington did take her child away from its natural father.

"It appears you did."

The carriage began to slow.

"And your correct choice is waiting for you inside that church."

Her father was right. Inside the church, Boyd stood at the front waiting for her with his son at his side. There were very few present to witness the event. There were her parents, Mrs. Feasby, Susan, Mr. and Mrs. Dootson — from whom her father rented the cottage — and Mrs. Adams. However, it did not matter to Felicity who was there to fill the front pews so long as Boyd was there.

It did not take long for the service to be read, the

register to be signed, and the parson to pronounce them Mr. and Mrs. Hedrington.

Matthias tugged on his father's coat when all was said and done.

"Felicity comes home with us?" Words had begun flowing more freely, though only in small, measured bursts, from Matthias last evening – after Felicity had assured him that she was not leaving.

Boyd nodded, and Matthias clapped his hands.

"He is not the only one who is delighted by that," Boyd whispered as he and Felicity made their way to the door of the church.

"Matthias and Susan have agreed to accompany us to Grenwood, that is, if that is agreeable to you," Mr. Love said to Boyd. "And Mrs. Feasby has accepted a ride from Mr. and Mrs. Dootson."

Boyd smiled broadly. "That sounds perfect."

Mr. Love chuckled. "I thought you might think so. Do not be too long in arriving at Grenwood, however, or I will have surely fed your son too many biscuits." He continued to chuckle as he went to deliver the good news to Matthias.

"I had hoped to have you to myself." Boyd opened his umbrella and hurried himself and Felicity to his waiting carriage.

"Do you know why I had hope for such a thing?" he asked while handing Felicity in the carriage.

Felicity shook her head, though she hoped she really knew his intentions. She was no innocent after all.

"I believe I promised to kiss you properly on our wedding day," he said as he settled into his seat.

Felicity felt her cheeks growing warm. Her hope was correct. "Yes, I believe you did." And to be honest, she had been longing for a proper kiss ever since that day.

"Would you be shocked if I asked you to sit on my lap? It would make kissing you much easier." He fidgeted with the sleeves of his jacket. "I wish to hold you."

And she wished to be held.

"I admit I am surprised, but I am not displeased by your request." She rose as best she could. "How would you like me to arrange myself."

He smiled and with a shake of his head pulled her down onto his lap. "Like this."

Then, before she could do more than shift a leg to make herself more comfortable, he had cupped the back of her head and claimed her lips. His kiss was tentative and gentle at first but quickly became more ardent.

Finally, with a groan, he broke the kiss and rested his forehead against hers. "Do you remember how I told you that I was not sure if I could love you as a wife should be loved?"

Her forehead rubbed against his as she nodded.

"That will not be a problem." He pulled away from her and gave her a lopsided grin. "I would be most pleased if you would allow me to love you in such a way, starting tonight."

"Is it safe?" She would willingly welcome him to her bed, but she must not think only of her own desires. She had to consider her child.

He placed a hand on her cheek. "I asked that of the midwife when Anna was pregnant with Matthias. It poses no danger to your child or you. Will you allow me the pleasure of being your husband in every way?"

Felicity leaned forward and pressed her lips against his for a quick kiss. "Yes," she whispered before kissing him one more time as the carriage began to slow and lurched to the side when it turned into Grenwood's drive. Then, she retook her proper seat so that she would not be found sitting on her husband's lap when the carriage door was opened.

~*~*~

The table in Grenwood's dining room was festively decorated, and plates and bowls laden with food stood waiting on the sideboards with footmen standing ready to be of service.

Boyd led his bride to her place beside him at the top of the table. Matthias was on his other side. However, he kept Felicity's hand in his and did not allow her to sit down as she had expected him to do.

"Before we begin eating," he looked at his son, "or continue eating."

The few guests gathered around the table, the same ones who had been at the church, chuckled.

"I have a gift to present to my wife."

Felicity's eyes snapped away from observing her guests to look at him. "A gift? For me?"

He smiled at her but then, turned his eyes toward the table. "Mr. Dootson, do you have what I require?"

"I most certainly do." The elderly gentleman rose and approached Boyd. "Tied up with a pretty bow," he said as he presented a packet of papers to Boyd. Then, he returned to his seat, and Boyd handed the papers to Felicity.

"What are these?" What sort of gift could possibly be concealed within a stack of documents?

"Open it."

Felicity pulled on the blue ribbon that held the papers together. Carefully, she removed the binding and put it aside. Then, she unfolded the papers. Her brow furrowed. Were these what she thought they were?

"The cottage is yours."

They were what she thought they were! Her hand flew to her throat. "The cottage? Mr. Dootson's cottage?"

"The very one," Mr. Dootson said.

"I know how much that cottage means to your parents," Boyd began, "and I wanted them to be able to stay there whenever they wished and for so long as they wish."

"You do?" Words were having trouble forming in her mind. Husbands gave their wives necklaces and hairpins. They did not give them wonderful things like cottages.

"I do."

"A cottage? For me?"

"And your child," he added softly before turning to the gathered guests. "Mrs. Adams, I think you are the only one here who does not know already that my wife is with child."

"Oh!" Mrs. Adams's eyes were wide.

"It is not something we will be able to hide for much longer and there will be more whispers than there already are."

"It is not Mr. Hedrington's doing," Felicity said. "I was seduced by the pretty words of a charming gentleman who promised to marry me. He lied." Her cheeks were burning from the shame of such an admission. "Nor did I trick Mr. Hedrington into marrying me." She smiled sheepishly when her mother gasped. "I also heard that whisper the day we were buying lace."

"When I offered for Felicity," Boyd inserted, "I promised her father that Felicity's child would become mine. As your father already knows, Felicity, this cottage will be a portion of your child's inheritance."

"Truly?" she looked from him to the papers she held and back.

"Truly."

She shook her head and placed the papers on the

table. How had she been so fortunate to be loved by a man like Boyd? "And I thought I could not love you more. I do not deserve you, Mr. Hedrington, but I am very glad I have you."

"We are of one mind on that, Mrs. Hedrington." He cupped her face between his hands. "I am so very glad you are mine."

"Mine, too," Matthias said, causing everyone, including Boyd and Felicity to laugh.

"Yes, yours, too," Boyd assured his son. "Now, may I kiss your new mother?"

"Yes, please."

Again, everyone chuckled while Boyd kissed Felicity, removing all doubt from anyone's mind who witnessed it that Mr. and Mrs. Hedrington had only married out of convenience – he to secure his inheritance and her to claim a home for herself and her child.

From this day forward, no one would question the love this pair had for each other, for it would never diminish but would only grow brighter. Their neighbors and acquaintances would even soon forget that Hope, the second oldest Hedrington child and the mirror image of her mother, was not a Hedrington by blood but only by birth.

And that precious daughter would become, from birth, dearly loved and cared for by both the only man she would ever know as her father and her elder and rarely silent brother.

The cottage would be well-used, for Mr. and Mrs. Love would continue to come to visit – often more than twice a year – so that they could spoil their six Hedrington grandchildren. Eventually, even Mr. and Mrs. Blakesley would also come to stay at the cottage with their three children and wonderful tales of Bath and its entertainments, as well as a few stories which were whispered from Mrs. Blakesley to Mrs. Hedrington about the unhappy state of Mr. Ramsey's marriage and whom he or his wife had been seen being cozy with on their last visit to the city.

Felicity, who had once lived for a house party and the delights of the season, never once missed those amusements. She and Boyd did not always remain at Grenwood as they did travel to Kent to visit the Loves, to Bath to visit the Blakesleys, and to a little school for girls in a distant county. But no matter where Felicity travelled, she always was happiest when she returned to Grenwood Hall where she had, once upon a time, found her best self and her convenient, and very happy, forever.

Before You Go

If you enjoyed this book, be sure to let others know by leaving a review.

~*~*~

Want to know when other books in this series will be available?

You can always know what's new with my books by subscribing to my mailing list.

(There will, of course, be a thank you gift for joining because I think my readers are awesome!)

Book News from Leenie Brown

(bit.ly/LeenieBBookNews)

~*~*~

Turn the page to read an excerpt from another one of Leenie's books

Other Pens, Mansfield Park Excerpt

[Have you ever wondered what happened to Henry Crawford after *Mansfield Park* ended? How about his sister or Tom Bertram? What about his friends who were never at Mansfield Park? If you have wondered about such things, you'll want to read my *Other Pens, Mansfield Park* series, which mixes Jane Austen's classic characters with a cast of original ones in situations never found in one of Miss Austen's novels. Below is an excerpt from the second book in the series, *Charles: To Discover His Purpose*, a story about how Henry Crawford's rakish friend Charles Edwards finds his happily ever after while attempting to steal a kiss.]

Chapter 1

Charles Edwards squinted into the late afternoon

sun – it was an action that he could almost do without any discomfort. The swelling around his eye had subsided, and soon, the bruising would fade to a nasty yellow and then disappear. Until that happened, he would continue to take his rides by wandering from one street to the next rather than face the taunting and questioning looks he was guaranteed to receive in the parks.

While it was an excellent way to avoid censure from his peers, it was dashed boring trotting up and down streets without so much as a single friend with whom to converse. Had he earned his scars more gallantly, perhaps he would not feel the need to hide them. To have been injured in a boxing match or defense of some lady's honor would make his bruises more of a badge than a blemish. However, since everyone in town had likely read that blasted article in the paper, the raised eyebrows from overprotective matrons and giggles from their charges would be unbearable. And then, there would be the gentlemen. He shook his head. Had he received a blackened eye from Trefor Linton for actually doing something inappropriate with Linton's sister, Constance, his friends would just laugh and clap him on the shoulder before filling his glass with some libation at his club.

But, he had not been caught doing anything improper. In fact, it was much worse than just not being found dallying with a debutante. He had been attempting to be gallant. He would do his best not to be put in such a situation again! Honourable actions and favours to ladies who were offering none in return must be avoided, for they only led to broken noses, disgrace, and lonely rambles up less well-to-do streets.

"Mr. Edwards?"

Charles drew his horse to a stop just in front of a carriage that was standing at the ready to receive a lovely young woman. He had not bothered to take note of her since this was not the part of town where the finest flowers of the season resided.

"Miss Linton," he said doffing his hat. "Is Crawford with you?" He nodded to the carriage.

"No," Constance Linton replied with a smile, "though he very much wanted to be. It is just Evelyn and I."

His brows furrowed. Evelyn? The name sounded familiar.

"Miss Barrett," Constance clarified.

"Ah, Miss Barrett. Of course. How negligent of me to not remember." How had he managed to forget her name? He certainly had not forgotten her perfectly pink lips or lithe figure...the same figure that was exiting the house to his left. She was perhaps the most enticing creature he had ever met and never sampled.

"Oh!"

Miss Barrett's lips formed such a wonderfully kissable *o*.

"Mr. Edwards," she greeted with a small curtsey. "Are you here to visit Mrs. Verity and the children?"

His brows furrowed again. "Mrs. Who?"

"Verity," Evelyn repeated. "She runs this home for children." She motioned toward the house.

"I did not know this was a home for children." His left brow rose in question. "Why are you here? None of these children are yours, I would assume."

Her eyes grew wide, and she gasped. "We are not all as reprobate as you, Mr. Edwards."

He leaned forward, nonchalantly admiring her look of utter indignation. "Then, what, pray tell, are proper young ladies such as yourself and Miss Linton doing here?"

"Charitable work. You do know what that is, do you not?"

He chuckled. Miss Barret was not the sort to shy away quietly to her corner and leave him be. He liked that. "I have heard the term."

"But have you ever experienced it?" asked Constance.

He shifted his gaze to his friend, Henry Crawford's, betrothed. "No, not beyond what is expected on my father's estate."

"It's rather fulfilling," Constance replied. "Today, we taught some children their letters. It was remarkable, was it not, Evelyn?" She wore a look of sheer delight.

"And Linton approves of this?" Charles asked.

"Both he and Henry do."

Delight did not begin to describe the look in Miss Linton's eyes as she said the name Henry. One day, when he was ready to take up his mantle of responsibility, Charles hoped to find a lady who would look even half as happy saying his name as Miss Linton did at this moment.

"Trefor," Constance continued, "thought this would be a safe way to keep me occupied. My last scheme, you see, did not leave him favourably disposed to allowing me to find ways in which to make my life more interesting."

There was a mischievous gleam in both her eyes and those of her friend Evelyn. Curious, that. He had not expected anything akin to impishness from Trefor Linton's sister or any of her friends. Constance Linton was the most proper chit he had ever met, and he suspected, to be her friend, Miss Barrett must be the same.

"Is your eye feeling better?" Miss Barrett asked.

"It is, but I'll not be doing either of you any favours in the future," he replied with a smirk. "At least not unless I receive something better than a broken nose and a black eye in return."

"I can neither apologize or thank you enough," Constance replied.

She had apologized over and over and over again as she stood holding a compress to his eye in the Linton sitting room those many days ago. "I think you have said the words enough," he replied softly. "I merely jest." He would not have her feeling guilty for his injuries when it was not her doing which caused them.

Miss Barrett tipped her head as she looked up at him, a puzzled look on her face. Then, she shook herself and smiled. "We are expected at your house soon, Connie. Mother will be waiting."

"As will Trefor," she smiled, "and Henry."

Much to Charles's surprise, Miss Evelyn Barrett rolled her eyes at the tone her friend used to say Henry's name.

"Do not let me detain you. I would not wish to run afoul of any of them." He winked at Miss Barret. "At least, not until I am healed."

She gasped. "My mother has warned me about you, Mr. Edwards."

"As well she should," he replied easily. "I am dreadfully charming."

Constance had entered the carriage, but Evelyn, who remained on the street, laughed. "That is not how my mother said it." Her eyes sparkled with impertinence. Then, with a small curtsey of parting, she boarded her carriage.

Charles looked after her and tipped his hat as the door closed on those shining eyes and teasing smile. Oh, he could find great pleasure in evoking such a look from her on a regular basis. Not that he wished to spend great amounts of time with her. No, he was not the sort of gentleman to trot around behind a lady hoping for her to smile at him or laugh at his jokes. He danced; he flirted; and he stole kisses. He did not become attached. Attachments were dangerous. They led to marriage and, he fought the urge to shudder, responsibility. He was far too young for such things as that just yet.

Still, he wondered where she would be this evening and if there would be any dark corners into which she might be persuaded.

He blew out a breath. Hiding himself away from society was perhaps not the best idea in the world. It apparently was wreaking havoc on his well-ordered, carefree existence. A rogue such as himself did not stalk his prey. He simply looked for the opportunity and took it. Planning anything was far too much like being responsible. Rules, guidelines, ledgers, accounts, and all the rest that went with being a gentleman of standing belonged to his father, not Charles.

In front of him, the carriage stopped, a man jumped down, the door opened, and a pretty face peered out, looking back to where he was.

He nudged his horse forward as Miss Barrett waved him towards her.

"Do you require help?" he asked as he drew near.

"No, no, we are well. Connie and I were just

talking, and I thought as we were discussing how dreadful it is that you were injured on Connie's account that it would be charitable of us to offer you a place in the Linton's box at the theatre tonight."

Charles began to shake his head.

"Hear me out. Do not refuse until I have made my full request. And come forward more, I feel as if I am going to fall out of this door and onto the street."

Charles chuckled. This young woman sounded more like Linton's cantankerous Aunt Gwladys than a young lady of the ton. Most young ladies who presented themselves during the season went out of their way to appear demure to one and all – always.

"Do you scold everyone?" he teased as he did as she said.

If he had expected her to be offended, he was once again going to be surprised, for she merely smiled, batted her lashes, and replied, "No, I scold very few beyond my brother actually."

"So, I am special," he returned.

She shrugged. "Perhaps you are. Or perhaps I just find you as troublesome as Griffin."

"I think I will insist you find me special."

"Do what you will; it matters not one jot to me," she retorted.

Her words might have said she did not care, but her tone clearly said she was annoyed.

"As I was saying..."

"Before you began scolding." Charles smiled at her huff.

"Before I had to pause to give instructions."

Charles chuckled. "Continue. I shall not refuse until you have said your piece."

"Refuse? You intend to refuse?"

"Most likely. But, I have not heard your request in full, so I cannot be certain I am correct until I do. I have been wrong before."

Her brows rose, and her lips pursed for a moment as if she were holding back some retort.

"There will not be very many people in our box. If you slip in a side door or something and scurry up to the box, you will not have to have many people gawk at you."

"You think I am worried about being seen?"

"I would be if my eye were the colour of yours. That *is* why you are riding here and not in a more populated place, is it not? And, I have not seen you at any events since...well..." she pointed to her eye.

"I will admit that I do not relish the whispers." Why he felt he needed to admit such a thing was beyond him. He could come up with any number of reasons to be riding where he was and for not having been at any soiree she had attended. A smile slipped slowly across his face. "Have you missed me?"

"What?" She shook her head vigorously. "No. I just noticed that I had not seen you slinking from shadow to shadow."

"If you say so."

"I do." She scowled. "Now, will you be joining us? I am certain no one would be in the least put out if you did."

"How reassuring," Charles muttered.

"Please," Constance added from the interior of the carriage. "I do feel dreadful that you have been out of society. It must be terribly boring sitting at home instead of going out."

"Who said I was sitting at home?" He smiled a lazy, suggestive smile.

"Henry," Constance replied.

Blast! Did Henry tell her everything?

"Very well, I have been hiding away. Are you happy to know my shame?"

"Only if it means you will join us," said Miss Barrett.

"Can you not muster an ounce of sympathy?" he asked in surprise. Were not young ladies – especially those who did charity work – supposed to be compassionate?

She shook her head. "No. Not a morsel. While I am awfully sorry you were injured, I do believe you have escaped more times than you have been caught."

The lady might look like an angel, but she had a heart of ice. However, ice could be melted. In fact, it could be quite a marvelous lark to attempt to melt that ice.

"Very well, I will join you if you will but attempt to feel an ounce of pity for me."

The way her lips pursed with contained amusement was tempting. "A full ounce?"

"Yes." He moved closer to her door. "A full ounce." He repeated the words in a low, sultry tone – slowly and deliberately. Satisfaction curled his lips as he saw her pretty nibble-worthy neck rise and fall when she swallowed.

She licked her lips. "I shall make an attempt."

"Then, I shall see you at the theatre."

"Very good."

He chuckled at the uncertainty in her voice. Again, he tipped his hat to the closed carriage door and watched it drive away before continuing on his way home to prepare for an evening of entertainment – and a play.

Acknowledgements

There are many who have had a part in the creation of this story. Some have read and commented on it. Some have proofread for grammatical errors and plot holes. Others have not even read the story, and a few, I know, never will. However, their encouragement and belief in my ability, as well as their patience when I became cranky or when supper was late or the groceries ran low, was invaluable.

And so, I would like to say *thank you* to Zoe, Rose, Kristine, Ben, and Kyle, as well as my Sweet Tuesday readers on Patreon and my blog, who followed this story as it developed and waited, as patiently as one might do, from one Tuesday to the next to read a new chapter. I feel blessed through your help, support, and understanding.

I have not listed my dear husband in the above group because, to me, he deserves his own special thank you, for, without his somewhat pushy insistence that I start sharing my writing, none of my writing goals and dreams would have been met.

Other Leenie B Books

You can find all of Leenie's books at this link
bit.ly/LeenieBBooks
where you can explore the collections below

~*~

Other Pens, Mansfield Park

~*~

Touches of Austen

~*~

Dash of Darcy and Companions Collection

~*~

Marrying Elizabeth Series

~*~

Sweet Possibilities, A Darcy and Elizabeth Variations Collection

~*~

Willow Hall Romances

~*~

The Choices Series

~*~

Darcy Family Holidays

~*~

Darcy and... An Austen-Inspired Collection

~*~

Nature's Fury and Delights (A Sweet Regency Novelettes Series)

About the Author

Leenie Brown has always been a girl with an active imagination, which, while growing up, was both an asset, providing many hours of fun as she played out stories, and a liability, when her older sister and aunt would tell her frightening tales. At one time, they had her convinced Dracula lived in the trunk at the end of the bed she slept in when visiting her grandparents!

Although it has been years since she cowered in her bed in her grandparents' basement, she still has an imagination which occasionally runs away with her, and she feeds it now as she did then — by reading!

Her heroes, when growing up, were authors, and the worlds they painted with words were (and still are) her favourite playgrounds! Now, as an adult, she spends much of her time in the Regency world,

End Street Volume 1

e Case of the Cupid Curse & The Case of the Wicked Wolf

n Bradley, Cover design by Meredith Russell,

5645648

playing with the characters from her favourite Jane Austen novels and those of her own creation.

When she is not traipsing down a trail in an attempt to keep up with her imagination, Leenie resides in the beautiful province of Nova Scotia with her two sons and her very own Mr. Brown (a wonderful mix of all the best of Darcy, Bingley, and Edmund with a healthy dose of the teasing Mr. Tilney and just a dash of the scolding Mr. Knightley).

Connect with Leenie

E-mail:

LeenieBrownAuthor@gmail.com

Facebook:

www.facebook.com/LeenieBrownAuthor

Blog:

leeniebrown.com

Patreon:

https://www.patreon.com/LeenieBrown

Subscribe to Leenie's Mailing List:

Book News from Leenie Brown

(bit.ly/LeenieBBookNews)

For everyone who loves End Street, and always for our families.

The Case Of The

Cupid Curse

End Street Volume 1

Chapter One

Sam Enderson stood outside his building and smiled with pride. The fresh sign painted on the door in crisp black letters read 'End Street Detective Agency'. Examining the overall effect, he nodded in satisfaction. This move to becoming a private investigator was as far from being a timid bookseller as he could get. No one would walk all over someone who investigated crimes for a living.

Three months of correspondence school and a shiny new multi-weapon license had given his confidence a much-needed boost. After the hellish past year in which he'd found his boyfriend in bed with his now ex-best friend, followed by the death of his favorite uncle, Sam was ready for a new start in life.

Uncle Hanson. Just thinking about him made Sam feel sad. He had fond memories of visiting his uncle at work. The man had always liked Sam. He evidently had carried that affection into Sam's adult life. After all, he had left Sam an entire building in his will, the building Sam now stood in front of. An office with accommodations over the top, worth quite a bit of money despite its proximity to an undesirable area.

"You should sell," his friend Oscar had said. Oscar had no love for Uncle Hanson. In a sniffy tone, he often consigned Hanson to the idiot pile and called him 'odd'.

"I don't want to sell," Sam had protested.

"What are you going to do with it?" Oscar had asked.

"Open up my own agency."

Oscar still wasn't speaking to him, even now, three months later.

Sam sighed at the memory and mentally pushed it all to one side to admire his property. The lower half consisted of a business office and reception area, with the upper two floors divided into four apartments. Three were empty, but his uncle had filled the fourth one with notes from his own investigative practice. That room was high on Sam's list of things to sort out, but he first needed to concentrate on renting out one of the empty apartments.

Sam might have inherited the house, but it hadn't exactly come with a burgeoning bank account to match. Forty years of being a detective and all Uncle Hanson had to show for it was this building, a small bank account, and a room full of papers. Sam was determined he was going to be different. He had a five-year plan in place. Sam didn't doubt for one minute that he knew exactly why his uncle had little money to speak of. Uncle Hanson had done too much pro bono work for *them*.

Filing cabinets and boxes overflowed with notes from years of being a private detective. A lot of those papers included cases involving aspects of the paranormal, things Sam thought better left alone. Sam didn't have a drop of supernatural blood in his entire body, and he didn't plan on associating with those who did. It hadn't exactly worked out well for his uncle.

Paranormals had their place. Hell, they owned half the city. Vampires and werewolves, witches, fae, and pixies—they all had their own parishes. Neighborhoods where they lived amongst their own kind. Like enjoyed living with like, and although they often mixed and matched, no one in Sam's family had ever crossed the romantic boundary between the magical and the not.

Sam didn't count his second cousin Christa, who had taken up with a blood demon. There was a bad seed in every batch.

Worried he'd use up the rest of his small inheritance, Sam had put an ad in the local paper to rent out two of the four apartments. They were empty but spacious rooms that had no one currently occupying them. After a quick mop and dust, they were ready for renters. Why his uncle had a space with no one living there didn't make much sense. Of course, if his cousin Erik hadn't been estranged from his father, Sam wouldn't have inherited anything. A twinge of guilt went through Sam, but he hadn't heard from his cousin in years and had no way of getting hold of him.

"Excuse me!"

A soft voice had Sam spinning around to see an old lady looking up at him. Her wrinkled skin and the way she leaned against her cane betrayed her great age.

"Can I help you?"

She squinted at him as if trying to make him out through her foggy white eyes. "You owe me a favor."

"What?" Sam examined the lady carefully, but he hadn't ever met her before in his life. What possible kind of favor could he owe her?

"The man here before. He promised he'd help me out," she explained.

"I'm sorry—"

The old lady didn't give Sam a chance to explain. She jabbed her finger into the air at Sam, pursed her lips, then began shouting. "He owes me. He owes me!" she repeated twice, her voice rising to a screeching pitch.

Ahh, now it becomes clear. "You must be talking about my uncle. Why don't you come inside and we can discuss what I can do for you." Although he didn't feel the need to keep a dead man's promise, if he could help the woman out, he would.

After opening the front door, he motioned for her to go ahead of him.

She settled into his visitor chair while Sam scooted past her to sit on the leather chair opposite, patting his uncle's gargoyle statue as he walked past. Uncle Hanson had the strangest collection of art he'd ever seen. Eventually, he'd get rid of it all, but right then the weird pieces reminded him of his beloved relative and better times.

"My name is Sam Enderson. How can I help you?"

Scowling over at him, she shook her head. "The guy here before never told you not to share your name, did he?"

"The man here before was my uncle. No, he didn't tell me not to share my name."

She shook her head as if not understanding Sam's stupidity. "You never share your name with a witch unless you want her to do a spell."

Sam jerked in his seat, appalled at what he'd let through his front door. "You're a witch?"

The woman slammed her cane onto the wooden floor. "Of course I'm a witch. I've got the wrinkled skin, the hunch, the cane, and the rheumy eyes. What did you think I was?"

He shrugged. "I-I thought you were just an old woman." An old scary woman who gave him the creeps, but an old woman nonetheless.

"Old!" the witch shrieked. "How dare you call me old? I'm only a hundred and sixty!"

"Forgive me." Sam raised his hands in alarm. "I didn't mean any offense." Secretly he wondered how old a witch had to be before she fell into the 'old' category.

"Well, I *am* offended," she snapped.

"Sorry. I don't know much about *your* world." Witch or not, he couldn't help the little slip of derision into his tone.

The witch regarded him carefully. "What are you?"

"What do you mean?"

"What blood flows in your body?" she asked, as if expecting him to come up with some sort of interesting paranormal cocktail.

"Human. Just human," Sam answered.

"You don't like paranormals, do you?"

"No." Sam saw no reason to deny the fact.

"So what are you doing here?" she asked suspiciously.

"I've inherited this building."

"And you intend to do what?"

"Carry on business as usual. Private investigations. It's what I'm qualified for." And he had the multi-weapon license to back him up.

"Then you'll have to do paranormal cases." She gave him a taunting smile.

Sam's stomach churned. "Why?" He didn't plan to ever take a paranormal case.

"Because the law states no business can discriminate against a paranormal due to his or her status," she explained. "It'll get you shut down, it will." There was definite glee in the old woman's expression.

All Sam wanted to do at that moment was place his head in his hands and curse. He didn't. He was much too professional for that. Instead, he shrugged. His mom always said if you had nothing good to say, then don't say anything.

The witch cackled in true witch fashion, and Sam shuddered inwardly. The scent of something dead and decaying pervaded the room. Add in the crooked teeth and the rags for clothes and he couldn't understand why he hadn't immediately pegged her as something *different.*

"Now about that favor…" she continued.

"What?" He couldn't look her in the eyes. Maybe if he didn't look, whatever she said wouldn't be real. He was comfortable with his denial. In fact, he might just lock the door, pull down the shades, and wallow in it for a few days.

"I need help tracking down a werewolf."

Sam looked at her. "Why?" Paranormal hunting paranormal? That couldn't end well.

The witch scowled at him while tapping her cane on the floor. "What do you mean, why?"

Had he stuttered? "I mean, why do you need a werewolf?"

"It's none of your business *why* I need a werewolf, boy. I just do," the witch snapped.

"It is, if you want me to do your dirty work." Sam knew all kinds of uses witches had for werewolves and none of them was nice. "Not to mention hunting werewolves is illegal."

"Pfft." She waved away the law as if it were nothing. Probably was since *she* didn't plan on breaking it but had asked Sam to do it instead. "I've got a rare potion to make, and I need some werewolf bones."

"No." Sam might not like paranormals very much, but he wasn't going to hunt one down, either.

"Your uncle owes me!" she screeched.

Sam wanted to cover his ears at the high-pitched noise. "My uncle is dead," he began to explain as patiently as he could. "I was willing to hear you out, but I'm not going to go kill an innocent werewolf so you can make a potion." Were werewolves actually innocent? Hadn't there been that whole rampaging werewolf-pack mess last year? Sam seemed to remember people—human, non-magical, regular people—getting killed in that little incident. Still, whatever issues he had with werewolves, he didn't do that kind of work. He had enough problems without getting jailed for killing werewolves, innocent or not.

"This potion can save a loved one!" the witch announced dramatically. "I need those bones."

"Find a different potion. I'm sure any given werewolf is someone's beloved too."

The witch scowled at him, then abruptly leaned back in her seat and smiled. The smile exposed a mouthful of yellowed teeth, and Sam winced inwardly at her lack of dental care. "Do you have anyone you love, Mr. Enderson?"

Sam's mind shifted back to the image of his boyfriend of ten years screwing his best friend. "Not anymore." Despite his ex pleading for forgiveness, some things Sam wouldn't forgive. He'd moved out and away from his lover within days and blocked both work and mobile numbers from his phone. His uncle had been his last close relative that had stayed in his life. So really, with his uncle dead, at this point in time, he had no one he could call a loved one. But he'd give her his own bones before he admitted the extent of his loneliness.

The witch stood with a purposeful air. "When you're on the verge of losing someone you love, come find me and maybe I'll free you. Until then, enjoy my present."

With a poof of smoke, the witch vanished.

Gasping, Sam tried to wave away the stench that accompanied the smoke, acrid and with a hint of burnt almonds. Finally, when that didn't work, he rushed over and opened a window to let the ashy smell out. Great start to his first day as a PI.

"You're an idiot."

"Ahh!" Sam jumped back from the window to face the empty room. What the hell? Was she still there? Was the witch invisible?

"An idiot," the voice repeated. This time Sam confirmed the source, emphasized when the statue on his desk turned its head and regarded him with eerie yellow eyes.

"What the hell are you?" he managed to ask coherently.

The statue's stone wings moved, creating a sound like gravel underfoot. "I'm a gargoyle. What are you?"

"I-I'm a human." Sam swallowed rapidly, trying to get some moisture into his dry throat. "What are you doing here?"

The statue stretched out of its crouch until it stood about a foot tall on the corner of the desk. Its baleful glare pinned Sam to the spot. "You're an idiot. That witch has something planned for you, and it isn't good."

"H-how do you know?" Sam's heart beat faster than a rabbit chased by a werewolf.

The gargoyle rolled his eyes. "You're not too bright, are you? Your uncle trafficked with that witch."

Sam frowned. His uncle had been a kindly old PI, who hadn't seemed to actually do much from day to day. There was no way he had trafficked anything. He had been the type of man who always had a ready supply of candy for eager young visitors like Sam.

"The sweet old man who brought you candy didn't exist," the gargoyle answered his thoughts. Wait? How the hell...?

"How did you know what I was thinking?"

The gargoyle ignored the question, "He would've had that werewolf for the witch by the end of the day and walked away with enough cash to eat for months." He didn't sound like he approved, and there was sadness in his tone.

"N-no, that can't be true." Sam shook his head in denial. Surely the gargoyle had his facts wrong?

"Have you actually looked at the paperwork upstairs yet? I heard you banging about. I assume you actually read some of them?"

"I was moving furniture for my future tenants." Sam shook his head. "And no, not yet. I thought they were just old case files that needed organizing."

Defending himself to a freaking gargoyle made Sam feel like an idiot. The damn thing had been sitting there every time Sam had visited, and never once had it appeared to be anything more than an ornament. The creature must be wrong. Sam would have seen it if Uncle Hanson had been a bad guy. He wasn't stupid. How could he not have understood his uncle's true nature? Nope, this 'gargoyle thing' had to be wrong.

The gargoyle clomped across the desk. "Look at the files and check out the back closet in the file room. Your uncle had more going on than anyone knew about. That includes exposing himself to a lot more than just a witch with teeth problems and a ready hand with curses."

With those parting words, the gargoyle sank back into his original position. A loud, crackling noise filled the room, and the creature became a statue once more. Sam poked at it with his index finger, but it didn't move again.

"Huh."

Maybe he was in the middle of a dream, one where he

was going to wake up in his sun-lit apartment in Johnstown with his boyfriend in bed with him.

File room.

The gargoyle's words sank in. Maybe he did need to check out the apartment with all the files a little more carefully. It wouldn't hurt to see what other pies his uncle had his fingers in. As he stepped out of the office, a knock on the front door had him turning away from the stairs and back towards the front door. Why would someone be knocking? The door was unlocked. At least, he didn't think he'd locked the door. But then, it was an old place. Maybe the latch had closed behind him when he'd escorted the witch inside.

His mind still on the files upstairs, he opened the door and stopped, frozen.

Vampire.

The man could be nothing else. Tall, elegant, and having an unearthly beauty, the vampire gave him a smile that exposed his fangs. "I hear you have an apartment to rent." The vampire's voice was like scotch over ice and dripped with sensuality.

A vampire here? In the daylight? Sam glanced past the vamp. Yep, the sun shone brightly in the sky.

"Ah, you're not used to us." The vampire flashed another smile. "We don't actually burn up in the sun."

That's a shame. That would be one less paranormal to cause trouble.

"Um, you need an apartment?" Sam had never heard of a vampire living in an apartment. "I thought you people had mansions and crypts and stuff."

The vampire threw back his head and laughed. "That's only in the movies. Now, can I see your place?"

"...Umm" Sam searched his mind for a good excuse.

Anything to keep the skeevy, blood-sucking supernatural out of his house.

The tall vampire smiled. "You know that part about vampires reading your mind?"

With a sinking stomach, Sam nodded.

"That part's true."

Sam sighed. "You'd better come in. It's right this way."

The day had started out so well, too. Now, Sam just wanted to go back to bed and hide under the covers.

"I'd be happy to keep you company," the vampire said in a low, sultry tone. For a second, Sam didn't understand what the hell the vampire was talking about, and then he recalled what he had just thought about beds and covers. Sam looked over his shoulder to see the vampire checking out his ass. Rolling his eyes, he headed up the stairs, leading the vampire to the top floor. He pulled an old-fashioned key from his pocket, unlocked then opened the door.

"No spell locks?" the vampire asked with concern in his voice.

Sam shook his head. Like he'd had any time to do things like that. The vampire was lucky the room had been tidied and cleaned. "You're welcome to add your own, of course." Fuck, he was going to rent to a vampire. He could hope the creature didn't want the place. "It's nothing fancy."

Please want something fancy.

Before Sam could take more than two steps into the apartment, the vampire pinned him to the wall. "I'm not a creature. I'm a man, and I'd be happy to show you exactly how manly I am."

To Sam's shock, he could feel the vampire rubbing his erection against him. "U-um, s-sorry." Was this what vampires did just before they drank every drop of blood from your body?

"I don't want you sorry. I just want you to want me."

Sudden, inexplicable desire burned through Sam and his body hardened in reaction to the proximity of another man. The vampire smiled, exposing a flash of fang. A shiver of fear trembled down Sam's spine.

"No!" He shoved at the vampire, who, surprisingly, broke his hold and released Sam.

The vampire watched Sam with a wary look. "What are you?"

Why does everyone keep asking me that?

"I'm human, okay? Just human." Sam scowled at the vampire.

"No human has ever shattered my glamor." The vampire sounded thoughtful, and his appraising look unnerved Sam.

"Well, good for me." Sam folded his arms. He might not like paranormals, but he knew enough about vampires and their way of controlling people to know he didn't want that within six feet of him. "I'm not going to rent a room to someone who tried to glamor me. You might as well go."

The vampire smiled. "My name is Bob."

A snort of laughter burst out of Sam. "Your name isn't Bob."

The vampire tilted his head, and his eyes glowed with amusement. "How do you know?"

"Because I just had a witch tell me not to share my name with a paranormal so I doubt you would be telling me your real name."

Bob grabbed Sam's wrist. His grip was firm, and instinctively Sam yanked his arm to try to break the vampire's hold. "There was a witch here?" Bob snapped urgently. "What did she look like?"

"A witch." What did it matter what she looked like? "She

was old, crony, and witchy. You know—" He gestured expansively with his free hand— "A witch."

"What did she want?" Bob still hadn't let go of his wrist. The vampire didn't know his own strength. One last tug and Bob finally let him loose. Idly, Sam rubbed at the sore skin burn.

"From what she said, werewolf bones."

Bob scanned the room as if he expected the witch to jump out of the wall or something. "Never trust a witch and never, *ever*, tell a witch your real name."

"Okay, um… Bob." Sam could barely hold back the laughter building inside him.

"My real name is Roberto, but I go by Bob," Bob finally said. "Vampires don't have last names outside a coven. Your last name reveals the group you belong to. I am an independent."

Sam couldn't hold back the laugh inside him. Dire warnings about witches aside, he couldn't wrap his head around a badass vampire calling himself Bob. Hell, a vampire named Bob. That was wrong on so many levels.

"Vampires are supposed to be sexy. There's nothing sexy about a Bob," Sam finally managed to say without laughing. Why he cared what the vampire called himself, he didn't know, but there was no way he was going to call a vampire Bob.

Bob seemed to forget his need to warn Sam about witches and names and instead pulled Sam into his arms. Evidently he had returned to his first agenda. "I'm sure I can convince you I'm sexy," he drawled. What was it about this man—vampire, whatever—feeling like he could manhandle him at every turn?

Sam narrowed his eyes at the vampire. The man might be

the sexiest thing Sam had ever seen, but he wasn't going to admit it…

Damn. He had just thought that. And damn—Bob had heard him. Shit. Bob was definitely smirking.

"Do you have a multiple personality disorder or something? You bounce around more than anyone I've ever met. From scary vampire to smirking idiot in a second."

Bob smiled and didn't appear to take offense at Sam's comment. "You'll have plenty of time to examine my personality when I move in. How much is the rent?" The quick change of subject threw Sam, but it didn't keep him from trying one last time to stop Bob from moving in. He mentioned an exorbitant amount for the monthly rent to attempt to deter the vampire.

Bob released Sam, and then walked through the living room and down the hall. There were two bedrooms and a small kitchen, though Sam doubted Bob would need a kitchen. Vampires didn't eat real food. Right? But wouldn't he need a fridge or something for all the blood? Or would he be one of those vampires with a live donor?

What did Sam know? He had thought vampires could only come out at night.

Sam pushed aside thoughts of blood.

Bob returned to Sam's side in long, confident strides. "I'll take it."

Shit!

Chapter Two

NOT FOR THE FIRST TIME, AS SAM INHALED THE DUST IN HIS uncle's storeroom, he wondered if he should have worn a mask. Dust was everywhere. The damned stuff covered years of undisturbed chaos piled in the corner of his uncle's filing system. Spider webs, dark and thick, coiled in and around files that were faded with age. The top one, labeled Aster vs. Aster, was dated fifteen years ago, so God knows what the rest was like.

Throwing back the full black drapes brought light into the otherwise dismal space. He finally got a good look at the room his uncle had always called 'the bookroom.' Objects, boxes, letters, and photos covered every conceivable surface. A pile of notes here, a file of case observations there. With no discernible organization at all, the sight of it almost sent Sam running back out and shutting the book room door behind him.

He opened Aster vs. Aster and traced a finger down the spidery writing.

"Edgar Aster, Elf, aged…" He peered closer. "Aged one hundred eighty-three. Against Agnes Aster, daughter of…

pursuant to… what the hell?" Even with his reading glasses perched on the end of his nose, it was difficult to work his way through both the handwriting and the legalese. The notes were sketchy, and then all of a sudden there was a switch in language. He couldn't understand the English parts, let alone the symbols that lined the page.

"Edgar Aster cheated on his wife." The voice came out of one of the other dark corners, and Sam spun around, brandishing the file in front of him.

"What the hell?"

"He cheated on his wife. It says so on page fifty-seven. That is the conclusion reached." The voice was so damn formal. Sam squinted at the shadowy corners but didn't see anyone. Not even a little gargoyle statue sitting around waiting to come to life.

Just as he decided he'd lost his frigging mind, the disembodied voice was joined by a body. Well, half of a body so far, actually. The full form was manifesting from wisps of smoke, and a man's figure formed in front of Sam's eyes.

He'd seen ghosts before. On television. Not real ghosts; make-believe ghosts. He knew they existed for real, but they generally kept to themselves.

"Then you'll never guess what he did." The ghost floated nearer as a nose joined his face and ears aligned on each side of his head. The ghost's voice dripped with the tone of someone sharing salacious gossip. Glee danced in his pale misty eyes. Definite glee. "He got his wife and girlfriend pregnant at the same time."

"At one hundred-eighty-seven years old?" Sam blurted, painfully aware he was having a conversation with a ghost, who appeared trapped in a time from centuries past. The britches and a flowing white shirt put the ghost a few hundred years earlier than current, and the long ringlets cascading to his shoulders gave him a more feminine look than the man's voice suggested.

"That's nothing," the ghost said conspiratorially. Sam found himself unconsciously leaning closer to hear. With a snort of disgust, he pulled himself back. The ghost didn't appear to notice, now fully formed and standing—floating—in front of him. "Turns out he had seven mistresses and…" His voice trailed off as he raised his eyebrows. "He had so many children, he ran out of elvish names to call them."

"Oh," Sam offered helplessly. The ghost held out his hand as if to shake it, and Sam, on instinct, made to grasp the offered fingers only to watch his own hand pass straight through the misty one. The ghost giggled. Seriously chuckled with mirth. Then, to Sam's shock, he floated straight through Sam.

Sam shivered at the icy sensation that passed through him and jerked forward as soon as it was done. Swiveling on his feet, he turned to face the ghost, who was staring at him with an odd expression.

"I didn't like that," the ghost said quietly.

"*You* didn't like it?" Sam spluttered. He felt violated and mildly nauseous. "I feel—"

"What are you?" the ghost asked.

"What? I'm the owner here. My uncle—"

"No. *What* are you?" the ghost repeated his question in a slow, patient manner as if he were talking to a child.

"What? Why does everyone ask me that? I'm the normal one here. I'm human."

"Oh." The ghost looked puzzled. Then he wrinkled his nose and shrugged. Apparently he didn't understand that Sam was the human here. "Sorry about the…about before—you know the whole, umm…"

"Ghosting through me and violating me?" Sam snapped

the question. The ghost appeared offended and perched on the side of one of the desks. Sam could see the files through the pale form, like some kind of weird special effect.

"I was just teasing you," the ghost said idly. "I'm Theodore McCurray Constantine III. For some reason, your uncle Hanson liked to call me Teddy. I'm the file keeper." His voice spilled over with pride as he straightened his ethereal shoulders. "It's a big responsibility."

"The file keeper," Sam repeated carefully.

"Can I join in?" The voice was a welcome respite from making sense of why there was a ghost sitting on his desk. A ghost whose name appeared to be a mishmash from different continents. Teddy looked across to the door, and with a girly shriek, he vanished from sight, leaving only a few random wisps of smoke that trailed around where he had been sitting.

Sam ran his fingers through his hair and sighed loudly.

"You may be renting from me, Bob, but this is my room and vamp…tenants are not allowed in this part of the building."

Bob looked around the space, with its tangle of files, boxes, and books, then, disregarding Sam's statement, he strode the few steps to Sam and took the file from his hand.

"Aster? I remember him." Bob looked up at the ceiling with a smile on his face and reminisced. "What a guy."

Sam immediately reacted negatively. This Aster, if he could believe the ghost, had been a serial adulterer. There was nothing remotely fabulous or amazing about that. "He sounded like a bastard. Cheating on his wife."

"Wives," Bob corrected quickly.

"Wives? It gets worse."

"So you don't like the idea of a cheat?" Bob asked thoughtfully. Sam's mind wandered to thoughts of his ex. He narrowed his eyes as Bob stared, suddenly remembering the vampire could read his thoughts.

"Did you know that vampires mate for life?" Bob began conversationally. "We don't cheat. Ever. A cheating vampire is a dead vampire."

"Yay for vampires," Sam replied sarcastically. Bob took one step closer, and Sam took a measured step backward. His ass hit one of the filing cabinets, preventing him from backing up any further. "You scared Teddy." Changing the subject was probably a good thing at this point.

Bob waggled a hand from side to side. "Vampires don't get on with ghosts and vice versa."

"They don't?" *Why? Why did I give him the chance to explain? He's freaking me out, and he's between me and the door.*

"I think the veil is thinnest between a vampire and a ghost," Bob offered in explanation.

That was possibly one of the most insightful things Sam had heard since he had been a child sitting through interminable hours of remedial paranormal studies with Mr. Esterhoon.

"Because you're both dead people," Sam offered.

Bob took that final step forward until there was nothing more than a single breath between them. Damn it. There was a flash inside Sam, a curl of lust that climbed higher while sweat trickled down his back. His dick was so hard he could swear it was going to break the zipper on his pants. Bob had the most incredible eyes. Amber and gold, they shone with an unearthly light, and Sam could see every striation of color in the irises. And the scent of him? Of Roberto? A mix of earth and sky and oh so damn intoxicating.

Placing his hands on either side of Sam, Bob pressed into him, clearly just as hard. Bob bent his head, and instinctively

Sam tilted his head in response. Bob brushed a gentle kiss against Sam's exposed neck. He couldn't stop himself. He was going to let Bob feed on him, kiss him, fuck him and…

Bob pulled back with a smirk on his face.

"I can promise you I am not dead."

Sam pushed at Bob. "Stop that," he snapped. "You're up in my space, and I don't like it." Sam made his words firm and unyielding. Bob would have to understand exactly where he was coming from. *No touching*. Bob narrowed his eyes then shrugged. Evidently, Sam's firm stance had hit a chord. Bob took a few steps back, and, crossing his arms over his chest, he only stared. They locked gazes. Bob's focused look made Sam more and more nervous. In the end, Sam snapped.

"You can go now," he said.

"I'm happy here." Bob resolutely stood his ground, and Sam could feel the tension knotting inside him at the brooding vampire and his inability to just go.

"This is my office and—"

"You have a visitor," Bob interrupted. He tilted his head to one side and closed his eyes. "Two actually. Of the same mind."

Sam hadn't heard the door, but moved past Bob to peer over the banister and down the stairs anyway. Bob was right. Two figures stood huddled together in the wide entrance hall. Jeez. If Bob hadn't said anything, Sam wouldn't have known they'd arrived. There and then, he resolved not to spend time trawling through the file room at the expense of possibly losing a paying customer. He needed a bell, an alarm, or something.

"You have visitors," a voice whispered in his ear. Sam cursed in surprise as he turned to find Teddy, half there and half not, with a look of concern on his pale face.

"I know, thank you," Sam said sharply.

"Are you going to ask them what they want?" And now Bob was there as well, right up next to him and tracing one of his long fingers down Sam's arm. "I'm not sure you should leave clients standing in the hallway."

"Your uncle would have been down there already," Teddy warned.

That was the final straw. "Enough. I'm perfectly capable of dealing with clients."

Ignoring the sigh from Teddy, Sam pushed past Bob and went down the stairs as calmly as he could. Excitement built inside him as he observed the two tall, slim gentlemen, currently with their backs to him, talking quietly. With short blond spiky hair and dressed in jeans and sweaters, they looked normal. He could handle normal. Normal was easy. They apparently hadn't noticed him arrive behind them, and it gave him a chance to brush the dust off his clothes.

"Can I help you?" he asked. They stopped talking and, in perfect unison, turned to face him.

Twins.

Twins with narrow, delicate features and wide, silver-blue eyes.

Twins with runes and other markings tattooed in exact replica on each perfectly sculpted right cheek. Not to mention the pronounced widow's peak and the silver threaded into their short hair. He racked his brain, trying to remember a classification for this particular type of non-human but failed. Tall. Slim. Silvery. Tattooed faces. Sighing inwardly, he realized now was the test of his promise to himself to only work for humans. The twins didn't seem so bad. No fangs or huge sharp teeth, no fur, and they appeared fairly harmless.

"We have lost our third," one of the twins said directly. He held out a hand, which Sam instinctively grasped to shake.

"Our third is lost," they said together to emphasize the reason for the visit. Sam shook his hand also. Sparks chased up his arm, and he felt curiously dizzy for an instant. The twins looked at each other, and the first took a step forward to release the other's handshake.

"Not now," he said.

"Not now," the second repeated.

Shaking off the dizzy feeling and not at all understanding this strange conversation, he gestured with a hand toward the office. The two visitors walked into the room first. They stopped just inside the door, and Sam shuffled around them as best he could before sliding into his chair.

"Please. Sit." He wondered if he should have offered coffee, but after casting a quick look at his uncle's old coffee machine, he wasn't entirely sure he could work the damn thing. Nothing led him to imagine for one minute that he could fix a proper cup under the watchful gaze of the strange silver-eyed twins. They sat in perfect unison, and both wore the same expectant expressions on their faces. Pulling his brand-new notepad from the side of his desk, he sat poised with the pen hovering over the paper.

"You said you're missing your third. Can you elaborate at all? Your third what?" It was a safe question. They had mentioned losing a third.

"Us," Twin on the left said.

"Us," Twin on the right repeated.

"Us. You. Um…" Sam scribbled in the notebook. One word. 'Us'. A good start.

"Can I maybe get some more details?" *More lucid details that actually made sense, maybe?*

"We created a list."

"A list," he repeated. This was going nowhere fast.

Left twin passed the paper over along with a photo of a

man who looked just like the two men sitting across from Sam. He set aside the picture, grabbed his reading glasses, and peered down at the writing. He didn't know what he'd been expecting, but it wasn't this simple list written in English No runes or hieroglyphics, but actual writing. Of course, the normality ended there. He didn't understand one thing on the list.

"Places he was seen."

"Places he went."

Sam did recognize one name as that of a local nightclub, but it could be a coincidence. He looked back up at the twins. Both of whom appeared to be close to tears. Hell. He hated it when people cried. He never knew what to say or do.

Okay. The third is a person. Someone who means a lot to two men who look like twins.

He sat back in his chair and steepled his fingers. He had seen his uncle do that on more than one occasion, and he had always thought it made his uncle look brilliant and considering. Finally, he put his thoughts into words.

"So," he started carefully. "Your third, your brother or triplet, is missing, and these are the places he has been spotted. You are hiring me to track down your missing brother."

"With haste," left twin intoned gravely.

"Utmost haste," right twin enforced.

Sam looked back down at the paper. "Can I get some contact details for you?" He looked up, but the twins had stood and were already at the office door. "Wait." Clambering to stand, and cursing his leg that somehow had become trapped between chair and desk, he finally stumble-tripped out to the hallway.

Gone. Both ethereal twins were gone. Throwing open the front door, he stepped out into the sunlight and blinked at the sudden change in brightness. Scanning the street for a car, or at least two walking men, he stared up and down the road. Nothing. Totally gone.

Damn it. He had nothing much in the way of information, no names…and no money. Maybe that piece of paper would reveal more than he thought, but he hadn't even agreed to a damn fee. Shit.

Freaking paranormals.

Chapter Three

SAM WENT BACK INTO HIS OFFICE AND THREW HIMSELF INTO his chair. Nibbling on his fingernail, he reviewed the list.

"You shouldn't take this case."

He looked up to see Bob watching him with a worried expression in his eyes.

"What? Why not? I need this." He wasn't going to turn away his first client, especially since they looked so distraught. Paranormals might not be his favorite type of people, but he wasn't going to ignore anyone looking for their missing relative.

"They lusted after you." Bob frowned at Sam as if it were his fault.

"Bullshit. They barely looked at me. They want me to find their brother."

Bob shrugged. "Fine, don't believe me, but don't go anywhere alone. Make sure you have backup."

Where the hell was he going to find backup?

"Okay, whatever you say," he placated the vampire.

Bob rolled his eyes. "You are a terrible liar, especially with someone who can read your mind."

"Oh, yeah." He'd sort of forgotten that part. "Listen, Bob. I know you're only trying to help, but frankly, I don't have any backup. I'm alone and probably going to stay that way. I just want to take enough cases to pay my bills and be independent." He'd hoped to avoid paranormals, but they appeared determined to find him.

"Take me with you."

Sam laughed. "I don't need a big, dangerous vampire to watch my back."

Bob shook his head. "You need someone to look out for you more than anyone I've ever met."

Sam ground his teeth together. "Get out of my office!"

"Remember what I told you!" Bob pointed his finger warningly at Sam. "Don't go anywhere alone."

"Go!"

"Fine!" Bob stomped out of the room.

"He has your best interests at heart." The gargoyle's feet made a grinding noise against the wood of the desk. Now Sam knew where all the gouges on the surface had come from.

"Shhh, go be a statue," Sam told the gargoyle, making a shooing gesture with his hand.

With a shrug as if he'd done his best, the gargoyle turned back to stone.

Sam plopped his chin in his hand and proceeded to look over the list the twins had left.

"The gargoyle is right, the fae triad is trouble." Bob stood in the doorway, scowling. The vampire hadn't stayed away long enough for Sam's peace of mind.

"Fae? Is that what they were?" The power pulsing off the twins had sent tingles through Sam's body. He almost didn't want to know how strong they would be with their third.

Bob rolled his eyes. "You don't even know what they are

and you're dealing with them?" His tone indicated that Sam lacked the brains of a gargoyle in stone form.

Sam shrugged. "I'm not dealing with them. They want me to find their third. It's my job to find missing people, even if they are the weird third of a freaky paranormal triad."

"They won't leave you untouched."

Bob's serious tone had Sam setting down the list to give the vampire his whole attention. "What do you mean?"

"I mean, the fae always mark those they consider valuable. If you're successful in finding their third, they'll never let you go. You'll be considered a resource, and they'll come back time and time again."

"What's the alternative? Let their brother disappear? I might not like paranormals, but I won't turn away someone in need." That was the crux of it. As much as he didn't want to become involved with the otherworldly, he wouldn't ignore people genuinely in distress. The twins might be odd, but he could tell they were deeply disturbed by the absence of their third.

"Then I'm going with you." Bob folded his arms as if that had settled the matter.

"Um, no. Why would I take you along? I don't need you following me like a vampire bodyguard. I need to blend into the crowd."

Bob threw back his head and laughed. "You will never blend, baby."

Blending had never been a problem before. Hell, even his lover had considered him invisible enough to have an affair, as if Sam didn't even exist. Sam scowled. "Don't call me baby. And there's no reason why I can't melt into the crowd."

"You might have been ignored by your loser ex, but to me and most paranormals, you glow like a homing beacon. I'm not letting you go into any club without backup."

Sam rolled his eyes, even though he could tell the vampire meant what he said. "Fine, but if you get in my way, I'm going to try out my staking skills."

Bob gave him a fang-tipped smile. "I'm at your command." His low, seductive tone had Sam shaking his head. The last time he'd heard a voice that seductive was in college when he'd accidentally walked into a succubus bathhouse.

"Are you sure you aren't part succubus?" Sam asked.

Bob walked over, planted his hands on Sam's desk, and kissed him on the cheek. "Not that you can prove." Straightening, he turned and left the room.

No matter how he looked at it, Sam was in trouble.

HOURS LATER, after it had reached proper club-hopping time, Sam decided to start at the only clubs he recognized from the list. Not that he'd been inside the place, but he'd driven past Club Virgo several times on his way home from his old job selling books. Club Virgo straddled two worlds and sat on the border of normal and paranormal territories. Sam's investigation showed there would be a mix of human and non-human there tonight. A good place to start. Humans he could talk to.

After much internal debate, Sam dressed in his old club clothes, an outfit he hadn't dusted off in at least a few years. Damn, maybe there was more than one reason his ex had gone elsewhere for excitement.

The jeans fit Sam like a second skin and the shirt skimmed his body with avid devotion.

"You don't look too bad," he told his reflection as he added some gel to his hair and contemplated his appearance.

At least the gym membership looked to be paying off. He might only be sitting behind a desk so far, but he'd started working out in the mornings and some of his soft parts were firming up.

"Not too bad is one hell of an understatement," Bob spoke from the doorway.

"Hey, how did you get inside my apartment?" Sam's ire faded as he took in Bob's outfit. Where Sam wore jeans, Bob's lower half was encased in leather that faithfully followed every line of his body while his top half was covered in a red silk shirt that looked extremely touchable. Sam's mouth watered. He might not want to become involved with a vampire, but there was nothing that said he couldn't admire the scenery.

"I'm a vampire. I can get into anywhere." Bob's wicked smile told Sam he didn't need to voice his admiration—the bastard had read his mind.

"I don't suppose I can get you to stay here?" He didn't need a bodyguard, and he doubted anyone would think the vampire belonged to Sam. He didn't have the striking good looks to attract a man with Bob's otherworldly beauty.

"Nope." Bob shook his head. "Trust me—you don't want to go to that club without me. You want to appear claimed by someone, or you'll be too much of a target."

"Fine, but if you grope me, hug me, generally be all over me, or pinch my ass, I'm going to punch you," Sam warned.

"If I get my hands on that ass, it'll be worth a hit." Bob smiled. Sam didn't trust the hunger in Bob's eyes. He only wished the answering need in him could be tamped down as it was messing with his control.

"Let's go," Sam sighed, hoping Bob read his frustration but not his attraction.

Bob remained silent as Sam gathered his wallet, and then

left the apartment. He ignored his companion as he headed to the club, which was only a few blocks away. He could see its neon sign glowing up ahead. As they passed an alley, a low growl stopped him in his tracks.

The hairs on the back of his neck stood on end as a pair of glowing yellow eyes peered out at him from the darkness. At that moment, Bob's presence didn't feel so suffocating. When the vampire put his hand on Sam's back to let him know he was there, Sam felt relief rather than resentment.

"Are you Sam Enderson, the detective?" a deep voice growled.

"Yes." He didn't offer further information. The scary yellow-eyed creature already had the advantage. The paranormal who stepped into the light might have odd colored eyes, but the rest of him made Sam's libido jump up and take notice. Dark, shaggy hair topped a ruggedly handsome face. The stranger had wide shoulders and wore a stretched T-shirt that tried to confine his bulk. The jeans he wore fared little better, as they had tears here and there at the seams, but it was the hunger in his eyes that made Sam take a step back into Bob's arms.

"Is there something we can help you with?" Bob asked. The chill in his voice should've caused icicles to form in the air.

"Not you," the werewolf growled. "Him." He pointed a finger at Sam.

Sam cleared his throat. He tried to step away from Bob, but the vampire held him tight. "Um, what can I help you with?"

Bob's fingers dug into Sam's shoulders. "We're together," he snarled at the man-beast.

"No, you're not," the werewolf insisted. "You might want to be, but he's not yours yet." He sniffed the air like Sam had seen bloodhounds do on television. "He doesn't carry your scent."

Sam shoved Bob away from him and stepped forward. Any other time, he might worry about approaching an unknown paranormal without at least a gun in his possession, but curiosity won out over caution.

"What do you want with me?"

"I heard you don't like paranormals, but I have enough money to persuade you to help me anyway." The man tilted his head as if he could hear something out of the range of a mere human.

"I'll help anyone for a price," Sam agreed.

"What's your price?"

"What's your case?" Sam countered.

Surprisingly, the werewolf pulled a picture out of his jacket pocket. "My daughter is missing."

Sam accepted the photo. The image of a smiling girl with her daddy's yellow eyes hit him in the gut. She couldn't be more than five. "H-how old is she?" A lump stuck in his throat made it difficult to speak. Shit, it didn't even matter that the man wasn't human. Sam had a soft spot for children.

"She's four. She disappeared two days ago. I'll give you anything if you find my little girl. Her name is Shelby."

"Where was she last seen?" Sam racked his mind for all the proper questions. He doubted he could find a werewolf girl, not if even her father couldn't catch the scent.

"Wolf Creek Park on Seventh."

Shit, it was deep in the shifter park; Sam doubted the werekin would appreciate him poking his nose into their private business. "Who was with her when she disappeared?"

"Her nanny. Her mother and I aren't together, and we both work. We hired a nanny to watch her during the day until she can go to school."

Sam nodded. Werekin had the same problems as any other parents. Gone were the days where there were big pack nurseries and pack subsidized housing. These days, most packs were happy to earn enough money to afford the taxes on their hunting lands. Sam doubted even if he found the girl alive and healthy that he would get much money from the man standing before him. Looking up at the yellow-eyed shifter, Sam saw for the first time a concerned father instead of a werekin waiting to eat an unwary human.

"What's your name?"

"Hartman Hunter."

Crap.

Sam might not recognize the man, but he did recognize the name. Hartman led the biggest pack in the state. His list of enemies probably circled the globe. Sam sighed. "I'll see what I can do."

"Can I have your hand on it?" Hartman held out his hand.

Giving a werewolf your handshake on a deal was as good as a blood bond. If he broke it, Sam knew his blood would decorate the streets, the sidewalks, and probably splatter the sides of buildings as a warning to others. Bob held him back. Sam glanced up into Bob's worried eyes. Sam shook his head subtly. There was a child involved here.

"A little girl, Bob," he thought. Bob closed his eyes briefly then released his hold on Sam, as good as giving his approval. Taking a deep breath, Sam took the werewolf's hand. Hartman shook it gently as if worried about harming Sam.

"Thank you." Hartman turned to leave.

"Before you go, could you tell me who sent you to me?" Sam hadn't been there long enough to earn a reputation.

"Some ghost who said he worked for you," Hartman said.

Then with a quick nod and a growled "I'll find you," he disappeared into the night.

"Huh." Sam didn't know if he should thank Teddy, his friendly neighborhood ghost, or give him a firm talking-to.

Bob slid his hand around Sam's arm. "I don't think you should've taken the case."

Sam held up the picture for Bob to see. "You think I should stand by and let something happen to this little girl?"

Bob nodded, unperturbed by Sam's sharp tone. "You heard him. She's been gone a few days. Odds are, if she hasn't been found alive yet, you aren't going to find her."

Jerking his arm out of the vampire's hold, Sam stepped away from Bob and toward the club. "Excuse me if I care." Annoyed with the vampire's attitude, Sam strode off to the club entrance.

The bouncer looked down at Sam. "Do you have an invitation?"

"Damn, I didn't know I needed one." Before he could think of a good excuse, Bob spoke up behind him.

"He's with me."

The bouncer stepped aside. "Go right in, sir."

Bob's lips formed a smirk as he turned to Sam. "I told you, you need me."

"I guess, for once, you were right," Sam retorted. Inwardly cursing, he made sure his face didn't reveal his turmoil. What kind of detective didn't investigate the place he planned to case out for a client? He should have known he would need an invitation. He really had to work on the basics if he didn't want to get killed.

"You'll learn." Bob placed a hand on Sam's back, leading him toward the bar. "The best person to answer questions is always the bartender."

"I know that," Sam snapped. He'd watched enough detective shows and heard his uncle's stories.

Bob kissed him on the cheek, and Sam barely resisted the urge to punch him.

Approaching the bar, Sam smiled at the perky brunette who whipped out drinks faster than the naked eye could follow. She didn't give off a paranormal vibe, but Sam decided her speed showed she was a bit more than human.

"What can I get you, gentlemen?" She looked from Sam to Bob and back again.

"Whiskey," Bob said before Sam could speak.

"What?" He turned to face the vampire.

"Detectives drink whiskey, everyone knows that."

"I hate whiskey."

Bob shook his head sadly. "You'll never be a proper detective."

"I'm going to punch you before the night is over," Sam vowed. He turned back to find two glasses of whiskey lined up on the bar.

The bartender slid one toward Sam. "This one is on the house," she said with a wink.

Rolling his eyes, Sam tossed back the drink, trying to make sure none of it actually hit his tongue.

"And Sam?"

Sam snapped his gaze to the bartender. He hadn't given her his name, he was certain of it. He must have misheard her. "Sorry?"

"Grandmother says hi." With a cold smile, she turned around and walked to the other end of the bar.

A strange tingling shot through Sam's body. "Oh hell, what the fuck did she give me?"

Chapter Four

"SAM… SAMMMMMMM." BOB'S VOICE WAS ELONGATING INTO a mess of syllables inside Sam's head. Lights spun behind his eyes, and he grasped at the nearest thing he could hold. The feel of leather and material in his hands and the strength of Bob were the only things stopping him from giving in and fainting like a girl on the club floor.

Has she killed me? Is it poison? Bob?

"Sam." Bob was shaking him like a rag doll and nausea rose in Sam, threatening to add an unpleasant decoration to the vampire's shirt.

"St-stop shay-ayking me," Sam managed to force out. Bob did. Then he did something worse—he held Sam so tight that Sam couldn't breathe. Sickness gave way to panic as his claustrophobia hit him hard, and he began seeing spots behind his eyes. Using every ounce of his strength, he pushed at Bob and staggered backward and away until the bar was behind him.

"Sam? Sam. Sam… Sam!"

"Shhhh," Sam pushed the plea out there as the cacophony of *SamSamSam* was making his head hurt. Whatever was in that drink felt like ice trickling through his veins. Experimentally he flexed his fist and attempted to focus on his fingers as they clenched together. Peering close, he swore he could see silver tracing through his skin, but when he blinked to focus, it had gone.

"Are you okay?" Bob asked worriedly. He had a firm hand on Sam's arm, clearly concerned that Sam was going to keel over at any minute. He pulled his arm out of Bob's grasp.

"I need a drink," he said firmly. The words sounded okay in his head, and he hoped they were making sense. "Not whiskey. Water."

"Water," Bob ordered imperiously. Sam looked back over his shoulder at the short guy who was staring at Sam and Bob like he had never seen a vampire or a poisoned human before. "I said water," Bob emphasized. The guy, some kind of derivative of a dwarf clan by the looks of it, scurried over to the bottles of water and filled a glass. In seconds, he was back to Sam and slid the full glass across the wooden surface of the bar. Bob snatched it away before Sam could reach it. He swallowed two gulps then waited.

"It's okay," Bob said, before handing Sam the water.

"Don't you have different chemistry, being… not being alive?" Sam waved a shaky hand to indicate what he meant, which in no uncertain terms was about Bob being dead anyway.

Bob huffed but didn't argue the point. "Drink the water."

So Sam did. Cool and wet, it slid down his throat like an icy balm. Shaking his head of the residual fuzziness, he peered down at his hand again. He really could have sworn he saw silver strands under his skin. He opened his mouth to tell Bob, but his vampire keeper wasn't there. Curiously, he scanned the groups of people in the immediate area, none of whom seemed to have noticed the fact that someone had tried to kill Sam. Kill him, or poison him, or…shit, anything.

"Hello, gorgeous." The voice was low and very close to Sam's ear. So close it took him by surprise and he yelped in shock. Jeez, his nerves were hanging by a thread. Spinning on his heel, which wasn't that clever considering his head was a mash-up of dizzy and spaced out, he turned to face the owner of the voice.

Stunning. That was the first word that came to mind. Six feet of ethereal perfection was inches from him.

"Hello," Sam said politely. All the while he was shuffling along with the bar at his back an inch at a time. He was stopped by the feel of a hard body behind him, and he relaxed slightly, thankful Bob had returned. He wasn't sure what this guy with the long dark hair and the body to die for wanted from him, but now that Bob was there, he could handle it.

"They have rooms in the back." The voice was a new one. Belonging to the strong body he was leaning on. Which clearly wasn't Bob.

With another unmanly yelp, Sam spun to face the new guy and for his sins had the first guy pressing against his ass.

"I think I love him," the owner of the hard dick at his back said. Sam's head spun.

"I love him as well. He's everything I want—"

"He's everything I need—"

"He is so beautiful—"

"He smells so good—"

"I want him forever—"

"I would die for him—"

"Guys," Sam interrupted the one-upmanship and wriggled to free himself from the men. Where was Bob? Sam was starting to feel hemmed in. Hands wandered up his body and around the front of him. But this wasn't a casual club feel-up.

This was something very different. He attempted to push himself away, but whatever was in that drink had left his limbs like jelly and they refused to cooperate.

"Come with me," the second guy crooned. "I love you. We could be so happy."

"No, with me."

"Guys." Another voice interrupted both men. A statuesque blonde with wild hair, who was dressed in little more than a necktie and a transparent sheath, pressed her ample breasts up against Sam's arm.

"Gay…" Sam said weakly. This was getting out of hand.

"You need me," the blonde simpered. She pressed harder, and her scarlet-tipped nails tracked a path from Sam's temple to his navel. Sam could feel his balls draw up almost inside his body in fear. "I want you. We could make the most amazing children."

"Hang on…." Sam was trying to be polite. Children? Love? Need? What the holy hell was going on here?

He only had one thought as he continued to extricate himself from grabby snugglers. "*Bob, where the hell are you?*"

"Tracking whoever did this to you." Bob's voice was like a spring breeze in his overheated thoughts.

"Come back." Sam sent the plea as directly as he could. "*Help*." He didn't stop to think why he could hear Bob's voice inside his head or how he suddenly felt it was okay to answer.

Bob was back at his side in seconds. His strong grip removed the three who were entwined with various parts of Sam's body. The tall, strong, and very insistent vampire was a damned effective barrier to the rest of the club who, one by one, were turning their attention to Sam.

"You can't do this. It's against the law to use love spells

in open spaces," the barkeeper snapped at them. Sam raised his eyebrows and knew he stood there with his mouth wide-open. Love spells? What? Like a love potion? Is that what he had drunk? He turned to Bob, who had a face like thunder. "You'll have to go," the barkeeper insisted.

"Your girl did this," Bob explained, with the emphasis on the *your*.

"What girl?"

"The barmaid," Bob said.

The short guy looked pointedly left and right. "It's only me here. You need to take your human and remove him from my premises before I call an enforcer."

Sam listened to the exchange, but the press of bodies against him was suffocating. He could feel the familiar tightness in his chest as the air stopped circulating around his face. More and more people were coming closer.

"Bob!"

"Back off!" Bob roared in an uncharacteristic way. Bob was all about silent and sardonic; he wasn't this demanding, emotional mass of fang-tipped anger. Yet another face was up in Sam's space, demanding that he love him, and Bob actually hissed his disapproval. If Sam weren't close to losing consciousness, he would find angry Bob damn sexy.

Bob's hands were on him, under his arms. In a smooth movement, he was pulled out from the clawing hands with their declarations of love, need, babies, and marriage, then shoved behind the bar. For a second, it appeared to be a good place to be; the solid counter between Bob, him, and the barkeeper held back the masses. Until the first of them placed a hand on the counter and hoisted themselves up and over.

"Back door?" Bob asked urgently. The barkeep, whose expression had changed from annoyed to suddenly enamored, gestured to the other end of the bar. He actually took a step toward Sam, but Bob's snarl had him stepping back again. In seconds, Sam was outside the club and away from the people. He was stumbling, being half supported and half carried. Only with the late night air hitting his face did Sam feel able to inhale deeply and clear his lungs. Bob took more of his weight; he felt drunk and uncoordinated. The sounds of the club were dissipating, but Bob didn't stop walking at his faster than normal speed, and Sam's feet barely touched the ground. Finally, it appeared Bob was happy with the distance between them and the club, and he deposited Sam on a bench.

Glancing around, Sam recognized the place as Victory Park, a well-known hangout for younger wolves. The old fenced fields with sparse coppices of old oak trees were not the place for a lone human to be wandering, especially one who appeared to have some kind of attraction poison in his blood.

"I need to go home," Sam groaned. He rested his elbows on his knees and bent his head, inhaling fresh air as if his life depended on it.

"You need a keeper," Bob grumbled under his breath. Not too low that Sam didn't hear him.

"What was in that drink?"

Bob frowned and crouched down on the ground between Sam's knees. Sam had a flash of what Bob could do properly on his knees at this level. He pushed the image down ruthlessly. Not before Bob heard his thoughts, though, if the vampire's fang-tipped grin was anything to go by.

"I imagine that first bartender wasn't really someone who worked there," Bob began thoughtfully.

"You think?" Sam couldn't keep the sarcasm from his tone.

"I also imagine her grandmother must be someone you have wronged, and she was just the provider of justice."

"I haven't wronged a single damned person," Sam snapped. Hell, he apologized for things if they were his fault —he was the last person to wrong anyone.

"Well, whatever." Bob shrugged. "It wasn't my whiskey that was spiked."

"Love spell—he said that. The bar guy. I don't know much about magic, but you can't tell me love spells are real. Why would they do that to me anyway? People don't go around dumping random spells on people."

"But they do," Bob said earnestly. He placed his hands on each of Sam's forearms, sending a jolt of heat through Sam's body. Bob's touch unnerved him. Sam had always imagined vampires to be icy cold, but Bob's hands were heated and insistently firm. "What about that witch who wanted the werewolf bones?"

"What about her?" Sam asked. A sense of foreboding swept through Sam. "Oh my God, she did say for me to enjoy my present. I bet she arranged this."

Bob nodded. "You cross a witch, and you're lucky to escape with your life. Consider yourself fortunate you got dumped with a Cupid's curse."

Sam lifted his gaze and met Bob's expressive eyes. "Cupid curse," he repeated. He really tried to inject humorous disbelief into the two words, but, he had nothing.

"It's what they call it. Love spell, or love potion, is what you probably know it as. At the root of it is a very real curse bound to the magic."

"So I somehow wrong a witch, and I end up with some guy in diapers dancing in my head?" Bob gave another of his frowns as if he hadn't understood the reference to the god Cupid and artists' renditions of him. "Whatever," Sam added. "How do we break this, and what the hell does it do?"

"It renders the observer immediately in love. They will

feel as if their life is incomplete without you and they face nothing but a chasm of despair should their love not be reciprocated. The whole point of a Cupid curse is to encourage murder and suicide and other not so savory results. The curse itself is ancient, but you can buy watered down versions of it from pseudo-witches. They're just never usually good enough to actually work."

"This one clearly works," Sam moaned. Then it hit him. "Why aren't you all over me?" he asked.

Bob shrugged. "Maybe it's slower at affecting vampires?"

"How long does this curse last?"

"The original witch needs to remove it. To begin the spell, all she needed was something of yours, and of course, your name."

Sam groaned as the realization hit him. "I bet it is that witch I met when I first opened. She said my uncle owed her. Said she wanted me to catch her a werewolf. She spouted some nonsense about needing werewolf bones."

Bob tightened his grip on Sam's arms momentarily, but otherwise he gave no sign that he found Sam's statement important. Only clearly he did, because, in seconds, he'd scooped Sam up off the bench and was striding out of the park.

Okay, so Sam wasn't little, and he sometimes loved it when a man got all toppy on him, but being carried around didn't make him happy at all.

"I can walk," he protested. "Let me down."

"I need you safe," Bob insisted.

"I am safe. I'm with you." As Sam said it, he realized he truly did feel safe with the tall man who held him as effortlessly as he would a small child, despite feeling humiliated over not being allowed to walk.

Bob stopped and allowed Sam to slide down his body to a

standing position. Slightly dizzy, Sam placed a supporting hand on Bob's chest. The vampire pulled him in for a tight hug before quickly releasing him. Cupping Sam's face in his hands, he looked down at him. Fear created shadows in his eyes as he locked gazes with Sam.

"If this witch is trying to track down werewolf bones, then a little Cupid curse is the least of our worries," Bob said.

"What was my uncle involved in? How did he owe a witch? And… Shit." Sam stepped away from Bob's touch, too antsy to stand still.

"What?"

"Would the witch have asked someone else when I said no to hunting down a werewolf?" Energy drained from Sam, leaving him shaky. He couldn't get his thoughts together. "What about the missing girl?" Horror filled him as Sam imagined Hartman's little girl taken for her bones.

Bob shook his head. "Stop it," he stated firmly. "None of that is on you. The wolf girl has been missing for two days. Before you met your witch."

"But could it be connected?" Turning down a witch didn't mean she wouldn't select the next on her list to do her dirty work. Nor did it mean she hadn't asked someone before him and had a child delivered to her.

Bob shook his head. "I don't know." They started walking again. Sam wasn't entirely sure about the route they were taking to get home, but somehow Bob avoided meeting anyone. Sam wondered how long this damn curse would last. Was it permanent? Or maybe something to teach him some kind of weird witchy lesson?

"We didn't exactly get any further on finding the fae third either," he grumbled. They turned down the road where the agency was located, albeit from an entirely different direction than they had gone to the club. A man stood by the bushes lining the path, and Sam instinctively moved closer to Bob. The last thing he needed was someone going all psycho wannabe lover on him.

"Wait here," Bob said. He propped Sam against the gate and pulled the other man away from the lights of the house and into the dark. Sam watched from his spot in the shadows and didn't move. He wished he could hear what Bob was saying. He tried the whole telepathic link, but Bob glanced back at him and shook his head. Clearly he didn't want Sam in his head. Great.

Sam turned his attention to the other man. Slightly shorter than Bob, he was fair-haired where Bob was dark. There was something about his stance that spoke of a connection to Bob. *Probably another freaking vampire.*

They exchanged words, and the guy didn't seem overly happy. He, too, glanced back at Sam, then crossed his arms over his broad chest, openly staring. He really was one hell of a stunning man, aristocratically gorgeous. Sam felt the impulse to straighten under the observation. Bob said something else, and with a shrug, the second vampire walked toward Sam, turning direction at the last minute to brush past him with a muttered curse. He headed back the way Sam and Bob had come, leaving them alone at the threshold of the agency.

"Mikhail will take care of the problem of you being tracked," Bob explained. "Otherwise you will be besieged here, and it will only get worse."

"How is he going to help?"

"He's half vampire, half siren," Bob said as if that explained everything. Too tired to ask for clarification, Sam fumbled with his keys a bit before Bob took them and unlocked the door to let them both in. Teddy floated across the entryway, wringing his hands as he drifted from one side of the wide hallway to the other. He stopped when Sam slumped tiredly on the bottom step of the staircase.

"I tried to stop them," Teddy said immediately.

"Stop who?" Bob asked. Teddy went back to wringing his hands and moving from wall to wall. Bob stepped into his path. Sam imagined the ghost would pass straight through the vampire, but instead, Teddy stopped and wrinkled his nose in distaste. Clearly ghosts didn't like to pass through vampires. Sam smiled at the thought and realized he really was heading for exhaustion.

"Stop. Who?" Bob repeated.

"They forced their way in, without a by-your-leave, and passed straight through me. Said they wanted Sam and some files." Teddy frowned and tapped an ethereal finger to his pale lips. "Or was it the files and Sam?"

"Who?" Bob walked away from Teddy, opened the door to the office, peered inside, then moved to stand at the bottom of the stairs and looked up into the darkness beyond. "There's no one in the house."

Teddy puffed out his chest. "They left when I threatened them."

"Just tell us who it was, Teddy," Sam intervened.

Teddy's expression changed from proud to anxious again. He knelt at Sam's feet, or more like disappeared into the floorboards until he was at Sam's level. Sam instinctively leaned forward as Teddy hissed one word, dripping with horror and grudging respect.

"Sirens."

Chapter Five

"SIRENS?" SAM DIDN'T LIKE HOW OFTEN SUPERNATURAL beings were showing up in his life. For a man who'd planned to stay away from the non-human population, he was failing spectacularly.

Teddy floated closer to Sam. "You look really good. Your aura glows."

"Back off, spook," Bob snarled, flashing his fangs as if that would do anything to a spirit.

"What? I'm not doing anything. Besides, what can a ghost do?" Teddy asked.

"We both know the sort of damage a ghost can do," Bob replied in a hard tone.

Sam wanted to ask, but exhaustion sank into his bones as he leaned against the railing.

"Come on, babe, we'll discover what's going on tomorrow. The sirens left, so whatever they were after is already gone. We can look around for it later. You need some rest." Bob wrapped his arm around Sam's waist and helped him upstairs. As soon as his head hit the pillow, Sam tumbled into sleep. He thought Bob said something right before darkness took over, but he only caught a few words about watching him while he slept. Sam didn't know if he should be reassured or creeped out.

A SOFT HUMMING broke into Sam's subconscious. The sound, soft and alluring, drew Sam out of the comforting darkness of sleep. Reluctantly, Sam opened his eyes to see who caused the tempting music.

"Shh," he said irritably. He needed more rest. Nestling into his pillow, he tried to block out the seductive sound.

"Wake up, beautiful." A smooth, masculine voice spoke in his ear.

"Aagh." Sam jolted awake and jerked away from the speaker.

Mikhail's gorgeous face came into view. "Good morning," Mikhail said.

"Um, good morning." Sam searched the room frantically, looking to see if anyone else had snuck in during the night. He barely remembered climbing into bed.

"You sleep like a child, without fear," Mikhail commented.

Sam frowned. "Until now I didn't think I needed to worry about someone attacking me in my sleep." Before, Sam hadn't worried about people attacking him while awake.

"What are you doing here?" Bob entered Sam's bedroom, a look of disapproval on his face as he took in Mikhail's presence.

Sam had never been so happy to see a vampire in his life.

Mikhail shrugged. "I came to see what I was protecting. He's awfully pretty." The vampire reached out to touch Sam, only to have his hand smacked away by Bob who had moved with supernatural speed to intervene.

"Don't touch him!" Bob growled. "Don't ever touch him."

"What makes you think you're the one he wants?" Mikhail taunted.

"Oooh, Mikhail, you know Bob'll kill you," Teddy said, floating up through the floor.

"Everyone get the hell out of my bedroom!" Sam shouted. How could his room be busier than a subway system and he still didn't get any action?

Both vampires stopped their spat midsentence and turned to face him.

"What?" Sam snapped.

"If you want some action, sweetheart, I'd be happy to help you out." Mikhail's eyes glowed with lust as he raked Sam with his gaze.

"You can wait outside," Bob said to Mikhail pointedly. He tilted his head at the door.

"Fine. Next time you want a favor, I'm going to remember how you didn't want to share." Mikhail slid off the bed and marched out of the room.

Sam didn't let out his breath until the other vampire had left.

"Hey, it's all right," Bob said in a calming tone. "I wouldn't let Mikhail touch you."

Before Sam could decide if that was a good thing or not, Bob kissed him. Sam expected a jolt of heat or excitement. What he received was more like coming home.

Bob's mouth brushed across his over and over, until Sam grew dizzy from the lack of oxygen. Reluctantly, he grabbed Bob's shoulders and pushed him away. Gasping for air, he examined Bob's expression.

"Sorry, I need oxygen," Sam explained.

Bob smiled. "It's been a while since I bedded a human."

A chill went through Sam's body. Hearing his growing affection reduced to the level of mere sex was like throwing icy water over his arousal. He scooted away from Bob's touch.

"Aww, don't be that way." Bob was evidently not taking Sam seriously. "I scared off the big, bad vampire-hybrid. Don't I get a reward?" Bob gave him a pleading look like a puppy waiting for his treat.

"I'm not a reward," Sam snapped.

"You are underselling yourself. You are definitely a reward." Bob leered at him, and Sam had about had enough.

Rolling his eyes, Sam slid out of bed, surprised to find he still wore his underwear.

"Nice look," Teddy said, drifting around Sam to check him out. Jeez, Sam had forgotten the creepy ghost was still in the room.

"Leave, ghost-boy," Bob snarled.

"I'm going." With a scornful look at the vampire, Teddy floated back down through the floor.

Sam grabbed his jeans off the floor and slipped them on, feeling better with more than a thin bit of cotton covering his ass.

"Sam! You should get back into bed," Bob said in a coaxing tone. "We were connecting. I'll be happy to show you how good it can be with a man who doesn't need to breathe."

A laugh burst out of Sam, breaking the tension of the moment. How could he be angry when Bob came out with one-liners like that? "As tempting as that is, I think it best if I resist. I've got too many complications right now without sleeping with someone."

"Don't worry, we wouldn't sleep," Bob reassured him.

Shaking his head, Sam snagged a shirt and put it over his head. "Let's gather everyone and find out what we can do next. I think we need to go after the werewolf girl. If the witch is hunting werewolves, we should at least warn them they are about to become spell components."

Bob lost his sunny smile. "They might not be quick to accept a warning from a human. Your species isn't known for your concern for the welfare of other beings. If you're not careful, you'll get a reputation," Bob warned.

"As what? The happy werewolf friend? I've got enough on my plate with the curse. I'm not going to worry about appearing too friendly to a supernatural. We need to find Broomhilda and have the damn spell curse shit reversed. We can't expect Mikhail to guard me forever."

Sam didn't know how he felt about the other vampire guarding him. He'd never needed protection before, and now he had a supernatural bodyguard to protect him from crowds of people swarming to have sex with him.

"Don't worry about Mikhail; he owes me. He'll watch over you until the end of time if I need him to," Bob said confidently.

"O-okay." Sam didn't know what else to say. Too much appreciation towards the other vampire brought out Bob's territorial instincts. He slowly headed for the door. He didn't see the vampire move before Sam found himself pressed against the wall.

"What?" He leaned in close. "No goodbye kiss?" Bob teased.

"I'm going downstairs, not off to war," Sam countered.

"You shouldn't leave your man hanging." Bob pinned Sam's wrists to the wall and plastered a kiss on his lips. The banked fire from the kiss they'd shared before had tripled in strength, bursting through Sam's body like an inferno. Bob was pushing, guiding, kissing him deeply, and holding him so tightly against the wall he couldn't move. Fuck. He'd never felt anything so erotic in his life.

When Bob released his hands, Sam dropped them to Bob's shoulders and fisted the material of Bob's shirt to hold him close. He couldn't get enough of the vampire's taste, and when Bob pulled back, Sam chased him for more.

"Wait," Bob said. He bowed his head, his hands flat against the wall on either side of Sam's head, and inhaled deeply. Did Vampires even breathe? Whatever Bob was doing he was attempting to find control.

"What?" Sam asked. His voice sounded unnaturally hoarse.

Bob smiled. No, wait. It wasn't a smile. Bob's canines had extended. Sam watched in fascination as the vampire ran his tongue over them. Was Sam supposed to be scared? Gently, he reached out and touched one very sharp tip. Teeth like this could rip through his skin. Sam tilted his head to expose his neck. What he was asking for, he didn't know—his body was calling the shots.

"No," Bob said. Using Sam as a balance support, he sank to his knees in front of Sam, looking up at him, amber eyes filled with questions. Bob began to unzip Sam's pants, pulling his boxers to one side and finally holding Sam's erection in his hand. Sam wasn't able to talk as he watched the tip of his dick disappear into the hot, wet cavern of Bob's mouth. Was he imagining the scrape of teeth on the tip, or catching on the thick vein that ran the length of his cock?

"Fuck," he managed to force out. Bob swallowed him down, all the way to the root. God, there were benefits to having a blowjob from someone who didn't need to breathe. The combination of Bob's fingers fondling the weight of his balls and the rhythmic suction had Sam close to coming before his brain caught up with his dick.

"Bob… Bo—I'm…—"

Bob increased the movement, more erratic than systematic, and Sam couldn't tell what was next, a move or a sucking swallow, then it was game over. He tried to push Bob off, but the vampire wouldn't be moved and Sam could swear he could hear Bob telling him to come echoing in his head. His orgasm ripped through him, and only Bob's tight grip kept him upright. Slowly, Bob stood, and as he did so, he kissed every small part of exposed flesh between his buttons and Sam's throat. Finally, he captured Sam's lips in another heated kiss, and the taste was there between them. Would he ever get enough of Bob's taste and touch? Sam sighed, boneless, completely drained of energy.

"You need to…" His voice trailed off. He wasn't a selfish lover and, hell, for that blowjob, he would do anything in return.

"No, babe," Bob whispered. "Watching you lose control got me off. That hasn't happened in hundreds of years." Bob spoke very low, with those sharp fangs literally a breath from Sam's ear and throat.

"Mmm," Sam hummed. He really needed to build a stronger immunity, but Bob's lips were softer than Sam could ever remember another man's lips being, certainly softer than his ex's…

Bob tore his mouth away. "I'd prefer if you never compared me to your ex ever again," the vampire drawled.

"If you stayed out of my head, you wouldn't know who I compared you to," Sam pointed out.

"Then I'd never learn all the other interesting things that go through your head." Bob kissed him again.

Sam's cock hardened again, as he fought to keep things

cool between them. His body wanted naked time with Bob, buried deep inside Bob, owning him. Sam wanted to feel.

"We should go and see what the sirens were after last night," Sam gasped. He struggled to find the words while Bob ground his equally hard body against Sam. That earthy, piney, have-to-have-now scent of the vampire filled Sam's nose, and he couldn't stop the groan from passing his lips.

"I'm sure the siren problem can wait a few more minutes." Bob nipped at Sam's throat.

Oh, yes.

Coherent thought evaporated from Sam's mind as Bob proceeded to show him how nothing held more interest than the vampire's touch. For a brief, mad moment, he wanted to urge Bob to bite him, but when Bob's fangs grazed Sam's throat, he jerked back out of reach.

"I don't think so," Sam said. He pulled his scrambled thoughts together and tugged at Bob's hold. "Release me."

"You don't really want me to let you go," Bob said in a persuasive tone.

The vampire's sincere expression had trapped Sam for a second before he realized what was happening. Bob was inside his head. He had to be. Fury surged through him. Sam watched with satisfaction as he proved beyond a reasonable doubt that a knee to the groin worked just as well on male vampires as it did with human males.

Bob crumpled to the floor.

"You ever use your glamor on me again, and you'll be lucky if that's all I do," Sam said. Disappointment made his chest ache. He'd thought Bob a different type of vampire, but apparently when push came to shove, Bob would do anything to get his way.

"Ow, I wasn't…" Bob whined.

Sam ignored the pitiful man on the floor and left the room.

He had made it to the hall before Mikhail joined him. "Where's Bob?"

"We had a difference of opinion," Sam said.

Mikhail peeked around him to where Bob was curled up on the floor, cursing with his hands clutching his balls. "Ouch," Mikhail replied.

"You vampires should learn a little discretion. Humans don't always appreciate being manipulated." Sam continued down the stairs, not caring if Mikhail followed or not.

Bob's actions upstairs had proven to Sam that even the most sincere vampire would revert to his true behavior if he didn't get his way.

Mikhail's hand on Sam's arm pulled him to a stop. "Don't judge. You don't know what it's like to be us."

Sam jerked his arm away. "And you don't know what it's like to be human. I think that understanding can work both ways."

"Good point," Mikhail agreed. "We'll both try to be more accommodating of each other's quirks."

"I don't consider trying to control my mind a quirk. I consider it damn rude!" Sam frowned at the vampire. He could see Mikhail truly didn't understand the problem, and Sam had too much to do to waste any more time on vampire-human relations. "How are you keeping the masses away from my curse?"

Mikhail gave a twisted smile, not as cheery as his usual expression so far. "My mother is a siren. I've learned a lot of distraction spells from her. I cast a siren call around the block so anyone who thinks to follow you will suddenly want to go in the other direction to follow my song."

"But what if a client wants to find me?" Sam asked.

"It only affects those under a spell. Usual clients shouldn't be a problem. Besides, from what Bob told me, having enough clients right now isn't a problem for you," Mikhail said pointedly.

"True. What happens when I leave the area of the spell? Will I be inundated with followers again?" Sam wondered how he'd be able to make a living if he constantly had to fight back admirers.

"I thought of that." Mikhail pulled an object from his pocket and waved it towards Sam proudly. "This will keep the majority of them at bay. It has a siren call built into it to neutralize the curse."

The necklace, made entirely out of shells, looked like tropical tourist trap merchandise. Sam almost shuddered at the thought of putting the thing around his neck, but Mikhail's hopeful expression had him quickly accepting the jewelry and sliding it over his head. He definitely wouldn't be called up to decorate the cover of any fashion magazine anytime soon.

"Why do I need the spell on the block if I have the necklace?" Sam truly didn't understand this entire curse thing. It didn't seem fair that the one person who vowed to avoid supernatural people was now neck deep in their affairs.

"The necklace is only good for about six hours at a time. After that, it will need to come back here to recharge. I enchanted the silver tray in your office to refresh the spell when you're not wearing it. Set it there when you get home for about an hour, and it'll be ready to use again. Be careful not to stay out past six hours, because when the siren spell stops, the Cupid's curse will take hold again." Mikhail's serious expression had Sam nodding his understanding.

He shuddered at the thought of being out there exposed to dozens of people when his spell took effect again.

With a quick thanks to Mikhail, Sam headed for his office. After he was certain Bob had left, he'd take a shower and get ready for the day. Right then he wanted to see what the sirens might have done to his stuff.

Opening the door, Sam didn't have to be a psychic to figure out the problem. A dagger stabbed into his chair held up a picture of the missing member of the triad. The words '*Stay Away*' were written in red pen.

"Damn," Sam muttered. Why would one set of paranormals not want him to find another of their kind?

"I think because they're the kidnappers," Bob said, walking into the office behind him.

The vampire limped a bit, but Sam refused to feel guilty.

"Why would they kidnap a member of a triad?" Sam asked.

"Because you completely unbalance their power. I'd say they either want to stop the triad from doing something or get them to agree to something in return for their third," Bob commented, looking at the picture.

"They didn't need to attack my innocent chair." Sam scowled. "After this is over, I'm only going to take cases from humans. I don't care who threatens or sues me, it isn't worth the hassle."

"Yeah, because humans never fight amongst themselves," Mikhail said dryly.

"Or have different factions," Bob added.

"Go ahead, enjoy your amusement," Sam muttered. "But I bet a gangland war would be a mere inconvenience compared to this damn curse."

"Possibly," Bob agreed. "What are you going to do now?"

"Concentrate on the kid. She's the only real innocent in this thing. I don't know much about the triad, but if the guy left the other two to trawl clubs, then surely he isn't much of a priority. The werewolf girl's only crime was being born a shifter. We need to find her before the witch does and rescue her before it's too late." Sam could feel a sense of rightness in his decision settling in his bones.

"You'll want to start at the Hunting Grounds," Teddy said.

Sam almost jumped when the apparition appeared beside him. Damn, Teddy would give him a heart attack someday, the way the guy floated between floors and appeared unannounced.

Instead of screeching like a girl during a horror flick, Sam took a deep breath before addressing the ghost.

"What are the hunting grounds? A park?" Sam had hoped for a park, but the malicious glee on the ghostly face didn't put his fears to rest.

"It's the best werewolf bar in the city. All the werekin go there to let off steam," Teddy replied.

"I somehow doubt a werewolf child is going to be at a bar," Sam scowled.

Teddy shook his head. "You're pretty, but kinda stupid. If any werekin saw your missing girl, they'll be at that bar. It's two days before the next full moon, and they always start to congregate a few days before the main event. You're going to want to find her before then."

"Why?" Sam had a feeling he wouldn't like the answer, and he wasn't disappointed.

"Because if the witch took the girl and she's mature enough to shift, then the witch is going to want to kill her at the height of her power," Teddy said.

Sam frowned. "Her dad didn't say she was able to shift…"

"Wolves don't generally share private information like that, but she's an alpha's daughter so she'll be strong." Mikhail sounded thoughtful.

"Then we have a short window of time to find her, don't we?" Sam said. He wasn't going to admit he had no idea what he was doing or how the thought of entering a werekin bar made him twitchy.

"You don't need to go, Sam," Bob spoke up. "I can go and report back here."

"Don't be an idiot." Mikhail scowled. "You know not a single werewolf will talk to a vampire. We've been at war for far too long."

That was news to Sam. He'd read the newspapers and seen TV documentaries, but he tended to avoid discussion regarding supernaturals for most of his life. So there was tension, but being at war didn't sound good....

"He doesn't mean war," Bob said. "We don't like each other."

"Why don't you like each other?"

"Because once upon a time, we used to fight for the same food. Mikhail's eyes flashed with menace. "Humans."

"Oh." Sam swallowed, trying to get moisture down his suddenly dry throat. "Well then, it's probably best that I go alone."

He didn't want to think about werewolves eating human flesh or vampires fighting them for blood rights. The more he didn't think about it, the better life was. Yep, that was going to be his new approach.

Denial.

Chapter Six

SAM HAD EXPECTED IT TO BE DIFFICULT TO GET INTO THE Hunting Ground. He wasn't stupid. Werekin bars and humans didn't mix.

"And you probably smell like vampires have rubbed all over you," Teddy announced.

"I'm human. Impartial. And I don't smell like a vampire," Sam snapped.

"Humans and werewolves are about as friendly as vampires and werewolves," Mikhail added helpfully. "The last group of humans who wandered too close to the club?" He shook his head. "Two of them were never seen again."

Sam attempted to ignore them all and focus instead on what he was going there to do. He was as close to a cop as he could be without actually carrying a badge, and he was working on a case for Hartman Hunter, the biggest baddest werewolf of them all. Surely that would count in the not-eating-him column. The gargoyle on his desk sided with whoever was talking, which helped not one bit.

Bob was suspiciously absent from the general advice and warnings, and Sam hoped he would be able to leave without running into the vampire. He didn't need his self-proclaimed protector upping the fear Sam already had inside him with dire warnings about becoming werewolf kibble. Ushering out both Teddy and Mikhail, he locked the door to his bedroom, then opened his closet and looked in.

Deciding on clothes took his mind off the fear eating away the lining of his stomach. He chose jeans. Boots. A black T-shirt and a red button-down. His leather jacket with his license tucked in the pocket…and the completely tacky shell necklace. A final look in the mirror and he was ready to go. For a second, he leaned on his dresser and closed his eyes. He needed to focus.

"Sam?"

Sighing, Sam turned. A solemn looking Bob stood at the threshold. He'd locked the door, for God's sake. How the hell had the vampire opened a locked door? *Probably some kind of freaky mind trick.* Bob frowned and held out his palm.

"No tricks. I, um… have a key," he explained. Clenching his fist around the large ornate key, he pocketed it, not taking his eyes from Sam.

"Of course you do," Sam said. Now was not the time to worry about where the hell Bob had found a freaking key to his room. He turned on the spot and held out his hands. "How do I look? Is this more or less likely to offend anyone and get me eaten?"

"Don't joke about things like that." Bob's uber-serious voice, his narrowed eyes, and his thinned lips conveyed his true feelings. Great. The triple whammy of Bob being serious, pissed, *and* worried.

"You *know* I've been asked to investigate this by Hartman Hunter himself," Sam explained. "He's alpha of the biggest pack in the state. No one is going to hurt me."

"Sam, you don't understand. His name may not carry as

much weight as you think. A wolf not able to protect his family is considered weak. The word on the street is that Hartman is vulnerable and if people learned he begged for your help—"

"He wasn't exactly begging, Bob."

"He went outside the pack, so he may as well have begged for human help."

Sam pinched the bridge of his nose and sighed tiredly. "What are you saying? That I need protection? I can't take you or Mikhail in case you all kill each other. Teddy can't leave the house, and the stone ornament on my desk can't move more than five inches. I'm on my own. I'm going in unarmed, but *I am* going in and I am asking my questions."

Bob began pacing from the door to the bed and back again. It looked curiously like a kind of dance. *Step step turn step step turn*. In the end, Sam moved in front of the vampire and stopped him with a hand on his chest.

"No one has to know Hartman asked me for help," Sam began. "How about I play it that I stumbled on a link to a missing werewolf child by accident? How about I just case the place?" He was constantly amazed that he was picking up the whole PI language so quickly—casing, logging, and tracking weren't words he had much use for before. Bob lifted a hand and placed it on Sam's, over his non-beating heart. Sam pressed a little harder, anything to get this final connection before he ran off into God-knows-where and faced God-knows-what.

"I'll be close. You know that, right?" Bob looked so serious, and if Sam didn't know any better, he would have thought he saw fear in the vampire's beautiful eyes.

"Not too close," Sam said. He couldn't help the worry in his voice any more than Bob could stop the fear that nearly radiated from him. Gone was snarky, confident Bob, and in his place stood a man fearful for Sam's life. He didn't think vampires could feel fear—weren't they at the top of the food chain?

"We only fear when we don't have control," Bob whispered.

Sam leaned in to hear Bob's soft response to his unspoken thought. For a second, they stood close and Sam wanted to touch. He didn't think it was Bob using his glamor, this felt very different. A real connection.

"You'll be close," Sam confirmed. "And we have this thing." He tapped his head with his free hand then tapped Bob on the end of his nose. "This link. I'll call you, okay?"

Bob subsided with a sigh of acceptance. "Are you sure I can't make you stay here?" he asked.

"Not unless you tie me up," Sam said. He wished he could take the words back as a lustful glow appeared in Bob's amber gold eyes. Sam sighed heavily. "No, you're not tying me up." Bob released the grip he had on Sam's hand and stepped back.

"Ready?"

Sam took one last look in the mirror and straightened his shoulders.

"As I'll ever be."

FROM THE OUTSIDE, the club couldn't be more opposite from Club Virgo. That place had been neon and flash; this place was nothing more than a pair of double doors in a long wall. Only a small sterling silver plaque identified it as the Hunting Grounds, defined it as a business. Striding confidently to the door, Sam pulled at the handle. Locked.

"You'll need to be moving on, human," a voice came from the darkness to his left.

"I'm here on business," Sam explained to the shadows. He pushed down the instant fear at the low, growly voice. It probably belonged to a seven-foot monster wolf with fangs and claws. Of course he'd watched the Discovery Channel and had seen all the informational documentaries. Everyone knew a wolf was merely human-looking when unchanged. Still didn't stop him from feeling suddenly like his bravado was leaving faster than Sam could ever run.

"There's nothing but trouble for non-wolves here," the voice boomed. Sam peered into the darkness, and the glow of yellow eyes looked back at him. They seemed awfully low down for his imagined werewolf.

"Nevertheless, I need to get in," Sam insisted.

Suddenly, Sam faced the second werewolf he'd ever met. He relaxed. Standing a good few inches shorter than him, the slimly built man/wolf looked harmless enough. Okay, so his hair was thick and black and long, but other than that, he wasn't very wolf-like. In fact, nothing like Hartman Hunter. Nothing to be scared of here. The small wolf scented the air and wrinkled his nose.

"A Night Man," he said dismissively. "You reek of him. Wait. Two of them?"

Sam kept his cool. Bob and Mikhail could be smelt on him. Big deal. They weren't here now. "I need to get inside," he repeated. Say it enough times and the door wolf might just back down. He took a step toward Sam and scented the air again. He had the most stunning bright green eyes, and he reached out a hand toward the tacky necklace Sam wore around his neck. At the last moment, he pulled his hand back as if burned.

"Something's wrong… What are you?" he asked with a curious tone. He tilted his head to one side as if sizing Sam up. Sam swallowed his fear and placed a hand protectively over the necklace. He was a God damned cursed human, and he couldn't do a thing about it. If this thing came off in the middle of a werewolf club, there would be a bloodbath. But, if he didn't go in, he wouldn't get jack-shit about where the little girl could be.

"I'm human," Sam snapped. "Now let me in."

The small werewolf finally reached a decision. He placed his hand on the door.

"On your head be it, human."

Sam heard a click, then the door silently swung inward. As it opened, he was hit by a virtual brick wall of noise. For a moment, he didn't move. Only when the werewolf pushed at his back did Sam take his first cautious step inside, into a world that he knew would be alien to him.

Except, as his eyes adjusted to the bright lights with dancing beams cutting the dark, he realized it wasn't alien to him at all.

In fact, inside it was like any other club. A sea of bodies on the dance floor, music, and drink. Groups of guys, groups of girls, some guy on guy, some girl on girl, others where you couldn't tell where one person started and another ended. Nothing different than any other place he had been to. Making his way around the edge of the dance floor, he kept his head down and focused entirely on reaching the bar. That was always the place to start; go to the man who held the secrets of many a disgruntled, or tired, or talkative patron.

The bartender, definitely not a werewolf type, was tall, impossibly thin and incredibly pale. The guy fitted the description of a dryad that Sam had learned about in his paranormal studies class. They often became bartenders once their trees were cut down for bar tops. Renowned for their empathic skills, they made very good barkeepers. The dryad got to remain with its tree, and its calming aura helped keep peace among the bar's clientele, a beneficial relationship for both parties. The dryad didn't blink an eye when Sam ordered a Coke, just slid it toward him and took the money. Sam noticed a slight narrowing of his expression, but he didn't ask questions. Like any good bartender, he kept his own counsel.

Pulling out the photo from his pocket, Sam placed it face up and toward the dryad.

"I'm looking for someone to talk to about a girl," Sam said. The barkeeper frowned. "A missing girl, a werewolf child," he qualified. Briefly the dryad looked down at the photo.

"I don't know her," he said with a shrug of indifference.

"I need to ask some questions, and I thought you may be able to point me in the right direction as to who I should be talking to?" He was shouting when the music chose that moment to go quiet. For a second, his question hung between them, then Sam became aware he no longer stood at the bar on his own. Two seriously muscled werewolves surrounded him in a buff man sandwich. The music started again, but that didn't stop Sam getting the very heavy-handed message. He scooped up the photo and placed it back in his pocket. Evidently, he wasn't going to get anything else from the dryad.

"Boss needs to see you," Big Wolf One said succinctly.

Sam looked into his face, but there was definitely no smile of understanding or indeed a glimpse of anything other than steely-eyed determination. As they walked away from the bar, Sam gauged the possible success of darting through the heaving crowd to the door. He couldn't see it working. Then he wondered if he should call for help. Not one wolf in the whole establishment would meet his gaze or acknowledge the human being led out of the main club and into a corridor. A dark corridor at that.

"Guys, I'm not sure—"

"Here." The second wolf spoke, or rather began to issue a set of monosyllabic orders along the lines of *inside, now*, and *stay here*. They left him in a room lit by two small lamps in a corner and containing luxurious leather office furniture. When the door opened again, Sam flinched.

"What the hell are you doing in my club?"

Face to face with possibly the biggest person he'd ever seen, bigger than Hartman Hunter, Sam felt his knees lock to hold him in place. Fuck. The guy gave a new definition to huge.

"I need to ask some questions," Sam said. He knew he sounded shaky, and refused to call for help, but when the werewolf flashed a toothy half grimace, Sam took a few steps back.

"No humans in here," the wolf said. "You're lucky my Beta found you before you became an appetizer."

"They'd eat me?" Sam believed it.

The wolf sighed. "We don't eat humans anymore. I meant appetizer in a sexual way. Never mind." Thrusting out his hand, the big guy introduced himself. "Evan Wolfe—with an e—owner of the Hunting Grounds."

"Sam Enderson, uh, human. Sorry, no, that isn't what I… Hell… I'm a private investigator, following a lead."

"A lead here?"

Sam held out the photo of Hartman's daughter.

Evan's face went from interested to blank in an instant. He turned to his fellow wolf who was hovering by the open door. "Zach, get me someone in here from the Hartman pack."

"Yes, boss." With a nod, Zach disappeared into the darkness beyond the room.

"Sit," Evan instructed. He indicated a chair at the edge of the room. Sam didn't argue. Evan began pacing just like Bob had done earlier. He only stopped when a man entered the room and tilted his head in a werewolf sign of respect.

"Alpha," the new wolf said firmly.

"Marcus, you need to take this human home."

"Wait. No. I'm not going anywhere until I get some answers," Sam objected. He was not going to be passed on to another wolf simply to be escorted off of the premises.

"You'll find nothing here," Evan said. "No one will discuss another Alpha's daughter with you."

"But she's a missing child."

Evan inhaled deeply and exchanged looks with the only slightly smaller Marcus, who was watching the exchange avidly.

"I promise you I will look into it," Evan said. Sam looked into the wolf's dark brown eyes and thought he caught a glimpse of compassion in their depths. It disappeared so quickly that he might have imagined what he had seen.

Sam sat back down. "I'm not going anywhere."

"Interspecies and pack rules dictate—"

"Rules mean nothing when there is a missing child. The longer we sit here and argue the point, the less likely it is that we find her alive," Sam snapped immediately.

Evan reared back as if Sam had physically assaulted him. Sam imagined that being the big bad Alpha meant everyone who talked to Evan were all "yes sir, no sir". Well, Alpha or not, it meant nothing to Sam. Evan leaned over him, to the point where Sam could feel the soft puffs of breathing against his skin. He was being scented, and, seriously, that was something he would never get used to.

"Go home to your Night Men," Evan spat, "and leave wolf business to the wolves." He backed away. Sam pushed himself up and out of the leather chair until he stood toe-to-toe with Evan.

"If a human isn't wanted in wolf business, why did the Hartman pack approach me for help?"

Evan frowned, but this time it was Marcus who spoke.

"He is talking nonsense. No wolf would lower themselves to request human help," Marcus dismissed. "Come on, *little man*," he said. Sam drew himself to his full height, refusing to be intimidated. "We are going."

Someone wasn't telling him everything here. Marcus looked both focused yet uncomfortable. Evan was pacing again. Sam admitted he had clearly crossed some invisible paranormal line that no one could see except wolves, but this was ridiculous.

"I'm not leaving until I ask some questions." He really was not going anywhere with anyone.

"You are leaving," Evan said almost gently. "Marcus will take you to the vampire who waits outside for you, then you need to go elsewhere. The Alpha's daughter is lost to him, he can only learn to bear that loss."

An unspoken message passed between Evan and Marcus, and in the space of a heartbeat, Sam found himself out on the street. The cold air was welcome after the heat and confusion of the club. Sam saw Bob immediately as he detached himself from the shadows.

Marcus growled low in his throat as Bob approached, and they circled each other warily until Bob had his hand on Sam's arm and Marcus was back at the club exit door.

"See to it he doesn't come here again, vampire." The last Marcus spat with disdain. "I can't vouch for him leaving alive next time."

Bob stepped toward him with a fang-tipped snarl, but the wolf simply turned his back, the ultimate insult, and slammed the door shut.

In the quiet of the midnight street, Sam felt nauseous as the energy that had flooded him began to leave.

"And?" Bob asked carefully.

"And what?" Sam couldn't focus.

Bob continued patiently. "Did you get what you came for?"

Sam shook his head. He didn't know what he had learned, but what he hadn't received was an answer to anything. Another Alpha warned him off from Hartman Hunter and a Hartman pack member told him to go home. In fact, he'd got nothing except trouble.

There were no leads and a little girl, a wolf child, still missing only two days before full moon. There was the witch who wanted werewolf bones and who for some reason felt he owed her a favor. He had a case with no leads, where there was a missing fae from a triad, and a threat stabbed by sirens to his office chair. Not to mention the curse that meant wearing a god-awful necklace, and a vampire that followed him everywhere.

Let's face it. I'm shit at this detective stuff.

"No, you're not," Bob said. Sam sighed. He'd forgotten to add that to the list—someone who could read his damn thoughts.

Sam crossed his arms over his chest and looked back at the closed club exit door. "I get the feeling there was more going on in there than I was getting a read on. Some kind of pack thing. Evan Wolfe-with-an-e knows more than he's letting on, and Marcus had this overwhelming—I don't know —sadness or something about him."

"Sam, we need to go home, regroup, and see what we can

find in the files. Maybe we could trace the paper or draw a board of information up or something."

"You've been watching too many cop shows," Sam said. Although to be fair, regrouping and pulling together facts was probably the best way forward.

"We need to stop and think," Bob replied thoughtfully.

It was only when Sam and Bob reached the front door of the office that Sam realized Bob had said 'we'. Not only that, but the thought of 'we' left Sam with the warm fuzzies.

It was late. He was clearly losing his marbles. *Freaking paranormal monsters and their creepy lives.* Too late he realized what he had thought. Bob glanced back at him briefly, and his eyes were narrowed.

"Tomorrow" was all Bob said before climbing the stairs. His tone was final and pissed. Great. That was all Sam needed. A complete bust on one of his cases, a threat on the other, and now an offended vampire. He hadn't meant to hurt Bob, but his head was full to bursting with crazy and he had reached a limit.

Going into his office, he avoided the desecrated chair and instead slumped on the small sofa in the corner. Exhaustion stole over him. Laying his head back on the headrest, he closed his eyes. He told himself he wasn't going to sleep there, but ten minutes to think before he went to bed would be good.

Maybe he would get inspiration with his eyes closed.

Chapter Seven

"WAKE UP, SAM. YOU'VE GOT A PACKAGE."

Sam blinked awake. He was tired of people standing over him when he woke up. This time, the person wasn't real. He'd made it up to bed a little after four am, and even in bed, his sleep had been at a minimum.

"Go away, Teddy," he grumbled. He rolled over and pulled the blankets over his head to block out the apparition.

"I think it's about the missing fae," Teddy persisted.

"Why would you think that?" Sam didn't really care. He only wanted the ghost to go away. Maybe if he pretended interest, Teddy would float back to wherever the hell he came from.

"Because it has a siren emblem on the box."

Sam could almost hear the snotty smirk in the ghost's voice.

Sighing, he threw back his covers and stood. "Fine. I'm coming."

"Nice boxers," Teddy taunted.

"Shut up," Sam snarled. He was tired, and he hadn't had

coffee yet. Teddy was lucky he was already a ghost, or Sam would've helped him along.

Sam ignored the apparition while he pulled on his favorite jeans and a green T-shirt. Living at his uncle's old place apparently didn't come with any privacy.

"I need some coffee," he muttered as he pulled open his door and stumbled over the threshold.

"Morning, beautiful," Bob said, coming out of his apartment.

Sam rolled his eyes at the vampire and continued toward the stairs. There wasn't enough coffee in the world to deal with Bob in the morning. He gave Bob an absent wave, not stopping to talk and walked down the stairs.

He entered his office and stared at the package. Gold paper covered a small box with a stream of silver ribbon wrapped around it and tied in a pretty bow.

"Someone likes you," the gargoyle chanted.

"No one likes me," Sam denied. His ex hadn't thought he was interesting enough to keep, and he certainly didn't send him pretty packages. He cast a look over his shoulder at Bob.

"I didn't send it," Bob growled.

Sam could tell the vampire didn't like the thought of anyone sending Sam presents. Curious, he walked closer. He didn't trust presents appearing out of nowhere.

"Have the gargoyle open it," Bob prodded.

"Can I?" The gargoyle's eyes glowed with excitement.

Bob leaned over Sam's shoulder and whispered in his ear, "Gargoyles can't resist shiny things."

"Go ahead and open it," Sam told him.

The gargoyle's stone feet clunked across the desk with a loud knocking sound. For a hard creature, he used surprising delicacy as he pulled on the ribbon. He let out a sound of delight when it easily slid apart and tumbled off the package. Grabbing the lid with his gnarled hands, the gargoyle yanked it off in one swift motion.

A loud song filled the room—calling, tempting, twisting Sam's gut in a weird curlicue. Sam watched in surprise as the gargoyle and Bob fell to the ground screaming.

"What's wrong?" Sam searched for the reason for their screaming. Reaching over, he peeked inside. A pink seashell glowed in the middle of the box, pulsing along with the notes of the song.

Sam put the lid back on the box, cutting the noise. The silence echoed almost as loudly as the music had before.

Bob's hands appeared at the edge of the desk as the vampire dragged himself to his feet. His skin had an ashy hue. "What the hell did you do to the sirens?"

"Nothing," Sam denied. "I've never met a siren before."

He tried to stay as far away from the paranormals as possible, a task much easier when he didn't live and work at the edge of their territory. He might have to resort to selling it all and moving if he couldn't get them to find someone else for their problems. Why couldn't a hapless human wander into his office? Was it too much to ask for a divorce case or a bit of embezzlement?

The gargoyle fluttered back to his perch at the top of the desk. "Crap! Fucking mermaids!"

"Why weren't you affected?" Bob narrowed his eyes at Sam.

Sam shrugged. "It sounded like loud music. My ears are ringing, but it didn't bother me much. Are humans more immune than paras to siren song?"

Bob's wide eyes told Sam that was the wrong question. "You're not entirely human, are you?" the vampire asked.

"What are you talking about?" Sam didn't appreciate Bob's insinuation. His bloodline ran true. "I'm human. Completely, normal and 100 percent human."

Bob raised an eyebrow at Sam's vehemence. "I had no idea you were so prejudiced."

Sam's mouth dropped open. "I'm not prejudiced."

Cautious maybe, but not prejudiced.

"You called yourself normal, and you were quick to deny any paranormal roots," Bob reminded him.

Sam shrugged. "I'm just saying I'm all human. Nothing against the paras."

"A human can't withstand a siren call," Bob insisted.

"Well, apparently some humans can. I can." Sam knew he was digging the hole deeper, but he refused to admit anything. Surely those family rumors were just …rumors

The gargoyle cocked his pointed head and stared at Sam with piercing eyes. "Your uncle was pure human. I'm not sure what you are."

"How about we address the important issues? Why would the sirens send me this box? What's their message?" Sam examined the box, making sure not to open it again.

"I think it's a warning to back off. Maybe they thought your little trip out last night was more on the missing third triad member case?" Bob said. "If you were like everyone else, the noise would've knocked you on your ass. I wouldn't be surprised if you had a little siren blood in you."

"Enough. I don't want to hear anything more about my blood," Sam snapped.

"Fine, no more talk about your questionable ancestry," Bob said with a scowl. "Now, we need to think. What is the connection between the missing fae and the sirens?"

"I don't know. I only have two cases. It either has to do

with the missing fae or the missing wolf girl. Either way, I don't know how the sirens fit into this. Do you think Mikhail is involved?" Sam didn't like to think the half vampire, half siren could have anything to do with the box, but he had just met him. "He's a siren, isn't he? Maybe it's him sticking the knife in my chair and sending me freaking seashells."

"No." Bob sounded certain.

"How can you be so sure?" Sam asked.

"I've known Mikhail for many years. He has little to do with that part of his family. He's chosen to live on land instead of the sea. It estranged him from his mother's relatives," Bob explained.

"And you don't think he'd do something to get on their good side?" Sam asked.

Some people would do anything to make amends to their relatives.

Bob shook his head. "No. They got his little sister killed. He never forgave them."

"Huh." That ruled Mikhail out. "Can he contact any of them to determine why they might send me a siren call in a box?" Sam still didn't understand what message the box was supposed to convey. A warning to stay away from the case? A message to go see them? What did they want with him? Why couldn't paranormals talk normally? Preferably by phone or email. "I need to talk to them."

"Oh, hell no." Bob folded his arms over his chest. "No way am I going to take you to the sirens."

Sam blinked at Bob in surprise. "I wasn't asking you. I'm going to go ask Mikhail to go with me. You would be useless if they started singing."

Bob gripped Sam's arms. "There's no way you're going without me. I will wear earplugs if necessary."

The urge to grab his weapon tingled through Sam's fingers. One shot, he could stun Bob and be gone. However, the concern in Bob's eyes couldn't be faked. The vampire truly didn't want Sam to leave without him.

"You need me?" Mikhail's rich voice floated from the doorway.

Sam turned to see the gorgeous man saunter into his office.

"Is this one of those things where I say your name and you show up?" Sam arched an eyebrow at the vampire hybrid.

Mikhail grinned. "I'm not the devil. I was heading over here to tell you I heard that the fae you're looking for was spotted at Bite, the new bar in the south end."

"The one bought by that werewolf-human couple?" Bob asked. He looked at Sam, and there was definitely a blatant message in his smirk. Sam didn't care if other humans were with paranormals, it still didn't make it completely right in his head. He returned the stare calmly. Bob continued, "I didn't think they were open yet."

"They had a soft opening last night. Your fae dude was apparently there," Mikhail insisted. "He was dancing with a siren, but they left early. They didn't look like they were getting along."

"He was with a siren, or *with* a siren?" Sam asked. He added in smart quotes with his fingers. Mikhail narrowed his expression.

"How would I know? This is secondhand news," he said. "Anyway, I thought I heard a siren call when I came in here."

Sam nodded toward the box. "I got a little present."

"Shell," Mikhail guessed.

"Yep. A really loud shell," Sam agreed.

"They really must not want you messing with the fae," Mikhail said. "Sirens only send sound shells if they want to warn people away or wreck their ships."

"As I'm on land, I guess it was a warning," Sam said dryly.

"We'll go to Bite around nine and ask around," Bob stated.

Sam held back the urge to argue. Telling the vampire to mind his own business wouldn't have any effect.

"Where's your necklace?" Mikhail scowled at Sam's bare neck.

Sam frowned. "It's in the silver dish recharging. I'll make sure to wear it when I go out."

"You do that." Mikhail patted Sam on the back. He grinned at Bob on his way out the door.

Bob growled. He reached out and grabbed Sam, slamming their bodies together. "You might think you're going to sneak out without me, but I will not be a happy vampire if you do."

"Don't you have anything else to do besides follow me around?" Sam asked. "Bodies to drain dry? People to play bogeyman to?"

Bob grinned, his teeth flashing with his amusement. "Why would I do that? I don't want you to feel neglected."

Sam opened his mouth to argue. Bob swooped down and captured Sam's lips with his own. Sam's heart skipped a beat in his chest. He clutched Bob's shirt, pulling the vampire even closer.

A moan filled the air, a combination of both their breaths, tangling their mouths against each other. Need gripped him in the gut like a body blow. Craving gnawed at him until he didn't know if he needed air more than a good hard fucking.

"Out!" a gravelly voice shouted.

Sam pulled away, blinking at the passion-filled gaze focused on him. Like he was the center of the universe, and gravity pulled the vampire towards him.

He leaned forward for another kiss.

"Stop! I don't need to see this," grumbled the voice.

Sam shook his head to dispel the passionate haze filling his mind.

Turning, he caught sight of the gargoyle, his wings tucked tightly to his body and a definite sulk in his eyes.

"Sorry," he replied.

"I'm not," Bob answered, stroking a hand down Sam's back.

Sam arched into the vampire's touch. More. He needed more touch, more contact with Bob's fingers stroking across his skin.

He wondered for a moment if the vampire had a siren call of his own. One that affected Sam in ways the genuine article did not. He didn't fight or argue or make any protests when Bob grabbed his wrist and pulled him up the stairs.

Sam let Bob lead him to Sam's apartment and into his bedroom.

"Strip!" Bob growled.

Sam paused for a minute, entranced at the smooth flesh appearing with the removal of clothes. Piece by piece dropped to the floor until Bob stood before Sam with nothing covering his perfect body.

"Wow," Sam said. He didn't have any words to cover seeing a model-beautiful naked man in his bedroom. Bob was almost too perfect. How could Sam remove his clothes and live up to the high standard Bob had set?

"I already think you're gorgeous, Sam I don't need perfect; I need you naked, now!"

Still, Sam hesitated. His hands trembled slightly as he reached for the bottom of his T-shirt to pull it over his head.

"I'll help." Impatient, Bob yanked Sam's shirt off and flung it over his shoulder. His eyes glowed with appreciation. "Very nice."

Without giving Sam any more time to get nervous, Bob ripped open Sam's jeans and yanked them down to his thighs along with his underwear.

"Even better," Bob growled. He dropped to his knees.

Sam's breath caught in his throat.

"Easy, beautiful," Bob soothed. "I'm going to take your shoes off. I don't want you to get all tangled up."

Having a naked man kneeling at his feet fed all sorts of fantasies into Sam's mind.

Bob laughed. "Maybe later we can be more adventurous. I need to fuck you now."

"No," Sam said firmly.

The vampire looked up at him. "What do you mean, *no*? You don't want to have sex?"

Sam shook his head. "And I thought you could read my mind. I want to have sex with you, but I want to top."

Bob didn't speak for a moment. He helped Sam out of one shoe then the other before sliding off Sam's socks, then his jeans.

Unlike Bob, Sam couldn't read anyone's mind. "No? Yes? You want me to leave you the fuck alone? What's your answer?"

Bob rose to his feet, confusion swirling in his eyes. "I've never bottomed before."

"Never?" Sam stared at Bob in disbelief.

"Never," Bob confirmed.

"Oh." Sam didn't know where to go from there. He'd bottomed before, but he'd never really enjoyed it. Then an idea came to him, one that would benefit them both "How about you bottom, but I let you suck my blood?"

"Really?" Bob grinned.

"Really," Sam agreed.

"Deal." The vampire turned around and threw himself on the bed, spreading his arms and legs wide. "I'm yours for the taking."

"Hmm, that was too easy. I have a feeling I've been had," Sam grumbled.

Bob laughed. "I'll never tell. Now come fuck me so I can have my snack."

Sam rolled his eyes. "Do I need a condom?"

"Nope. Though I'd prefer you use lube."

As much cheer as the vampire exuded, Sam could read the anxiety hidden underneath. "I'll use lots of lube, don't worry."

Reaching into the drawer, he pulled out the bottle he'd bought recently. "This would go easier if you rolled over," Sam advised.

Bob shook his head. "I don't want to hurt you. If you are behind me, I might instinctively attack. Besides, I can't bite you if you're behind me."

"You could bite me afterward," Sam said.

"No. It'll taste better if I bite you in the middle of orgasm. It will give me an extra rush of energy."

"Oookay." There were so many things Sam didn't know about vampires, he could fill a library. He refused to consider that this was a very tidy excuse for Bob to bite him.

Taking Bob at his word, Sam popped the lube cap and coated the fingers of his right hand. To ease some of Bob's anxiety, he first turned his attention to Bob's cock. Wrapping his hand around Bob's shaft, he slid his hand up and down until Bob squirmed and moaned. Satisfied he'd eased the vampire's nerves, Sam slid a finger into Bob's hole, twisting and circling until Bob relaxed. Adding more lube, he pushed in two fingers and scissored them around until he hit a spot that had Bob squirming from his touch.

"Oh," Bob cried out. "More."

"I'll give you what you need," Sam assured him.

He added a third finger, making sure Bob was fully prepped. Pulling out his fingers, Sam lined up his cock and slid inside. Bob tightened around him, his eyes wide with lust.

"Easy, easy. I have you." Sam hooked Bob's legs over his shoulders. His eyes locked with Bob's, checking for discomfort. Only seeing the passion in the vampire's eyes, Sam snapped his hips, moving in and out of the tight, blissful cocoon of Bob's body.

Sam closed his eyes, absorbing the sensation of taking a new lover.

"So good," Bob sighed. "Now fuck me like you mean it."

"My pleasure," Sam replied.

Gripping Bob's hips, Sam moved in and out of Bob's ass, setting a fast rhythm. "Touch yourself," he demanded.

Bob wrapped a hand around his erection and began pumping furiously. "Oh fuck… Sam!" Bob shouted as cum spurted from his cock.

Sam groaned as he gave into his orgasm. He lowered his body across Bob's, tilting his head back.

Bob struck. Fangs sank into Sam's neck. Sam convulsed as pleasure took over the initial pain of sharp teeth slicing through his skin. He slid carefully out of the vampire, sighing as the sensation of sucking vibrated his throat.

Bob gave a low growl then he lifted his mouth and licked his lips. "You are simply delicious," Bob said with a sigh. "And not entirely human."

"Shut up," Sam growled. He didn't want to deal with whatever Bob thought he'd found in his blood. "I'm basking in the afterglow. Don't ruin it for me."

Bob said nothing. He simply kissed Sam on the neck and snuggled him close.

Chapter Eight

For a club still a couple of days away from an official opening, Bite was buzzing. The signs at the door proclaimed there were wards inside to stop enchantments and that Bite was a class four establishment, which Sam knew meant it didn't distinguish between species. Inside these doors would be vampires, werewolves, fae—you name it. Humans as well, Sam guessed.

As soon as they were in, they had to fight through groups of people to get to the bar. Sam felt like he stood out in the same jeans and shirt he had worn to the Hunting Grounds. All kinds of beings wandered around the club. Designer labels rubbed up against leather, vampires stood solitary and watchful, werewolves clustered in groups, and the guy behind the bar had what looked like a permanent grin on his face. Tall, skinny, and blond, he ticked the boxes for Sam. Well, the old boxes. The ones he had before he met Bob.

Damn. Did I *think that?*

He chanced a glance at Bob, who nodded back at him. Yep. Clearly he had thought that very thing.

"Hi, welcome to Bite. What can I get you?" The blond

was all energy and fire and hyped up happy. Sam didn't need to be an empath to see that.

"Three beers," he said.

The guy moved away to pull out beers, and Sam looked to his left at Bob, who was leaning casually against the bar. Dressed in those damn leather pants and that tight woven silk shirt, he was perfection. His amber gaze flickered across the club, scanning the crowds of paras and normals that mixed and moved around them. Mikhail was to his right. Utter beauty in similar leather pants and a scarlet shirt, he, too, was watchful and focused.

"Your beers."

"Thanks. I wonder if you've seen this guy?" Sam slid the small photo of the missing fae across the counter, and the barman looked down at it curiously. At least he was looking, which was more than the Dryad had at the Hunting Grounds in the search for the wolf girl.

"Yeah, he was in last night. Caused quite a stir for a while, but Alec had words with him and they left." The bartender slid a beer to a werewolf a few feet away.

"Could you point out Alec to me?" Sam asked.

"Uh-huh…" What the barman had started to say was lost when he was interrupted. A tall, broad wolf shifter with dark, shaggy hair and deep brown eyes stalked up to him and literally lifted the human barman off the floor. There was the most graphic display of public kissing Sam had ever seen. Definitely enough erotic content to fuel a few minutes of future jerk-off material. Not helped when the barman wrapped his long legs around the other guy's waist, who clung like a limpet, then deepened the kiss. After at least thirty seconds and a whole crowd full of catcalls, the big werewolf dropped the barman to his feet and hugged him close. The human pushed at his lover, grinning widely.

"Someone wants to talk to you, Alec."

That was Alec?

Sam held out a hand, and Alec immediately shook it. He shook hands with Bob, who had quite pointedly held out his hand. Clearly the wolf/vampire relations here were not as strained as at other clubs.

"How can I help?" Alec asked.

Sam pushed the photo closer to the broad werewolf and tapped it.

"Your barman said you spoke to him last night?"

"You a cop?"

"A PI, trying to track down a missing person." Sam considered pulling out the photo of the wolf child as well, but something stayed his hand. Not asking a wolf about another wolf was one of the lessons he had learned. Maybe he could grab the bartender at the end of his shift. If the guy were human, normal, he wouldn't be so damn territorial.

Alec looked at the photo and wrinkled his nose. Then he frowned. "Nate is better with faces than I am," he began. "The fae all look the damn same to me, but if he says this was the fae I spoke to, then it must be." He was near shouting over the noise of the music. Sam suddenly wished this case wasn't one where he spent so much damn time in clubs; maybe more time in nice, quiet coffee shops.

"Can we go somewhere and talk?" Sam said loudly.

"Yeah, go to the end of the bar. We can talk in my office."

Sam smiled his thanks, and with Bob following, he made it through the door marked private. The music still provided a bass line that thumped the door and vibrated through the floor, but he could at least talk at a normal level. He still had his beer in his hand, and he took a fortifying swallow. Bob leaned against the door and crossed his arms over his broad chest, ever the watchful guardian.

"So how can I help?"

"Your barman, Nate—"

"Owner. My partner in business and in life." Alec said this with no room left for anyone to argue. Perhaps he had a lot of people recoiling from him at the mention of a wolf/human pairing. Sam recalled more of his remedial paranormal studies. Didn't wolves have mates? Mates that they scented and went all animal on? Like, for life and all that?

"Your mate is a human?" Sam asked curiously then immediately regretted it when he sensed Bob moving to stand to his side. Shit. Was he expecting trouble? Sam should never have asked such a personal question.

"Yep," Alex answered instead. "Who'da thought it?" He smirked. "A big, bad wolf man and an itty bitty human, eh?"

Sam knew enough to know he was being teased at asking the personal question and felt suitably ashamed. Who was he to judge? Jeez. When he recalled what he had begged Bob to do…

"My apologies," Sam offered. "That was a personal question, and I didn't mean to offend."

"You didn't," Alec answered with a wry smile. "We've had worse, but yes, Nate is my true mate, and yes, we love each other, and yes, we stick out like a sore thumb. You'll get used to it."

"Sorry?" Sam replayed the sentence. Used to what?

"Being a human with a paranormal."

"I'm not—"

Alec shook his head and snorted a laugh. "His scent is all over you," he said. He nodded to Bob in recognition. Sam looked directly into Bob's hurt amber gaze. What did he expect Sam to do? Climb Bob like a tree to prove to the world they were having sex? Vampires didn't have mates. Right?

They were sharing incredibly hot and satisfying sex. Bob's expression became impassive, and his gaze shuttered. Sam appreciated he had probably fucked something up without realizing.

"We'll talk later," he thought. Bob nodded his understanding.

"Anyway," Alec interrupted Sam's thoughts. "This guy was in here last night. He was trying everything. Dancing, kissing, talking, drinking all kinds of different drinks. Not that his minder was impressed with it, some tall, skinny siren dude. You know how most fae are, uptight with their all-seeing eyes and cozy triads. Your guy? Uptight? Not so much. The thing is, he lost it big-time for a while. Then the siren stepped in and got verbal with one of my staff. So I tossed them out. Why do you need to find him anyway?"

"The other two in his triad have reported him missing." Sam didn't mind sharing details if it helped. "Can you tell us what was said?"

"Couldn't make much sense from the fae, but the siren was all cultured vowels and apologies." Alec shrugged. "Don't have a lot of time for sirens so what I say may be colored by what I think. Be warned."

"Okay." Sam knew all about prejudice. It's what had used to keep him safe and away from paranormal areas.

"Seems to me the fae was on a tight leash. I pulled him away from the siren dude and asked him if he needed help of any sort. Nate and I do some work with the Fifth Street para shelter, and we could have got him there, siren or no siren."

"Did he want to leave?" Bob asked.

"That was the strange thing. For all the alcohol he had drunk, and for all the out of character behavior, he was adamant that the siren was the one he was going home with. What else could I say?"

"Could the fae have been under a siren spell?"

"You saw the signs on the way in. We have a state of the art, brand-new surveillance and blocking system. No way could either enter if a siren song were being used."

"Then they left?"

"Just after midnight. I followed them to the road. That was the last of it. Although I can certainly give you the number of the cab company that came and picked them up. If it helps?"

"Thank you." Sam meant it. A cab company meant a driver who might remember a drop-off. That could be the break they needed.

The door flew open, and Nate entered the room then slammed the door shut to keep out the noise.

"Hey," he said. "All done in here?" He looked curious and wary and immediately stood right next to Alec, entwining his hand with the big wolf. Had he come in here to protect his lover? That was kind of sweet in a suicidal way, given he would be getting in the middle of a vampire/wolf standoff if things had gone south.

"Everything's cool. They were looking for the missing fae, and I told them what I knew."

"You should ask them, Alec," Nate said firmly.

"Not now, Nate." Alec extended his hand, and first Bob then Sam shook it. Sam ignored the last strange comment made by the other human in the room.

"No…wait," Nate commanded clearly. Sam had his hand on the doorknob but stopped.

"Nate. I said no," Alec said. There was warning in his voice.

"No one else is listening," Nate snapped.

"It's no one else's business—"

"It's my business," Nate said gently. Sam turned back to

face the couple. Nate was looking up at Alec with an imploring look on his face. Alec looked stony and way past pissed and moving up to furious. "She's my pack, too."

At those words, Alec visibly slumped, then sat down in the leather chair behind the desk. Gone was the confident club owner, and in his place was a wolf with tension and regret pasted on his face. When Nate slid to his knees next to the wolf, it was clearly his undoing.

"Ask them then," he said quietly.

Nate touched Alec on the face; gently he pressed Alec's lips, then at each eyelid. Sam wondered at the touches. Was it a wolf thing or just something this couple did? Nate placed his hand over where Alec's heart would be.

"I love you, Alec," he said. Sam felt he was intruding.

"Tell us what?" he encouraged.

"There's a wolf child missing. A little girl. She's four, and we think the mother has something to do it. The pack is covering it up."

Sam waited for Alec to defend his pack's actions, but the wolf simply shrugged. He knew packs were closed and territorial, but if what Nate was saying was about the same girl he was looking for, then all these closed doors were getting beyond ridiculous.

Taking out the photo of the little girl, he hesitated when he was about to place it flat on the desk for both Alec and Nate to see.

"Are you Hartman pack?" he asked instead.

Alec took the photo from Sam, then nodded. "That's her. That's Shelby."

"We have a working theory that she has been kidnaped by a witch—"

"No." Alec surged to his feet with a growl and a snarl, and Nate clambered to stand. He rounded the table, and Sam stepped back. He didn't need to worry, Bob was there, an immovable object between him and the snapping wolf. "We thought it was her mother hiding her from Hartman to scare him. She's done it before. A witch? That can't be right. The pack wouldn't be hiding things like that—"

"How do you know this?" Nate interrupted. He had a calming hand on Alec but looked just as distraught. Sam peered around Bob.

"It's only a working theory," he said. "We need to track her down and every single wolf we try to speak to is a dead end. What can you do to help us?"

Suddenly all thoughts of the missing fae were pushed to one side. The missing child was the important thing here.

"How did you? What did you?" Alec looked lost for words. Everyone was startled when the door opened, and this time Mikhail stepped in the room. The door closed out the noise, and Mikhail stood, looking around the room with narrowed eyes.

"He's Hartman pack," Mikhail announced. "The missing girl is his sister's girl." He waited for reaction and frowned when there was none.

"Hartman Hunter is your brother-in-law and pack leader?" Sam summarized carefully.

"And Shelby is his niece," Nate said gently. "We've been looking, but the doors are slammed in our faces as much as yours. When Alec met me, it was only through Hartman's involvement that I was accepted as Alec's true mate. We don't live with the pack, and they don't trust us."

Alec pulled Nate close and buried his face in Nate's blond hair, inhaling deeply. The scent appeared to soothe him, and he went from temper and teeth to calm and patient in an instant.

"My wolf hates that the pack won't let me do anything.

You never abandon a pup, but they want to keep everything so close to their chests. My sister is brainwashed that only wolves can help wolves. That's part of the reason she…" His voice trailed off. "Hartman is a good man trapped in a net of pack politics and fighting off challenges left, right, and center. Used to be that a pack had nothing more than territory to defend. Now the Hartman pack has global holdings, schools, college funds, and so many others try to fight the Alpha for that. We thought it was a rival pack Alpha that took her to provide some kind of leverage, but we tracked nothing."

All the fight had left Alec as he leaned back on his desk and bowed his head.

Bob took a step forward and laid a hand on Alec's arm.

"Can she shift yet?" he asked.

Alec raised his eyebrows. "Not yet. Although it won't be long," he added proudly. "Not this full moon, but maybe next? Is that important?"

Bob glanced back at Sam, and it was all Sam could do not to leave the room and keep from breaking Alec's heart by telling him what he thought. In the end, he couldn't turn and run. He had to tell Alec the truth.

"The spells that the witch would need her for? It calls for the bones of a wolf, but only the bones of a wolf able to shift."

"We think," Bob added quickly.

Nate twined his arms around Alec, and it was his turn to bury his face into Alec's neck and hold him close. Sam watched this shared support and suddenly wished Bob would hold him. The strength of emotion in the room was so intense it hurt.

"Find her…" Alec stuttered. Emotion choked in his voice, and he looked broken. "God. We have to find her."

"We'll find her. Together we can find her," Bob said simply.

"A vampire and a wolf working together? Against the pack system," Alec murmured. He spoke more to himself than to the rest of the room. "Will wonders never cease?"

SAM and his vampire wingmen left the club with no more real information about the missing girl but with at least the chance of working with others to find her. They could do nothing until they met in the morning back at the club. The scents of the city were too much at night, and they all agreed they needed calm heads. No one had said a thing when Alec said he would be out scouting that night. He had gone from an uncle thinking his niece was some kind of pawn in a game between Hartman and his wife, to believing his niece was really missing. He'd left a silent Nate at the bar when it had closed. Nate was destroyed, and Sam wished he had words to encourage the other human. A simple 'it will be okay' was like putting a Band-Aid on a bullet wound. No use at all.

Walking back home, he was way past discouraged and allowed support from Bob, who squeezed his hand in silent care. Mikhail was whistling a tune under his breath. The notes left his pursed lips and hung momentarily in the deep night air before disappearing. The sounds were another form of comfort, he guessed, and he didn't call Mikhail on it. Once they were back at the house, he immediately went to his office. There was no way he was letting the trail on the fae cool.

Two calls later, he had a cab number scribbled on a piece of paper. Apparently the guy who drove it, Doug, was a good guy with an eidetic memory. That would help. He was back on duty in the morning, and as much as Sam had tried, he couldn't prise out a home address or number for this Doug guy.

"You should get some sleep," Bob said. He was leaning against the doorframe and looking gorgeous. Well, gorgeous and also concerned. Sam stretched at the desk. There was nothing he could do there for a few hours, and Bob was right: he was tired. Bob was on his heels and Sam fell face forward on his mattress, fully clothed. He allowed Bob to manhandle him, even permitted him to pull the covers over him. He didn't argue when Bob climbed in as well and slotted his warm body against Sam, spooning him from behind.

Sam was too tired to argue.

Anyway, it was kind of nice.

Chapter Nine

SAM WOKE UP WITH ONE GOAL IN MIND—TO FIND THE missing fae. He had to resolve something, and though he desperately wished to find Shelby, he had more information on finding the fae third.

Bob's eyes were closed, but since he didn't breathe, it was hard to tell if he was sleeping or in a coma or whatever vampires did to rest. He slid out of Bob's embrace and quickly dressed. Downstairs, he settled behind his desk and dialed the cab company. Doug was already at work and more than happy to tell Sam where the siren and fae went.

"I'll come by and take you to that address," Doug offered helpfully. "I didn't get a good vibe when I dropped them off the other night, but hey, he's an adult, and it wasn't my business."

"I understand, thanks. There will be a little something more for you if I can find him." Sam didn't have a lot of funds, but the cabbie deserved a bit of extra money for his willingness to help out where no one else cared. Sam gave Doug his address and was told he'd be there in half an hour.

"What's going on?" Bob appeared in the office doorway. His eyes blinking, and shirt unbuttoned.

Sam's mind derailed for a minute as he admired the body on display. Bob might be a pushy vampire, but there was nothing wrong with the man's body.

"Still think I'm only into you for the sex?" Bob asked.

Sam shook his head. "Nope. I'm not that good in bed. You're in it for the blood, too."

Bob pushed away from the doorway to walk closer. He went around Sam's desk and lowered his head until his lips brushed Sam's ear as he talked. "You can distance yourself and claim it's only sex, but when you walk around town and decide to flirt with another person, you are going to reek of me. Anyone with a bit of paranormal blood will avoid you like the plague because they will know to touch you will mean their death."

Sam shouldn't find that sexy. He shouldn't. He shivered at the possessiveness of Bob's tone. The vampire meant every single word he uttered. For a man who'd once been tossed aside by his ex-lover as if he were as disposable as a tissue, it boosted Sam's ego immensely.

"I wasn't planning on flirting with anyone else," Sam said, leaning away to meet Bob's eyes. "I like you, Bob. I really do. I don't know where this relationship of ours is going to go, or if it will go anywhere, but I enjoy my time with you."

Bob's smile, slow and sweet, lit up his face. "Good. What's the plan for today?"

"The plan is: I've got the cabbie coming over to take me to where he dropped off our elusive fae. Right now, I'm going to grab something to eat, then go and see if I can rescue a fae who may or may not need to be rescued."

"He needs to be rescued," Bob said. "Fae are born into

their groupings. For them to break away and be independent is unheard of. He will start to feel his triad's absence if he hasn't already. If this siren has undue influence over our missing fae, then we need to deal with him first."

Sam shrugged. "Maybe the fae is in love with the siren."

Bob laughed. "Sirens don't fall in love. They are born with icy hearts and colder minds. Anything they do is for their pod. If a siren is with a fae, then that fae is being used for something."

"What about Mikhail? He didn't have to help me, but he did," Sam pointed out.

"Mikhail is half siren and half vampire because his siren mother wanted to have a son who could live on land. The sirens are always trying to manipulate genetics and see what will make the strongest combination. Their biggest goal is to take over a chunk of land. However, with Mikhail, his vampire half is stronger so he has at least half a heart."

Bob's words resonated deep inside Sam. Could the answer to the disappearance of the fae be this easy to solve?

"That's it!" Sam shouted. Excitement shot through him as he figured out the question bothering him this entire time. "The sirens must be using the fae to breed. They want him to make a fae-siren child." Hope rose in Sam, knowing this might resolve the entire case.

Bob regarded him with a narrowed gaze.

"Good idea, but why is he with a male siren?" Bob asked. "Surely a female siren would've been a better choice."

Sam deflated a little. That was a very good point. He considered the theory, then the perfect solution for that problem jumped to the forefront of his mind. He snapped his fingers.

"Not if they found out too late that the fae they kidnaped

only liked men," he suggested. "Perhaps they didn't know that at first."

Bob nodded. "And once they had him enthralled, it was too late to try to grab a different one," Bob added.

"Maybe that's why the fae was drinking at the bar. He knew he'd displeased his siren, maybe the very being he'd fallen in love with, and he's depressed." Sam could almost see the entire situation spreading out before him. "Poor fae. He might have gone out with the siren to try something new. To break away from his triad for a while, maybe? Instead found himself trapped by a siren who wants a breeder."

"They might kill him," Bob said, "if they can't use him."

Sam frowned. "But wouldn't the retaliation from the remaining two in the triad be huge? I mean, the others would feel it if he were dead, wouldn't they? I think they'd be furious if their third were murdered."

"Yes, but that doesn't necessarily mean the siren won't kill the fae. They don't always use the most sense. You forgot this." Bob pulled Sam's necklace out of his pocket and dangled it in the air. "It was recharging overnight."

Sam cursed inwardly, grabbed it and slipped if over his head. "Thanks. I don't want a mob. Do you think this spell will eventually wear off?"

He didn't want to be wearing a cheap tourist trap necklace for the rest of his life.

Bob shook his head. "No. I think you'll have to find someone to break the spell. I'll ask around after we get the fae safely home."

"Thanks."

Bob leaned down and kissed Sam. "There's nothing I wouldn't do for you, love. You might think we're just fucking, but I'm staking a claim. You'll always be mine."

"Well, not always," Sam interjected. "I'll die way before you."

Bob shook his head. "Not if I bind you to me. If you become my human mate, you will live as long as I do."

"Oh." Sam didn't have a response to that. In fact, his mind went completely blank. Did he want to live that long? His life so far hadn't exactly been such a blast he wanted to prolong the experience.

"Sam, Sam, why do you have to analyze everything? Let things happen where they may. I'm not going anywhere, and with your business, you're not going anywhere. We don't have to make any decisions right now."

"True." Sam couldn't argue with that logic. "But you looked hurt yesterday when I said we were just having sex." He couldn't get that look out of his mind.

Bob cupped Sam's face between his hands. "I've never had a connection with anyone as I have with you. To me, it is much more than sex. I can't make you feel the same for me, but I'm also not going to play down my affection for you just to make you more comfortable." Bob's voice held so much determination that Sam couldn't argue with what the vampire had said.

"Fair enough," he finally said. Bob smiled at him, and for a second, Sam lost himself in the vampire's beautiful amber eyes that held so much emotion.

A honk outside had them separating.

"That's Doug, the cab driver, I bet," Sam muttered. "Damn, I didn't get anything to eat."

"We'll get something on the way," Bob soothed.

"We?"

Bob flashed a smile. "Did you actually think I'd let you go after a possibly unbalanced siren without me? You're just now starting to have fun."

Sam checked the charge on his multi-weapon and grabbed his jacket off the back of his desk chair.

"Let's go catch a fae," Bob said, his eyes lit with the joy of the chase.

Laughing, Sam took the hand held out to him and let the vampire lead him out of the building.

"HERE IT IS," Doug pronounced as he parked his cab at the end of a creaky wharf. The smell of the sea permeated the area with a salty perfume as gulls screamed out their wish for more tourist French fries.

The place was isolated and in need of repair, old nets and lobster baskets discarded on the worn concrete pathways. An air of sadness and loss of hope pervaded the pier.

No one was around.

"You dropped them off here?" Sam asked.

"Hey, he was a siren," the cabbie said. "I figured he had a hideout in the water or something, and you don't wait around to ask a siren questions." The cabbie appeared unconcerned about having dropped two people off in the middle of nowhere in the dark.

"Oh, okay. Can you wait while we look around?" Sam asked. He doubted calling another cab would get one to arrive very quickly, if at all.

"Nope, sorry. I've got another pickup. You can call me when you're ready, and if I'm available, then I'll swing by." Doug handed over a receipt with his business card.

"Thanks, Doug."

They left the cab and headed toward the wharf. A loud slurping noise had Sam spinning around.

Bob opened his mouth and let the straw drop. "What? It's a really good blood shake."

Sam rolled his eyes. "That's the last time I let you pick the drive-thru."

"Oh, come on, admit it. You enjoyed the tofu veggie crepe on a stick."

"I admit to nothing," Sam argued.

Bob tossed his cup in the trash and joined Sam on the pier. He wrinkled his nose. "It stinks of sirens around here."

"Does it?" Sam took a deep breath, but all he could smell was salty air and dead fish.

"You probably can't smell it, but it's there."

Bob headed to the end of the pier, Sam followed. They stopped at the edge of the wood and looked down. A face looked back at them from under the water.

"I hope that's a siren," Sam said. "Otherwise we have a dead person watching us."

The person blinked.

Siren.

Sam crouched down. "Can we talk to you?"

The siren floated to the top of the surface. "What do you want, human?" Bob fell to the pier.

"Whoa." Sam rushed to Bob's side. The vampire's eyes were rolled up, and only the whites showed.

"He'll be fine." The splash of water hitting the pier had Sam looking up to see that the siren had joined them on the pier. Pale blond hair with a hint of green framed a narrow face with pale green eyes. When he smiled, razor sharp teeth like a shark's appeared. The siren's pale white skin almost glowed with its translucency. Water sluiced off him as if he were a fish, his skin quickly drying.

"What's wrong with him?" Sam asked the siren as he shook Bob, trying to get him to wake.

The siren tilted his head. “He can’t handle the siren’s allure. What’s really surprising is that you can. Why is that, human?”

“I don’t know.” Sam didn’t understand this strange immunity he appeared to have for certain paranormals. He wasn’t about to talk to a siren about it, either. “Who are you?”

The siren wore swimming shorts that hung low on his hips and ended just above his knees.

“I’m Sturgeon,” he said. Sam held out a hand to shake, but Sturgeon ignored the social nicety. Sam dropped his hand and coughed to cover his unease.

“I’m Sam,” he offered. “I have something I was hoping you could help me with. Would you by any chance have seen a fae around here?”

Sturgeon narrowed his eyes and glanced from Bob to Sam, then back to Bob again. He was unsettled by the question. Any PI worth his salt could see that.

“Yep,” he finally offered. Sam waited for more information, but Sturgeon said nothing. Time to put his PI skills to good use.

“I imagine having a fae around here is a little worrying, what with the other two in his triad wanting him back.”

Finally, Sturgeon got with the program. “Silverfish is in big trouble for grabbing the dude,” he said.

“I’ll take him back if you don’t want him.”

Sturgeon smirked. “He’s gay, but we can still take his magic. He’s useful to us.”

Sam frowned. “You keep him and you’ll be starting a war with the fae. Is that what you want?”

Sturgeon huffed a laugh. “Like they can do anything to us. What are they going to do? Grow fins and swim in the water?” Sturgeon asked.

“Where’s Silverfish now?” Sam asked. He didn’t like the

cold, emotionless expression on the siren's face. It seemed that nothing bothered him about possibly draining another being for his magic.

Sturgeon shrugged. "I saw him at the Rockfish, the siren bar down the street."

Sam examined Sturgeon's expression. "Doesn't it bother you that your people kidnap others to experiment on combining their genetics?"

"Why should it? It's survival of the fittest. We need to do what we can to increase our numbers."

"Even if it means destroying other people, other paranormals?" Sam didn't understand this divide and conquer approach.

Sturgeon laughed. "We don't kill them. We steal some magic and sperm. They survive to go on with their petty lives." Sturgeon tilted his head and narrowed his gaze. "You would be an interesting candidate."

Sam raised his hands, palms out in denial. "No. I'm gay, and I have no interest in becoming a sperm donor."

"Shame." Sturgeon's cold gray eyes raked Sam up and down as if searching for his weaknesses.

"Can you wake him up?" Sam nodded towards Bob.

"He'll wake up when I leave. Some people can't handle the power of a siren even when we're not singing." Sturgeon's sneer conveyed how little he thought of those who couldn't resist him.

"Thank you for your help," Sam said, as he wondered if the siren had actually helped him. He might have handed over the third fae's possible location, but he'd also given no sign of compassion in any of it.

"Anytime, pretty human. Any time at all." Sturgeon jumped back into the water without causing a single splash.

"Uhhh…" Bob's moan dragged Sam's attention away from the water.

He crouched down beside Bob. "Hey, sleeping beauty, how are you doing?"

"What happened?" Bob asked, blinking at Sam.

"You are apparently unable to resist sirens. I'll have to send you home when I go to the siren bar."

"I'm not letting you go to a siren bar by yourself," Bob growled. He pushed himself to a sitting position and clutched at his head.

"Well, you can't go with me!" Sam pointed out.

"You're not going alone. I'll send Mikhail with you," Bob replied. "He can easily resist sirens."

Sam thought about it for a moment. It would be foolish to go in without backup. "Okay, you're right. I'll take Mikhail with me."

"Good." Bob got to his feet and gave Sam a sheepish smile. "I guess I'll have to sit this one out, love."

Sam nodded. "Understandable."

SAM STOOD outside of the Rockfish bar, waiting for Mikhail. Bob hadn't wanted to leave him alone, but Sam had insisted. The vampire had looked unsteady on his feet and getting close to the Rockfish had turned his skin an odd shade of green. Not a good color on a vampire.

The number of sirens checking him out on the way to the bar unnerved him a little. Even with his necklace on, he worried maybe the spell had eaten through the enchantment.

"No!" a scream tore through the air.

Sam spun on his heel and stared at the bar. The scream

had definitely come from inside. Where was Mikhail? Why wasn't he here?

"Noooo!" This time the awful, heart-rending scream made Sam move. Mikhail here or not, he was going in. He pushed in the door and raced through the bar, dodging around the people who tried to get in his way. Another scream and Sam located the source of the awful noise. The fae he'd been hunting lay on the ground, the runes on his face glowing brightly.

"They're hurting me. Make them stop!" the fae screamed.

Sam dropped to his knees. Instinct had him reaching for the fae's face. Energy zapped up his arms, causing the fine hair on his arms to stand on edge.

The fae calmed beneath his touch immediately. The runes dimmed slightly, and the fae closed his eyes.

"Shhh, you'll be fine," Sam soothed.

"You can't have him. He's mine," a petulant voice interrupted Sam's concentration on the man on the floor.

Sam looked up to see a blue-haired siren scowling down at them.

"He's coming with me. He needs to go back to the other parts of his triad," Sam stated.

"No!" The siren slammed his foot to the floor in a petulant stamp. "I found him, he's mine!"

Sam saw the other sirens in the club were starting to mill around. He didn't know if they would side with him or the siren, but he didn't want to stick around and find out.

"Come on, let's get you out of here." Sam wrapped the fae's arm around his shoulder and helped pull him to his feet. "Let's get you back to my place."

"You aren't listening to me!" The siren screamed. The siren was losing his shit big-time in a tantrum to top all tantrums. "It's nothing to do with you. He's mine."

Sam lost his temper in an instant. He'd been told one too many times to mind his own business regarding paranormal matters, as they pulled him in. He carefully set the fae down in the closest chair and walked up to the siren until they were face to face. The siren took a step backward. Clearly, they weren't so big when faced with someone who didn't get all unconscious at the first sight or sound of them.

"He's mine!"

"You are a spoiled, frustrating moron, and you need to back off before I punch you."

"I dare you!" the siren screamed.

Sam punched him in the face.

"Ow! Fuck!" the siren whimpered.

Sam scanned the room, but none of the other sirens came closer to interfere or defend the siren with the now probably broken nose. Leaning down, Sam retrieved the fae and headed for the door.

"Nice job, detective!" Mikhail stood in the doorway. Sam didn't know how long Mikhail had been standing there, but he could tell the vampire would have been ready to step in if needed.

"Thanks."

Knowing Mikhail had his back against any reprisal, Sam helped the fae out of the bar.

Chapter Ten

SAM COULDN'T GO ANYWHERE IN THE AGENCY WITHOUT THE found-fae following him about an inch away.

"You can sit in my office," he said on more than one occasion. The last being when he'd nearly tripped over the immoveable mass as he pulled files out of the cabinet.

"I can't," the fae answered. Sam sighed. He couldn't keep thinking of the fae as 'the fae', especially if he needed to tell the guy to step away from Sam's personal space.

"What's your name?" Sam asked.

"They don't have names," Teddy pointed out. The ghost was yet another shadow that didn't appear to want to let Sam have any time on his own.

"We do have names," the fae protested. "They're secret to anyone but the ones that matter to us." He moved closer to Sam then, in an odd move, tilted his head and rested his left cheek on Sam's chest where his heart was. He was pressing quite hard, and Sam was literally pinned between the cabinet and the fae. Sam gently pushed the fae away and slid out from between him and the cabinet.

"I'll tell you my name, though." The fae made to follow him and Sam held up a hand.

"What is it?" he asked.

"What is what?" the fae replied.

"Your name?"

"Oh, that. Sindri," the fae replied.

"Well, Sindri, I need to concentrate on a few things. How about Teddy takes you to the office and shows you where the coffee is?" Did fae drink coffee? Sindri had certainly drunk an awful lot of everything else in the human/wolf bar, so he guessed offering coffee wasn't too odd.

"Can you touch me again?" Sindri asked. He moved closer, but this time Sam had managed to get the door behind him and could make a run for it. He passed Mikhail on the stairs, who stood back and out of his way.

"What's wrong?" Mikhail asked.

"Sindri is all over me like a rash," Sam snapped. "He wants to keep touching me."

"You do have an effect on him I haven't seen before," Mikhail offered. "You calm him."

Sam pushed away the thoughts of what that meant. He'd already assigned the cat-like rubbing to the fact that Sindri was grateful to Sam for the rescue. Thinking about any other reason for the action had him questioning his heritage, and he was so not going down that path.

"Whatever," Sam summed it up neatly. Sindri appeared at the top of the stairs and looked down at Sam with a yearning expression on his face. Sam positioned Mikhail between the two of them then carried on down to his office. Closing the door at least gave him some illusion of privacy.

How come it was taking the other two fae so long to get there? Sam had contacted them over an hour ago, and Sindri needed to go home.

"Mikhail has that fae cornered on the landing," Bob announced as he barged into the office.

"Good," Sam muttered. "He was freaking me out."

"Mikhail?"

"No, the fae, Sindri."

"Why?"

"He was all up in my space and rubbing himself against me."

Bob considered the words for a moment and very deliberately closed the door. "Used to be if a fae owed you they bestowed the gift of sexual gratification on you."

Sam blinked as he listened to the words coming from his lover's mouth. "What the hell?" he asked.

Bob shook his head. He didn't look any happier about what he had said than Sam did. "You rescued him," he said. "And for that reason, he thinks he owes you."

"I don't need owing."

"It's kind of dangerous to turn a bestowed gift down."

"I am a human. I'm not part of this fucked-up paranormal world. No one is bestowing anything on me that resembles sex without my permission." He couldn't stop his anger and Bob visibly recoiled.

Shit.

"Not you, Bob," Sam added helplessly.

"Why wouldn't it be me, Sam?" Bob said sadly. "You've made it clear that what we have is sex, and you don't trust that I am not using my glamor on you." He shrugged. "I will buy the house next door to stay close to you, but I won't force you into anything you don't want to do."

Exasperated with himself and his mouth and Bob's self-sacrificing attitude, Sam pushed himself up and away from the desk and pressed Bob back against the door.

"I don't want you to go anywhere," Sam said.

"Okay," Bob said uncertainly.

Sam reached up and cupped Bob's face in his hands. "I think we have something that scares me. You and me together feels right. When I was inside you, when we cuddled, when you protected me." He closed his eyes and rested his forehead against Bob's. Out of all this craziness, the one thing he didn't want to happen was for Bob to go. Somehow feeling something more than lust for this gorgeous amber-eyed vampire had sneaked up on him.

"I'm sorry if I said something wrong," Bob offered softly. "I don't want to be like the fae, always in your space and forcing you—"

"I love you," Sam interrupted. As soon as the words were out, he almost wished he could snatch them back. Was the love spell responsible for him saying these words? Was Bob entirely unable to use his glamor on Sam?

"Sam, I love you more than I was ever supposed to," Bob said simply. Sam considered the odd way the admission had been worded and filed it away to think about later. Bob carried on talking, "I always will."

The doorbell sounded, and Sam stepped away from Bob. He examined the expression on Bob's pale face; a mix of love and questioning and sadness. He leaned in and kissed Bob and melted into the kiss that deepened between them. The door moved behind them, and reluctantly they pulled apart.

The remaining two members of the triad came into the office, hot on the tail of an agitated Teddy, who was muttering under his breath, something about mess and cats. The last thing Sam wanted was to have an annoying Teddy hanging around his clients.

"Thank you, Teddy, that will be all." Teddy narrowed his gaze then huffed noisily before disappearing in a trail of wispy smoke out of the room. Mikhail and Sindri entered the room, and the three fae embraced for a long while. They were talking, but Sam couldn't understand the soft words. He waited patiently while Bob and Mikhail hovered by the door, watchful. Sam smiled as Sindri turned to him. But the smile disappeared when, in a smooth move, Sindri swept him backward in a kiss worthy of a black and white film. The kiss tingled, burned, then a sensation ran through Sam like no other. Ice, followed by fire, chased by dizziness.

When Sindri released him, Sam's eyes went to Bob and Mikhail. They stepped closer, but something was stopping them dead. They were standing there like mimes pressing against a sheet of invisible glass. Some kind of magical barrier, Sam thought. Sindri was replaced by Fae Two, whose kiss was like a summer's day, fresh and bright. God, Sam felt so dizzy. Feebly, Sam pushed at Fae Two, but that only meant Two was replaced by Fae Three, who muttered an incantation low and soft before stealing a third kiss.

Then everything went black.

"SAM? SAM, WAKE UP, BABE." Something slapped his face.

That hurts.

"Hell, he's not coming round," Bob said.

"He's opening his eyes," Mikhail pointed out.

"Wha' happened?" Sam asked. He blinked as his eyes adjusted and saw it was only him and the two vampires in the room. "Where did the triad go?"

"They did their thing, then left," Mikhail said. Between him and Bob, they managed to get Sam sitting up on the sofa. Bob gripped his hand. Sam felt the pressure and welcomed it. The touch grounded him, and he began to feel less dizzy.

"Their thing?"

“Turns out, directive twenty-five seventy-three of the Paranormal/Human Bylaws means they can’t bestow a ‘thank you’ through full sex,” Mikhail summarized. “But they can kiss you.”

“They bestowed… what? … I don’t understand…”

“You’ve been fae blessed,” Bob said in a small voice. Reaching out, he touched a finger to Sam’s cheek. “They’ve left their mark on you.” Sam stumbled to stand and crossed over to the mirror. Bob was right. On his left cheekbone was a tiny star that glittered when he turned his head. Using a finger, he rubbed at the mark, but there was no removing it.

“They can’t just tattoo me,” Sam protested.

“The fae carry runes on their faces. They saw no reason not to mark you in a similar way,” Bob said.

“But… what does it mean…?” Sam was confused. “What does it mean to be fae blessed?”

Bob shrugged. “We’re not completely sure. They left before we could ask for full details.”

“If it’s anything like what happened to Viktor, Sam’s blood is now marked as being special in the fae world.”

“Viktor killed himself as soon as he received the blessing,” Bob said instantly. He grabbed hold of Sam and held tight. “You’re not killing yourself.” Bob was desperate.

“Viktor couldn’t handle the touch of the fae,” Mikhail placated. “It took him three weeks to gain consciousness. Look at Sam, he’s awake and he feels fine. You do, Sam, don’t you? Feel fine, that is?”

Sam considered his body. He felt tired and tingly and his cheek was numb, but other than that, he didn’t feel particularly bad, much less suicidal at this point.

“I’m fine.”

“One good thing, though,” Mikhail continued. “The triad broke the Cupid curse. You can go out in public now.”

"Thank God for small mercies," Sam muttered. "No offense but that shell necklace was awful."

"None taken," Mikhail laughed. "I'll leave you two alone now." He left and shut the door behind him.

"I couldn't stop them," Bob whispered into his ear. "I tried to."

"I know, I saw."

"If anything happened to you, I would go with you. If you died, you wouldn't die alone." If the words had been spoken loudly with great theatrical *vampireness,* Sam would have dismissed them, but Bob's voice was calm and full of emotion. That was the moment Sam knew the love building inside him was real.

Epilogue

THE FAE CASE FILE WAS CLOSED, AND SAM WASN'T FEELING that bad. Okay, so he still had the missing wolf to find, but a win was a win and he would take that while he decided what to do next to find Shelby. The doorbell sounded again, and when no one answered the door, Sam went to find out what mystery might turn up on his doorstep next.

There was no one there. Well, no person at least. There was a cat. An ebony cat with wide green eyes… and a box. Sam didn't think anything of the cat, but he was intrigued by the small, plain box with his name written on it.

"Siren spells don't work on me," he called out, in case what was in the box was some kind of weird siren revenge or a warning like the shell he'd received before.

"Of course they don't," a voice replied. Sam narrowed his gaze and looked around. There was no one there, and he dismissed the words as a product of his hyped-up imagination. He brought the box in and closed the front door before heading into his office.

The box had a loose lid. Curious, he opened it. Inside there was a note and a single red ribbon. A chill ran up his arm when he touched the silky material. He thought he heard a child crying and felt fear rip through him. Not his fear, but hers. It stopped when he took his fingers off the scarlet strip. Weird. He touched it again, and the crying resumed. Freaked, he backed away, but not before grabbing the card and turning it over to read it.

It was signed by Hartman Huter. The message was simple.

This was sent to me. My daughter's blood is on this. I can't scent it, but I hope you can track where it came from. Find her. Please.

Sam slumped on the sofa. Surely a werewolf would be better suited to tracking down blood. The door flew open, and Bob rushed over to him, worry stamped on his face.

"What happened?" Bob demanded.

"Hartman dropped off evidence, at least I assume it was him. I don't understand why. It's a ribbon with blood on it. Surely he can use it to scent?" Sam asked.

Bob picked up the box and inhaled deeply.

"Magic is cloaking this," he summarized. "I can scent nothing but the blood group. Nothing of a wolf, child or not."

"Then why can I…" Sam didn't want to say it. But why could he touch it and hear crying?

"Why can you what?"

"Pick up the ribbon for me?" Sam asked. Bob removed the ribbon from the box, and it coiled into his hand. He peered down at the scarlet material. "Do you hear anything?"

Bob frowned. "No."

"I can. I can hear crying, and feel her fear."

Bob replaced the ribbon in the box and crouched down in front of Sam and gripped his hands tightly.

"It's probably a fae thing," Bob began carefully.

"So, what, you're saying I can hear distress and feel other's pain? That isn't a gift, Bob."

Bob appeared lost for words. "I'll go and make you some coffee," he said finally. "Then we'll sit and think about this."

"Okay," Sam replied. He waited until Bob left the room then buried his head in his hands. He didn't want to experience other people's pain. Yes, he could almost sense a location for the girl. Yes, if he concentrated, he could feel the cold in her bones and the temper of the person screaming at her. But he didn't want any of that.

"Well, you need to suck it up," a voice told him in no uncertain terms.

Great. Now his uncle's gargoyle was talking at him. But not in his usual growling grumbling voice, and hell, when had he begun to read Sam's thoughts? Opening his eyes, Sam focused on the gargoyle, but the stone was not moving in any way to indicate that it was animated.

"Down here," the voice pointed out. Sam looked down at the floor, to the same black cat that had been on the doorstep. He was going mad, he thought.

"I'm going mad," he said out loud. "Hearing things."

"*Real*," the cat said. Well. Thought, at least. The cat's mouth didn't move. He was staring at Sam with a focused green intensity.

Bob came back in the room carrying two mugs and set them down on the desk.

"The cat talked to me," Sam said.

Bob raised his eyebrows and glanced down at the feline twisting in and out of Sam's legs. "I was wondering when it would turn up."

"He," the cat thought.

"It's a he," Sam repeated. Then he shut his mouth. What was he doing, talking about a hallucination like it was real?

Bob shrugged. "It was inevitable he would find you."

"What?" Sam was confused. The cat stretched then leaped up on the side of the sofa next to Sam. "What do you mean find me?"

"As soon as the witch's curse was broken, her familiar would be looking for a new home. Looking for stronger magic than his current witch."

"A familiar? The cat is like a supernatural entity that assists a witch?" He recalled what he had learned from his college days. Didn't crony old witches have black cats? Evil black cats that did their awful bidding?

"My name is Smudge," the cat thought. "I'm black, but not evil." Smudge stepped delicately onto Sam's lap and curled into a ball. "I'm staying, magic-Sam-human."

Bob appeared to take the whole thing in stride. Passing Sam a coffee, he settled with his own drink next to Sam and leaned in close.

"You okay?" he asked. He was concerned. Sam could see that through the fog of what-the-fuck that was in his head. Sam's thoughts tumbled in his head with no direction, but he knew he wasn't okay.

"I have a witch's cat as a pet who talks to me," Sam began. "Not to mention, I have a ghost who is permanently annoying and grumpy, and a gargoyle who sulks. Then there are the werewolves who threaten to remove my head from my body if I interfere in their pack business. And two vampires; one who flirts with me and one that I've fallen in love with. No, Bob, despite the fact that this time three months ago I was all for paranormal and human staying in separate areas of the city, I'm really not okay."

Bob patted his arm gently. "I think you're in shock," he said helpfully.

"You think?" Sam snorted.

"Everything will be okay. Once you accept this new path of yours. Anyway, the ribbon is a clue, though. That's good, right?"

Suddenly determined, Sam pushed Smudge off of his lap. The cat mewled in protest as Sam stood up. Bob moved with him.

"Okay," Sam stated firmly. "We can't afford to stop this now. Shelby is due to be able to change soon, she needs rescuing, and for some reason, a fair number of people think I may be her only hope."

Bob crossed his arms over his chest and nodded in agreement. "What do you want me to do?" he asked.

Sam sat behind his desk, placed his coffee on a coaster then pulled the ribbon toward him, using a pencil.

"Get Mikhail in here, and Teddy."

"Okay."

"We have a case to crack."

THE END

The Case Of The Wicked Wolf

End Street Volume 1

Chapter One

Sam Enderson sat back in his desk chair and looked at his notes with annoyance. The strip of ribbon Hartman had sent him sat on the corner of the desk. As long as he didn't touch it, he couldn't hear the girl crying. Despite what Bob had said, he knew the ribbon belonged to the missing werewolf girl. Who else would be crying out in pain? The only thing that made Sam question his judgment was Bob's statement that he didn't sense any shifter scent on the ribbon.

"It's a puzzle."

"Yes, it is," Sam replied to Smudge, the black cat familiar curled on the pillow beside his chair.

Smudge flicked his long tail as he groomed his black fur in long, languid strokes. When he spread his legs to lick his privates, Sam turned away. "Can't you do that elsewhere?"

"You're just jealous because I'm bendy," Smudge taunted.

Searching for a distraction, he turned his attention back to his sparse notes. He read them from beginning to end. Shelby Hartman, young werewolf and the daughter of a pack Alpha, was missing. All he had was the ribbon that had been sent to him, and the strange feelings of hearing her crying when he touched it. They had no other leads.

Nothing made sense. Where had Shelby gone? Bob had talked to his contacts, but people weren't talking. Seemed as if being a big bad alpha like Hartman Hunter was enough to keep everyone well away.

Sam wished he could interrogate the werewolves, especially Constance—Shelby's mother and Hartman Hunter's ex-wife. From the little Hartman had told Sam about her, she seemed a prime suspect. Hartman kept insisting none of the shifters would do that to a little girl, but Sam had his doubts. Shelby's mother had two sons from a previous marriage, both old enough to challenge for Alpha. Even Hartman had admitted she was power hungry. What better way to bring down the Alpha than to crush his spirit? Hartman denied his pack had anything to do with Shelby's disappearance, but Sam noticed the Alpha hadn't asked for his pack's help in locating his lost girl.

He sighed as he looked at the miniscule amount of information he had to work with. If the case hadn't involved a little girl, Sam would've passed on taking it. However, he couldn't refuse to help out an obviously broken-hearted person even if he was a werewolf.

Unfortunately, this new job didn't do anything to help foster a good reputation among the human population. So far, paranormals were the only ones interested in Sam's services. The witch was still complaining to everyone she could find that Sam hadn't lived up to his uncle's promise. Since word had also traveled that she'd cursed Sam and that he'd recovered the missing fae, his name was becoming rather well known among people he'd rather avoid.

A knock on the door drew Sam's attention away from his futile endeavor.

"Yes?" Sam called out.

A large hulking man with hair popping out of every visible crevice stomped into Sam's office. He wore a surprisingly stylish suit, but Sam figured if you were that large, everything was probably custom-made.

"Are you Sam Enderson?" he asked in a voice so deep Sam thought he felt the floor vibrate beneath his chair.

"Yes." Sam stood to greet his guest. The man-creature-being—whatever the hell it was—towered over Sam. However, he looked to be a bit slow in the walking department and Sam's confidence raised a few notches when he realized he could probably flee the building before the visitor reached him. "Can I help you with something?"

Smudge hissed from his perch.

"Troll."

Sam had never met a troll before. Fascinated, he watched his visitor with open curiosity. He hadn't known trolls ever left their bridges. Of course, what he knew about trolls could be stuffed in a brownie's pocket.

"I need something removed." The troll spoke in slow, drawn-out syllables, as if each word had to be dredged from his soul.

All the various things that could be stuck under a bridge flashed through Sam's mind. What could a troll not be able to move?

"How can I help you?" he asked neutrally. He wanted to fix whatever bothered his visitor and send him on his way. It wouldn't help Sam's reputation for anyone to spot another non-human being wandering into his office.

"I heard that you solve people's problems." The troll frowned as though Sam was the slow one in this conversation.

"I try to. Why can't you move whatever it is? I'm not any

stronger than you so I doubt I'll be much help." Sam hoped the troll would take the hint and leave.

The troll held up his enormous hands the size of serving trays. "It's alive."

Sam's mind froze as he wondered what kind of creature a troll couldn't scare away from its home. "Um, how about an exterminator?"

"I don't want to kill it. It's only a baby."

Sam thought about arguing further, maybe suggesting Child Services, but it would probably be best if he went to see what the troll was talking about before he gave any more advice. His visitor didn't look like he understood much.

"Okay, I'll come look." What other option did he have? The troll didn't look like he would leave Sam's office without getting help.

"I pay first," the troll announced. He pulled a small velvet bag out of his pocket and dropped the payment onto Sam's desk.

The bag landed with a loud metallic clink.

Curious, Sam pulled open the drawstring and peeked inside.

Gold. Dozens of gold coins filled the small purse.

"Um, this might be too much," Sam offered hesitantly. He was almost certain he could buy the entire block with the wealth contained in the small sack, but he didn't want to hurt the troll's feelings.

The troll made no motion to take the gold back.

"How about we can decide a price after we see what you need done," Sam offered diplomatically.

"Okay," the troll agreed.

Sam returned the gold-filled bag.

The troll gave him a wide toothy smile. "You're a good man, Sam."

"Uh, thanks." Sam didn't want to take advantage of a creature that appeared to only have the understanding of a small child. Probably less than some of the savvy children he'd met in the past.

"Hey, Sam." Bob walked into the room. The vampire froze as soon as he saw Sam's visitor. "Trawl? What are you doing here?" he asked the troll.

"Bob!" The troll grinned at Bob. "I thought I smelled vampire."

Sam had forgotten that trolls were related to giants and had an advanced sense of smell. "You know this troll?"

"Trawl lived under the bridge by my house some time ago," Bob said.

"Nice bridge. They tore it down for newer one." Trawl wrinkled his bumpy nose in disgust. "Don't like new bridge."

Sam wondered what the criteria was for the perfect bridge for a troll. Trawl turned his attention back to Sam. He decided his curiosity could wait.

"Trawl is hiring me to remove something," Sam announced.

"Really?" Bob lifted an eyebrow at the news.

Sam could tell Bob was trying to read his mind and learn the details, but since Sam didn't know any, scanning his mind wouldn't reveal anything.

"Well, let's not waste any time. Let's remove Trawl's pest," Bob said cheerfully.

Sam opened his mouth to tell Bob he didn't need to come, but a sharp look from his lover had him holding his tongue. The vampire obviously didn't want Sam going alone. Unfortunately, because Bob was obsessively protective, Sam didn't know if Bob suspected something dangerous waited for them, or if Bob's obsession had taken new heights.

Sam followed the troll out of the door and down the street.

"Oof." The weight of Smudge landing on his shoulder pushed the air out of his lungs.

"Shush. I'm not that heavy," the familiar scolded.

"Says the cat who'll eat anything," Sam teased.

Smudge dug his claws into Sam's shoulder and wrapped his thick tail around Sam's neck for balance.

"If I choke to death, you fall," Sam reminded the cat.

Smudge released his grip a little so Sam could breathe.

"Thank you. Why are you coming anyway?" Since Smudge had arrived a few days ago, Sam hadn't seen the cat do anything more strenuous than take a bath.

"I'm here to help."

Sam didn't know how a black cat could help with anything, but then he still hadn't figured out what the damn animal was hanging around him for anyway. Sam didn't have any magical powers for a familiar to access or improve. Smudge had declared that Sam smelled good and that he'd stay a while.

As Sam followed Trawl down the sidewalk, he watched in surprise as citizens fled the path, allowing Trawl the full walkway without obstacles. Surely they'd seen creatures more imposing than Trawl? The lumbering giant appeared to have a rather calm personality for a troll.

Sadness emanated from Trawl. Sam wondered if his newly given empathic power from the fae was helping him sense Trawl's emotions. He still didn't quite know how the ability worked, but he did know now when Bob was watching him with something more than platonic affection and when the search for lube had turned critical.

Trawl's bridge turned out to be only three blocks from Sam's building.

“Huh, I didn’t know this was here,” Sam said.

“That’s because you never come down to the paranormal parishes if you can avoid it,” Bob said dryly.

“True.” Sam saw no point in denying it. Bob knew how Sam felt about paranormals. Sam might have a vampire lover and a growing collection of unusual associates, but he still hoped to build a business based in the human world. The world he understood.

Still, that didn’t stop his curiosity about what the troll had under his bridge.

Sam followed Trawl and Bob as they hiked down the slope to get beneath the stone bridge. The smell of mold and mildew filled Sam’s nostrils. He took slow breaths in through his mouth to combat the stench.

As soon as he was fully beneath the structure, a soft sobbing drew his attention. Frustratingly, in the dim light, he couldn’t see a thing. Darkness wrapped around them, pitch black and impenetrable.

“Who is it?” Sam asked, unable to make anything out.

“A naiad,” Bob replied. “A young one or at least she appears that way. You can’t always tell their age.”

“Why is it crying?” Sam’s knowledge of naiads could be put in a thimble with room for an encyclopedia on fairies to be tucked beside it.

“I-I’m lost!” the creature sobbed in response. Naiads must have excellent hearing since Sam hadn’t spoken very loudly.

Smudge gave a soft hiss. Sam didn’t know if it was over the naiad or the dampness, but he didn’t need the snarly cat to aggravate the naiad problem.

“Behave!” Sam warned the familiar. “Or we’ll find out if you can swim.”

A puff of air blew against Sam’s neck, followed by Smudge’s weight disappearing from Sam’s shoulder.

Sam spun around but couldn't see anything or hear a splash. Where had the damn cat gone?

"What's wrong, Sam?" Bob asked.

"Smudge disappeared. He was here, then he vanished." Sam squinted harder, trying to see in the darkness but failing miserably. Water soaked through his clothes up to his knees as he waded in deeper, looking for Smudge.

Bob grabbed Sam's arm. "Easy, honey. I'm sure he teleported home. Once he determined there wasn't any threat to you, he probably decided to take a nap or something."

"He could've warned me," Sam grumbled. "I didn't know he could teleport."

"Some can, some can't. Apparently yours can," Bob said philosophically.

"He's not mine," Sam argued. "He's on loan."

"From who?" Bob's voice held an amused edge that had Sam gritting his teeth as he walked closer to the naiad.

"Some idiot who misplaced his familiar, obviously." Sam trudged through the water toward the sobbing sound, pleased when Trawl chose to walk beside him. The troll's reassuring mass made the entire encounter less intimidating. Despite having just met Trawl, Sam found he liked the big guy.

"Hello there," Sam called out into the inky blackness, hoping not to startle the naiad. He could barely detect her faint glowing outline. "I wish I had more light," he grumbled.

A ball of fire formed in the air before him, illuminating the entire space beneath the bridge. Now he could clearly see everything, almost as if it were daylight.

"Human has powers," the troll gasped.

"No, human doesn't have powers," Sam snapped. He glared at the light, offended by its mysterious presence. "I don't know what that is from."

"We'll worry about it when we get back home," Bob soothed.

Sam nodded. He walked forward, a little disconcerted when the glowing ball floated ahead of him.

The naiad had blue hair and silvery skin with eyes as wide and innocent as a fawn Sam had once seen while hiking in the forest. Physically, she didn't appear much older than ten. Dressed in a cream-colored shift, she sat in the water with her arms wrapped around her legs, resting her cheek on her knees.

"What do you know about naiads, Bob?" Sam asked, not taking his gaze off the sobbing girl.

"They're dangerous," Bob warned. "She may look young and innocent, but she could be hundreds of years old."

"She looks like a pre-teen," Sam scoffed.

The naiad's thin shoulders shook while she sobbed as if her heart had shattered and the water had swept away all the pieces.

Sam crouched down so he wasn't towering over her. He tried to ignore the water seeping into the seat of his pants. "I'm Sam. What's your name?"

The naiad uncurled from the ball she had huddled in. "Are you a human?"

Sam nodded.

"They were humans too," she said in a shaky voice. She wiped at her tears with her wet fingers, adding more drops of water than she brushed away.

"Who?" Sam asked gently. He tried to keep his voice low and calm, afraid of scaring her further.

"The men who captured me and all of the others." She looked everywhere but at Sam.

"What others?" Sam asked. He could sense her fear—it

wrapped around him like a blanket of nails poking at him with its sharp tips.

The naiad frowned. "The other girls." Her tone indicated she thought he should've known that.

Fear shot through Sam at the idea of a bunch of young paranormal girls captured by humans. The horrible things men might do to the children froze his blood.

"Was there a werewolf girl among them? About four years old?" he prodded. Excitement over possibly getting a lead on their case had his heart racing.

The naiad narrowed her eyes. "Why? What do you want with her?"

Sam noted how quickly she went from sobbing to suspicious. "Her father hired me to find her. He's very worried," he explained.

"Oh." Tension sagged out of the naiad as if the stress had dissolved all her bones and she had nothing left to hold her together. "Yes. I saw her. I don't know her name. They kept her in a cage away from the others. I think they were going to keep her for a different reason, but they never said."

Sam's heart ached at the image building in his head. "I want to rescue them. Can you help?" At this point, Sam's new goal wasn't just to save the werewolf child. He also wanted to break up this kidnapping ring and bring the humans to justice. They were giving a bad name to humankind.

The naiad shook her head frantically. "I won't go back! I won't!" she shrieked.

"Shhh." Sam sent out soothing thoughts, hoping his new fae abilities worked in reverse. After a moment, she calmed down.

"Sorry," she whispered.

"I understand you don't want to return to your kidnappers. I don't blame you," Sam said. "But maybe you can help us figure out where they put the other girls, and in return, we'll take you home. How does that sound?"

A crafty expression crossed the naiad's face. "It sounds like a deal. Are you trying to make a deal, Sam the human?"

Sam hesitated. Her word choice had a ritualistic tone he hesitated to agree with. Not to mention, the naiad's change of expression from vulnerable to scheming had Sam thinking hard before he said anything else.

"Careful, Sam. Naiads are trickier than fae when cutting a deal," Bob warned.

Sam sighed. "Why isn't anything easy?"

Bob chuckled before addressing the water sprite. "What do you want, naiad?"

"A promise. Swear to me on my life shell that you will try to save the girls and I will tell you all you need to know." She pulled a necklace out from beneath the shift she wore. A large red shell was attached to a thick black rope.

Sam was surprised the kidnappers had let her keep it.

Bob wrapped a hand around Sam's upper arm. He leaned forward and spoke in Sam's ear. "If you swear on a naiad's life shell and break your vow, you will die in the water, eaten by the creatures that dwell beneath," he whispered. His breath brushed across Sam's ear.

Despite the frigidity of the water and Bob's ominous words, Sam's cock made a valiant effort to rise. He had to think of non-sexy things like Trawl's nose hair to keep his erection down.

"Wow. No pressure." Sam sighed. He really needed to get a paranormal handbook. Maybe he could find an edition of *Weres, Witches and Whatnots* in the library. His plan to only deal with humans obviously wasn't working.

Chapter Two

HARTMAN WAS ROOTED TO THE SPOT.

Danjal Naamah. The man that Hartman had promised forever to was here on this street. He'd be unaware that Hartman Hunter, Alpha of the Hartman pack, was standing outside contemplating the suicide of coming back into Danjal's life. It wasn't as if Hartman had told Dan he'd be visiting. They weren't on speaking terms, or meeting terms, or any other kinds of terms. Danjal hated him, with good reason. When Hartman had told Sam he'd get someone to help them, he hadn't realized how difficult that process would be.

Hartman sighed. He'd deliberately avoided this part of town for so long, but now, standing here, he wondered how he could have stayed away. So much was familiar. From the café on the corner run by fae to the theater at the other end, the short road of stores was one mystery after another. Here in this street, there was magic, and he'd spent one hell of a lot of time here before he had given in to pack pressure to produce an offspring. Back when it had been him and Dan against the world.

He examined the short block, trying to determine if anything had changed while he'd been gone. Nothing. Everything looked as if it had been frozen in time, waiting for his return. Werekin and Fae alike still walked the length of the sidewalk, while tables and chairs were scattered here and there from the café onto the pavement and across the cobbled road. Quarter Street was the last bastion of the old magic and the old ways, and Hartman's wolf howled in excitement at returning here. Of returning to the man his wolf had always considered his mate. Damn, he'd missed him.

The need to move became too strong to ignore. He could stand there all day and contemplate the sorrow of his empty life without Dan, or he could man up and beg his former lover for help. It didn't matter how long he stood there watching the ebb and flow of foot traffic, he had to see Dan and get the locating spell he'd promised Sam. He'd started to draw attention to himself, anyway. Who wouldn't notice a brooding hulk of a werewolf half in and half out of the shadows? With his luck, someone from his pack would see him, then everyone would know where he'd been. Hartman Hunter plus Quarter Street could only mean one thing—Danjal Naamah.

He walked the short distance to the second to last shop front and stopped outside the door. The windows were made of hundreds of small panes of glass that gleamed brightly in the mid-morning sun. He couldn't see through them very well, but to be honest, the description above the window told any curious onlookers exactly what was contained inside.

"Excuse me! I need to get out," a peevish voice demanded.

Hartman realized two things at once. He'd nearly stepped on an irritable dwarf and now the door to the Apothecary was open. Wide open. The smells of herbs and spices along with a hint of magic spilled out of the shop and showered Hartman's senses. He stepped aside to let the dwarf pass, then though he wanted to move, he was rooted to the spot. The scents, the warmth, the citrus spice combination—they pushed him back to a time when all that had mattered had been the love he could hoard for himself. Not a relationship bound by contract to ensure succession for his pack. Back when his marriage to Constance hadn't existed and his current divorce and threat to his Alpha status didn't hang over him like the Sword of Damocles.

Memories flooded him of blissful lazy mornings waking up next to Dan—the only man Hartman had ever loved.

Inhaling deeply to capture the familiar fragrance in his lungs, Hartman stepped across the threshold, then carefully closed the heavy oak door behind him. There was no one in the shop. No sign of Dan or of his assistant Everett—nothing. That wasn't unusual. When he'd visited before, he'd often found Dan buried nose deep in a tome of ancient magic or the latest gossip magazines. If that was where Dan was now, then Hartman needed to go deeper into the shop, back to the workroom where Dan conducted his more perilous projects.

"Can I help you?"

Hartman jumped. Werewolves didn't do that. Irritation at his nervousness pricked at him as he turned to face the owner of the voice.

"Everett," he said politely.

"This isn't good," Everett responded quickly. His gray eyes darted from Hartman to the rear of the shop and back again. The hobgoblin hopped back and forth on his bare hairy feet as he regarded Hartman, trepidation in his large brown eyes. "Not good at all."

Everett kept Dan's shop tidy and free of supernatural pests, and he also minded the store when Dan became involved in one of his projects. In return, Dan allowed the creature to live in the chest of drawers by the door. Hobgoblins liked to stay close to the places they took care of.

"Is Dan here?" Hartman interrupted the hobgoblin before he could go into his usual doom and gloom diatribe. He'd never warmed up to Hartman in all the time he'd been with Dan. Considering how they'd separated, maybe the little creature had had a point. In the end, Hartman hadn't been good for Dan.

"He's in the back room," Everett replied.

Hartman made to move, but Everett stopped him with a hand on his arm. For a second, he held on, then he simply nodded and released his hold. Everett didn't say anything else. Instead, he went to stand behind the antiquated register. Hartman frowned at the usually vocal hobgoblin's silence. Deciding to take the gift as a positive sign of acceptance, Hartman went to find his ex-lover, the man who would forever hold his heart.

Another reason his ex-wife hated him.

Walking the familiar path from the front of the shop, down the corridor to the back room, was like throwing himself into the past. To keep his focus, he mentally repeated his daughter's name over and over. *This is for Shelby. For Shelby.* The door was open and a delicious blend of citrus, cedarwood, and rosemary scents was his first confirmation that Dan was inside. Peering into the room, he spotted Dan hunched over a microscope. He was talking to himself, ticking off items from a list, and marking scribbles on the pad beside him. The lamplight in the corner lent a curiously shaped glow around the only person outside his daughter that could affect Hartman beyond his duty to the pack.

"Dan," Hartman interrupted gently. He wanted to walk up and demand that Dan tell him everything he might know about witches, werewolf bones, and magic. That was his head telling him what to do, with no time for niceties. His heart, on the other hand, wanted to take it easy on Dan. That lovesick organ longed for him to wrap Dan in his arms and refuse to ever let him go again.

Dan stiffened. Very carefully, he shuffled around on the stool until he was facing Hartman.

Hartman lost the rational power of speech and the ability to breathe. Dan hadn't changed one bit. He was as gorgeous as Hartman remembered, and he still had power over Hartman's wolf that no one else had ever held. Dan looked tired, and his red-tinged pupils were wide in his eyes. Obviously shocked was an understatement—the demon was speechless. The lamplight created shadows where the small horns on his head poked through his messy, tangled, jet-black hair. Hartman loved those eyes, and the horns. He loved Dan. Whatever happened, he would forever love Dan.

"What do *you* want?" Dan asked slowly and deliberately. His tone was completely empty of emotion.

"It's good to see you, Dan," Hartman said, attempting civility.

"What. Do. You. Want?" Dan repeated.

"Your help. Just your help." All the other things he longed for from Dan could wait until he found his daughter. He needed to find Shelby first. Everything else, including his love life, could wait.

"Five years. It's been that long," Dan said evenly.

Hartman wished he could get a handle on how well this was going. Or not. But the scent of Dan was overwhelming and he couldn't get a fix on Dan's underlying emotions.

"You know I wouldn't come to you if it weren't important," Hartman offered.

Dan leaned back on his stool, extended his long legs in front of him then crossed his arms over his chest.

"So important that you drag your wolf ass into my shop, where you vowed never to step again? To talk to the one person you also added you never wanted to touch, sleep with, or even see again?"

Sarcasm dripped from Dan's words, and Hartman winced. Yes, he had said all that. It had been his clumsy attempt at getting Dan to fall out of love with him, despite the fact that demons fell in love once and forever, much like wolves. He'd hoped maybe they hadn't bonded, at least on Dan's side. He'd wanted the only person—besides his daughter—whom he'd ever loved to move on with his life. Everyone deserved love… except Hartman, who'd had to push love to one side and instead let the weight of the pack rest on his shoulders. Leaving Dan had been his biggest mistake…but having Shelby was his greatest accomplishment.

"It's Shelby," he said. "My daughter."

"I know who Shelby is, Hart." Dan stood and stretched tall.

Hartman's chest tightened at hearing Dan's nickname for him. No one else called him Hart, like no one else shortened Danjal to Dan except for Hartman.

"She's missing," Hartman stated.

"Have you tried looking in the forest? If I were your daughter, I would have run too."

The words had been said so simply, and the hurt they caused ripped through Hartman and manifested with his barely held temper breaking free. In seconds, he had Dan pressed up against the wall with his hands around the demon's throat. Shock filled Dan's eyes, but he snarled and pressed back at Hartman, giving as good as he got. They pushed each other for a few seconds until Dan went limp in Hartman's hold. Hartman immediately let go, and Dan spun on his toes and, with one kick, had Hartman lying on the floor staring up at the ceiling strewn with diamond-shaped tiles.

"You always were slow on the uptake," Dan spat.

"Dan. Please. I just need information—"

"There are other apothecaries, Hart—"

"Not like you." Hartman rolled to all fours, then clambered to stand, using a display cabinet to balance him. Dan might be slight, but he was devious as fuck, and strong.

"Just leave," Dan said tiredly, then returned to his bottles and the microscope.

"She's been kidnaped," Hartman blurted out. "She's only a baby."

"She's four. She probably has the ability to shift and claws long enough to tear my heart out. She'll be back by nightfall." Dan didn't face him.

"You don't understand, Dan. She's been missing six weeks," Hartman snapped.

Silence.

After a long moment when Hartman thought the demon would continue to ignore him, Dan turned to face him. No glimpse of empathy showed on his face, but at least he was listening.

"I have a private detective working on it. He's human. I'm that desperate. I can't ask anyone in the pack because they'll think I'm weak, but I need more help." He was seconds from begging, but then Dan had always known how to bring Hartman to his knees.

"I bet your pack loves you coming to me." Dan's voice held a world of pain.

Hartman swallowed his instinctive apology. Later he could beg for Dan's forgiveness. Right then he needed to focus on his daughter. "The pack doesn't know I've come to you for help. Please. I just need a small location spell.

Somewhere for me to start, or give to Sam so he knows where to look."

"I'm listening. There has to be a very big reason why an Alpha would deign to be anywhere near a demon he says he hates with every fiber in him."

"I think she's been taken, and I suspect her mother has something to do with it. Constance has two sons from a previous mating and they are getting old enough to fight for Alpha. I think she's done something to Shelby so I'll be too heartbroken to fight and she and her sons can take control."

"Do you have proof?" Dan asked. For the first time, a spark of sympathy filled his eyes.

Hartman shook his head. "Only instinct. The nanny disappeared soon after announcing Shelby had vanished. I don't think I'll see her again. Constance is screaming that I can't take care of my family so I don't deserve to be Alpha."

"That's some wife you've got there," Dan said. "I can see why you'd want to ditch me for her. I mean, after all, I lacked that critical vagina that obviously brings you such joy."

"We're divorced. It was finalized eight weeks ago, just before Shelby's disappearance. Please, Dan, I need to know if a witch might have taken her. Or if you can at least point me in the right direction. I'm begging." Tears threatened Hartman's composure, but he held them back. He wasn't too proud to cry for his daughter, but he didn't want Dan to think he was trying to emotionally blackmail him into helping.

"A witch? You think she might have been taken for spell-making, don't you?" Dan didn't appear fazed by the suggestion that a witch was involved in Shelby's disappearance.

Hartman deflated and slumped into the nearest chair. He buried his head in his hands.

"I don't know," he said. "But Shelby and Constance never

bonded. I wouldn't be surprised if the bitch sold our daughter to get back at me."

"If she hasn't shifted yet, she'd be worth a lot more to a witch. Along with the other paranormals, a wolf comes into true power at the first shift. An absolutely perfect moment that can be captured and ground with the bones of that child to form the basis of a lot of dark magic. Bone powder can form a base for an almost endless combination of spells." Dan's voice had the scientific, neutral tone he used when he was analyzing things and working out a problem.

Hartman felt anguish crawl through his body and emotion choke his throat. Horror gripped him and he felt sick.

He couldn't speak.

"If she's been missing six weeks, you realize that it's likely she's already dead," Dan added.

Hartman's heart stopped for a second or two, and he looked up at Dan, who had resumed the position of arms crossed over his chest. There was no hope in Dan's eyes—there was nothing except the cold summing up of the situation. Where was Dan's compassionate nature? Had Hartman killed the part of Dan he had loved the most with his decision to place pack first?

Blindly, he staggered to his feet. He needed to get out of there. Get some air. Panic clawed at his throat, and though Dan was still talking to him, he wasn't able to listen. He reached the door of the shop, but it locked in front of his eyes. A haze of red surrounded the door and Hartman was compelled by the force of it to turn and face Dan.

"Dan, you need to let me go. I have to find her." Desperation filled his voice. He couldn't stop the images in his head of his little girl trapped by some sicko to use her bones.

"I wouldn't leave a child out there alone if I could help.

Even if she's indirectly responsible for breaking my heart," Dan said.

The visible haze of red around him, the remnants of the magic he had used, made him look more demon and less human. Hartman had seen this before, and it didn't scare him. Dan might hate him for what he had done, but he was a good demon.

"Dan—"

"Hart, we need to focus on Shelby," Dan countered gently. Stalking over to Hartman, he held out a hand. "I think what was in the past should be left there. Agreed?"

"You can do that?" Hartman asked. He wasn't sure he could leave Dan in the past. He'd tried it once, and he knew he couldn't do it again. If Dan knew the heartbreak Hartman carried with him every day, then he would never suggest forgetting the past.

"I can," Dan said firmly.

Hartman gripped Dan's hand and was startled at the rush of lust that sent blood straight to his cock. This beautiful demon held so much power over him, and that scared him more than he was prepared to admit.

"So where do we start?"

"There are places we can go. People we can talk to. Tracking spells—"

"I tried them," Hartman interrupted.

"Who with?"

"Stadtler on Fifth. Yesterday. He couldn't divine anything."

"You went to Stadtler before you came to me?" Dan's voice had an edge to it, and his narrow-eyed expression held disbelief.

"I was trying not to bring you into this. I didn't want to hurt you again." Hartman looked down at their joined hands and released his grip. The lust was still inside him and images of Dan laid out under him—arching into his touch, making the most exquisite sounds and pleas of need—were etched into his brain. *I loved you. You have to know that. I still love you. You are my fated mate.* When Dan frowned at him, Hartman hoped to hell it wasn't because the demon could read his mind.

"The hurt has already happened," Dan said. "We need to see if we can find Shelby. That has to be our focus."

"And you'll try your best for me?" Hartman hated how he sounded, needy and desperate.

"For Shelby? Yes."

Chapter Three

SAM EXAMINED THE NAIAD'S EXPRESSION. HER CHALLENGING look got to Sam because he could sense her vulnerability underneath. He quickly wrapped his fingers around her shell pendant. The last thing he wanted was for her to take his hesitation as him not meaning what he'd said.

"I promise to try and help all the captured girls to the best of my ability," he vowed.

The necklace hummed beneath Sam's fingers and flashed like a beacon for a second. Sam's hand tingled as if he'd been jolted with electricity. He snatched his fingers back and shook them to regain his circulation.

Bob growled. "I warned you about promises to paranormals, Sam. You've got to stop doing that."

"I was going to look for those girls anyway. It isn't like I promised to do anything I hadn't already planned to do." Sam didn't understand why Bob sounded so upset.

Bob grabbed Sam's arm and dragged him away from the naiad. Their feet splashed up waves as they walked. Sam anticipated a nice hot shower when he got back to his apartment.

A groan interrupted his thoughts. “Don’t imagine showering. I’m trying to focus here.”

“And I’m trying to wrap things up so I can be warm again. How are we going to get the naiad back home?”

“We’ll have to take her with us while we investigate where her family is located,” Bob replied.

“How? Can she even travel out of the water?” Sam had no idea of what a naiad needed other than water.

“I see someone needs a paranormal encyclopedia for Christmas,” Bob teased.

“No, I don’t. Because I’m not going to be working with paranormals,” Sam denied blithely, ignoring his earlier idea of needing a book.

Bob pointedly looked at the troll and the naiad. “And how is that working for you?”

“I’m really starting to hate you,” Sam whispered.

Bob grinned. “Then I guess I’ll have to change your mind when we get back home.”

The way Bob had said ‘home’ gave Sam a warm, cozy feeling inside, as if they were a couple who would be returning to their shared place after an outing. In a way they were, except they really only shared a building, not an apartment together.

Bob’s speaking broke into Sam’s thoughts. “I’ll carry her back to the office. We can put her in the apartment with the ghost so she doesn’t get lonely. She should be fine in your bathtub while we look for her family or whoever she’s searching for.”

Sam nodded. That made good sense. He still needed to find out where the other girls were so they could get them all back home, especially Shelby. “Can we go talk to her now?”

Bob didn’t speak a word—he splashed his way back to the naiad.

Sometimes Sam wondered if relationships were worth the hassle. His never seemed to be.

"Oh, I'm worth all the trouble and more," Bob tossed over his shoulder.

"Stop listening to my thoughts," Sam snapped. He hated it when the vampire did that. It didn't allow for a balanced relationship. Sam couldn't read a damn thing Bob thought.

"You don't have to listen to mine," Bob said, still not turning back around. "I tell you all the good parts."

Sam sighed.

The naiad gave Sam all her attention as he told her, "After we get the other girls safe, we'll find your family."

"I don't stay with family. We make our own places in the world as soon as we are born. I need to return to my water." The naiad frowned at him as if she didn't understand how he could come up with such a weird idea.

"Sorry." Sam vaguely remembered hearing about naiads and their attachment to their lakes and rivers. "Okay, do you know what it's called?"

Maybe they could resolve the naiad issue faster than Sam had dared to hope.

The naiad nodded. "Pretty-river-that-feeds-into-lake," she announced proudly.

"Of course it is." Sam barely held back a groan. That was exactly what he'd feared. On the plus side, there were only three lakes nearby—surely they could narrow it down quickly. After they found the girls, Sam would go and take pictures of all the places where a river intersected with a lake. There couldn't be more than a dozen or so spots. He mentally crossed his fingers.

"Where are the girls being held?" Bob asked.

The naiad ignored him.

Sam blinked at the intense stare the girl gave him. He

looked between Bob and the naiad. “What’s your name?” he asked gently.

“Springlilly,” she replied.

“Pretty name.” Sam thought he should say something. After all, she kept staring at him as if she expected him to come up with something brilliant to say. Sam didn’t know how to tell her she was doomed for disappointment.

“Thank you.” She beamed.

“For now, Bob and I are going to take you back to my place. I have a spare apartment you can stay in while we go and rescue the rest of the girls. Does that sound okay to you?”

Springlilly nodded. “Thank you.”

Sam turned to face the troll. “Trawl, thank you very much. I think your naiad can help me with my case.”

Trawl’s wide face cracked into a smile. “I’m glad I could help.”

Before Sam could say anything else, the troll dropped four gold coins in his hand. Sam held tightly to them so they didn’t drop into the water. “Um, thank you.”

Sam started to speak, but Bob squeezed his shoulder and whispered in his ear, “Don’t deny him. He’ll be very unhappy.”

He doubted an unhappy troll would be a good thing. After a pause, Sam gave the troll a short bow. “Thank you, Trawl.”

“Welcome, Sam. I will tell all my friends to go to you. You’re a helpful human,” Trawl said proudly.

“I’m glad I could help.” He didn’t want to appear too grateful. The troll might see that as a sign of encouragement. Sam didn’t want to know what kinds of friends Trawl had. He doubted any of them were human, since the bridge was positioned in the paranormal part of town.

He quickly shoved the gold coins into his pocket and

turned back in time to see Bob lifting Springlilly out of the water.

"I'll meet you at home," Bob said.

With a burst of speed, Bob vanished from sight. Sam didn't feel abandoned—he figured the naiad needed to be out of the water for the shortest amount of time possible.

Sam nodded awkwardly to Trawl and scrambled up the bank to reach the sidewalk.

It didn't occur to Sam until that moment that he didn't know where he was. He'd followed Trawl to the bridge not paying particular attention to the path they'd taken. Sam looked both ways, but neither direction looked right.

Damn.

If he had any sense, he'd go back down and ask Trawl which way they'd come. But, Sam didn't want the troll telling everyone that a detective couldn't find his own way back home. It was purely an ego thing, and he knew it was stupid, but Sam couldn't make himself ask. Turning around a few times, Sam finally figured out which way he'd gone down the bank.

"I can do this," he muttered. Resolute, he marched in the direction he hoped he had arrived from.

Fortunately, it only took him a few minutes to realize he had walked the right way. Ten minutes later, he walked through his office doors, relief rushing through him.

"Took you long enough!" Teddy snapped as he floated down through the ceiling. "Your water princess is in my bath!"

If the ghost had a solid form, Sam was certain he would've heard a stomp of his foot.

"Were you using the bath?" Sam asked. As far as he knew, spirits couldn't bathe.

"Of course I wasn't. What kind of question is that?"

Teddy crossed his arms. "But I don't like to be reminded that I can't."

"Well, that is one of the few rooms not currently being used, so it'll have to do."

Sam wasn't going to back down. This was *his* building, no matter how many other beings thought they'd make it their home.

"What about the empty one?" Teddy pointed out.

"I'm trying to rent that one out, and I didn't want her to be by herself. She's in a strange environment and kidnappers have frightened her. Would you want to be alone?" Sam appealed.

"No." Teddy lost some of his ire. "I should go check on her."

"That's a great idea," Sam encouraged. "And why don't you help me play detective and ask her where she saw those other girls?"

Teddy nodded. "I could do that!"

He rushed through the ceiling quick enough to make Sam's head hurt.

"Clever," Bob said.

Sam hadn't noticed the vampire leaning against the wall.

"I thought so. Did you get anything further out of her?" Sam asked.

Bob shook his head. "She doesn't like me. Especially after I raced her here. She didn't like the speed or the fact that a vampire carried her. Vampires and naiads don't really get along."

"Why not?"

"Mostly because vampires drain people of life to exist, while naiads spend bits of their life energy to encourage nature. We have opposing philosophies," Bob explained.

"Oh, I hadn't thought of it like that." He hadn't really

thought of it at *all* if he wanted to be honest. The less he thought of Bob, the more he could concentrate. "I doubt that Teddy will have better luck, then, since he's already dead."

Sam headed to the stairway. He froze when his front door opened and Hartman entered the building, a slim man trailing behind him. Spotting the horns on his second guest, Sam decided that once again a paranormal creature had walked through his door. At least this one was cute.

"He's not cute!" Bob snapped.

"Didn't I tell you to stop listening to my thoughts?" Sam asked mildly.

The vampire got what he deserved if he dipped into Sam's brain without permission.

"Who are you?" the strange demon asked.

"I'm Sam Enderson. Who are you?" He held out his hand to shake, only to have Bob yank him away from the newcomer and into his arms.

A low growl poured from the vampire like a rough purr.

"Hello, Sam. I'm Danjal, but you can call me Dan." The demon winked at Sam, causing Hartman to growl.

"He can call you *leaving*," Bob countered.

"I'm sure there's a reason Hartman brought him here," Sam replied, scooting out of Bob's hold.

"Dan's an apothecary, but he also has a special skill set. He can look at the ribbon I gave you and see if any potions have been used on it. He might also be able to divine the location of my daughter." Hartman sounded pleased with his friend's abilities.

Dan appeared to want to kick Hartman.

Sam smiled at the demon. "We'd love any help we can get."

"I'd love to help you any way I can." Dan's long lashes dipped down. He looked at Sam flirtingly through them.

"I've never met a demon before." Sam stepped a little closer to push Bob's buttons.

"Do you want to pet my horns?" Dan asked.

The over-the-top leer almost made Sam laugh.

The low growl from Hartman had Sam taking a cautious step backward. "Maybe later," he said.

"Maybe never," Hartman snarled in a gravelly voice.

Dan spun around to face the wolf shifter. "Did you think I was waiting in my shop for you to return to me this entire time?"

Hartman's head snapped back as if he were slapped. "No… I… tried not to think about it. I'd hoped you'd find someone else," he admitted.

Sympathy for the wolf had Sam taking another cautious step backward. Apparently Hartman and Dan had a history between them. Harmless flirting wasn't so harmless when other people's feelings were involved. He didn't worry about Bob—the vampire could tell if Sam was serious or not—but Hartman appeared crushed.

"I might have a lead on your daughter—" Sam began.

A piercing scream cut through the air.

"Springlilly!" Sam ran up the stairs toward the bathroom.

The naiad sat curled up in one corner of the tub, cowering away from the ghost.

"What's wrong?" Sam asked, searching the room for any dangers. He didn't see anything to cause such a commotion.

"I-it's a ghost." Springlilly pointed a shaking finger at Teddy.

"It's Teddy. He's completely harmless," Sam assured her.

Teddy scowled. "Not completely."

"Ted!"

"I mean you no harm," Teddy finally agreed as he settled on the toilet seat.

Sam found that a bit disturbing since he could kind of see through the ghost. "He really doesn't. I asked him to question you about the girls. We're especially interested in the young shifter in the cage. This is her father." Sam pulled Hartman up front so Springlilly could get a good look at him.

"She has your eyes," she said after a long silence. "She was very brave. She didn't cry like the others. She bit one of the humans so they put her in a cage. I think they were afraid of her."

A proud smile crossed Hartman's face.

"How did you escape?" Sam asked.

"They were marching us to a new warehouse. I jumped in the water," she said, lifting her chin. "It was really cold and most people couldn't have survived it."

"But you could because you're one of its guardians," Hartman finished.

Springlilly nodded.

"So, the warehouse is by the docks?" Hartman asked.

"It was. They were using vans to move us away. I don't know where. They were careful not to talk in front of us." She turned watery eyes to Sam. "You'll help them, right?"

"Can you tell us how many girls there were?" Sam asked. He didn't like how professional the kidnapping operation appeared. On the plus side, if they didn't want the girls knowing anything, then they probably weren't going to kill them for their bones. At least not right away.

Springlilly licked her lips as she thought over her answer. "I think about ten. They kept us separated until they tried to move us, but that's how many I think there were. I'm sorry I'm not much help."

She began crying again.

Sam crouched down beside the tub. "Hey, it'll be all right. We're going to work on getting the girls back. After we have them safe and sound, I'll find a way to take you home. Okay?"

"O-okay. You won't forget and leave me here, will you?"

"No," Sam said firmly. "Teddy is here to tell me if anything goes wrong. He'll watch out for you like a guard."

Springlilly looked at the ghost with a pleased expression. She gave him a tentative smile. "I'll wait as long as you keep your promise."

Her eyes took on a silvery glow.

"I said I'd take you, and I will," Sam replied.

"It doesn't work, does it?" Springlilly asked no one in particular.

"It never does," Bob said sadly.

"What doesn't work?" Sam wondered why it always felt as if there were two or three conversations going on and he only understood half of one.

"Persuasive magic," Bob said. "I've decided that's why siren songs, vampire persuasion, and now naiad charms don't work on you. They're all persuasive magic, and you have the strongest sense of self I've ever seen. You can't be swayed because you genuinely can't understand why someone thinks they can change your mind."

"Fascinating," Dan said. "I've never heard such a thing. I'd love to study you some time."

"No!" Bob and Hartman said in unison.

Sam sighed. "Let's get a map and see where we can find some warehouses. Maybe if we can discover where they were, we can figure out where they're going. Thank you, Springlilly. I'll be back to talk to you soon."

He hoped he'd be able to give her good news, but with the smoothness of the smuggling operation, Sam suspected the job would be much harder than he'd originally anticipated.

Chapter Four

"ARE YOU SURE HE HAS THEM IN HERE?" SAM GRUNTED AS yet another box toppled against him.

"He had everything in here," Teddy answered immediately.

"Well, I can't find anything." Dirt and cobwebs covered Sam's clothes, not improving his mood at all. At least he'd sneaked in a quick shower before they'd begun their search, and his clothes were no longer sopping.

"Maybe over here?" Bob asked.

He hefted a folding table on its side, then slid it along the wall. Moving the table had revealed three more shelves close to the floor, every single one overflowing with papers. Sam was suddenly overwhelmed with all the piles of boxes and papers that his uncle had hoarded. Surely maps would be obvious—they had to be large and in those familiar round tubes he'd seen in the library. Unless they'd been folded, then they could've been tucked anywhere.

He'd found all kinds of information—except what he was looking for—including literature on werewolves. He'd dumped those papers into a box, then added a hastily scrawled "Werewolves—to keep" on the side with a half-chewed pencil. He didn't want to begin to think about who had chewed it.

"Aha!" Bob announced loudly.

Sam turned to face his lover, and hope built inside him that finally they'd found what they were looking for.

"I knew Byron Bennatyne was the murderer." Bob waved a folder in the air. "Everyone said it was his brother Jim, but I always said Byron looked shifty."

"Bob," Sam said patiently. "Are those maps?"

Bob glanced over at him, then down at the folder. Dan chuckled from over in his corner and Sam joined him. Bob looked so happy to have found whatever it was he had found, and the warmth of affection flooded Sam.

"Idiot vampire," Dan muttered.

Only then did Sam realize the demon wasn't so much chuckling as sniggering. Bob evidently thought the same. He narrowed his expression and stood to full height.

"You have a problem, demon?" he snapped.

Sam stood between them when Dan simply shrugged and smiled. The smile made him look more handsome if that was possible. Sam remembered Bob could listen to his thoughts and would have heard exactly what Sam was thinking. When he turned to look at his vampire, there was an empty space where he'd been standing. *Great.* Dealing with a pissed-off vampire was not on today's to-do list.

"Uh-oh," Teddy commented.

"Was it something I said?" Dan said innocently.

"They're not in the attic," Hartman announced from the door. "Who upset the vamp?" he added.

"He's angry that Sam finds me attractive," Dan said. He crossed his arms over his chest. "He wouldn't be the first since you left."

Hartman snarled his opinion on that, and Sam huffed in disbelief. It was like standing in some kind of paranormal kids' playground.

"Yes, you're attractive—"

Hartman growled and took a step toward him.

"Let me finish," Sam ordered. "I want to get one thing straight here. Dan, I am with Bob and there will be no more using me as a way to upset Hartman or Bob." There. He'd said his piece.

Dan looked momentarily chastised, then he smiled widely. "Who said it was only to upset them?"

Hartman was taking another menacing step toward Dan when Teddy broke into the conversation with a loud, "Found them!"

"Saved by the ghost," Sam muttered. Pushing his way through paperwork, he finally made his way to Teddy's side. He couldn't see maps.

"Where?"

"Behind those boxes," Teddy said. Then he waved his hands. "Ghost, remember? I can pass through but not move them."

Hartman was at Sam's side in an instant, his thoughts very obviously focused on Shelby again and not on his irrational jealousy of Dan teasing Sam.

"I wish I didn't have to rummage through boxes to get to them," Sam groaned as a falling case hit him on the head this time. He sat back on his ass in surprise when the boxes disappeared, only to reappear neatly stacked next to him, revealing the eight map tubes Teddy had found.

"You have magic?" Dan asked from behind him.

"No!" Sam snapped. "I don't. Someone help me." He didn't want to think about this being the second time today that he had wished for something and it had happened.

Dan squeezed in between him and Hartman, and used his shoulder to lift the shelf above the maps so that they were finally free from being hemmed in. Sam gathered five map tubes, Hartman the other three, then they went down to Sam's office. Bob was nowhere to be seen, but Sam resolved to track him down in a while. To be on the safe side, he thought about his affection for Bob in case his vampire was listening in to Radio-Sam's-Brain.

Hartman pushed the chairs on the visitor's side of the desk to one side before moving the small coffee table. Together they dusted off the maps and laid them out roughly in position to join the roads.

"Half of the human area is missing from here," Hartman observed.

Dan leaned over the map and traced a long, slim finger from one corner of a paper to the next. "These are paranormal maps. The focus is on clusters of types of beings. Look." He stabbed at a certain point that was identified with a red star, and another red star farther down. "Werewolves," he said carefully. "Blue for vampires. Green… I can't see what that is. There's no key on these."

Sam peered down at an area marked with green, then another colored mark and a sudden inspiration hit him. "Water spirits," he guessed. "Look how each green star is lakeside, or by a river. And the docks."

"Other paranormals are at the docks," Bob said from the door.

Sam glanced up at his vampire. "*Sorry*," he thought.

Bob nodded in response.

"The connection with water is a good suggestion, though," Hartman said quietly. "Springlilly said the girls were taken to the docks."

"Why was my uncle cataloging groups of species like this?" Sam asked no one in particular.

Bob was the one who answered as he crouched down next to Sam and placed a firm hand on Sam's shoulder. "Your uncle wasn't good like you, Sam. You've seen for yourself that he dealt with witches. Why else would he be approached for werewolf bones?"

Hartman made a strangled noise of horror and sat back on his knees. He looked utterly devastated and broken. Sam opened his mouth to say something, but Dan beat him to it.

"Everyone except Hartman needs to clear the room for at least an hour or two. I can't get a proper fix on the ribbon and the maps if I don't have space."

Sam scrambled to stand and Bob rose in one lithe move. Sam envied the vampire his ability to crouch and not have wobbly legs. Bob gripped his arm as Sam swayed, then tucked Sam under his shoulder. Together they left the room. As they left, Smudge wound his way through Sam's legs, then darted into the office before Sam could stop him. He couldn't imagine a cat would cause an issue to the divination so he pulled the door shut behind him.

"About earlier…" Sam started.

Bob pressed him back against the wall and held him there with the weight of his body. He lowered his mouth and kissed Sam thoroughly.

"As long as you stay with me," Bob growled, then pressed his lips to Sam's throat. He scraped his canines across sensitive skin, sending all of Sam's blood south to his cock, which swelled uncomfortably against his pants. "Then I won't have to kill him," Bob finished the sentence and the note of complete possession in his voice didn't annoy Sam. If anything, it caused a new level of desire and want to stream through him.

"We have an hour," Sam said softly.

Bob gripped his hand and led him upstairs to their room, stopping only to check in on Springlilly and Teddy, who were chatting about everything and nothing as if they were old friends.

An hour was all they needed.

HART MOVED from the kneeling position to sit back against the wall with his long legs crossed and his hands resting on his knees. Danjal couldn't help but look as Hart moved, and he felt a familiar desire rise in him, which he thought he had long since dealt with. Hart had been his past. The wolf shifter had chosen to mate with a female to continue the pack line instead of staying with Danjal, despite his previous declarations of love. Hart had walked out on him, claiming Danjal was a waste of his time, a cruel demon who had misled him and used magic to bind Hart to him.

Danjal turned back to the maps. He picked up the ribbon again. He heard the crying in his head, but he heard it secondhand, as if someone had already connected to the trace memory before him. He sensed Sam's scent and his touch and knew for certain Sam was in possession of skills that he didn't want to acknowledge. There was something very different about the human who was at the center of this. The black cat sat next to him and Danjal wished it wouldn't stare so damn hard.

"These maps are so old," he said. "Conducting a divination with materials this dated and contaminated by others is going to be difficult." He didn't know why he said this out loud. Maybe saying something would stop the damn cat staring at him, because the intense green eyes were distracting. *Understatement of the century.*

His head was muddled, and in the end, he stood and shooed the hissing feline out of the door before shutting it tight. The buzzing in his brain only grew louder as he regarded the maps laid out on the floor. He removed the four on the right, under the window. They were largely unmarked by paranormal stars and he felt nothing when he touched them. Only four remained.

Taking sage from his satchel, he lit the end of the bundle, then placed it in a silver bowl he'd brought for that very purpose. The scent of it would help him focus his thoughts.

"You're struggling, aren't you?" Hart asked tiredly.

Danjal turned to face his former lover sharply. Hart looked exhausted, and sadness seeped from every pore of him. Anger built inside Danjal.

"I asked you to stay because of your blood bond, but all you do is stare at me and I can't shut you out," he complained.

"Do you want me to leave?" Hart moved to all fours, then stood in a single motion. "If I'm stopping you from seeing, I can go. Call me when you need me."

Danjal pressed his fingers against his temples. He couldn't envision the paths he needed when his head was so full of Hart and anger and pain.

"You left me," he snapped. Accused. Demanded answers.

"Now? You want to do this now? With my daughter out there scared and crying?" Hart asked in disbelief.

"I can't do anything with you in my head," Danjal said forcefully. "You're in there all the time. Your smile, your lips, your cock in my mouth, pressing me into the bed and making me yours. Every second of the day, I can smell you and sense you. You're a mess in my head."

"I'm sorry," Hart said.

Danjal knew he was being honest about that. If anything, Hart was overwhelmed by his contriteness and his whole "I take the blame for everything" minotaur shit. Frustrated, Danjal marched around the maps to the werewolf who invaded his dreams and stole his sleep.

"Five years!" he shouted and stabbed a finger into Hart's chest. "You walked out five years ago, Hart. You told me I was nothing, that we had nothing, and still I don't believe you." He paused before adding sadly, "I think about you and you ruin me for every other relationship."

Hart blinked, then very pointedly gripped Danjal's finger.

"Dan, I had no choice. I did what I had to do. I hoped you'd find someone else."

"Who?" Danjal snapped. Hart's face fell. "I loved you, wolf. Teeth, claws, and your whole Alpha shit."

"We need to… don't we…? Shouldn't we… be…?" Hart wasn't able to get out a coherent point.

"I can't," Danjal snapped. "There's something I have to do."

"Your eyes," Hart said.

Danjal knew what Hart saw. The build-up of tension inside him made his eyes glow with the scarlet of his magic. It was something Hart had seen before, but only when they were making love.

"We're not doing this here," Hart said hurriedly.

"Tell me the real reason why you left," Danjal asked.

Hart paused. "Shelby. We need to focus on my daughter—"

"No. I can't focus and help anyone until my head is clear of you," Danjal interrupted.

"Stop it, Dan." Hart shoved him away, but Danjal pushed

back and suddenly they were so close that every huff of breath Hart exhaled was warm on Danjal's skin.

"Hart. Tell me," he pleaded. For so long, he'd wondered what he'd done to make Hart leave.

"I had to. My pack needs a strong line and I am their Alpha. I had to select a female to carry on my genes."

"I get that. I can understand why you had to do this, but you could have had both of us." Danjal's voice lowered to a whisper, then he did what he had wanted to do since Hart had walked back into his life. He kissed him.

At first, it was nothing more than a gentle touch of his lips on Hart's, then he paused. He waited to see what Hart would do.

"Dan..."

The word was a strangled plea, and in an instant, Hart had him scooped close with his hands on Danjal's waist, pulling him and plundering his mouth in a soul-searing kiss. The more they kissed, the more balanced Danjal became. Allowing Hart to touch him like this, reminding them both of what they'd had, was the only way Danjal could feel settled and able to help. In a smooth move, Hart turned them so it was Danjal against the wall, then it was him leading the kiss and asking for more. Danjal hadn't been this hard in months, or as needy, or as insane for another's touch. Inside him, the heart of a demon harbored resentment and anger, but only Hart could break the shell and allow Danjal to let love inside.

"You still want me," Danjal whimpered as Hart pressed his legs apart, then ground himself to Danjal.

"I will always want you," Hart growled. "Forever," he added. As if Danjal wasn't already certain of that.

"You left me," Danjal repeated. "You tried to make me think you hated me. I know you did. Why would you do that to us?"

Hart forced cold hands up and under Danjal's shirt. The touch of ice to fire was intoxicating, and he deepened the kiss and swallowed any words that Danjal wanted to say. They rubbed against each other, the hardness more than Danjal could handle. With the scent of Hart in his nose and the taste of him cracking his barriers, he was coming so hard he stopped breathing. When Hart stiffened and at the same time released their kiss, Danjal saw something in Hart's eyes. Something he had wanted to see since the day Hart had walked away.

Love.

They rested against each other as Hart used Danjal for support. He was heavy, but Danjal relished the weight of the only person he had ever loved.

"Because I couldn't share," Hart said. His voice had sounded weird—choked and rough with emotion. "I couldn't expect you to want me when I had a child."

"You know demons mate for life, Hart," Danjal said sadly. "When you left, I thought I was going to die."

"I do know that," Hart whispered. His breath brushed across Danjal's skin. "I died inside. And the only good thing that came out of it was Shelby." He lifted his face again, his eyes shiny with tears. "Find her for me, Dan."

Nodding, Danjal walked away as soon as Hart released him. Ignoring the dampness in his pants, he crouched down over the first map and scattered the herbs he needed across the length of it. Intoning an ancient divination, he watched as a small tongue of fire followed the herb path to the center of the map. His mind was so clear he could almost see Shelby. Hart moved to sit beside him, and together they watched as the small flame separated into three and wound its way over to each of the maps. Finally, one of the flames flashed brighter and Danjal pointed at the place on the map ringed with tiny flecks of blue fire.

"There. In the old shipbuilding docks, a long way past the new docks. But look at that star." He pointed to the fire. Right in the middle of the ring was a silver star.

"We don't know what silver means," Hartman said.

"Betrayal, deceit, hate. Sirens."

Chapter Five

Bob pinned Sam to the mattress, his entire body aligned with Sam's. A sigh poured out of Sam at the perfect weight of the vampire pressing against him. He'd never had the bone-deep pleasure of knowing his lover would mesh up with his needs so perfectly before. A man who could read his mind while making love never had any wrong moves. The usual awkwardness and fumbling about didn't exist since Bob could anticipate Sam's needs. He just wished the rest of the time his lover would stay out of his head.

Bob smiled. "But I love visiting your mind," he purred. "It tells me much nicer things than your mouth."

Sam scowled. "Behave or you won't get to do anything with my mouth despite what lies my mind might tell you."

A hard kiss had Sam rethinking his stance. He wound his fingers through Bob's hair just because he could. Of all the things he missed about having a steady lover, the freedom to touch another person was the biggest.

"Stop thinking of past lovers when I'm with you. I should be all you think of." Bob's eyes took on a red tinge.

"Sorry." Sam agreed with Bob's statement. If he could

read minds, he wouldn't want to know his lover was thinking of someone else while they had sex.

He tilted his chin up for another kiss. Bob liked to take control. Most of the time, Sam fought him for dominance, but not today. This time he gave in to Bob's need to be in charge, letting the vampire reaffirm their connection and soothe Bob's wilder nature.

Sinking into the embrace, he relaxed beneath Bob's hard body, allowing the vampire to call the shots. So far, there'd been a lot of petting and not much action, considering they were both naked.

"You can start any time now," Sam prodded.

"I have started." Bob smiled down at him, exposing full fangs. "I'm taking things slowly."

"You know I have a finite amount of time on this planet, right? I'm not going to be here two hundred years from now when you finally decide you're ready to fuck." Sam raised an eyebrow at Bob. How much more clearly did he need to spell out his wishes? Did Bob need a diagram? Maybe sock puppets?

"I don't think puppets are necessary," Bob drawled. He slid to Sam's right, allowing more air into Sam's lungs. Bob wrapped a tight fist around Sam's erection, making Sam's back bow from the sensation.

"Oh, damn," Sam whispered.

"That better, love?" Bob asked. His tone was calm, but his eyes sparkled with mischief.

"Much." Sam gave in and let the gasp escape his lips. "More."

"No. I want to be inside you when you come." Bob removed his hand.

Sam thought hard about different ways to murder a vampire.

Bob laughed. "That's not very nice when I'm about to send you to paradise."

"You need to stop reading trashy romances," Sam muttered. "Paradise indeed."

Bob slid his big hands along Sam's body, mapping his skin with a slow intensity as if he had a geography lesson the next day and had to pass with flying colors.

"I thought we agreed to speed things up." Sam wiggled beneath Bob's fingers, eager to progress from touching to fucking.

"Patience," Bob teased.

Sam growled. He rolled over and pinned the vampire to the bed.

Bob's smile reflected in his eyes. For a second, Sam was caught in their beauty.

He pressed a hard kiss to Bob's lips, until he knew other paranormals would smell his scent on the vampire.

"Staking your claim?" Bob's laugh had a loud joyous sound Sam had never heard from him before.

"Absolutely." Sam might not be sure about his relationship with a vampire, but he didn't want anyone else to touch him either.

"I'm yours, babe. You don't have to worry about that." Bob rolled them back over until he pressed Sam against the mattress, their cocks rubbing together in a sticky, pre-cum-smeared kiss.

From the nightstand, Bob grabbed the lube, which Sam hadn't bothered to put away last time. He cursed with impatience when the cap didn't come off right away. He yanked off the top, and a blob squirted out of the container, landing with a splat on Sam's stomach.

Sam burst into laughter. "I think it's supposed to be used a little lower."

Bob grinned. He slid his fingers through the puddle, and thrusting his hands under Sam's ass, he pressed the first finger inside, then paused. "Thanks for the tip," he murmured.

"Another one," Sam demanded. His infuriating lover simply withdrew, then moved back in.

"Two?" he asked innocently. A second finger joined the first, then a third. "Three? Four?" He stole a heated kiss and Sam whined in his throat. "Could you take more?" he asked against Sam's lips.

"More," Sam said simply.

Bob chuckled darkly, then plunged in further until he rubbed Sam's prostate.

Sam groaned and his body instinctively pushed down for more friction. He could come from this—the insistent push of Bob's fingers inside him and his lips so close.

"I think I found the spot."

"Y-you found the spot," Sam concurred. It was difficult to actually talk at this point and he stammered as he replied.

"Good." Bob withdrew, took another scoop of lube with his fingers and spread it across his own cock. "You're beautiful. My Sam." The words washed over Sam, and he waited. Once he had everything slicked how he wanted, Bob lifted Sam's ass with his big hands, lined up his erection, and pressed inside.

"Oh, right there." A low crooning sound poured out of Sam. His body became nothing but sensation when Bob set up a bone-rattling rhythm.

"Hold on to the bed," Bob ordered. Sam did as he was told. Reaching up over his head, he closed his hands around the metal headboard and grabbed on for dear life.

"Bob, please," he begged.

"Don't move," Bob said as he shifted a little to change the

angle. Sparks burst behind Sam's eyes, and he closed them at the overwhelming pleasure. Groans, curses, and finally a shout of completion formed Sam's world. His orgasm pulled his balls tight, and he used the extra leverage of his hands on the headboard to push himself down so Bob was impossibly deep.

Bob grunted above him, releasing his seed deep inside Sam, and kept moving until finally Sam protested weakly. What this vampire could do with his cock was not something he could begin to describe, but it always left him boneless. Added to that the waves of satisfaction pouring off the vampire almost sent Sam to sleep. He sighed as Bob softened and slid out of him, then rolled onto his back to settle Sam more fully next to his body.

Sam took slow deep breaths, trying to get oxygen back into his lungs.

Soft kisses landed on the top of his head. For a blood-sucking creature, Bob was really quite affectionate.

Something occurred to Sam, and he frowned. "Do vampires have live sperm?"

"You think of the strangest things after you come," Bob replied. "Yes, I have sperm. How do you think vampires come into being?"

Sam shrugged. "I don't know a lot about vamps."

"Well, you should learn. I'm not going anywhere. Ever. If you don't let me extend your life, I'll be here until you die," Bob vowed.

The wave of despair rushing from the vampire had Sam rubbing Bob's chest. "Hey, it'll be all right." Sam tilted his head. "Bite me," he demanded, knowing how to distract the vamp.

He almost expected Bob to talk it over or argue or say

something. Instead, he gripped Sam's hair in a tight hold and plunged his fangs into Sam's exposed neck.

If Bob hadn't used such a strong grip, Sam might have jerked away and ripped out his jugular. Instead, he made loud noises he would deny to the day he died. Lust ripped through him as if he had been jolted with an electric prod.

Sam slid his own fingers deep into Bob's hair to keep him there. From the noises the vampire made, Sam had no doubts Bob was enjoying his taste.

After an eternity of pleasure flooding him, Bob slid his fangs out of Sam's neck and lapped at bite mark. "I've marked you again." Satisfaction filled Bob's voice as though he'd received everything he ever wanted wrapped with a nice bright bow. Sam felt energized and touched his fingers to the site of the wound. There was an uneven feel to the skin, and at that moment, he wished desperately that the mark would never leave him.

"You already knew I was yours," Sam replied.

Bob smiled. "And now everyone else will know it too."

Shaking his head, Sam climbed out of bed. "Let's go take a shower. We don't want to smell like sex when the werewolf comes to find us."

Bob nodded. "Good point."

"IT'S SIRENS."

Sam looked up when Hartman entered his office.

"What? I thought they were humans," Sam said. He ran his fingers through his still-damp hair.

Hartman sniffed the air. "I hope you weren't bored while we searched for the kidnappers."

"We found a way to entertain ourselves," Bob drawled

from his chair by the window. He didn't look the least put out by Hartman's statement, and he certainly didn't blush like Sam.

Sam cleared his throat. "Anyway. What makes you think it was sirens that took the girls? The naiad thought they were humans."

"Who said it can't be both?" Dan asked. "They aren't mutually exclusive. Your human uncle did a lot of work for paranormals. There's no saying humans can't be hired to do the sirens' dirty work."

Sam winced as he thought over what kind of work his uncle had actually been doing. "You think these humans are working for the sirens?"

Dan nodded. "If the humans are kidnapping girls and the sirens are involved, I'd bet money that the humans were hired by them."

"Why? What would sirens want with little girls? From the sounds of it, they are all different types of paranormals." A chill went through Sam. "How is their reproduction?"

"Low." Dan paled. "Are you thinking they are getting these girls for breeding purposes? But they are all so young."

"Wouldn't it be better to have time to brainwash them before breeding them?" Sam asked. His stomach threatened to revolt over the thought of what these young girls were going through.

"My poor baby," Hartman said. He sat down abruptly as if his knees had collapsed out from beneath him.

Sam watched with interest when Dan knelt beside Hartman's chair, offering a comforting touch on his arm.

"On the plus side, they won't want to hurt her," Sam offered. He sucked at the comfort thing. He always felt more awkward than wise.

Hartman looked up at him, hope growing in his eyes.

"That's true. They wouldn't want to harm them if they are planning on keeping them long term."

Sam nodded encouragingly. "We need to find out where they're hiding the kids. They can't take them underwater so they've got to have a home on dry land they plan to house them in. If there are almost a dozen kids, then they'll need some place relatively large. We need to concentrate on large buildings by the water that have recently been purchased or were granted permits for major renovations."

"Good thinking," Bob said.

"I've got to get back to my shop. But please let me know if I can help anymore," Dan said. He traced a light touch across Hartman's hair with his fingers before turning to leave.

Hartman focused on Sam. "Tell me when you have anything more and we'll go straight away." Then he grabbed Dan's wrist before the demon took more one step away. "I'll come with you, Dan. We need to talk."

Dan opened his mouth, and Sam was certain the demon would object. Instead, Dan's mouth snapped shut, and he nodded. "Okay, Hart. I guess we do have a few things to discuss."

From Hartman's expression, it didn't look like talking was on his agenda. "Let me know when you find anything out," he said.

"I'll go talk to Mikhail," Bob said.

The look he gave Sam should've burned him to his toes. Memories of their encounter earlier flashed like a ball of lightning through his body. Bob jerked in his seat.

Sam laughed.

"I'll make you pay for that later," Bob warned.

His tone told Sam he should look forward to the evening.

After everyone had vacated, Sam leaned back in his chair and let out a deep breath. He was way over his head and quickly drowning. What the hell was he thinking? Maybe he could sell the building and haul his human ass back to the normal world. A place where his desk ornaments didn't come alive and his lover couldn't read his mind.

"I wish no one could read my mind," Sam muttered. The idea of someone flipping through his thoughts still freaked him out.

A brief knock sounded on his office door, then Mikhail entered.

"Oh, hey, Bob was looking for you," Sam said.

Mikhail paused in the doorway, a frown crossing his handsome face. "What did you do now?"

"What do you mean what did I do? I'm trying to find out what the sirens are up to." Sam pulled his laptop from where he had tucked it into his desk.

"You have a computer?" Mikhail asked in disbelief.

"Yes, Mikhail. Why wouldn't I have a computer?" Sam had had enough with magic and paranormals. Frankly, he just wanted some peace and quiet, with maybe a simple cheating spouse case.

Mikhail shrugged and draped himself across the guest chair. "I can ask around, but I doubt the sirens will tell me anything. They hate me since I won't help them with their little projects."

"What kind of projects?" Sam asked.

"Last I checked, they were trying to take over the waterways and control the trade routes," Mikhail said. He narrowed his eyes at Sam. "Why can't I read you?"

"What do you mean read me?" Sam paused. "You mean read my mind?"

"Yes. It's like you're blocked or something now."

"Good. I don't like people inside anyway," Sam said firmly.

He pulled up company records to see if anything triggered an alert. A couple of buildings came up as new acquisitions, and three were having major remodels done. He printed up a list with the addresses.

Hopefully, one of them would pan out.

"Sam, there you are," said a voice Sam had hoped to never hear again.

Sam scowled. "What are you doing here, Josh?"

Now he had ex-boyfriends walking through the front door.

Things had reached a new level of weird.

Chapter Six

JOSH LOOKED AS GOOD AS SAM REMEMBERED. A SHADE OVER six foot, he had a runner's build and soft blond hair. His eyes were a pale gray that Sam himself had once described as magical. He had perfect teeth and an even more perfect smile, but that was the shell. Tall, blond, and sexy had nothing Sam wanted anymore.

"I found this address in some papers. I wanted to see you," Josh said.

"I don't want to talk to you," Sam said, irritated. The last thing he needed was a heart-to-heart with the guy who had cheated on him.

Josh stepped farther into the room, and Mikhail immediately moved between Sam and his ex. Evidently Sam's lack of enthusiasm for Josh was being picked up by Mikhail, despite the vampire not being able to get a read on him.

"Can I help you?" Mikhail asked firmly.

Josh leaned around Mikhail. "I'm here for Sam."

"Go away, Josh," Sam said.

"I don't think Sam wants to see you," Mikhail said. He

glanced over his shoulder at Sam and quirked his eyebrow. He was looking to Sam for a decision.

Sam sighed noisily. There was absolutely nothing to be gained here by Mikhail being a barrier between him and Josh.

Sam crossed his arms over his chest. "It's okay. I can deal with him, Mikhail."

"I'll tell Bob he's here," Mikhail said.

Great. Bob and the ex. That was not exactly what Sam wanted at this moment. He had leads to follow up on.

"Give me at least a few minutes," Sam said.

Mikhail brushed past Josh and left the room, no doubt directly on his way to Bob. Actually, Sam couldn't understand why Bob hadn't turned up on his own. Surely Josh arriving and the shock Sam had felt at his arrival should have been enough to bring his jealous lover running from wherever he was.

"What do you want, Josh?" Sam asked. Maybe if he found out why Josh had showed up, he could get him moving away that much quicker.

"To say I'm sorry—" Josh began.

"Okay, you've done that. Now you can go. I have work to do."

Josh didn't reply immediately. He glanced around the room, and his gaze settled on Smudge. The cat stared at him before switching his gaze to Sam.

"Nice cat," Josh offered lamely. He extended a hand to pet Smudge, but the cat arched his back and hissed. Josh snatched his hand back. "Is he not a friendly cat then?" Josh asked.

Sam scooped Smudge up into his arms. "He's a very friendly cat." As if to prove his point, Smudge purred and rubbed his nose against Sam's face before climbing and settling around his neck.

"Anyway," Josh started, "things ended quite awkwardly, and I wanted to clear the air."

"Awkwardly?" Sam replied. "I'm confused. Finding you balls deep in my best friend when you thought I was at work is simply awkward?"

"Sam—"

"What was awkward?" Sam interrupted. "Me finding you? You fucking Trent?"

"Sam—"

"I think you need to leave," Sam said firmly. He'd had enough of Josh's bullshit to last a lifetime. Every day, Josh had found a way to belittle Sam, to undermine his confidence and his enthusiasm, and Sam hadn't realized what was happening until it had all finished. He wasn't that man anymore who needed reassurance from a two-timing asshole.

"Sam. Trent, sleeping with him. It meant nothing to me," Josh said, as if that made it all better.

"No, I think you'll find I meant nothing to you," Sam corrected him.

"It only happened a few times," Josh retorted.

"A few? I thought it was once. That's what you said before."

"Well, Trent was willing and you were never home." Josh's voice had taken on a distinct whine, and that along with the crap Josh was laying on him irritated Sam.

"Someone needed to earn money to pay the bills. We weren't going to be eating on a writer's earnings, were we?" Sam couldn't help the condescension in his voice, but hell, he'd supported Josh since college and through four years of him finding the muse to get his first book written.

"You weren't home. Trent was there—"

"Yes, I know. He was willing. So you said." Sam had given up on his friendship with Trent—despite having known the man since he was three—the minute he'd found Trent on the bottom of a betraying, lying heap.

"He misses you. We both do," Josh said.

The door Mikhail had shut flung open and Bob made a grand and very growly entrance.

"Sam? Mikhail said you had company and I couldn't hear you…" His voice trailed away. He stepped around Josh and took up Mikhail's recently abandoned position of brick wall. Sam didn't need a protector. He needed his lover to give a life-affirming PDA.

Stepping forward, Sam snaked an arm around the immobile vampire. With a press of his shoulder, he encouraged Bob's arm around his back and Smudge jumped off him, onto the desk next to the gargoyle.

Let's make this good… Sam thought. He glanced up at Bob, who didn't move a muscle and clearly had not heard Sam's thoughts at all.

"This is Bob," Sam said. "Bob, this is Josh. Someone I knew once."

"His boyfriend," Josh said and extended his hand in welcome.

Bob snarled and his fangs flashed dangerously. Josh quickly withdrew his hand and stumbled back a step.

"Ex-boyfriend," Sam summarized. "Bob is my partner now."

Josh looked Bob up and down and frowned.

"You don't *do* paranormals," he observed. "You told me that paranormals were nothing more than monsters made real, yet here you are sleeping with a vamp?" Josh was still frowning, then suddenly his expression cleared. "Shit, Sam. You're working in an area you vowed never to visit again, with animals and monsters, and now you're doing what?

Sleeping with a blood-sucking bat? Hell, Sam, he has to be using glamor to convince you."

Bob stiffened and Sam tightened his hold on Bob's shirt. This could end a few ways, but every way was bloody.

"No one is using their glamor to convince me to do anything," Sam said wearily.

"Or a spell or something," Josh persisted.

"I love Bob. He's my lover and my partner and you need to leave."

"I'll find a way to break it," Josh said hurriedly. "Then you could come back."

"Back? To you?" Sam asked in surprise.

Why would Josh think he'd ever take him back?

"Why not? We're good together, Sam." Josh took a step toward them, and Sam was relieved when Bob stayed relaxed and in control.

"Have you run out of money? Why do you suddenly want me back in your life?" Sam knew there had to be an explanation he was missing in this entire encounter.

"Trent left me," Josh said, a little desperately.

Okay, so that statement was a killer. He hadn't realized that Josh had taken up with Trent after the great reveal. That hurt. Sam pushed down the instant temper that threatened to spill over and cause him to let Bob physically remove Josh from the office.

"So you lost his paycheck? Is that what this visit is for?"

"I think you need to take yourself out of the building," Bob muttered.

"It speaks," Josh said derisively.

Bob hissed in anger, and Josh, suddenly scared, stumbled back. When he was in the room, he appeared to regain some of his bravado.

"Just you wait, bat, I'll find a way to break your glamor.

I'll rescue Sam, and we'll be together again." He turned on his heel and left the house at a near run.

Bob made no move to follow him. Instead, he turned Sam in his arms and pulled him close.

"I can't hear you," Bob said softly. "I came in here and your lover was here—"

"Ex-lover," Sam said firmly.

"And I couldn't listen to your thoughts. That only happens when relationships end. The trauma of it causes the connection to stop. I wanted to kill him."

"I'm glad you didn't."

"I was going to," Bob said. He gathered Sam even tighter, "then you said…"

Sam guessed where this was going. "That I love you? I've said it before. I wasn't lying."

"I know."

"I do love you."

"I know."

"That's it? I know. Is that all I get?" Sam asked.

"It stopped me killing him," Bob said. "Do you think he'll try and find a way to hurt what we have?" Bob sounded worried, which wasn't like him.

Sam was quick to reassure him. "You've never been able to use your glamor on me. He can't hurt us by breaking something that doesn't exist." Sam paused. "You changed the subject," he said gently.

Bob pulled back and buried his hands in Sam's hair. They kissed deeply, and Bob sighed into the embrace. He pulled back and Sam chased for more kisses, but Bob stopped the motion.

"I love you too, Sam Enderson. So why can I not hear you anymore?"

Sam shook his head. He had no idea. It wasn't as if he had

wished that no one could get in his head. Wait. Hell. That is exactly what he had done without meaning to. First, the magically appearing light, then the maps, and now he had blocked Bob from his thoughts. What the hell was going on with him?

"I may need to see someone about a small wish infection," Sam said carefully.

Bob sighed against him.

"I knew it," he said. "You wished me out of your thoughts." His voice dripped with hurt.

"Only because sometimes it's like I have nowhere I can go where I am just myself."

"You should have said. There are ways you can block your thoughts from reaching me if you want them secret. Like at birthdays." Bob had added the last part with a purely hopeful tone, and Sam couldn't help but laugh.

Birthdays?

"Do you celebrate your birthday anymore?" Sam asked.

Bob shrugged. "Sure, but I don't bother with the candles. I could burn the entire house down."

Sam almost asked Bob his age but decided there were some things he didn't want to know.

"I wish you could listen to my thoughts again," Sam said to no one in particular, paying attention to the wording he used. He'd seen films with wishing powers in them before and they'd never ended well.

Bob tilted his head.

"Think something," he ordered.

Bossy man, Sam thought.

Bob smiled, then narrowed his eyes. "I heard that."

Sam moved to the table. "I have addresses. Where did Hartman and Dan go?"

Bob glanced out of the front window. "Last I saw, they disappeared out the front door to 'talk'."

"We need to find them. If they're serious about covering some ground in the search, then we need to decide who goes where."

THEY HAD WALKED QUITE a distance before Dan decided to talk. Hartman had a lot to say himself, but his instinct was to wait and let Dan clear the air of what he wanted to say first. They'd reached the end of the road and Dan stopped to sit on the short wall running the entire length of a vast green space.

Hartman's phone rang. He looked at its readout, then shoved it back into his pocket. He didn't want to talk to Alec. His brother-in-law couldn't help. Hell, he'd probably take Constance's side.

"Back there… was…" Dan said softly.

"Wrong?" Hartman offered dejectedly.

Dan looked up at him with a frown marring his face.

"Unexpected," he said firmly.

"Oh." Unexpected was not the word Hartman would have used, but he didn't want to use the word wrong either. He didn't think what they had between them was wrong. He never had. Pack pressure had split them apart and that had only been because tradition and superstition held the Hartman pack in its thrall.

"You're in my head all the time," Dan said simply. "I don't like it."

"So you said," Hartman agreed. "I don't mean to be." *Lame response.*

"It makes what I do very hard. That is why I needed to…" He waved a hand between them.

Hartman guessed Dan was indicating the wholly satisfying getting-off that had happened earlier.

"Yeah." Hartman sat down next to Dan.

"Doesn't mean I feel anything for you anymore." Dan half turned to face him. "It was necessary, but it will never happen again."

Hartman sighed inwardly. He had expected Dan to say that. Hell, he needed to stay away from Dan before he hurt him again. Things in his pack were too unsettled to test how they'd take his relationship with a demon. He knew that. Still, the knowledge of what he *should* do didn't change what he *wanted* to do. He half turned as well so that they were face to face. Gripping one of Dan's warm hands, he took a deep breath and began.

"I always imagined the things I would say to you if I ever had you near me again. The apologies I would make, the things I said to you that I would take back. What happened to us was wrong. I loved you so much. But… a pack Alpha has responsibilities that go way beyond what we had."

He wouldn't give Shelby up for the world… but the loss of Dan had almost killed him.

"Is this going to be a wolf history lesson?" Dan asked angrily. He attempted to pull his hand away, but Hartman gripped it tighter. Dan's eyes glowed red for a moment, and Hartman began to talk again before Dan went full-on demon.

"No. You have to listen to me—" Hartman insisted. He was going to have his say, then Dan could ditch him for good, but first he would tell Dan what was on his mind.

"I don't have to do anything."

"I was wrong. Okay?" Hartman was shouting, and he couldn't stop himself. "I admit it. I put my pack before my heart, and I will never be the same again. The only thing left in my life now that makes sense is Shelby, and I'm losing her too."

Dan's eyes brightened, and he tilted his head in question.

"The worst of it," Dan began. "Is that I understand. Instinct and the survival of your pack was greater than what we had."

Hartman shook his head, but Dan held up his free hand to stop Hartman from saying anything.

"Listen to me, Hart. I don't really blame you for the choices you made, which were forced onto you. I don't. But I selfishly wanted more from the lover who said he would die without me."

"I'm sorry," Hartman offered.

"Don't be sorry. Tell me what happened. I know the rumors, but wolves can be so isolated."

"I didn't produce a legitimate heir. Shelby is a girl, clearly. They're pushing me to re-marry another she-wolf and try for a male. I don't want to." Hartman paused for a while. He recalled the arguments that were so intense and loud in the pack. "You know I was working toward pack equality, and loving my girl was seen as wrong. We were never together, not in the real sense of the word, Constance and me. I was only with her a couple of times, enough to do the right thing. Once Shelby was old enough to understand her mother didn't really care for her, I divorced her. I didn't want her near my daughter. I still think she had something to do with Shelby's disappearance, but no one will listen to me. You have to believe me, Dan, I wanted to come back home."

"Home? Weren't you on pack lands anyway?" Dan frowned at him.

"Back to you, you're home. I was desperate for you, but

Everett told me you'd left. I realized you didn't want me, and I didn't blame you. There was no chance for us."

"I was away in London."

"He said you left for a long trip. I took that as a sign we were over."

"You broke my heart." Dan closed his eyes, then leaned forward.

Hartman mirrored the move until they rested their foreheads together.

"Can I ever make it right?" Hartman whispered.

"Do you want to?" Dan asked. He sounded so damn sad.

"More than you'll know. After we find Shelby, maybe we could give it a go? Meet up, talk, you could meet Shelby. We could be friends at least?" Hartman held hope in his heart that Dan would say yes.

"I can do that," Dan agreed.

They sat in silence for a little while longer, still as close as they could be and clutching hands. The feeling grounded Hartman, and he wondered if Dan felt the same.

"What do you think she is doing now?"

"Shelby?"

Grief carved through him. He wanted his daughter back. He wanted to know who had taken her and why. "Do you think she's still alive?" he asked. He wasn't expecting an answer, but Dan gave him one anyway.

"Yes," he said.

Just one word. But that one syllable held so much conviction that Hartman felt a lightness in him that he hadn't had before. Dan always had that effect on him.

"Hartman! Danjal! We have our first location!" Bob shouted.

Hartman looked up at the approaching vampire and knew this was it. They would find Shelby one way or another. Sam was following at a more sedate pace but just as intense in his concentration.

"I have four locations along the docks that could be possible sites," he announced.

"We should split up," Dan said firmly.

Sam handed over a sheet of paper with the details on it for two warehouses in mid-renovation. "Keep in touch," Sam said. Hartman nodded. He wanted to know the minute Shelby was found alive.

He couldn't bring himself to contemplate her being found dead.

Chapter Seven

Sam headed for the first warehouse with Bob tight on his heels. They'd decided to break into pairs. Sam and Bob, Hartman and Dan—each pair took two warehouses and each agreed to call the other pair if they found anything at all.

Gazing around, Sam didn't see any signs of life, paranormal or plain feathered. Nothing.

"Does it seem too quiet to you?" Sam asked Bob.

"Yes. Stay behind me," the vampire insisted, walking in front.

Sam pulled out his multi-weapon, hoping he wouldn't have to use it.

However, he wasn't going to hide behind his lover. That certainly wasn't the way to build up his reputation as a detective—hiding behind Bob while he shook in his shadow.

Sam straightened his shoulders and kept his weapon at the ready, scanning the area. The silence unnerved him. How could an entire dock have nothing there? Where were the workers, the boats…? Hell, where were the fucking seagulls?

They were the only people in the entire area.

"Do you sense anyone?" Sam asked. He'd kept his voice low in case something paranormal stalked about.

Bob shook his head, not turning around from his perusal of the area. "If there is, they'll be in one of the buildings. No one is out here, that's for sure."

Sam relaxed a bit, pleased he wasn't the only one who thought so.

"If they were here, they left," Bob said finally.

Sam sighed. "Let's go check out that warehouse." He nodded toward a building several yards away that appeared to be put together with metal flashing and bubble gum. Rust ate holes in several places and the few windows Sam could see were shattered. An emanation of despair oozed from the warehouse as if even the structure had given up all hope.

He desperately prayed they weren't there. As much as he wanted to find the children, this location practically radiated the promise that he wouldn't find any of them alive.

Bob lifted his head to the breeze. "My senses aren't as good as a shifter's nose, but I don't smell anyone. If someone was here, they left a while ago."

"If they were here, they might have left some clues." Empty, the warehouse might tip them off to where the kids had been moved. If they couldn't find anything, they'd move on to the second address on their list.

Ready for anything, Sam rushed to keep up with the vampire as Bob approached the metallic structure.

Bob paused before pulling on the door, which opened with suspicious ease. It didn't squeal on its hinges like its appearance implied it should. Anticipation tingled up Sam's spine. Someone had been there.

After Bob motioned him forward, Sam walked carefully through the doorway. He didn't want to hide behind his vampire lover, but he wasn't an idiot who rushed through dark doorways when he didn't know what might be hiding on the other side either.

Sticking close to the wall, Sam surveyed the interior.

It was a large empty area with little else but trash and a whole lot of space. Spots of oil dotted the floor as if machinery had once rested there, other than that, the building was clear.

"Smell anything?" Sam asked.

"No. Nothing." Bob scowled in the gloomy interior. Most of the windows were boarded over, and there was no chance of letting sunlight in to brighten the space.

Sam stopped for a minute, startled that he could see so well. When had he started to be able to see in near dark?

"Um, let's go back outside." Unsettled, Sam turned to leave.

"It's because we're mates," Bob said.

"What?" Sam squinted against the sudden brilliance of the sun as they stepped outside.

"It's why you can see better in the dark. You are seeing like me," Bob replied.

"Oh. Am I going to start craving blood?" Sam didn't know how he felt about this latest strangeness in his life. Every day seemed to bring something weirder.

Bob laughed, and Sam resisted the urge to punch him. "No. You aren't turning into a vampire, but you are going to be able to see better and will probably get stronger. Other than that, I doubt you'll have any other tendencies."

Sam sighed. "But don't you see? Not wanting to mix with paranormals doesn't mean I envy them and want to be one. I just want to be human."

Why did he keep finding himself saying that phrase? It was as though he thought if he said it enough, he'd go back to being the uninformed normal he used to be. It was too late to be what he had been before. Now he had to move forward to whatever waited for him. He wouldn't give up Bob, even if it meant going back to fully human.

"It won't, you know," Bob said.

"Won't what?" As the words left Sam's mouth, he knew what Bob had meant.

Bob stepped forward and settled his hands on Sam's waist, holding him close enough that he could feel the heat from the vampire's body.

"If you dump me—which I won't let you do—we will still be linked. We've bonded. You'll belong to me until the end of time." The conviction in Bob's voice twisted Sam's gut.

"I did want a faithful boyfriend," Sam replied weakly. How could you argue with anyone who only wanted to love you forever?

Sam rested his head on Bob's shoulder, pulling his lover close. For a long moment, they stood there with Sam inhaling Bob's scent and enjoying the minute of peace.

"We need to find the girls," Sam said, reluctantly pulling away.

"Yeah, I'll call Hartman and tell him this location is a bust."

Sam nodded. "Good."

Restless, Sam walked to the edge of the pier. Even though they hadn't seen anything in the old warehouse, he still found the entire situation strange. Even the seagulls and pigeons had abandoned this place.

Looking into the dark water, Sam let out a sigh. "I wish I knew where the girls were," he whispered.

A glow sparkled in the water. First a subtle light that Sam brushed away as sunshine reflecting on the waves, but then became a brighter glow that didn't belong.

Crouching down, Sam could just make out the scene.

Another building, this one made of peeling white wood, appeared on the water's surface as if a photo had fallen into the sea. Young girls tied together by rope sat in little sad clusters like withering grapes. Along the back wall, he could see some cages stacked together. Appalled, Sam realized a few figures moved in the metal traps.

He wondered if Shelby was one of them.

Trying to get every detail he could, Sam scanned the size of the structure. From the height of the roof, it was a place not unlike the one they had just inspected despite the different construction. Sam was about to give up gathering any additional clues when the image shifted a few feet to the right and Sam saw a row of canoes on a large frame along a wall.

"They're in a boathouse," Sam muttered.

"What's that?" Bob asked.

The picture shattered as Sam's attention wavered.

"My wish powers that the fae gave me. I wished to know where the girls were, and they appeared. It looks like they are kept in a boathouse with white paint not in particularly good condition."

"Hmm, probably more a boat construction place than a yacht club then," Bob mused.

Sam returned his gaze to the water and gasped. Half a dozen faces looked back up at him.

Sirens.

"Oh shit, Sam, run!" Bob grabbed Sam's arm and yanked him away from the edge of the pier as hands slapped against the side and sirens began to leave the sea.

Now he knew why there weren't any other beings on the docks. They had all fled.

The wooden walkway trembled beneath their feet. How many were there? Sam stepped carefully back, not willing to turn around and leave himself vulnerable to attack. The weapon shook in his hand, as he didn't know where to point it. Bob's tight grip on Sam's arm would undoubtedly leave vivid bruises in the morning, but Sam couldn't make himself care right at that moment.

If they got out of this alive, they could worry about injuries then.

"Sam, remember I love you," Bob said as the wet sirens continued to come in the same direction they were running. Damn things moved fast.

"We're going to get out of this," Sam said. He refused to consider any other option. They were going to escape this and move onto less stressful endeavors like flame swallowing or chainsaw juggling.

"You have interfered too much, Samuel Enderson," the leader of the group of sirens said. "The queen has issued your death warrant, and I've volunteered to collect your head."

Her long hair had a sea-green cast and her almond-shaped eyes could have been beautiful with their coral glow. Problem was she looked to be contemplating the best way to sever Sam's neck.

Sam shot her in the leg.

Screaming, she tumbled to the wooden planks.

The others stepped over her as if she were another piece of seaweed to ignore. Sam wondered if this species completely lacked compassion.

"Where are the girls?" Sam asked the group at large.

There were only five of them remaining. He was confident that with Bob's help, together they could take care of the rest of them.

A male siren in the front gave a cold smirk. "You won't need to worry about that after you're dead."

"You're Sturgeon," Sam said. He remembered the siren from the other day.

"Knowing my name won't save your life," the siren sneered.

Sam shot him in the foot. He screamed but continued his approach.

"I will make you pay for that injury. You have no idea what you are doing. We have fought too hard to find the perfect matches to let you ruin it for us." Sturgeon limped forward, but the determination and hatred in his eyes made him appear more formidable than a hundred vamps.

The ground shook beneath them. To Sam's horror, fingers were rising through the planks. The sea around the boathouse was filled with more sirens—they were calling, singing, their voices meshing into one loud sound.

Bob toppled to the pier, his eyes glazed and tears trickling from the edges.

"Stop it," Sam snapped. "You're torturing him."

To Sam's surprise, they did. The ensuing silence disturbed him more than the singing.

"How are you still immune to us?" Sturgeon asked.

Sam shrugged. "Lucky, I guess."

He wanted to flee so badly his muscles twitched with the urge, but he couldn't leave Bob behind. Keeping his eye on the sirens before him and trying to ignore the ones under the dock, Sam grabbed Bob's shoulder and tried to pull him up.

The grunt yanked from his chest didn't result in anything more than a slight shift in Bob's positioning.

"Bob, you've gotta wake up. We have to get out of here," Sam pleaded.

The planks beneath his feet began to tremble again. Sam swallowed back further words.

"You tore those girls from their homes, their families. Don't you have any morals?" Sam asked.

Maybe if he stalled them long enough, they'd forget the whole bring-Sam's-head-on-a-platter idea their queen had. Starting a discussion about morals seemed like a good idea at the time; attempting to reason with kidnappers and killers might be stupid, but he had to try.

Sturgeon shrugged. "If they wanted their children, they shouldn't leave them lying about where anyone can steal them. We will take better care of our offspring." Sturgeon gave absolutely no apology. He seemed shocked that Sam would ask. Then he stepped closer.

Spooked by the closeness of the sirens, Sam leaned down. He slapped Bob hard across the cheek, intent on snapping his lover out of his haze.

"Ow." Bob blinked a few seconds before his eyes focused. He stood quickly, with his vampire strength lending him speed. "What did I miss?"

"The sirens took the kids to make mutant offspring, to create their own little genetic laboratory. I can imagine humans doing something like that, but I'm surprised a supernatural would turn on another one." Sam couldn't hold back his surprise at how disappointed he truly was about the sirens' behavior. "The others will be upset when they find out sirens are involved."

"Um, Sam, you might not want to phrase it that way," Bob replied.

"Why?"

"Because we will stop at nothing to keep our secrets," the leader added.

Wood splintered all around them as the sirens broke through the pier from below. Their shrill screams had Sam flinching. "Stop it!" he shouted.

Silence.

Beautiful, blissful silence.

Bob stared at Sam. "I think you took away their voices," he said quietly so the others couldn't hear him.

"What? I didn't wish anything," Sam said defensively.

"Maybe you don't have to use the word 'wish' now?"

Sam turned back to the sirens only to see them clutching at their throats and glaring at him.

Oh hell, the sirens were going to kill them slowly, painfully, and with great enjoyment.

Bob stepped in front of Sam.

"In exchange for the location of the children, we will return your vocals to you. Do we have a deal?" Bob asked.

Sam rested the top of his head against Bob's back. How far did these powers spread? How could he get rid of them? Humans weren't meant to have magic—that's why they were born without it and only a small percentage could wield it without consequences.

The sirens nodded.

"If you go back on your agreement, we will take your song forever," Bob warned.

Sam peeked over Bob's shoulder in time to catch the look of terror on their faces. Apparently to a siren, the worst threat was to not be able to sing.

"Sam?" Bob prompted.

"I wish they had their voices back," he whispered. He'd kept his tone quiet so they couldn't understand what was happening. If they knew he could wish things to happen, they might want to kidnap him and take him for observation too. If only he could wish back the children as easily.

"You won't be able to get to the children anyway," Sturgeon challenged.

"Why not?" Bob asked.

"Because the humans are well armed and are under orders to kill anyone who tries to take the girls." The siren sneered in triumph.

"Where are they?" Bob asked. "We'll deal with the fallout."

"On pier sixty-four on the south side of the docks," the siren confessed reluctantly.

Bob nodded. "Good. We'll be on our way."

"What makes you think we'll let you leave peacefully?" the siren challenged.

"Because if you don't, we'll make you silent again. You want to try?" Bob asked.

The sirens shook their heads.

"Our queen will know of your crimes against our species," Sturgeon announced in a loud, pompous voice.

Sam wondered if the sirens truly had no volume control. They always sounded so freaking loud.

"Go tell your queen that we won't be happy until all of your victims are freed," Bob said firmly.

The siren laughed. "They aren't victims. They are treated very well."

Sam walked around Bob to glare at the siren. "If by treated well, you mean torn from their homes and caged, then you have a different idea of what it means to be treated decently."

Too angry to say anything else, Sam spun on his heel and walked away. He would get the car and go find this other warehouse. The humans there had best not try to stop them. Sam would have no problem using his minor wishing powers to get rid of men who thought kidnapping children would be a good occupation.

As they rushed back to their car, Sam asked Bob a question that had been weighing on him. "Do you think I can wish for the girls to be home?"

"No." Bob's tone didn't allow any room for hope. "Wishing spells are generally minor. Teleporting an entire group of people will take a lot more than a wish."

"Too bad."

Bob hugged Sam to his side. "This is one time we have to do things the human way, just like you prefer."

Sam sighed. He figured that the one time magic might come in handy, it wouldn't work.

Chapter Eight

HART POCKETED HIS CELL PHONE AND IMMEDIATELY TURNED back to the car.

"Sam has a lead on the warehouse," he announced.

Danjal nodded that he'd heard. So far their two warehouses had been a bust. The first was being renovated into luxury flats overlooking the water, and close inspection revealed no evidence of anything to do with missing children. One of the workers there had shown a little too much interest in Hart, though. And hadn't that been an interesting thing to see. The slim, elvish fae had evidently decided she wanted the big bad wolfie to warm her bed. Danjal couldn't believe how much he'd given away when he'd stepped between them in an overt show of possession. She'd backed off, and Hart had been way too focused on finding Shelby to probably care. Still, it was revealing to Danjal that he had done that.

"Where are we going?" Danjal asked as they peeled out of the parking lot.

"The north side. Sam said we should look out for humans and sirens."

Danjal sighed. He really hated sirens. They smelled

wrong, and were always at the root of every nasty thing that happened in this town. They were so keen on taking over land like they lorded it over the sea. He rummaged in his pocket but came up empty.

"Stop the car at the next corner," he said as inspiration hit him.

"No. I'm not stopping the car, Dan. You want out, then I'll drop you at the warehouse and you make your own way home—"

"Shut up, Hart. Let me get into the trunk. I need my bag."

"Why?"

"Siren protection. One sound and you'll be on your back and unconscious. I need some sage and eucalyptus and I can cast something that will muffle the sounds."

"Sam says we're not just up against sirens, but humans as well," Hart said.

"You're joking?"

"I wish I were," Hart said.

"Why are humans in bed with sirens?" Danjal couldn't imagine a worse scenario than this. Sirens with all their plans to dominate other paranormals, or humans with their weird ideas about segregation and species superiority. The two together didn't bode well.

"Sam didn't say how he knew, only that we need to get there. I'm not stopping the car. I'll take my chances with the siren song."

"Stupid," Danjal huffed. He unbuckled himself as they turned into a side street and the motion forced him into Hart.

"What the fuck, Dan?"

"Keep driving." He scrambled into the back and yanked at the partitioned seat to pull down the middle. Channeling a little extra strength with a tiny amount of magic, he yanked the bag through the opening in the backseat. Finally back in the passenger seat, he pulled the belt across him, then opened the bag. The familiar scents of sage and rosemary, and the underlying note of brimstone, comforted him.

"What the hell have you got in there?" Hart asked as he slowed to check a blind junction.

"Just some stuff. Concentrate on driving." Hart had never really got his head around the whole brimstone thing, but it held powerful magic that Danjal could get to with very little effort. Of course, every time he used it, he got in trouble, but what his dad didn't know wouldn't hurt him. Into the confines of the bag, he whispered the correct words, then allowed a little heat from inside him to bind the herbs and the energy in the stone. Finally, he had a workable solution. Without warning, he flicked some of it at Hart's face.

Hart immediately sneezed, and the car swerved a little for a moment. He got it back under control and wrinkled his nose in disgust.

"Dan—"

"Do you want to be able to get to Shelby or not?" Dan snapped quickly. He rubbed a little of the charcoal mess on his own forehead, then tipped the rest into a small bag. Sam and Bob would need protection as well.

Hart focused back on the car and within minutes had pulled up sharply behind Sam and Bob. Both were standing by the car and Bob looked really unhappy. Danjal climbed out of the car and immediately threw some of the mix at Bob. Not even his vampire reflexes could avoid the throw of it, and he stood dazed, with eyes crossed, attempting to see what had landed on him.

"Protection against sirens," Danjal said simply. "Sam, you'll need some as well."

"I don't," Sam said. He backed away and held a hand up in front of him.

"It doesn't hurt," Danjal said.

"He doesn't need it," Bob interrupted. "He's immune."

Danjal narrowed his gaze on the human. That couldn't be right. Humans were more susceptible to siren song than vampires and werewolves.

"What are you?" he asked suspiciously.

Sam frowned, then shook his head. "No time to talk about that."

"Where are they?" Hart asked.

"A block down. I'm thinking we need backup," Sam answered. He glanced at his cell phone, which was in one hand, then to his multi-weapon, which he gripped tightly in his other.

"No." Hart stopped Sam as he raised the cell to his ear. "No backup, or anything like that. I'll take Bob and we'll do the first search."

"I'm going as well," Danjal insisted.

"And me," Sam added.

Hart poked Sam in the chest with a finger. "You're human. You die too easily."

"Well, I'm going." Danjal slung his bag over his shoulders.

"And you," Hart said softly. "I'm not losing you again."

With a nod to Bob, the vamp and the wolf sprinted away and Danjal was too shocked at what Hart had said to react. Sam grabbed his arm, and in a daze, Dan focused back on the here and now.

"We're not staying here," Sam said.

"No." Danjal focused on Sam's brown eyes. He was talking at him, but Danjal could only think about the fact that Hart had said he didn't want to lose him. What was all that about?

"Dan? Snap out of it. We'll take the other side. You with me?"

"Uh-huh," Danjal pulled himself together and realized Sam had already left. Quickly catching up, he fell into the easy rhythm of the run.

"Stay behind me," Sam said. He was a little breathless, but he had his weapon out in front of him, aimed high. Sam clearly had no idea what a demon could do, but there wasn't time to discuss this. Danjal might not be a kickass wolf or a fast-as-lightning vampire, but he had mad skills.

They rounded the warehouse, taking care to skirt the edge and keep out of sight. It looked empty. Weeds grew up through broken concrete and the scent of the ocean pervaded every inch. But not in a blustery, salty way—more in a decaying fish kind of way.

Danjal crouched behind Sam at the end of the final wall. "What's inside?"

"Intel says humans. Instinct says sirens too."

"Sirens don't stay out of the water long," Danjal commented. "It's the heat thing."

"What heat thing?" Sam whispered back.

Danjal frowned. "The whole sirens-don't-like-fire-and-kind-of-melt thing?"

Sam nodded, then adjusted the setting on the weapon he held. "Good to know."

"You didn't know that?" Danjal asked.

Wasn't an investigator supposed to know the A to Z of paranormals before being given a license?

Sam shrugged off the question. With the count of three on his fingers, he rose from the crouch and ran to a rusted side door. Danjal followed him and slipped through the crack that Sam had opened, until finally they stood just inside the warehouse.

Suddenly, with his eyes becoming accustomed to the low lighting, everything inside became very clear.

HARTMAN SLID TO A STOP, then swerved to avoid the first human guard. His speed had put him right up in the man's face far too quickly and the guy shouted in surprise before Hartman took him down with a crunch of bones.

"We don't need to kill everyone," Bob hissed.

Hartman ignored him. His daughter was in there, and as far as he was concerned, everyone died if it meant he had Shelby back in his arms. He darted away down to the next level of the warehouse and realized that it had doors that opened to the estuary. That explained the sirens using it without being seen. Not that a lot of visitors probably ever came down to this corner of hell in the city anymore.

Bob jumped the next flight of iron steps and landed lightly below Hartman. He held up a hand and clenched it into a fist. Had he seen something? Cautiously, Hartman followed him down and there, laid out in front of him, was a sight he'd never thought he would ever see. The sheer horror of children chained, all silent with some in cages along the far edge of the warehouse, was enough to send a father to his knees. He spotted five human guards and dismissed them. They would be easy to take out. Bob indicated with two fingers that Hartman should go left, and he didn't argue. Left or right—none of it mattered. The five were his target and the children would be free.

He approached the children from behind and took out two guards from his side with quick twists of their necks. He saw Bob doing the same thing on the other side. A moment's indecision, then he left Bob to deal with the remaining guard. He needed to find Shelby. He scented the air, but the strong stench of fear and despair overwhelmed his ability to find his own child. Three groups of five children chained together—vampire, wolf, fae—another six cages fixed to the wall, each with a child inside. Twenty-one souls stolen and trapped. Far more than they'd expected.

"Daddy!"

Shelby's voice broke into his horror, and in seconds, he was at the cage, reaching for his daughter. He heard a thud to his left and saw the last guard topple sightless next to him with a knife in his neck.

Bob looked over his shoulder. "We need to get them all out. The guard said the sirens are on their way."

"Daddy!"

Hartman ripped the cage door off its hinges, and in seconds, his daughter was in his arms.

"Hart. Are you okay?"

Dan crouched at his side, and Hartman had an overwhelming relief that Dan was there next to him. Shelby was so light, and Hartman could feel her shivering. Filthy, with her beautiful long dark hair matted and her skin dirty. It was only the fire in her brown eyes that convinced Hartman that he was holding his daughter alive in his arms.

"I told them, Daddy, that you would come for me."

"Hart, we need to go," Dan insisted.

He leaned over Hartman and touched the hinges and the locks on the next cage. All melted and the door fell off. The small vampire child inside huddled further into the back. All around them, children were being released and Hartman could hear Sam and Bob encouraging them out of the floor level side door. Nodding, he gripped Shelby tight and moved to join the exodus.

"Come on, sweetheart," Dan encouraged the little vampire out of her cage. "We're here to help."

"I—I—I—can't," she stuttered.

Shelby wriggled in his arms and pushed to be let down. Finally, he released her but kept his fingers only inches from his baby.

"C'mon, Mal," Shelby said. "Let's go home."

"They killed my momma," Mal whimpered. "I wanna stay here."

"Come with me," Shelby raised the tone of her voice from pleading to stern.

That appeared to galvanize the vampire, and Mal finally wriggled forward. Dan grabbed at the vampire, and with his arms full, he stood.

"Sirens!" Bob shouted from the door.

Hartman could hear the eerie sound of their song, but it was muffled and he only felt a little dizzy. Evidently brimstone and whatever else Dan had thrown at him worked. Dan thrust Mal at him, and Hartman instinctively pulled the other child into his hold.

"Take them," Dan snapped.

"Let's go," Hartman replied. "We need to go."

"Look after them," Dan said forcefully. "The kids need to get out. Help Bob and Sam, I'll hold off the sirens."

"Dan. No—"

"Just go."

Dan pushed him, and at the sudden calm and peace in Dan's eyes, Hartman knew he had no choice. Every single thing he had never said to the demon flooded him. *I want you. I need you. I love you.* But nothing actually came out of his mouth. He stumbled backward as Mal twisted in his arms and screamed. Glancing over his shoulder, he could see twenty or more sirens rising wraithlike from the seawater and climbing the steps.

"What are you going to do, Dan?"

Dan tilted his head and his eyes flashed a bright red. Then he clicked his fingers and a small flame hovered at the tip.

"Fight water with fire," he said. "Go."

"Dan—"

"I'll be right behind you, Hart."

Hartman turned and ran toward Sam and Bob and the last of the children being helped out of the warehouse. The force of the blast behind him pushed him to his knees and a wall of flame sent heat over their heads. Bob grabbed Mal, Sam had Shelby, and in a desperate lunge, he was beyond the wall of the warehouse. He turned. In the center of the fire, standing with the element of hell in a twist behind him, was Dan. He had formed fire between him and the sirens who were rushing back to the water, which steamed and churned from the heat. There was terrible screaming from the sirens and some of them fell dead to the floor, husks of what they had once been. Sam passed Shelby to him.

Flaming, Dan looked like the demon he was. Powerful. Stunning. Slowly the heat dissipated, and Dan fell to his knees. The sirens had gone, and everything in the vicinity was a blackened, charred mess. He faced Hartman, clearly exhausted. But he grinned and Hartman couldn't help returning the grin with one of his own.

"Daddy?" Shelby clung closer. "What is he?"

He knew what she'd meant. She maybe wouldn't have seen his small horns, and it wasn't as if there were more than a handful of demons in the city. She wanted to know his species. But he was much more to Hartman than just a demon.

"Aww, baby," he said softly. "That's the man I love."

Chapter Nine

HIS BUILDING WAS INFESTED WITH CHILDREN. SAM SCURRIED across the hall into his office and slammed the door shut behind him. The dark coolness of his private space settled the pounding panic in Sam's chest. His apartment had been taken over by Hartman to settle the werewolf children, while the vampires, fae, and other assortment of paranormals were tucked away in the spare apartment.

The rampant emotion spewing all over the place was getting on Sam's nerves. It wasn't that he didn't like kids. He had just never spent any time with them. Not to mention paranormal kids had a lot more special needs than the regular type.

After taking a look at Sam's pale face, Bob had suggested he might be more comfortable in his office.

Sitting at his desk, Sam let out a long, relieved breath. He couldn't remember the last time he'd been able to sit and relax. No one had ever told him being a detective was so hard on the nerves.

His ass had barely hit the seat before a knock at his door made him sigh.

"Enter!" he shouted.

The trio of fae he'd dealt with before entered his office.

"Well met, Samuel Enderson," the middle fae spoke.

They looked as Sam remembered. Eerily beautiful and disturbing in their synchronicity.

"Hello. If you're here for the fae kids, they're upstairs," Sam offered. Surely they would scurry away now. He almost wished they would before he suddenly remembered to be careful of what he said.

"We have them already on their way home," the fae on the left spoke.

Sam frowned. "Then why are you here? Oh, did you come to take off the wishing spell?"

He was of two minds about losing the gift. He didn't like having magic attached to him without his permission, which he would never give, but it was damn useful.

Identical scowls crossed their faces.

"We gave you no such spell."

The fae moved as one closer to Sam.

"Come here, let us look at you," the middle fae said.

Despite his unease, Sam didn't feel any animosity coming from the fae. Cautiously, he stood and approached them.

A light fingertip touch brushed against the underside of his jaw.

"Interesting. Did you recently acquire a familiar?"

Sam nodded. "Um, yeah."

"Then I would look to your creature. Familiars often place protective wards on those they have claimed. Yours appears to be particularly powerful." The fae tilted their heads at the same time and angle.

Sam didn't think that would ever stop being creepy.

"Thanks. I'll talk to Smudge about that."

Damn cat.

"The magically gifted are drawn to you, Samuel Enderson. You need to be prepared for all kinds of creatures seeking you out. Some will be friends, others will not. We have brought you a present to thank you for retrieving our kin."

Remembering Bob's warning about refusing fae gifts, Sam tried to be gracious. "Um, thank you." He knew his tone had been more inquiring than thankful, but it was the best he could do that day.

"Hold out your arm," the fae on the right ordered.

Obediently, Sam lifted his arm toward the fae. He knew this was going to be a colossal mistake, but he couldn't imagine of a way out of it. He didn't think they wished him any harm. He hoped he was right. Truthfully, even with the gift of empathy from the fae, he couldn't sense anything malicious from the trio.

A soft click returned his attention to the fae's latest gift.

"What is that?"

A one-inch wide metal band adorned his wrist. The entire thing shone with a silver light. Turning it around, he saw nothing but smooth, glowing metal.

"This is a human treaty bracelet. It was how people used to claim affiliations to different paranormal entities. Now it has been tossed aside by more modern ways, but those of the blood remember its uses."

"And what are its uses?" Sam asked. He gnawed his bottom lip as he wondered if he was going to be stuck with more abilities.

"Relax. It only announces to others that you have powerful allies who will watch out for you."

Sam didn't know which fae had spoken because he was still regarding the bracelet. Despite its light glowing, it didn't emit any sound.

"As the givers, we get to place the first mark."

"What?"

Before Sam could ask what they were talking about, the trio each put a finger on Sam's new bracelet. A ribbon of gold flowed from their fingers and slid around the band. A low chime filled the air.

When they removed their hands, a small symbol shimmered on the band. As Sam moved his wrist back and forth, the shimmer stayed in one spot.

"That is our mark. It says you are connected to the triad and to harm you is to bring our wrath."

Sam looked up and all three pairs of eyes were glowing at him.

"Umm, thank you."

"You're welcome. We will see you again." With a nod, they walked back out the door.

"At least they didn't give me any more powers," Sam muttered.

"What were they?" a tiny voice asked.

A shout left Sam's lips as he spun around to face the new intruder. He clutched his chest as if that alone could keep his thundering heart in place.

With his new sight, it only took a second to separate the person from the shadows. A small girl sat curled up in a corner of Sam's office between his printer and a stack of files dangerously teetering on the floor.

"Who are you?" Sam kept his distance since the girl had wide, frightened eyes, as if she thought he'd attack her at any moment.

"I'm Malerie. My friends call me Mal," she replied. She lifted her chin as if daring him to call her something else. She had the same way about her as Bob.

Vampire.

"Why aren't you with the other children?" Sam asked.

"Shelby already left," she said as if that explained everything.

"There are other vampires up there," Sam offered. He would've thought all the children would want to stay together, but obviously the trauma of the event had affected the kids differently, even if they were the same species.

"I don't like other vampires. They always make fun of me." The little girl had her arms wrapped around her legs and had curled into a tiny ball. No wonder Sam hadn't seen her before.

Sam leaned forward. "Why would they do that?"

He knew they didn't really need a reason—little kids were sometimes cruel. Sadly, they often didn't improve as adults.

"'Cause I'm different. I don't drink blood."

Sam frowned. Maybe the little vampire was a half-breed.

"What do you eat?"

"Energy."

Bob's voice had Sam spinning around.

"Mal's a psychic vampire. She feeds off the energy of the people around her. She's probably feasting off of you." Bob's anger pulsed at Sam. "She's dangerous."

"No! I'm not," Mal said quickly. "I don't want to hurt anyone."

Tears flowed down the child's face.

Sam stood, protectively placing himself between Bob and the young girl. "If you can't be nice, you can leave."

"What? You don't like paranormals. Why are you sticking up for her?"

"She's a little girl," Sam protested. "No matter her species."

"I've asked around, and no one knew much about her family. No father, and her mother was killed by the sirens.

They must've wanted her badly. I guess the temptation of combining a psychic vampire with the siren allure was too much for them. We'll have to send her to the orphanage. Maybe they can find someone to watch over her."

Sam turned back and saw the raw pain reflected on the small vampire's face. Her sorrow beat at him with more force than a hurricane.

"No. She can stay with me," Sam replied.

Relief poured off her so strongly Sam's knees almost buckled from the sensation. For a moment, he wondered if maybe *he* was the psychic vampire as he fed off her sudden joy. The room spun for a bit, but he blinked and the sensation passed.

"Sam, are you sure about this? I didn't think you liked kids." Bob stared at Sam as if he'd never seen him before.

"I can't let her go to an orphanage. Those places are terrible."

"Have you ever been to an orphanage for the supernatural?" Bob asked. His words had been slow and careful, as if he were feeling his way around the argument and didn't want to say the wrong thing in case Sam's last attachment to sanity snapped.

"No, but none of those can replace a home. We need to find her a good set of parents. I'm not going to let her go somewhere that will traumatize her further. She can stay here while we look."

"While *we* look?" Bob's expression said Sam had lost his ever-loving mind.

Sam stepped toward his lover. "You don't want to help me?"

He trailed a finger down Bob's chest as he looked at him through his lashes.

"Just call me putty," Bob said. "Everyone knows I have no willpower when it comes to you."

Sam bit his lip to suppress his victorious smile. He didn't want to push Bob away, but he wouldn't abandon a person in need even if she weren't exactly human.

"She can use my apartment. I'll move in with you."

Sam could've objected to Bob's pronouncement—they'd only known each other for a little while and Sam enjoyed his independence—but it wouldn't fool either of them. According to Bob, they'd already bonded. If Sam *was* gaining Bob's abilities, then whether they were in separate apartments or not wouldn't make any difference.

"Get away from him!" someone shouted.

Sam was thrown against the wall as Josh attacked Bob. A flash of metal alerted Sam that his ex-boyfriend had brought a knife to his vampire fight.

Josh flew across the room with the force of Bob's punch. He ended up crumpled against the door.

"Ow," Josh whined. "Sam, help me."

"Help you?" Outrage sparked through Sam's body. "You come in here and attack my boyfriend and you want help? You're lucky I don't call the police and have you arrested for assault."

Josh's red face paled as he realized Sam wasn't going to take his side.

"But Sam, we were so good together," he blustered.

Anger burned through Sam quicker than the demon's flame he'd seen in the boathouse. "I thought we were until I discovered you fucking behind my back. Bob might be a vampire, but at least I can trust him!"

The rush of pain still took Sam by surprise. He thought he'd be over it by now, but no—the memory of the betrayal still cut deep.

"I should rip out your throat for hurting my Sam." Bob's hard tone had Sam's cock perking up with interest. He'd deny it with his last breath, but he loved it when Bob became protective. He'd never had anyone want him with as much passion as Bob showed for him.

"No. Don't hurt me," Josh pleaded. He scrambled backward, dropping his knife as he went.

"Get out, Josh. Don't come back." Exhaustion had drained Sam.

"B-but, Sam, what about us?" Josh protested.

"There is no us. I foolishly thought you cared for me, but you taught me differently. Get out and don't come back, or I *will* let Bob rip out your throat."

Josh's mouth opened and closed like a guppy out of water. "You really mean that, don't you? You prefer this monster to me."

"This *monster* will be faithful to me until I die. Oddly enough, I've discovered I can overlook a pair of fangs when the rest of the package is far superior."

"You've changed, Sam." Josh scowled. "And not for the better."

"Get out." Sam didn't want to discuss his emerging opinions of supernatural creatures. He'd come to learn that they weren't all the same. Like humans, some were good and some weren't. He still hoped to have more human clients, but he couldn't in good conscience deny anyone in need.

Sam watched dispassionately as Josh pulled himself to his feet. His ex ran out of his office as if the hounds of hell were on his tail.

"You mean that?" Bob asked. He came up to Sam and placed an arm around his waist.

"That I like you despite your fangs?" Sam asked, turning to face his lover. He let all his thoughts about Bob float through his head. "We might not have a perfect relationship, but it works for now."

Bob tightened his grip. "It will work forever," he insisted.

"Wow, you two make a lot of energy." Mal had left her corner and approached them. She had on a shift similar to the one the naiad wore. Her pointed chin gave a sweetness to her heart-shaped face that should've looked odd on a vampire.

Sam blushed as he wondered how much energy he and Bob made when they had sex.

"Enough to light up the whole damn city," Bob whispered in Sam's ear.

Sam laughed. "Why don't you go and show Mal where she can sleep? If you tell Bob where you lived, we can go and retrieve your belongings."

Mal's eyes teared up again. "They destroyed our house. We lived on the beach. They flooded everything. I don't have any belongings left."

Sam didn't consider himself an overly violent man, but if a siren had walked into his office right then, he would've been more than happy to snap their neck.

"Easy, babe." Bob massaged the back of Sam's neck. "We'll go shopping after we get her settled."

"Can I have a bath?" Mal asked hesitantly. "I feel grungy."

"Absolutely," Bob replied. "I got some new fluffy towels too."

Bob ushered the little girl forward. He gripped the back of Sam's neck and gave him a hard kiss. "I love you too."

Sam would've replied, but by the time he unscrambled his wits, Bob had already left.

"Vampires do like getting the last word." The gravelly voice could have only come from Sam's gargoyle.

He turned to see the stone figure waddling around his desk.

"He does at that," Sam agreed. He sat back at his desk, then pulled out the map with the waterways.

"What are you working on now?" the gargoyle asked, settling at the side of the map and helpfully preventing it from curling up again.

"I'm trying to figure out where to return our naiad. She needs to go back to the proper waterway, and I'm worried if we pick the wrong one she'll be out of water too long."

"I know you were going to go take pictures but some of them you might be able to pull up online. You can find just about anything on the Internet these days," the gargoyle said.

Sam stared at the gargoyle. "What do you know about the Internet?"

The gargoyle grinned. "I know that the passwords on your computer aren't that good, and that you are definitely gay."

Sam blushed. He really needed to remember to delete his search history. "Stay off my computer," he snarled.

The gargoyle had the nerve to look hurt. "But what else am I going to do stuck in this office?" the creature protested.

Sam sighed. "I'll get you your own." He could spring a few hundred if it would keep the stone beast away from his laptop.

"Really!" The gargoyle's ears flicked with joy.

"Yes, really. I'll pick it up tomorrow when I go shopping for Mal," Sam offered.

"Oh thank you." The gargoyle clapped with uncharacteristic glee.

With that plan in place, Sam organized the best path to visit the waterways.

Chapter Ten

Alec, Hartman's brother-in-law, had said he wanted to talk. Alone. Given Shelby was asleep on the sofa in the main room and that the upstairs apartment where Alec and Nate lived was small, it had been Alec's idea to talk in the club itself.

Hartman, as the pack Alpha, could have ignored the missive, but he knew Alec had a say in this whole mess. The club was empty, and with the lights up, the night club, Bite, looked very different than it would later. When darkness fell, the place teemed with paras and humans alike. In this light, it was easy to see the dance floor was scuffed and the ceiling a mass of steel, but add in darkness only broken by flashing lights and this place would be paradise at night.

Nate, Alec's human mate, walked down with them, and for a moment, Hartman thought he was staying, but he only fetched the accounts ledgers from the small office behind the bar.

"I'll be upstairs," he said.

Alec pulled his human lover close and kissed him thoroughly, then with shared grins and a sketched wave at

Hartman from Nate, he left them. Hartman had always been slightly jealous of the easy affection Alec could share with Nate. Although his relationship to Constance had been rocky, Hartman considered himself close to Alec. They had grown up together, and he trusted Alec with his life. Probably one of the reasons why, when it had come time to choose someone to have a child with, it had been Alec's sister that he had picked.

Unfortunately, that had turned out to be a big mistake.

"It was interesting that Shelby told us it was her mother's face that she saw last," Hartman began. "I'm not sure what I am doing with this information, but I'm not letting Shelby out of my sight for another second."

Alec stayed quiet. Evidently, he had nothing to say on the matter. His expression of happiness had disappeared as soon as Nate left and the veneer of calm slipped. "If I don't get this out in the open, it's going to fester," he growled. "I need to speak to you freely, Alpha."

Hartman frowned. This sounded serious. "Of course. You don't have to ask."

"You should have freaking said something to me," Alec snapped.

"I couldn't—"

"You ignored nearly every one of my calls and you vanished the minute I came anywhere near you…" He was pacing the length of the bar and agitated was too small a word for what was carved into his expression.

"Alec—"

"I love Shelby. She's my niece. Damn it, I was as scared."

Hartman doubted that. He didn't imagine anyone would wish for death as badly as he would have if Shelby had died. Instead, he said what he imagined Alec needed to hear. "I know that, but Constance is your sister and I didn't know if she had influenced you."

Alec shook his head. "I would never help her do something like that. I was looking for Shelby. I could have helped. What did you think you were doing, going to that warehouse by yourself?"

"I wasn't ready to put other people in harm's way—"

"Don't give me that." Alec came to a dead stop in front of him and jabbed him in the middle of his chest.

Hartman's wolf snarled, and he knew the instant anger showed on his face. Still, Alec didn't submit, and for a second, Hartman had to hold himself back.

"I knew what I was doing, and I couldn't tell the pack I had involved a human in hunting for Shelby. Adding Dan to the mix would be more than the pack could take. I had to do this outside of the family since I still don't know how many support Constance."

Alec stared at him and his deep brown gaze was troubled. "This is me you're talking to."

Hartman crossed his arms over his chest. "What do you want me to say, Alec? You know one suggestion of me taking this issue outside of the pack and I would have another challenge for Alpha."

"You know damn well that being with Nate makes me isolated from everyone. I would have understood. Why not ask for my help? You were happy for an excuse to go to that demon."

"Don't bring Dan into this, Alec," Hartman said tiredly. "He was the only reason we managed to get the kids out of there alive."

Alec considered the words for a second, then exhaled noisily. "I need a drink," he said.

He vaulted over the bar and landed on the other side.

When he stood back up, he had two ice-cold beers in his hands and gestured to Hartman, silently asking if he wanted one. Hartman nodded and deftly caught the tossed bottle. A beer sounded like a damn good idea at this moment in time. He focused on removing the cap with his pack ring, then downed half of it in one go. Alec didn't jump back over, but it was probably a good idea for the bar to be between them because Hartman's emotions were right on the surface.

"Danjal is part of this. Tell me how you are going to explain Danjal to the pack as your lover and… what? Joint dad to Shelby? Tell me so I can tell you what you are facing based on what you say."

"It's easy. He's the man I love."

"And there you have the problem. Man. Demon. Whatever. But no childbearing capabilities. The pack is demanding a male heir and they are listening to what Constance is saying. That you refuse to give her another child, so why don't they have Ed as their pack Alpha?"

"What do you want me to do? Give up everything I had with Dan? Like I did before? I can't do that again. I *won't* do that again, and the pack will see it's for the best when everything is settled. I'll deal with Constance. Shelby may not remember much of what happened before she woke up in the warehouse, but if Constance was the last person she saw…"

"Agreed." Alec gave a lopsided smile. Then he rested both elbows on the smooth marble of the bar and let his beer dangle from one hand. "But, you're going off topic. See, I happen to agree with you. I don't know why you ever gave in to pack pressure in the first place."

"I'm Alpha," Hartman said.

"You think it means you have to give everything up? Including the man you love?"

"Yes."

Alec shook his head. "And this is where your problems started, Hartman. Shelby is case in point."

Hartman frowned. "Shelby isn't a problem."

"I didn't mean it like that." Alec sighed noisily. "You've been angry for so long. Telling the pack how things were going to be. Then giving in to what they wanted. That wasn't a smart move."

Hartman took a step toward the bar, but Alec held up his free hand in a gesture of peace. He tilted his head a little in a subtle submissive move that settled Hartman's lupine self instantly.

Alec continued, "When Constance's first husband died, she was devastated. It wasn't like we were close, even though she's my sister—she's so much older than me. But I knew enough to see the greedy, manipulative liar she had become. I think you should never have chosen Constance to bear you a daughter."

Hartman huffed. "Jeez, Alec, it's not like you were there to ask."

"I know. But Nate is the other half of me. I don't regret leaving the pack to be with him. The only thing I do regret is that I let my friend down when he needed me most."

"It is what it is," Hartman finally summarized.

A wealth of unspoken information passed between them. Years of history and of the pain both men had gone through when Alec had left. Hartman had finally overruled everything and Alec had been welcomed back by most. Significantly, his sister had been one of the most vocal against the cross-species lovers.

"When Shelby was born, the pack lost you. Don't get me wrong, you were always there for Shelby. But, I think you felt she should be with her mother and I don't think you really saw how much negativity Constance had for Shelby."

Constance was a force to be reckoned with. A stubborn, intractable thorn in Hartman's paw. He thought of Shelby, and the accompanying anger at the way Constance and her obnoxious oldest son were so involved in Shelby's life. A familiar twist of grief stole his breath for a moment.

"I try to have Shelby with me as much as I can," Hartman protested.

"You didn't know she had been gone for twenty-four hours," Alec said softly. "You were there, but not there."

Despair washed over Hartman. He was a good dad—always part of Shelby's life. He loved her. She loved him. But hell, Alec was right.

"She needed a mother," Hartman argued. He sat at the nearest table and stared down not seeing the beer in his hands. The drink that had felt like such a good idea a few minutes ago now felt bitter on his taste buds.

"I'm not blaming you," Alec offered. "I don't need to. After Shelby was born, you retreated into yourself. I also don't have any excuses. I should have been in Shelby's life more. Maybe then she wouldn't have been taken."

"None of it was your fault," Hartman said. He didn't want Alec feeling as if he had to take any of this on his own shoulders. *He* was Alpha, it was his job to make sure his pack was happy and settled. He'd been the one to play final advocate when Alec had approached the pack to introduce Nate, a human and an ex go-go dancer at that.

"You have to spread some of this around. You're not seeing what's in front of your face."

"Which is?"

"That you and Danjal belong together. Any idiot can see that. So stop telling yourself that it's okay to be without him."

"What will the pack say? Will they let us live in peace? Will I lose respect? I don't want to spend the rest of my life watching my back and proving my worth," Hartman explained.

"I think you'll be surprised at the sway of opinion. It's only the Aston family that is really solidly agreeing with everything Constance says."

"Okay. Thank you." Hartman was happy to hear it, but he had something else to think on. "I have to go to Sam and tell him what Shelby said about her mother. See if he can drag anything up about the human kidnappers."

"I don't believe Shelby was taken," Alec said carefully, and he winced as he spoke. Obviously, he was aware that his thoughts were going to get Hartman's famous temper to make an appearance.

"What do you mean? Not taken?"

"I think there is more at play here than you think."

"Like?"

"Have you considered Constance and her two boys? Ed, her oldest, is strong and determined. He turns twenty-one in a month and I see the gleam in his eyes for pack control that is only matched by the desire for more in hers. She wants him as Alpha. What if they gave Shelby away. She's said things to me, nothing overt, but over the past few weeks, she's been soliciting my help with things, even talking to Nate. You know she hates Nate, so why would she talk to him now?"

"You think she wants you on her side in a challenge for leadership?"

"She wants you weak, and what better way to do that than to push that final nail into your coffin? First you left Danjal, then Shelby disappeared. What if you had been too late? How quickly would you have lost the will to lead the pack?"

"Alec, please…" Hartman moaned. He couldn't listen to

anything in which his beautiful vibrant tomboy daughter was dead. The rest of what his friend was saying hit him squarely between the eyes. "That's your theory?"

Alec shrugged. "It's one that we could follow up on."

Hartman didn't want to admit he'd thought the very same during the long weeks he'd searched for his daughter. It went against his nature to think a mother could be this evil to her own daughter, but worse things had been known to happen.

The door to upstairs opened, and Nate walked out, followed closely by Dan. Shelby was sleeping in his arms. She'd done little more than sleep since they'd got her away from the sirens.

"You told him?" Nate asked Alec.

"He told me," Hartman answered for Alec.

Nate looked relieved.

"Told him what?" Dan asked. He cast glances between Alec and Hartman and shifted Shelby a little higher on his shoulder. She murmured in her sleep, and Dan smiled down at her.

At that moment, Hartman saw everything with clarity. Constance never smiled at Shelby. She berated her, told Hartman that Shelby was not like a proper wolf child. That she didn't like the things a typical four-year-old girl should enjoy. Shelby preferred climbing trees to anything like girls' toys. Why had he never seen it before? He'd been blind. Swiftly, he moved to Danjal and pulled him and Shelby close. He had something to do and it had to be now.

"I love you, Dan," he said softly. "Promise me you will always have Shelby with you. Protect her with Alec and Nate. Whatever happens?"

"Hart?"

"I have something I need to do. I'll be back. But, if I don't come back… promise me."

He stepped back, and Dan looked confused. His eyes momentarily darkened into their red hue. Hartman felt his stomach sink. Was he asking too much of his lover when they had only reconnected for a day?

"Always, Hart."

Peace stole over Hartman, and he dropped a kiss on Shelby's freshly washed hair. She smelled of apple and Dan smelled of citrus. He thought he would remember their combined scents forever.

In an instant, he'd left the club and all that he loved. He had to find Constance and see if Alec was right.

Chapter Eleven

Sam took the pictures he'd printed off the Internet upstairs to the naiad. Turned out the gargoyle was right and there were photos available of each of the sites Sam thought were a possibility. He found Springlilly splashing happily in the tub. She stopped when she caught sight of Sam.

"Can I go home now?" she asked, her eyes shining with excitement.

"I've got a few pictures I want you to look at so we don't end up traveling too far with you out of water."

"Oh, you don't have to do that. Once I know the place for certain, I can transport there." Springlilly smiled at Sam.

"Why didn't you do that already?" Sam kneeled beside the tub.

"I can't transport just on a memory. I need a visual," Springlilly replied.

"Oh." That made sense.

Sam showed the pictures he'd printed out. He'd almost given up when she gasped.

"That's it. That's my home!" she said, excitedly pointing

to a picture that had a long swath of flowers growing beside it.

He set the other pictures down. "What can I do to help?"

"Step back so you don't get hurt," Springlilly warned, sounding older than her years.

Sam quickly rushed to the doorway so he wouldn't get any kind of spell backlash but could be there if she needed anything. He barely made it to the edge of the tile before the sound of water splashing caught his attention.

Sam spun around. His mouth dropped open. In his formerly nondescript bathroom now sat a tiny waterfall that stretched to the ceiling and covered the entire wall. A tide pool of swirling water had replaced his cream-colored tub and rocks jutted out of the floor surrounding the water.

The naiad was nowhere to be found.

"I have a waterfall in my bathroom," Sam said in awe.

Surprisingly, the water didn't pour over the rocks but stayed in the little circle.

"Springlilly!" Sam called out. He walked to the very edge of the pool but didn't see any sign of the water sprite.

"What happened?" Bob entered the bathroom and examined the new addition.

"Springlilly. I'm going to have to go and check that she made it safely," Sam said.

"How do you know where she went?"

Sam held up the picture. "She supposedly went here."

"I'll drive," Bob offered.

IT TOOK two hours to reach the spot in Sam's photo. With each mile, Sam's anxiety increased. Until he saw Springlilly happy and well, he wouldn't be satisfied. Bob pulled up at the edge of the road and Sam jumped out of the car, not even waiting until it came to a complete stop.

"Springlilly!" he shouted.

A shape emerged from the water. Springlilly waved cheerily. "Hey, Sam."

Sam dropped to his knees at the edge of the river. This part had little flow and mostly consisted of deep, still water. A small waterfall trickled down the mountain and directly into Springlilly's watery home.

"Is this the right place?"

The naiad nodded. Her skin and hair were brighter and she was clothed in a dress of shimmering fish scales instead of the dull shift she'd worn in Sam's tub.

Her glowing vitality calmed Sam's nerves. "I'm glad you made it back home."

"Thanks, Sam!"

"You're welcome."

Sam started to straighten up only to have her grab his wrist and place her hand over the treaty bracelet.

"I owe you, Samuel Enderson, and a naiad always pays her debt," the little girl said solemnly.

A blue flash blinded Sam briefly. When he blinked his vision clear, his bracelet had a tiny whirlpool swirling on the surface like a semi-precious stone.

"Oh… um… thanks." Sam didn't know what else to say.

Bob grabbed Sam's arm and pulled him away from the water. "Naiads are dangerous, Sam. Let's go before she decides to keep you."

Sam peered back over his shoulder in time to see Springlilly bite the head off a live fish. A shudder went through him. She'd definitely lost some of her cuteness.

He rubbed his suddenly queasy stomach.

"You got her back to her home. You did your part," Bob said.

Sam nodded. There was one paranormal he didn't have to see again.

He took long, slow breaths as he tried to make it back to the car without throwing up.

Bob didn't speak for the first half of the trip. "You know she can't help her nature," Bob said in a soothing tone.

"I know." Sam didn't want the naiad to change her nature—he didn't want anything to do with a creature that could bite off the head of another creature.

"We have one more girl to deal with when we get home," Bob reminded him. "Maybe we can put her in the window and place a free vampire sign around her neck?" he teased.

Sam scowled. "She's not a homeless kitten."

"She kind of is," Bob argued. "Well, not a kitten but homeless."

"She doesn't have any parents that we're aware of and the other vampires aren't going to treat her nicely because she's different. I promised her a temporary home and I meant it."

The car swerved under Bob's capable hands, but he quickly straightened the vehicle. "You were being serious? We can't keep her. She must have a family."

"Then you find Mal's family. Until then, I'm not handing her over to any of those bloodsuckers who want to hurt her." Sam might never have planned to be a father and certainly not to a paranormal, but he wouldn't back down from the challenge either. It would be wrong to send a child, already traumatized, to live with someone who might belittle her. From what Sam could determine, because she wasn't a bloodsucker, living with a traditional vampire wouldn't be in her best interests.

"Fine! I'll find her family," Bob vowed.

"Good." Sam looked out of the window and tried to figure out how he got himself into these situations.

All he'd wanted was a peaceful life as a detective with regular cases.

Bob reached across the seats and squeezed Sam's hand. "I think you'd be bored with regular cases," Bob said.

Sam sighed. "Somehow I doubt I'll ever know."

THE OFFICE HAD people leaving in droves. Sam nodded to the vampires and shifters who were exiting the building.

"Are you Sam Enderson?"

Sam stopped as a tall blond vampire blocked his path.

He knew he'd regret admitting it as soon as the words were out of his mouth. "Yes."

"I'm Reginald Drewhaven and I lead the Northern coven of vampires. Perhaps you've heard of me?"

The vampire gave Sam such an expectant look that Sam almost lied. "No, I'm sorry, but I'm new to the territory."

"Oh, yes, of course," the vampire agreed. "Well, I wanted to say thank you. My Maggie could've disappeared forever and we never would've found her."

Reginald wrapped an arm around a tired young girl who kept her head down.

"I'm happy I could help. You might want to make sure she gets some counseling," Sam offered.

Reginald nodded. "Yes, yes, of course I will. Maggie will get whatever she needs."

From the cut of the vampire's suit, Sam doubted monetary concerns were ever a problem for the vamp. Sam was more worried about emotional ones. "You're very welcome for any help I might have given," Sam assured him. He wanted to tell

Reginald that a demon had done most of the final saving, but he didn't know of the relationship between demons and vamps.

Bob stepped forward. "I'm sure Sam is excited he could help you, but he's very tired and needs some rest."

"Of course, of course," Reginald agreed. "Humans are so fragile."

"Yes, I need a nap," Sam agreed, hoping to move this little encounter along.

He scooted around the tall vamp only to have his wrist grabbed. "A treaty bracelet! I haven't seen one of these in ages. Please allow me to add my family to those wishing to aid you in the future."

Sam couldn't think of any way to get around it, and the vampire's hold on his wrist was firm.

Reginald gripped the bracelet and muttered some words Sam couldn't really make out. A flash of white light indicated something had happened.

Before Sam could say anything else, Reginald gave a slight bow and led his daughter out of the door.

Sam looked down at his wrist. Beside the water spiral was a picture of a drop of blood.

"Lovely," Sam said in a dry voice.

Mikhail turned around from Sam's desk when they entered the office.

"Mikhail, what are you doing here?" Sam hadn't seen the vampire hybrid since this entire debacle had started.

Mikhail's beautiful face had an unusual sternness to its features.

"Sam, you have to stop interfering with siren politics," Mikhail warned.

"If by politics you mean stealing innocent children, then no, I won't stop interfering," Sam answered.

Mikhail walked around Sam's desk, then dropped into the closest seat. "They're going to kill you," he muttered.

"Who's going to kill me, the sirens? I know I'm on their bad list for saving the fae from them before. I didn't think taking their abducted children would suddenly put me on their good side. Sturgeon pretty much told me to expect my death by their watery hands," Sam said, trying to lighten the mood.

Mikhail sat straight up. "You talked to Sturgeon?"

Sam nodded. "Is he a relative of yours?"

"Ex-boyfriend," Mikhail admitted.

"Hmm, well, I don't have any moral high ground to stand on over that," Sam confessed. "I know you're worried, but there's no way I could have left those kids or that fae to a fate at a siren's hands. What would you have me do?"

No matter how much Sam reviewed his last few cases, nowhere would he have acted differently. He didn't have it in him to leave a little wolf girl to be used as a breeding ground for sirens.

Mikhail raked his fingers through his hair. "I heard through a trusted source that the sirens are going to be looking for your blood. They blame you both for stealing their breeding girls and taking the magical fae."

Sam gritted his teeth. "They can blame me all they want, but the fact of the matter is they didn't deserve to keep either set of people. If they continue in this way, I will make it my life's work to make things difficult for them." The sad expression on Mikhail's face almost had Sam wishing he could retract his hardline approach, but too many lives were at stake. "I'm sorry if this doesn't help your relationship with the sirens." Sam didn't know what else to say. He wouldn't compromise his ethics even if it led to his death.

Bob growled. "They'd best learn to keep away from you.

I'll kill every last one of the bastards if I have to. Except Mikhail, of course." He nodded to their friend.

"Of course," Mikhail said dryly.

"I hope Hartman gets things straightened out with his pack." Sam smiled at his vampire lover. They were finally in sync. Sam had his lover and maybe even a child of his own. If he could get cases that didn't involve tangling with the sirens again, his life would be so much better.

Chapter Twelve

SET IN THE HILLS ABOVE THE CITY, THE PACK LANDS sprawled from the peak of Mission Mountain at the farthest point and down into the valley to the main freeway to the north of the city. A loose collection of buildings and a thriving horse training business kept the pack busy, but over half had jobs outside the pack lands. Hartman's father had pushed for the pack to expand past what tradition dictated.

Some trained as nurses, doctors, teachers, and bankers. In this way, Hartman was Alpha of a wealthy pack. He'd been subjected to more than one challenge for his position. It was good that his father had also seen fit to train his son in defense as a human, and to strengthen his nature as a fighter. He had been challenged before, and no doubt if Ed did the same today, it wouldn't be the last challenge Hartman faced.

No more than an hour from the detective's house and he was at the place he called home, back to his sprawling house and the various buildings built around the main area. He went straight to Constance's place, but the only person there was her younger son Logan, who he caught around the back of the house as he was attempting to sneak away. There was a short scuffle, but Logan, at nineteen, was a skinny shifter and hadn't really grown into his body. All long limbs and clumsiness, Logan was still a good-looking and popular young man like his Uncle Alec. He had a gentle way about him that reminded Hartman of Dan. He had his jacket on, a motorbike helmet in his hands, and a rucksack over his shoulder. In seconds, Hartman had the boy up against the side of the house with his fingers wrapped around Logan's throat.

"Where's your mom?" Hartman said without introduction.

Logan made a noise halfway between a choked gasp and a gurgle. Hartman loosened his grip just enough so he could talk. Instantly, Logan tilted his head to expose his throat as a sign of respect. When Hartman didn't immediately exchange the usual pleasantries of wolf introduction, Logan suddenly appeared terrified and more than a little confused.

Logan refused to meet his gaze, and Hartman wasn't sure whether Logan was merely shy or was hiding something. He hoped to hell the young man wasn't involved in whatever Alec thought was going on. Hartman released him completely.

"Look at me," he ordered.

Logan did what he'd been told. His sapphire eyes were wet with tears, but he drew back his shoulders and dropped his helmet to the ground.

"I swear to you. I thought she was talking nonsense. I didn't know before," Logan said strongly. "I was coming to find Uncle Alec—"

"Why?" Hartman raised his hands again, but to give him his due, Logan didn't move a muscle though there was fear in his liquid gaze.

"I overheard… no… I know… I…" He didn't seem to be able to string together the words.

Hartman gripped the young man on his biceps and shook him gently. "Tell me."

"Mom and Ed… I swear, I never put it all together. They've been working on something that meant Ed could challenge you as Alpha. I didn't think anything of it. Mom is always talking about how her family was superior to yours, how Ed would be a better Alpha. But… it was all talk. Until yesterday."

"What? What happened yesterday?"

"Shelby. I heard them say they had dealt with Shelby. That they got good money for her. Said it would be more than you could bear and that Ed would be able to use your grief to be Alpha by the next moon." A single tear rolled down Logan's face. He was close to Shelby—she called him Uncle Lo. "We have to find Shelby."

"I have Shelby. She's safe," Hartman said, confused.

Logan's eyes widened. "You do? She's back with you? Safe?"

"She's safe."

Logan struggled free of Hartman's grip and pulled his rucksack off his back. He had it open and was reaching inside. "I wrote it down, although not much of it made sense. Sirens, and fire, and your… Danjal…" Logan lowered his gaze and a blush reddened his cheeks. "And Shelby. That they needed to take advantage because they may lose their chance. Ed wasn't arguing—it was like him and Mom were in some kind of bloodlust. I couldn't understand a lot of what they were talking about, but Ed caught me listening. They said Shelby had to die if they had any chance. I asked them what they meant. Ed just laughed at me. I tried to leave, but he took me down and tied me up. I couldn't fight, they injected me with something. It was chaos, then everything went black."

Logan looked a little ashamed, and the Alpha in Hartman rose to the challenge. For the first time, Hartman saw the marks on Logan's wrists and he knew that Logan was imagining he should have done more.

"But you got free. I'm proud of you, Logan," he said.

Some of the tension in Logan left, but he was still agitated and his words began to spill haphazardly and fast. "I was going to Uncle Alec and Nate. They'd know what to do. Ed and Mom were talking about a challenge. I have names. The Astons, Coren James and his brother Silvus and Mom and Ed. They wanted me. I wouldn't. They're meeting now. I wanted to grab my phone and contact Uncle Alec, get him to find you. Find Shelby. I didn't know what else to do—"

"So I need to go then," Hartman interrupted calmly. "Break up this meeting and take the challenge if it's given to me."

Logan's eyes widened. "On your own?"

"Where are they meeting?"

"The Aston's barn," Logan said quickly. "But you don't know how many are involved. There may be half the pack. Alpha, you can't do this on your own."

"It's my job to take care of this. I'm the Alpha," Hartman said firmly. Striding away from the house, he headed in the direction of the Aston barn. He heard running footsteps behind him. Logan caught up. He had intense focus in his expression.

"I'm coming with you."

For a second, Hartman wanted to send the young man away, but some emotion in his blue eyes translated to a plea to let him help Hartman make things right.

"I won't forget it," Hartman said quietly. "Stay with me and don't do anything stupid."

Together they quickened into a jog and reached the barn

in minutes. For a moment, Hartman considered scoping the place out, but the Alpha inside him told him he needed to get in there, whatever the price, however many wolves were inside. Throwing open the main door, he stepped inside the dusty interior and his wolf eyes quickly adjusted to the inside gloom. No windows were open, and a group of only seven stood in the center. The names that Logan had given him. Hartman quickly identified Constance, Ed, the Astons, and the James brothers. They all turned as one to face him. Their expressions ranged from anger to fear to outright terror. In fact, the Aston family slunk to the back of the barn then disappeared. When they did, the James brothers took their cue and left too, until only Constance and Ed stood in the barn with Hartman and Logan.

"I'm guessing you have something to say?" Hartman asked. He was already unbuttoning his shirt, and Constance simply sneered at him.

"You are a weak Alpha," she spat.

"No he isn't, Mom," Logan defended. He stepped forward, but Hartman stopped him.

"See how you let him push you?" Constance snapped. "You're pathetic and weak. You'll never be more than a beta. I should have known you'd roll belly up for Hartman."

"You don't have to do this!" Logan shouted. "He's our Alpha."

Hartman held up a hand and Logan took a step back and away. Blessedly, he didn't say anything else.

"Contact the beta," he said under his breath. Only the sounds of a cell phone had Hartman sure that Logan was calling. His beta, John, would bring wolves that could be trusted. They might arrive to see Ed victorious, but they needed to see the outcome either way. If Ed was a true Alpha and defeated him, then the pack had to follow.

"You really want to do this, Ed?" Hartman asked. He directed this at his challenger and not at Constance, who stood next to her son with lips pressed tightly together. He didn't mince his words. This was a challenge, and when Ed began removing his own shirt, his actions underlined what he wanted to do.

Constance visibly vibrated with excitement. Hartman knew it was because, as mother to the pack Alpha, she would have a position in the pack that was a lot better than what she had as Hartman's ex-wife. Not only that, but she would have direct influence over pack finances. She scurried back against the wall.

Shifting wasn't a given in a challenge. Many challenges were taken in human form, but today Hartman needed his wolf, and as Alpha, it was his right to demand that they follow what he ordained. Shifting from man to wolf in a smooth movement, he shook the human away from his head and everything changed to a singular focus. Ed shifted as well and paced toward Hartman. His wolf was as black as night, and his blue eyes flashed fire. They were similar to Logan's eyes, but whereas Logan had empathy in his, in Ed's there was only hate.

Hartman pushed away the pain in his heart and the anger that could cloud his mind. He needed to know if what Logan had said was true. Were Constance and Ed part of a group responsible for taking Shelby and giving her to the sirens? Not giving… selling? He wasn't sure how he was going to do this, but he decided to let things play out as best he could.

Ed made the leading move, but Hartman had expected that. Claws extended, they met in the middle with snarling, snapping jaws, and knife-like scrapes to fur and the skin beneath. Ed drew first blood, and when they backed off momentarily, Ed's eyes held a maniacal gleam of achievement. Hartman had let him have the first blood deliberately—it would make this young alpha wannabe reckless and thoughtless. This wasn't Hartman's first fight.

When they met the next time, Hartman feinted to the left and took his own mouthful of scarlet, smearing it across fur and snout and pinning Ed.

Ed was strong. He pushed back, and they rolled across the floor in a battle for dominance. Hartman sensed his beta arriving, and hell, Alec was there too. They wouldn't interfere, but he hoped to hell Alec being there didn't mean Dan was with him.

Please let him have stayed with Nate and Shelby. I don't want them to see me if I fail.

Ed clamped his teeth into his rear right flank and Hartman yelped in pain. When Ed shook his head and tore into muscle, Hartman had a momentary doubt that he was strong enough to defend himself. He wasn't a young wolf anymore. Had he underestimated Ed? A wound that bad to his thigh would make it difficult to push using his back legs. As suddenly as he'd doubted himself, the tide turned. As Ed probably thought he had the winning edge, Hartman was back up and pushing. He snapped, bit and tore until he had an exhausted Ed beneath him, belly and throat exposed and very real fear in his eyes.

"Fight harder, Ed!" Constance screamed demonically. "Kill him."

Hartman closed his strong jaw around Ed's neck and pressed firmly. Ed immediately went loose under him. Complete submission.

"No!" Constance screamed. "I killed Shelby! You should be weak. You can't win."

Hartman heard her words. She was trying to get inside his head with her suggestions.

"I took her screaming and shouting for her daddy and I sold her to the sirens. You're nothing. You couldn't even protect your daughter." She ran toward Hartman, a knife in her hand. He wasn't sure who reached her first, him or Alec.

With her throat ripped out, she lay dead in seconds. There was blood on Alec, blood on Hartman. She was gone.

Hartman shifted and pulled himself to full height. Alec shifted back, then fell to one knee in front of him, tilting his head in respect. The wolves formed a circle around him as he stood over Ed, showing their loyalty. Ed whimpered on the ground and shifted back to human with blood all over him.

"Go," Hartman said calmly. "While you still can."

Ed gathered his clothes and stumbled the same way that the Astons and the James brothers had gone. Hartman would track the others down and deal with them another day, but as far as he was concerned, Ed was finished with the pack.

"Hart?"

Hartman tracked the voice. Dan stood in the doorway, silhouetted by the sun behind.

"Where's Shelby?" Hartman asked quickly.

"Nate has her out at the car. I didn't want her seeing this if you were… Are you okay?"

Hartman realized that they were having a conversation over the heads of his pack. This wasn't where he wanted to be when he told Dan how he felt, but it had to be done this way. He wanted to see Shelby, but his pack had to know what he was doing. He held out a hand and Dan picked his way through blood and wolves until he grasped Hartman's hand. For a second, they stared at each other. Dan knew how this had to be. It was what Hartman should have done years before.

"I love you, Danjal Naamah," he said forcefully. "I have always loved you."

"I love you too."

"I claim this man as my mate," he confirmed to the wolves.

Now was the point where they either spoke up or by their silence accepted Dan. Not one of them moved from their positions. It was done. An incredible lightness filled Hartman—he could finally be free.

Hand in hand, they left the barn and as soon as Nate recognized Hartman, he allowed Shelby to scramble free of his hold.

"Daddy!" she shouted happily. Running to Hartman, she climbed him like a tree, and once in his arms, she gripped him tightly. She still smelled of apple.

"I should never have left you," he whispered into Dan's ear. "I'm sorry."

Dan wrapped his arms around them both and together they stood.

Family.

Epilogue

HARTMAN PACED THE FRONT ROOM. THREE DAYS HAD PASSED since Shelby had been found and the challenge had been dealt with. He hadn't wanted Shelby out of his sight and that had made things difficult and tense. On the one hand, he wanted to spend time with his daughter… On the other hand, he needed to reconnect with Dan. The demon had spent long hours at the apothecary shop, and they hadn't managed to complete the mating ritual that would settle Hartman's lupine self. He wanted Dan so badly, but having his daughter in bed with him was not the way to get alone time. The clock showed five in the morning, and he hadn't really been to sleep yet—no wonder he was anxious.

A loud knock on the door startled Hartman from his thoughts.

"Alpha," Logan said nervously. The young wolf visited every day, begging to do something that would make him useful. "You wanted to see me?"

"Will you watch Shelby for me? For a few hours?"

Logan's eyes widened. "Yes," he said softly. "It would be an honor."

Hartman nodded quickly. The fact that Shelby adored Logan made Hartman's decision easier.

"She's still asleep. When she wakes up, you'll need to sort out breakfast for her. Nate is coming over at ten. You think you can handle it?" He was aware his voice held impatience, but if he didn't see Dan today, he was seriously going to lose it. Dan had been all, 'I'll give you space to connect to Shelby,' but the enforced separation was killing Hartman.

"Absolutely," Logan said immediately.

A sudden tug of familiar fear pulled at Hartman. What had happened to Shelby had changed him. He growled at Logan, who immediately tilted his head in submission.

"I am trusting you with her life," he began, his voice low and deep. He had to say this. He blamed the incomplete bond and missing sleep for his lack of confidence.

"Yes, Alpha," Logan reassured.

"If anything happens to her, I will hold you to blame and I will rip your throat out."

Logan blanched but didn't back down.

There. Enough said.

In minutes, he was out of the door, and with no traffic, he was soon outside the apothecary shop. The early morning was clear and cool and the road empty of pedestrians or vendors. He knocked on the door and didn't have to wait long. Everett peered out through one of the panes of glass, and Hartman could see the hobgoblin's irritable expression. When the door swung open, Hartman immediately stepped in and Everett stumbled back with a huff.

"Do you know what time it is?" he asked with a snarl.

Hartman ignored the question. "Is Dan here?"

Everett sighed and nodded, then shut and locked the door. Hartman didn't wait around to talk to him. He had a focus to his actions and purpose in his stride. He was up the spiral staircase to the attic in seconds and, not long after, pushed open Dan's apartment door with a firm shove. As he stepped over the threshold, Dan sat bolt upright in bed with a startled yelp and a red aura sparking from him.

"It's me," Hartman said quickly. After seeing the whole hellfire and brimstone thing at his lover's hands, he really didn't want to become grilled wolf just yet.

"What the hell, Hart?" Dan asked blearily. He glanced over at the clock. "You realize it's really early." Suddenly his expression changed. "What happened? Is it Shelby?"

"Shelby is fine. Everything is…" He stopped and ran a hand over his smooth skin. "I need you," he said. Hurriedly pulling at his clothes, he was naked before Dan could answer. His cock was hard and leaking pre-cum, the same as it had been for three days. He was desperate. It had been too long since he felt his lover's naked skin beside him. He yearned for the glide of warm bodies straining to reach a common goal of indescribable pleasure.

When Dan simply stared at him, an unfamiliar feeling of uncertainty spread through him. What if Dan had changed his mind? What if he didn't want to be with Hartman? What if Dan decided Hartman had put him through too much and he was done? Panic surged through him, his entire body shook with a fine tremor as the strain of the past few days came back to haunt him.

Dan pushed aside the covers, revealing his naked body. Hartman couldn't have stopped the groan that tore from his mouth if he tried. Dan was beautiful. Perfect. His. When the demon rolled off the bed and padded into the attached bathroom, Hartman followed him closely. He watched as Dan brushed his teeth, then pulled open a drawer and removed lube.

Hartman was determined to do this right. He was going to go slow, be firm, make Dan beg for their union. They had to be mates. Hartman had given up too much to let Dan deny him now. If Dan made Hartman choose between him and the pack this time, he'd make the right choice. He loved his pack, but he loved and needed Dan.

Patience. He would give Dan all the time he required to get used to the idea, but they were mates and mates stuck together. Hartman might have denied that truth once before, but he was done depriving both of them.

Dan turned to face him, his eyes glowing red and his mouth open slightly.

"Three days, Hart," Dan murmured.

Hartman yanked the demon toward him and their lips met in a heated, clashing kiss. So much for control. The taste of Dan—heat, passion, and need—all rolled into one touch.

Mate.

When Dan simply melted against him, Hartman's wolf rose to the surface and gripped him tight. Suddenly all he wanted was to be buried deep inside and biting down on Dan's smooth shoulder. His mouth watered as his fangs tried to poke through his gums. In quick, stumbling movements and amid harsh fervent kisses, they made it to Dan's bed and Hartman finally had the sexy demon exactly where he wanted him. Dan crawled to the top of the bed, then stopped on all fours.

Hartman wanted to see his eyes—had to watch the scarlet fire when Dan was impaled with Hartman's cock and shouted his completion. But this time, he let his animal nature take control. This time was about permanency and a bite that would never fade from his mate's skin. Everyone would know Dan belonged to him and Hartman would protect what was his.

He grabbed the lube and concentrated on preparing Dan. With one finger inside, he had the demon squirming and begging for more—with the second and third, Dan was silent and arching into his touch. Sex with Dan—making love with him—had always been this way. Whereas Hartman would be incoherent with need, Dan would suddenly go quiet and focus entirely on pleasure… until Hartman was inside. He would beg and plead and want more. The change from calm to writhing on his cock always added more excitement.

"Now." Dan moaned. "Inside me now."

He wasn't stretched enough. Hartman had to object, "You're not—"

"Now!" Dan demanded with a hiss. He looked over his shoulder at Hartman, and his scarlet eyes were so freaking beautiful. Hartman whined low in his throat at the sight. No one but Dan ever looked at him with such need as if he would die if Hartman didn't fuck him right then.

"So perfect, Dan," he murmured. He pressed inside; froze once he pushed in deep. Dan needed to adjust to Hartman's size. It had been too long since they'd been together. Dan arched again, lowered his shoulders and shuffled a little.

"Move."

"I want to…" Hartman stopped. He wanted to claim Dan, wanted to fuck him into the bed, but he also needed it to last. The wolf in him demanded he mark Dan as thoroughly as possible until his scent saturated the demon and frightened off any potential challengers to their bonding. Dan tightened his muscles around Hartman's cock and Hartman reacted with a sharp slap to Dan's ass. "No," he said. He was finding it hard enough to keep control, let alone with Dan trying to push him. The demon always tried to take control. Hartman's wolf growled low, vibrating the air between them.

Dan went absolutely still, bowed his head in submission. Hartman began to move. He wasn't going to last—the heat and pressure on his cock was enough to make him want to come immediately, but he forced it down. The rhythm was hard, and Dan whimpered beneath him. Spreading his knees a little, he reached around Dan and pulled him upright so he was literally impaled.

"Oh," he sighed. Bliss had his eyes rolling back in his head. Taking a deep breath, he inhaled the amazing scent of the love of his life.

Hartman slid the fingers of one hand down Dan's chest and circled his lover's heavy cock. With deft movements, he was pressing up and into Dan and matching the movements with a firm grip. Raining open-mouthed kisses across Dan's shoulder, he nipped and sucked a path across his lover.

"So close," Dan panted.

At the last moment, while his orgasm swept through him, Hartman's canines descended. He sank them deep into Dan's shoulder. He could taste the blood and hear Dan's shout of completion as ropes of warm cum covered his hand.

He licked where he had bitten. The marks of his teeth would disappear, but the skin would remain colored in a perfect ring. Dan was his forever. His mate. His wolf settled inside, happy they'd finally claimed their man.

"I love you, Dan."

"Love. You," Dan said between breaths. Hartman pulled out and rolled Dan onto his back.

"Are you okay?" he asked carefully.

"Yours," Dan murmured. He smiled, then entwined his fingers with Hartman's and encouraged him to lie flat next to him. "Give me ten. We're so doing that again."

Hartman pulled Dan close in a tight embrace. The scarlet

strands of magic that hung in the air around them gave him a focus.

"Mine," he said gently. "Always together."

"Yours," Dan answered sleepily. "Always."

THE END

End Street Volume 2

The Case of the Dragon's Dilemma
The Case of the Sinful Santa

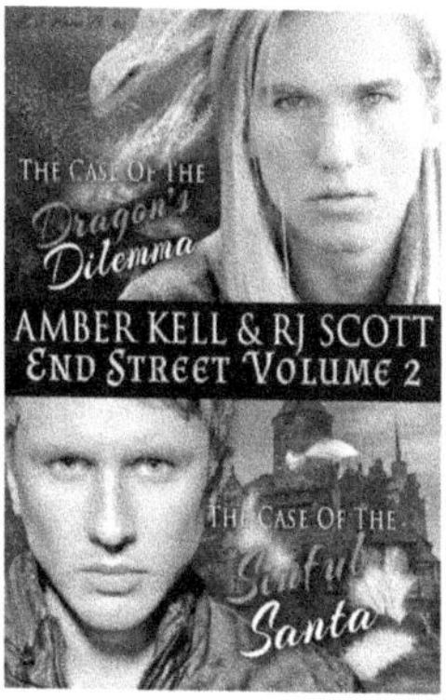

The Case Of The Dragon's Dilemma

Dragons, battles, a siren attack, and a deal Sam may come to regret, leave Sam and Bob in danger, and result in Mikhail finding a mate.

Bob and Sam take their kind-of-adopted-now vampire daughter Mal to look at new schools. Mikhail is left to babysit the last of the remaining rescued children while they are away. When sirens appear to steal her away, he is left facing the attack alone until a mysterious hero comes to his aid.

Ryujin, or Jin to his friends, is a dragon shifter and his role as Captain of the Dragon Guards puts him in direct conflict with Mikhail. The minute he sees Mikhail, he knows what he wants. Now if he can only get Mikhail to see the same.

The Case of the Sinful Santa

Zephariel, the Angel of Vengeance, Nick Klauson, nephew to Santa, Christmas magic, zombies in the school and a necromancer causing chaos…and at the center of it all—Mal.

Zephariel is the Angel of Vengeance and is tracking down his cousin Danjal for misuse of brimstone. When he walks into a bar and finds Nick Klauson drowning his sorrows, he is instantly drawn to him. Could this be his fated mate?

When Nick and Zeph join forces to deal with zombies in Mal's school, sparks fly. Add in a demon, a wolf and a necromancer, and Sam and Bob have a hunt on their hands.

Meet RJ Scott

RJ discovered romance in books at a very young age and realized that if there wasn't romance on the page, she could create it in her head. With over one hundred and fifty books published, she is a full time author of gay romance.

She lives and works out of her home in the beautiful English countryside, spends her spare time reading, watching films, and enjoying time with her family.

The last time she had a week's break from writing she didn't like it one little bit and has yet to meet a box of chocolates she couldn't defeat.

www.rjscott.co.uk | rj@rjscott.co.uk

NEWSLETTER - rjscott.co.uk/rjnews

instagram.com/rjscott_author

amazon.com/author/rj-scott

bookbub.com/authors/rj-scott

goodreads.com/rjscott

patreon.com/RJScott

Meet Amber Kell

Amber Kell has made a career out of daydreaming. It has been a lifelong habit she practices diligently as shown by her complete lack of focus on anything not related to her fantasy world building.

When she told her husband what she wanted to do with her life, he told her to go have fun.

During those seconds she isn't writing, she remembers she has children who humor her with games of 'what if' and let her drag them to foreign lands to gather inspiration. Her youngest confided in her that he wants to write because he longs for a website and an author name—two things apparently necessary to be a proper writer.

Despite her husband's insistence she doesn't drink enough to be a true literary genius, she continues to spin stories of people falling happily in love and staying that way.

She is thwarted during the day by a traffic jam of cats on the stairway and a puppy who insists on walks, but she bravely perseveres.

amberkell.wordpress.com
amberkellwrites@gmail.com